House

of

Clouds

Kristin Gleeson

Published by An Tig Beag Press
Text Copyright 2023 © Kristin Gleeson

Cover design by JD Smith Designs
978-0-9956281-9-9

PROLOGUE

Rome

The filmy white curtain billowed out behind her like a sail, full breasted, head to the wind. It was her sail, her ship, setting her on a different course, at least for a few days, taking her away from this room, this apartment, this city.

Below her and across the myriad tiled roofs, Rome was waking up, the sun just starting to cast canted light onto the piazza, finding the gaps in the old marble and granite buildings. At one end of the piazza, Maria entered, moving along the dusty cobbles, making her way to the weathered slate-blue door on the far side of the piazza, to prepare her employer's breakfast and get the children ready for school. Signora Benedetti, broom in hand, exited from another door, this one more a mottled green, a closed awning of red stripes above it that when unfurled, read "Benedetti's" in faded black cursive. The signora paused a moment, leaning on the broom before taking it up vigorously to sweep the small paved area in front of the little café at the end of the piazza. It was a familiar sight, a daily one, except Sundays, of course. The light, the colors, the people. It was Rome. Her Rome.

She felt him before she heard him, his bare footsteps silent across the tiled floor as he came to stand behind her. He pushed her dark auburn hair aside and kissed her neck. The kiss was soft, sensuous, with a hint of persuasion behind it.

"Come back to bed, Katerina," he said softly in Italian. He brushed his fingers along her shoulders, the persuasion stronger now.

She turned to face him. "Giancarlo, you know I can't. I have a flight to catch."

"In Italian," he said, a hint of admonishment in his tone. "Come back to bed, there's still time."

She sighed. She'd been too tired to speak in Italian, for once. Last night had been another late night. What charity had his mother chosen for the gala's profits this time? She brushed the question aside. It didn't matter. The faces were the same.

He kissed her now, his hands reaching under the flimsy negligee he'd only just bought her, tracing his fingers along her hip. "Come," he said. "I won't see you for a while. We must make the most of these last moments."

She sighed, already getting lost in his kiss.

ONE

The handle was the same worn brass, so scuffed and scratched by the countless fingers and palms that had grabbed and pulled at it over the years, there was no reflection to be had. Nothing to check herself in, to give herself a last-minute once-over before she entered, suddenly self-conscious in her Valentino suit, silk blouse, Ferragamo pumps, and sleekly pulled-back hair. Giancarlo had picked out the outfit for her, certain it would make the right impact on the New York City gallery owner. And now, she was afraid of the impact it would make here, in Somerton Lake. Two worlds colliding. Kate grasped the handle and entered O'Connor's pub. It was too late to change.

The music filtered to her as she made her way from the small foyer to the open room. Along the side opposite the door was the bar, a worn, dark mahogany- and-brass affair. Stools were pulled up to it like familiar friends clamoring for gossip, their surfaces worn smooth by people sliding on and off them over the years. The taps behind the bar showed the usual names, but also a variety of craft beers, something new to her. Above the optics hung the photos of long-ago Ireland and some faded shamrocks left from an ancient St. Patrick's Day. They were still there then. The Guinness mirror was foxed and mottled at the edges, as if it, like a few of the regulars she noted present, had taken too much alcohol over the years, and its once-clear view was now rheumy and blurred.

The wood floor was worn nearly bare of any protective coating through multitudes of shoes and boots treading its boards in all weathers. No change there. The tables, filled with enough people that made it a good crowd for a Thursday night, were as she remembered. High ones in the center, with matching chairs and lower ones over to the side, by the frosted windows that faced the street. All this she took in during the initial few seconds, her primary thought to find her father, who was always here on a Thursday night. Until it wasn't. Until the music penetrated the intention. The voice. His voice. Her eyes found the small stage area at the far end of the room, shocked, unbelieving. Ethan.

It was as if ten years hadn't passed. Or she was cast back in time. He was perched on a stool, his head bent over his guitar, his long fingers moving along the frets and strings. Low-slung jeans, a Henley topped by a flannel shirt. She could recite all the clothes, including the fedora that topped his head, coal-black hair curling from underneath. Coal-black hair. The Tennyson phrase had risen to her mind unbidden then as it did now, capturing its dark beauty. The glasses were new; black horn-rimmed. She grabbed onto that difference even as his voice, that smooth-as-silk baritone, reached out to her and melted her, but the difference evaporated in the face of his voice, those words, that song. Leonard Cohen's "Suzanne." A pain shot through her.

He'd sung it at the college's talent showcase the first week of her freshman year, before classes had started, when nothing was fixed and all the possibilities of what college might be were new and shiny, promising joy. The song "Suzanne" had confirmed it, shown her she was meant to be here, attending this college, finding her real path. He had confirmed it, singing that song. The song that was her mother's. The song that linked her father, her brother and her. His long, graceful fingers picked out the riff, finding the chords. Those hands, mesmerizing in themselves. She'd watched them, his fingers, finely crafted, loving them again already, before he'd even looked up. Before his eyes met hers. Ice-blue, rimmed with thick, dark lashes. She knew he was singing to her, then, somehow she knew that. The words, the music, his look. It was all hers. Until the song ended and he unbent the leg he'd propped on the stool rung, and nodded. He stood, gave a bashful nod, and moved to get another guitar propped on the rack behind him. It was gone, the connection broken. A brief, shining, moment. A moment only. And the last of the shining moments and bright promise that college had offered, on balance. All a mirage, brief and wavering in the distance, just out of reach and wholly false. But it was a long time ago. Another world.

Kate pulled her eyes away and resumed her search for her father. It took a few seconds only. He was up front and center as always, keen to listen and view the musicians who took the stage. She made her way over to him, careful to move as quietly as possible. When she arrived at his side, she laid her hand on his shoulder and bent over, kissing his cheek. He smiled at her distractedly and nodded before his eyes returned to the stage where Ethan had just been. She smiled. Her father's love of music would never die, she thought, fondly.

"I'm just going to get a drink," she whispered to him. She noted his glass of beer. It was half-full. She'd get him one anyway.

With a final pat on his arm, she turned and made her way

over to the bar, where a young, unfamiliar woman stood holding a glass under a craft beer tap, her eyes on the stage, dark head bobbing slowly to the song, as the frothy liquid filled the glass and overflowed. *A college student, probably*, Kate thought. The young woman's large eyes and full chest told the real story of her employment in Kate's opinion. Some things hadn't changed.

When the young woman had served the beer and taken the money, she turned to Kate. "What can I get you?" Her eyes already slid back to the stage.

Kate considered her choice, already revising it quickly after observing the young woman's skill. Or lack of it. Should she have wine? The quality of the wine probably hadn't changed either. This was a college town, where anything sophisticated was a pointless exercise. Though there was craft beer. More than before. The guys. That would explain it. There were plenty of guys who would go for that now. She eyed the bottles in the fridge and settled for a vaguely recognizable brand of craft beer.

"Just give me a glass and the bottle," Kate said brightly after she named her choice. "I'll pour my own at the table."

The young woman nodded, served her quickly, taking the money before she'd even retrieved the beer, and gave Kate the change and her beer with the glass upside down on the bottle at the same time. Kate hadn't even muttered her thanks before the young bartender already had her attention turned to the stage, despite the three women who had just arrived at the other end of the bar.

Kate quickly put her change away in her large Fendi tote that contained her laptop and made her way back to her father's table, wishing she didn't have to lug around her computer. At least she didn't have a suitcase. It had been a good decision, considering she'd taken a taxi from the train station and hadn't rented a car in New York. She hadn't told Giancarlo about her decision to wear clothes she'd left behind here, outdated though they were, rather than take items from her expensive wardrobe she wore in Rome. It had seemed for the best all around. For so many reasons. She was traveling light. No baggage. Her tote carried her essentials—simple makeup and toiletries. Anything more, and she would just grab it here. It was only a few days, after all.

When she reached her father, she placed the drink on the table and slid onto the high chair next to him, straightening her powder-blue suit jacket and the matching skirt. She scanned his face, checking for signs of change. The hair might be more gray than chestnut now, the jowl a little softer, but everything else looked the same.

The song finished, he turned his attention to her and grinned. "Kate, my Katydid. You got here."

She leaned over and kissed his cheek. "You know I wouldn't miss it."

He raised his brows and though there was a twinkle in his eyes, the gesture still made her wince inwardly. It spoke of the years she'd been away, the years that she had missed birthdays, Christmases, Thanksgivings, and other events.

"This is the big six-oh, Dad," she said, as if that explained everything.

He shrugged and took a sip from his beer. He nodded to her bottle and glass. "Nothing on tap appealed to you?"

She gave a wry smile. "More like the young college student's skill didn't appeal to me."

Her dad laughed. "Yeah, Carly started at the beginning of the semester. She does Tuesdays and Thursday nights."

A month and a bit, then. Long enough. "Someone needs to show her how to fill a beer glass."

Her dad's eyes were filled with laughter. "I think her mind's on other things." He nodded in the direction of the stage.

Kate rolled her eyes. "Doesn't she know that tips are linked to service?"

"I don't think it enters her mind," he said and chuckled. "Or that she has a problem with tips."

No, Kate supposed she didn't have trouble with tips. Still, it wasn't her concern.

A figure loomed over them. She looked up. Ethan.

"Hey, Frank," said Ethan. "Thanks for coming."

"Wouldn't miss it," said her dad. "You know that."

"Still appreciated, though," said Ethan. He slid out the chair on the other side of Kate's dad and sat down, her dad clapping his back. He looked at Kate and nodded to her, tipping his hat back a little. "Hey."

She forced herself to nod back, ignoring the knots in her stomach. Her father glanced over at her. "Oh, this is my daughter, Kate. Kate, this is Ethan. He's been playing here at the pub since late summer. He's staying over at the Zigler vacation place at the lake."

She flushed, her fair complexion betraying her as always. "Uh, we were in college together," she said in a low voice. "I think," she added impulsively and looked away.

"We were. Same year," said Ethan. "I think," he added a beat later, a hint of amusement present.

She glanced over at his face. Was he mocking her? But his face was impassive. Neutral.

"Really?" said her dad. He studied Kate. "I don't remember you mentioning him. A musician of his caliber, I'd have remembered that."

"I didn't really know him," she muttered, as Ethan said, "We had a few classes together."

• • •

"Did you read that Browning poem?"

Kate looked up. Ethan dropped the book on the table and slid into the chair beside her. Many of the seats around the classroom table were vacant. He'd chosen that seat. She nodded her head, gave him a tentative smile, but he was too busy taking out his laptop to see her nod. She cleared her throat. "Yes," she said, her voice sounding strangled.

"What did you make of it?"

"Uh..." She bit her lip, all the thoughts and inspiration she'd had when reading the poem vanishing under his attention.

"I'm a real fan of EBB, are you?"

It took her a moment to understand that he meant Elizabeth Barrett Browning, but then she nodded and was about to open her mouth when Caro took the seat on his other side.

"What a mad poem," Colleen said. "She's the biz, old Liz."

Ethan looked over at Colleen, nodded and grinned. Colleen took up her thread, talking about form and shape and illuminating areas of discourse, or something like that, when all that Kate had felt was the music of it, the images it had created, both so interwoven with the words. The experience had been so powerful that she'd thought that maybe, just maybe, her choice was the right one, going to Somerton.

"Oh, it's a pity you didn't know each other better back then," said her dad. "You two would have had so much in common."

Kate wouldn't look at Ethan, fixing her eyes on her father instead. She gave him a wan smile. "Hmmm," she said. Her father returned her gaze with a puzzled expression.

Ethan remained silent for a moment. "What did you think of the second song, then, Frank?"

Her dad looked over at Ethan, the brief puzzlement gone. "I

loved it. I can hear your influences, there, son. There's no mistaking Dylan, Leonard Cohen, and CSN."

Ethan laughed. "Yeah there's some of that in the mix. Though maybe more Crosby, Stills and Nash this time. But also a big dose of that famous band, American Sky."

Frank chuckled. "Flattery will get you nowhere." He gave a thoughtful nod. "But yeah, I could hear a few little riffs and phrasings that I could claim to be like mine. But that aside, I liked it, though you might consider lifting the chorus to the next key at the end. You know, bring it to a G major. That would give it a more hopeful twist."

Ethan gave him a wry look. "Maybe I wasn't looking for hopeful."

Her father shrugged. "Think about it. Think about what's best for the song."

Ethan raised his brows, but after a pause he nodded. "At the moment it doesn't feel like G major, but I'll think about it. You know I respect your opinion."

"But it's your song, in the end, Ethan," said her father.

"Thanks," Ethan said.

Kate stifled a yawn. Her head felt far too wired for sleep, this conversation, this encounter, anything but calming, but her body had other ideas. It was 4 a.m. by her body. And she'd endured a long day of travel, including the stop at the New York City gallery.

Her father looked at her, concern on his face. "You must be dead on your feet. Time to get you to bed." He turned to Ethan. "Sorry I'll miss your second set. See you tomorrow."

"No, don't worry about it, it's fine. Nothing new in the second set. Tomorrow then." Ethan nodded to Kate. "Good to see you again."

Her father slid off the stool, clapped Ethan on the back.

"Oh, and thanks again for "Suzanne." You know that gets me every time."

Ethan grinned. "Better than singing Happy Birthday?"

Her father laughed. "Ha. No contest."

Her father pulled her arm and Kate slid off her stool, glad he was directing her movements, her mind too stuck on the word "tomorrow." Tomorrow? Ethan was coming tomorrow?

Two

It was a kitchen full of warm smells and worn wood. The cracks and stains on the table, the counters, and the cabinets, all spoke of morning breakfasts, boisterous dinners, and rushed lunches. All memories that evoked so many complicated feelings for Kate.

Max nudged her arm, his wet nose tickling the skin near her elbow. From her seat at the kitchen table, Kate laughed and looked down at his baleful eyes, his head cocked slightly to the side. She could see there was white around his muzzle amid the golden fur, more evidence to add to the small sway in his movement and lumbering gait that told her things she didn't want to know. He was nearly fourteen, she calculated in surprise. The golden retriever in his prime that had been in her memory had grown old.

He nudged her again and she smiled down at him. "Still up to your old tricks?" She looked at the stack of pancakes on her plate, the maple syrup soaking the layers, and broke off a small chunk from the bottom one. She glanced over at her father, his back to her at the stove. The bacon in the pan that he held hissed and spat. She heard him mutter a little curse as a droplet of fat hit his hand. Kate smiled at the familiar sight and turned back to the dog, sliding the piece of pancake down her lap and in front of his nose. Before she could blink, the morsel was gone from her fingers and inside Max. She grinned at him and shook her head.

"He's still up to those tricks because you encourage them," said her father, his back still facing her.

She wrinkled her nose. "I can't see that it's all my fault. I mean, when was the last time I fed him?"

"Dogs have long memories," said her father. "Especially when it comes to food."

She forced a laugh. It was hard not to find hidden meaning in those words, that it was a dig at her long absence, though practically, she knew her father wasn't like that. To be fair, she'd been the one who had inferred her long absence with the statement about feeding Max. She felt momentarily annoyed at herself.

"Do you have everything you need for the barbecue today? Is there anything I can get from the supermarket?"

"Nah. It's all under control. Tom's bringing the steaks. Stokey's bringing burritos."

"You mean his wife is."

Her dad laughed. "Yeah. And Phil says he's got the beer covered."

"Any wine? Some people might want wine." She still hadn't decided what she would have to drink. Water? She wasn't sure she could stomach the kind of beer Phil would bring, or the wine that would be there.

"No, don't worry about the wine. Ethan's covering that. And bringing some beer, too."

"Ethan?"

"Yeah. And I almost forgot. Tamzin said she would make some kind of herby salady thing. We've got the macaroni salad already made up, but if you want to do the potato salad, that would be good. You know I always loved your potato salad. Only you could manage to make it just like your mom made it."

She hardly heard his words because her mind had tripped up on the name "Tamzin."

"Who's Tamzin?" Did her father have a relationship she didn't know about? After all, her mother had been dead for nearly twenty years. It was past time. Still, the thought of it made her uneasy.

"Tamzin? She's Tom's girlfriend."

It was the relief that made her laugh. She was nearly giddy with it, even as she berated herself for it. Her father deserved to have a woman in his life, after all. "Tom has a girlfriend?"

"Tom always has a girlfriend," said her dad. "Well at least that's what the girls think. Women. I keep forgetting that you two are adults now." He turned to her now, the spatula in his hand. He gave her a clownish grin. "Though you'll always be my little girl."

She snorted. "I'm a bit too tall to be considered little, let alone a girl." Her height had meant that she could look in the eye any man more than an inch or two under six feet. One factor that had kept the men in her life down to a minimum. That and other things.

"How long have they been going out?"

Her father considered for a few moments. "Six months? I think. She's some kind of glass artist from Boston. They met at an exhibition she had down here."

She nodded. So it could be serious. Tom hadn't had that many relationships that were serious. At least she thought not, since in the years since she'd left she hadn't heard about any. Or met anyone on her fleeting visits. His last one, to her knowl-edge, had been when he was in college at NYU, when he'd been with Sally, his long-term girlfriend from Somerton Lake. And

Sally was now a plump, happily married mother of three who lived with her husband, Joe, in the next town. No lingering heartbreak there.

The back door opened and Ethan walked in, clad in a leather jacket and jeans, a full-face motorcycle helmet under his arm. No glasses today. His hair, a casualty of the helmet, stuck out at odd angles. The ludicrous picture it presented did nothing to dispel his good looks or the shock Kate felt at seeing Ethan stroll in her back door.

"Morning Frank," he said. "Kate."

Kate, suddenly conscious of how of her appearance, looked down at the hole-filled overlarge T-shirt with her father's store logo, which matched the one her father wore. It now sported a faint maple syrup stain in addition to the holes. At least her dark gray sweatpants, though faded, weren't too embarrassing.

"Hey, Ethan," said her father. "Have you had breakfast yet? I've got more bacon if you want it. Or I could easily whip up a few pancakes. There's some batter left."

"No thanks, Frank. I'm good," he said, setting his helmet on the table and taking off his jacket. "Tom asked me to come over early to help with the setup." Ethan looked at his watch. "He should be here soon."

Kate sat speechless, taking in the exchange, its familiarity setting her off kilter even more. Not to mention the worn leather jacket, so obviously expensive, and the watch. Vintage Patek Philippe. A watch that should be insured and placed behind collector's glass. She knew that Ethan came from a prominent New England family, but she hadn't realized how prominent.

"You came on your motorcycle, then," said her father, serving up some bacon on a plate and handing it to Ethan. He pulled out a chair at the table and pushed Ethan into it. "Eat."

Ethan gave him a wry look and took the proffered seat. A fork was placed in his hand.

"Do you want Kate to pop over to your house and pick up the wine and beer?"

Ethan put a forkful of bacon in his mouth and shook his head. "No," he said after he swallowed. "It's all in hand. Zig is bringing it later."

Kate forced herself to take another bite of her pancakes. Anything to convince herself and the other two that she didn't find this unnerving. That the exchange didn't fill her with a multitude of feelings, some of which she couldn't bear to even examine. Not to mention that this exchange she'd just witnessed seemed to emphasize how much she wasn't an integral part of her father's life. She didn't want to consider why it was upsetting that it was Ethan who seemed more familiar with her father's everyday minutia.

"Congratulations on your exhibition," said Ethan.

She looked up to find he was regarding her closely. She opened her mouth to ask him how he knew about her show, but shut it before she could say a word. Her father, of course. Or maybe Tom. They seemed like good buddies. Both thoughts confused and angered her at the same time. For so many reasons. Reasons she really didn't want to resurrect.

Before she could answer Tom burst in the house, the door slamming open against the wall. His arms were full of grocery bags, his chestnut hair shaggy and tousled. "Morning," he said from behind the paper bags. "Coming through."

"Put them down over there," said her dad, guiding Tom to the vacant space on the smooth pine kitchen counter.

Tom moved toward the counter, revealing the petite woman behind him. "Hey, Mr. W," she said. She greeted Ethan. She looked at Kate and beamed. "You must be Kate. I'm Tamzin."

Kate nodded, almost overwhelmed with the vision Tamzin

presented. She wasn't like any of the other girls Kate remembered Tom dating. Her rust-colored baggy sweater and olive-green baggy pants made her caramel-colored skin glow and set off her golden-brown doe-shaped eyes. All this was amplified by the nose stud and the glorious dark hair braided into piles of tiny plaits gathered at her neck and hanging down to her hips. Tamzin's whole persona shouted statement.

"Hi, Tamzin," Kate said. "Nice to meet you."

Ethan rose from his chair. "Let me help you unpack that, Tom. Frank, why don't you go relax? We'll see to the rest in here."

Her father nodded and headed out of the kitchen.

Kate rose, too. She was done with breakfast, regardless of the half-finished state of her pancakes. It was time to get herself out of here. "I'll just change a minute and be down to help."

Tom came over to her. "Hey, give your old bro a hug, Katydid." He pulled her into his arms, and she tentatively put her arms around his back. It was no longer a lanky youth's back, but a man's, with the musculature to go with it. When had this happened?

"Katydid?" said Tamzin, snorting. "Great name."

Tom chuckled. "Yeah. She got it when we were little. When we were caught misbehaving I'd always say, 'Katy did it' and it morphed into Katydid."

"And of course I didn't," said Kate, trying to keep her humor. She put her plate in the dishwasher and edged her way out of the kitchen.

"Oh, Kate," said Tom. "Guess who's coming this afternoon?"

She turned and looked at him, shrugging. "Who?"

"Your old flame, Simon."

She reddened. "He's your old best friend, not my old flame."

"But you had a crush on him, though. For years."

"In high school. Briefly. That was a long time ago."

He waggled his brows. "Not too late to kindle old sparks."

Was he really thirty-three, thought Kate. She sighed. "Tom. That was high school. I'm in a serious relationship now."

He gave her a playful shove, laughing. "How would we know? We've never met him. Your man could be a total invention."

Kate glanced at Ethan who was shoving hamburger rolls into the fridge. She returned her gaze to her brother. "Giancarlo is not an invention. He lives in Italy. That's why you haven't met him," she said in a firm voice. Before he could say anything more, she turned and left the kitchen.

———

Kate balanced the three bags of chips on top of the platter of raw hamburgers she held and made her way carefully down the wooden steps of the back porch. The backyard was spread before her, a string of lights hanging between the few trees at the back, pine picnic tables topped with citronella candles strewn across the grass along with numerous lawn chairs of mismatched colors and various states of repair. Neighbors' outdoor furniture? On the side, near the porch, was a large folding table covered with a plastic checkered table cloth that was already groaning under the weight of the food it contained. The pungent odor of the simmering coals and cedar chips filled the air.

"Here, I'll help you with that." Tamzin reached for the bags of potato chips.

"Thanks," said Kate. "Stick it over there on the table, will you, while I give these burgers to the chef?"

Tamzin snorted, the humor filling her face. "Yeah, Tom is

really getting into the role. Your dad doesn't usually allow him full rein at the barbecue."

Kate smiled, looking over at her brother standing with an intent look on his face, his thick chestnut hair held back from his face by a bandanna.

"A special day for him, then, as much as it is for my father." Kate scanned the backyard a moment. There were several people here already, mostly neighbors nearby, though one or two she recognized from the lake.

"Have you seen my dad?" she asked Tamzin. Kate had been so busy madly making potato salad, burger patties, and relish and organizing the napkins, cups, and all the other minor details she felt she had to do, she'd lost track of everything but her tasks. She felt a momentary flash of guilt. She hadn't phoned Giancarlo yet since her arrival. The time difference had made impossible anything but a brief text to let him know she'd arrived last night. And this morning, well, it had fled her mind.

"I think he's down in the basement with Ethan and Phil organizing the beer to bring it up."

"Phil's here?"

"Yes. He just got here. His wife is around somewhere too."

Kate hadn't seen Phil or her dad's other band member, Stokey, in years. She wasn't certain how she felt about seeing them again. The band. Missing her mother, of course, but it was still American Sky, for all that. They'd been cornerstones of her childhood and even the years after that, until she left.

She was suddenly conscious of the platter of burgers in her hands. "Oh, I'd better give this to the chef before he throws a kitchen fit."

Tamzin grinned. "Oh definitely. He's the man with the knife, fork, and spatula. Deadly weapons in his hands."

Kate moved toward her brother, noting his flushed cheeks under the heat of the barbecue. Or was it the pressure of this great responsibility? Looked like it was hot in the kitchen for him, she thought with a laugh. Plates covered in foil were on the wooden table beside him, their contents ready for the grill.

"Here you go," she said when she reached him. She set the plate down beside one of the others. "The burgers are all ready to go."

"Thanks, Kate," said Tom distractedly. "Do you think the coals are hot enough now?"

She looked down at the coals glowing bright at the bottom of the large barrel-shaped grill. No gas barbecues for her father. Nothing but the real thing. "Authentic," he called it. Tom called it stupid.

"I think it's ready," she said.

"Is it too soon to start?" he asked, his eyes still intent on the coals.

She looked around. She could see another surge of people entering the backyard by the gate at the side. "Nope. Perfect time to start."

He frowned, glanced around. Straightened. "Right then. Let's do this."

Kate patted his back. "Yep, I think it's barbecue time."

She left him there, a smile on her face, and turned back to the house. There were still a few more things to bring out. She brushed her hair out of her eyes. Already the humidity was creating havoc with it, the curls and frizz starting to form, her sleek hairdo of the day before long forgotten. Still, the current hairdo went with the strange outfit she'd scrounged earlier. Her own clothes seemed to have disappeared, so she'd had to make do with an old pair of jeans from her brother held up by a tightly notched belt, and a Henley shirt from when he must have been ten, given its tight fit, and a flannel shirt from her father. Her mother's brown Fry boots circa about 1990 were the only things that weren't either too large or too small. She definitely had a statement look. A statement that would be a kindness to label "wacky," unlike the effortlessly cool look Tamzin achieved. But she would go with it. And try to own it. Isn't that what Giancarlo always told her? Though she wasn't sure this was a look he would ever want her to own.

Once inside the kitchen, she noted that the worn pine kitchen table was empty except for the clutter of old cloths, odd utensils, and some outsize bowls from under one of the wood cabinets next to the stove. Where was the stack of paper plates, cups, and napkins she'd left here just a few moments ago? She saw the open door to the basement.

"Dad!" she shouted. There was no answer.

She went to the head of the basement stairs, leaned down and shouted again. "Dad!"

A dark, shaggy head appeared.

"Ethan," she said, startled. "Is my dad there with you?"

"Yeah, he's just there with Phil. They're unearthing some old equipment. Want me to get him for you?"

She blinked, his words distracting her a moment. Equipment? She shoved the thought aside and focused on Ethan's patient gaze. "Oh. No, if you could just ask him if he knows where the paper plates, cups, and napkins went, that would be great."

"There on the dining room table," he said. "We just put them there out of the way so we could put the equipment where they were."

There was humor in his eyes, the lack of glasses making his gaze even more unnerving in the filtered light.

She forced a nod. "Thanks."

She turned quickly and left, heading toward the dining room where she was brought up short by the sight that confronted her. Gone was the familiar old dining-room set of mismatched pinewood chairs with broken rungs and a table marred and scratched from years of poorly aimed knives and spilled liquids, and in its place was a large rectangular table and six ladder-back chairs of maple. The table, French polished to a warm glow, showed off the simplicity of the style and matched the subtly turned table legs echoed in the arches of the chair backs. It was beautiful. But where had it come from?

She looked around the room for clues. The family photo taken just before her mother died still hung on the far wall beside the china cabinet filled with her grandmother's Beleek collection and an old tea set she'd brought with her from Ireland. The cheese plant was in the corner, looking ragged around the edges, and Max's bed that he never used was in the corner by the door that led to the kitchen. The table and chairs made the rest of the room's contents seem dowdy. What was it doing here? She shook her head and moved to collect the pile of paper goods sprawled on the table. She'd ask Tom.

Voices caught her attention. Hands full, she made her way to the kitchen just as her dad emerged, followed by Phil and Ethan. Her dad's arms were taken up with a tangled mess of extension cords. Phil's arms held a couple of large boxes, and Ethan carried speakers.

She narrowed her eyes at her dad. "A little late for a sound system, isn't it?"

"Nah, these are for later," said her dad. He put the extension cords down on the kitchen table and started clearing the rest of the space.

"Katydid!" said Phil. He set the two boxes on the table. "Come give old Phil a big hug."

She moved into his arms, fitting against his large frame that had grown even heftier in the intervening years, along with the thinning blond hair. But the earring was still in his right ear, a small gold loop that he used to tug on when he was worried. And his trademark twisted double leather bracelet he used to wear was still on his wrist. It had matched the triple twisted one that Stokey had worn on both wrists.

He pulled back and grinned at her. "Look at you. You're all growed up," he said, echoing the phrase Kate had said to her older cousin long ago.

She wrinkled her nose. "I've been grown up for a while now."

He laughed at her. "No, surely it was only yesterday that you were hugging my knees wanting a swing up."

"That was Tom," she said with a laugh.

"Sure about that?" he said, eyes twinkling.

She disengaged and slapped his arm. "Stop. Or I'll sic your wife on you."

Phil's face darkened. "Good luck doing that."

Puzzled, she glanced at her dad. "Divorce," he mouthed.

Her eyes widened. Why hadn't she known this? Why hadn't anyone told her?

"Oh, Phil, I'm sorry."

Phil shrugged. "It was years ago. Ginny's grown now, lives in Boston, near her mom, so it doesn't really matter now. Pat moved to Boston after the divorce. Ginny is a doctor now. We see each other every couple of months when I make it up to Boston."

There was pride in his voice when he mentioned his daughter, but she could detect a lingering pain about the divorce.

She gave him a hug. "Well, it's good to see you."

He squeezed her back. "Have you seen Stokey yet?"

She shook her head. "Is he here?"

"He wasn't earlier," said her dad.

"When I talked to him this morning he said that they'd be here around 2:30," said Ethan.

She looked at Ethan. She'd thought that maybe he'd just

met Phil, but clearly he knew all the members of the band. The unsettled feeling increased. "You know Stokey?"

Ethan shrugged. "We've played together with your dad and Phil a few times."

She took a moment to absorb that piece of information, which added to all the others she'd had to take in since her arrival was perhaps the tipping point into an overwhelming sea of facts.

She looked up at the clock. It was already 2:45. She nodded toward it. "Well, he might be here already."

"I'll just go and check," said her dad. "He's supposed to bring an extra mike."

"An extra mike?" Kate asked. "Just what are you planning?"

He winked at her. "It's a surprise. You'll see."

She gave him a skeptical look. She'd had a few too many surprises since her arrival. She wasn't sure she was ready for another one.

THREE

The yard was awash in the noise of conversation, laughter, and children dodging and running in the area at the back. Some odd trees were shedding their leaves and one or two drifted in the sky like an aimless kite. Kate pulled her flannel shirt closer around her. A chill was starting to penetrate the late afternoon, signaling that fall was well and truly in place. She'd have to go and get a jacket or a sweater soon. The barbecue seemed to be on a hiatus. Those gathered had their fill and had settled down to their beers and wine. In the corner of the yard, sitting beside Tamzin, she spied Tom. She'd wanted to have a word with him since she'd left him with the plate of burgers, but they'd both been busy. She'd been grabbed by all her father's friends, including Stokey, who'd hugged her with a force that she hadn't expected. Cheryl, his wife had just laughed, punched him in the arm and told him that Kate wasn't his teddy bear. She'd found that encounter and the others unsettling, a feeling not helped by the fact that she hadn't had a chance to eat yet, at least nothing beyond a few potato chips and a carrot stick. In a way, the busyness had kept her mind at bay, and any need to worry about Ethan and his sudden appearance in her life. In her father's life.

But now was her chance to talk to Tom. She made her way over to him and took the seat on the other side of him.

"Tom."

He turned and looked at her. "Kate," he said, mimicking her tone.

"The dining room set. What happened to it?"

He raised his brow. "Are you asking if a fairy came along and transformed it from an ugly, scratched, and broken old set to an amazing and beautifully crafted dining-room set, the answer is no."

She narrowed her eyes. "Haha. No, I mean where did the old one go and the new one come from?"

He handed his plate off to Tamzin who was giving him an amused look and turned to face Kate, his arms crossed.

"The old one is where it should be. A dumpster, and is now probably ash somewhere." He held out his hands for her inspection. "The new one came from these extremely talented hands."

She stared at him. "You made that dining room set? When did this happen?" The question wasn't just about when the furniture was crafted, though she couldn't bring herself to say it.

He frowned at her. "Don't sound so disbelieving. I am capable of it."

She blinked and looked away, all the words that he hadn't said floating above her. The phrase "if you ever came home long enough or often enough you would know," was the most prominent. She tried to contain all the hurt, the pain and the confusion that the thought brought her.

She forced herself to smile. "It's beautiful, Tom. And I have no doubt that you're capable of making something like that." She leaned closer to him and tried to adopt a conspiratorial tone. "So not just selling the furniture like Dad, you're making it now? What does he think?"

He shrugged. "He doesn't mind. You know the furniture store was really just a job that Granddad forced on him."

She stifled her surprise. She didn't remember that. When had her dad told Tom that? She tried to let it go. "So are you selling your own pieces now? Do you have commissions?"

Tamzin leaned forward, her expression intent. "Tom's pieces are works of art. There's nothing commercial about them. They should be shown in spaces that show off their beauty."

Kate gave Tamzin a puzzled look and then shifted her gaze to Tom. "So are you exhibiting your pieces yet?"

"He's assembling a collection," said Tamzin. "There's a few galleries up in Boston interested. It's only a matter of time."

Kate studied her brother. His gaze was neutral. He looked at her and shrugged. "I'm still working out what I want to do with it. In the meantime, I'm still helping Dad out at the store, and I work in the back in the old storage area on my own designs."

She nodded. "Well, the dining room set is amazing." And it was. She'd seen that. Was it just that it looked out of place in the worn, comfortable house she grew up in that it made her uneasy?

Behind her, the porch screen door slammed open. She turned and saw that her father had propped it so that it hung wide. Ethan came through a moment later burdened down by a couple of the old low risers they used to use to make the old stage in the large living room when they were growing up. The one their dad said was their own concert arena. Phil followed closely behind with more risers and then Stokey, his tall, lanky frame easily visible behind the others.

She turned back and looked at Tom. "What's this all about? Is this the surprise Dad was talking about?"

"Surprise?" said Tom. "He's setting up the stage. They're going to have a kind of band reunion and sing along. Dad thought it would be fun."

A coldness settled inside her. "A sing along?"

Tom shrugged. "You know him."

She looked around at the large group of people chatting, drinking and idly eating, some at the picnic tables, some in the various assemblies of lawn chairs and folding chairs, others on blankets they'd brought. There was nothing alarming about any of it. It all spoke of enjoyment.

"What about the neighbors, Tom? Won't they complain?"

"The neighbors are here, Kate," said Tamzin, a bemused look on her face.

Kate frowned at her, but couldn't find a suitable retort for her. She sighed. "Whatever."

Tom laughed. "Oh, Katydid. You sound just like you did when you were sixteen. Whatever, Katydid." He laughed again, this time shaking his head.

Kate burned under his comment but managed to resist saying anything else. She rose. "Well, I'm just going to check on the food. See if there's anything that needs topping up."

"Oh," said Tamzin. "No need for that. I did it a little while ago."

"Right, well...I'll just go get myself something to eat, then. I really haven't had a chance to do that yet."

She rose and drifted off to the food table, not waiting for their response. She put aside her thoughts about what had tran-spired, determined to focus on the simple act of deciding what to eat. She was just loading her plate with a burrito and a helping of a green salad when Ethan spoke behind her.

"Your dad said that your guitar is in your bedroom. Do you mind if I go up and get it?"

She whirled around to face him. Standing next to him was

another guy. He looked familiar and then she realized it was Zig, Ethan's old college roommate. She blinked and looked back at Ethan.

"My guitar?" she said after a moment.

All other thoughts but panic left her as she studied his face. He wore sunglasses and a ball cap, so half his face was shaded, his mouth really the only indication of his expression, though it was giving nothing away.

He nodded. "Yeah. He's getting all the instruments together. To play. He said I could use your guitar. That's if you don't mind." He glanced over at Zig. "Oh, right. You remember Zig, don't you?"

"Oh," she said distractedly, nodding toward Zig. "Sure. Hi, Zig." She bit her lip and tried to focus on Zig as he greeted her.

"So, you don't mind?" asked Ethan.

She thought for a moment, trying to remember his question. "Oh, no, I don't mind. Take the guitar. It should be there. I think I saw it this morning, in the closet, though you might have to dig it out from all those flannel shirts and old jackets my father stuffed in there."

He grinned. "Yeah, he has quite the collection of flannel shirts. He even wore them when it was roasting, back when I first came."

"That's my dad, all right. The man with the flannel shirts."

An awkward pause arose. Ethan nodded. "Well, I'll just get the guitar, then."

She nodded. "Let me know if you have any problems finding it."

"Will do," he said and turned, striding off toward the house, Zig following.

She stood there and watched his retreating back, still holding her plate of food, her head swirling with unanswered questions and unacknowledged feelings.

———

She watched her father sing into the microphone, his eyes shut, his face intent. He held his acoustic guitar slightly raised on one side, the strap holding it close to his chest, just as she remembered. After all those years, his fingers found the chords with effortless ease, and his voice retained its gravelly, earthy sound. Dylan crossed with Johnny Cash. Phil stood to the one side, his own guitar slung loosely, his fingers sliding around the frets, always easy in his manner. In the back, Stokey sat at his drums, sticks playing a laid-back rhythm. On the other corner stood Ethan holding Kate's Martin guitar, now miked like the other instruments, while he offered discreet harmonies to the songs they sang.

So far it had been a mix of the band's own songs and covers of others'. Everyone's favorites. Their favorites. The reception had been enthusiastic, and despite her own mixed feelings of joy, anxiety, sadness, and trepidation, there was no denying it was special.

Tom came over to stand beside her, Tamzin joining him on the other side.

"They still have it, don't they?" he said.

She gave him an amused look. "You mean despite Phil's belly and Stokey's bum knee? Not to mention Dad's arthritic thumb?"

He chuckled. "Even with all that. They can still hold the crowd."

"They can," she agreed.

"It doesn't hurt that Ethan is up there, either," said Tamzin.

Kate looked over at Tamzin and frowned. "Sure, Ethan's good, but my dad's band can hold their own without him."

Tamzin shrugged. "I didn't mean they couldn't, I'm just

saying that eye candy like that which has talent to go with it adds a whole extra dimension."

Kate looked away trying to pretend she hadn't really heard the comments. She focused on her father instead. He was singing Crosby, Stills and Nash's "Just a Song Before I Go," Phil and Ethan harmonizing. Though her father was sweating a little and his color might be a little pasty, his voice was strong and he was grinning out at the group. He definitely still had it. The Yankee heritage with a splash of Italian had given him looks that had only matured and now, with his eyes twinkling and his stage persona in full force, she suddenly thought that her own father might be the real eye candy right now.

"Hey, Tom," came a low voice behind her. "Sorry I'm late, I got held up by a small emergency."

She turned to see Simon Callington tap Tom's shoulder. He nodded to Tamzin. "Hey."

Tom turned around and grinned. A complicated fist bump session followed. "Pull up a seat," he told Simon.

Kate watched Simon head off to search for a chair. He still had a full head of blond hair, but the sweatshirt and jeans did nothing to hide the fact that his once slim frame had broadened out into a more muscled and mature version of the Simon she remembered from high school.

A moment later he was back, a somewhat battered lawn chair in hand. He stopped short at the sight of Kate. "Wow, I didn't see you there. Long time no see. How are you?"

"Good."

Simon placed the seat on her other side and leaned forward. "No offense, Tomicles, but I see you all the time."

Kate smiled inwardly at Simon's old name for her brother. A nice bit of revenge for Tom using Katydid in front of Ethan. "You seem well," she said. "What are you doing these days?"

He smiled at her, studying her carefully. Appreciatively.

Kate blinked under his gaze and fought the urge to look away. Was he remembering her crush, or was it something more?

"Same old," he said with an easy manner. "I've taken over my father's medical practice."

She sat back. "Really? I had no idea you went to med school."

He gave her an amused look. "What did you think my major was in college?"

She shrugged. "I don't know. Playing around? Drinking? You know, same as Tom. You two were in the same fraternity, weren't you?"

Simon gave her a bemused look. "Tom dropped out of the fraternity after the first year. Not his thing."

"Oh, right. I forgot." Had she known about that or that Simon had been premed? She put the thought out of her mind. There was a lot she didn't remember from around that time.

A short dark-haired older man came up along Simon. "Dr. Callington, you going to be at the game tomorrow?"

Kate turned her attention back to the stage, glad that Simon's attention was no longer on her. The whole conversation had made her uncomfortable, bringing back embarrassing memories she'd rather forget of her freshman year in high school skulking near Simon's locker. She looked over at Tom and Tamzin, wondering if she could escape into the house for a while to steal some moments alone. Lots of moments. An hour's worth if that was possible, or better yet, until after everyone had left. The light was starting to go. Surely it wouldn't be long.

Her attention was caught by her father playing the opening riff to "If I Fall Behind" in a blend that called both Willie Nelson and Elvis Presley to mind instead of Bruce Springsteen. Her dad glanced back at Ethan, giving a little nod. It took her by surprise when Ethan stepped up to the front of the stage to take

Phil's place at the microphone beside her father's. Phil stepped to the back, resuming Ethan's former position. Ethan leaned toward the microphone and in deep, rich tones sang the opening words of the song. Her breath caught and the words that had seemed so much a part of her father and mother's world suddenly became his. Even more than "Suzanne," the anthem of her parents' relationship, their life together.

The music, the words and his voice held her there, suspended, her breath long forgotten as the song rolled over her. The way he sang, sunglasses removed in the fading light, the hat tipped back, she could see that he was lost into the experience as a musician, just as she was, only as a listener. His eyes opened at the chorus and his gaze caught hers, and for a moment it was as if the words were meant for her—*I'll wait for you.* Even as he moved to the next phrase, his gaze never shifted, and she sat there, transfixed.

She blinked away all the emotions the song, his look, the whole experience aroused in her. She was grateful when, as the song continued, his eyes moved to others in the audience, his expression earnest, reaching out to everyone, drawing them in. *Such stage presence*, she noted. It was irresistible. She'd hardly resisted it back in college, and now it was impossible. O'Connor's had been a mere taster of his current abilities.

She sighed and shook her head, forcing unwanted thoughts away. He was good, a perfect combination of musician and singer, no doubt about it, and she could see why her father had bonded with him so quickly. What had drawn him here exactly for such an extended time period? Was he a professor on sabbatical? He'd been a top student, she remembered that. He awed her in the couple of English literature classes they'd had together. His father had been some bigwig lawyer or politician, she thought. Maybe he'd followed in those footsteps, like Simon had his father's. It was a puzzle she didn't really want to think about. She glanced over at Tom, who was watching Ethan's performance, a smile on his face. Tamzin leaned over and said something to him, and he nodded. What a couple they were. Or not. She was such an odd choice for Tom. Any thoughts on that front were best left alone, though.

Ethan brought the song to a close to loud claps and a few whistles. He grinned out at the audience. Her father gestured toward Ethan. "That's right, give it up for Ethan Peterson."

Ethan gave another nod and pulled down the brim of his cap to its former position and retreated to the back of the stage. And that was it. Kate blinked and found that her father was speaking, sending out his thanks to everyone for coming and sharing the music with him and bidding the audience good-night. The spell was broken. The celebration finished. It was what she'd wanted earlier, but she wasn't so sure now.

"Do you want any food, Simon?" She'd suddenly thought he might not have had a chance to eat.

He smiled at her. "No, I'm good. I grabbed something on the way over here."

Tom leaned forward. "Stick around. You can help clean up, and then we're going to have an informal jam session inside with just the band."

Kate looked at Tom, a kernel of alarm suddenly forming in her stomach. "We are? Is that what Dad said?"

Tom looked at her, puzzled. "Yeah. He didn't say?"

She shook her head. Her father had either forgotten, or had he decided to keep it as another surprise for her.

FOUR

The silence in the living room was haunted with old songs, old voices that invoked laughter, sorrow, and spurts of temper that every family experienced. At the moment, it was the old songs that drifted around Kate, and they nearly overwhelmed her. Her breath tightened, the reasons for her decision to stay away so clearly evident at this moment.

Phil leaned back against the dining room chair, a mandolin propped up on his lap. He caught Kate's gaze and winked at her across the living room. She gave him a wan smile. She'd chosen the seat in the far corner on the small occasional chair covered in the old faded print she remembered from her childhood. It seemed a safe bet, away from everyone's scrutiny. She had immediately ruled out sitting at the piano set against the back wall, where she'd be out of eyesight of at least half of the group, because that would suggest things she didn't want them to think. She'd been unsurprised that Tom had no such reluctance and promptly took the piano bench and had subsequently banged out an accompaniment or two for the songs that had already been sung.

Stokey had taken one of the chintz-covered armchairs, abandoning his drums for a banjo that gave the whole sound a bit more country type of feel. Simon was in the other armchair, while her dad, sitting on the darkly upholstered high-backed sofa, had his old Martin guitar in his lap and Tom's Gibson at his feet by the side of the sofa. Tamzin had taken the seat beside him on the sofa, where she tapped her foot and sang along when she knew the words, or when she didn't, added some kind of dah de dah. Her voice was strong, almost strident, but at least she was on key. The fact that Ethan had chosen to carefully squeeze his dining room chair on the other side of the room, near Kate and away from the sofa, made her wonder if he had experience with Tamzin's forceful voice. It would explain Phil's wink, deployed just after they'd concluded Seals and Crofts' "Summer Breeze" sung by Phil, harmonies courtesy of Ethan, her dad, Tom, Simon, a faint Kate, and a distinctive-sounding Tamzin. Kate had dropped out when she'd seen Tom nod at Tamzin encouragingly after the first chorus. It had caused Stokey to grin, but her father and Ethan had been hard to read. And Phil, until possibly this wink in her direction.

"Okay, you two," her father said, looking first at her and then Tom. "Time for 'Our House.'"

Kate shook her head. "Tom can do the main bits. I'll just harmonize along with the rest of you."

"'Our House'?" said Tamzin.

"Yeah, you know," said Tom. "The Crosby, Stills and Nash song."

"Oh, yeah, that."

Kate hid a smile. The tone and the hesitancy told her all she needed to know about Tamzin's knowledge of the song.

"Come on, Kate," said Tom. "Both of us. That's how we always do it."

Phil, Stokey, and her dad joined the chorus, insisting she join Tom at the piano.

"It works best when you guys do it together," said Simon. "You just bounce off each other."

Ethan glanced over at Simon and then Kate. "I wouldn't mind hearing it myself."

"You can harmonize with us at the chorus, Ethan," said Phil.

Stokey got up from his chair and made his way over to Kate, grabbing her hand. "You should have a guitar, my girl, if you're not going to sit at the piano. Where's yours?"

Kate slid a glance to Ethan. "It was needed elsewhere."

Ethan stood and started to hand it over. "It's fine. I can use Tom's. I just thought he would be playing it tonight. He said that you would be on piano."

Kate looked daggers at Tom while she reluctantly allowed Stokey to pull her to her feet. "Tom shouldn't make assumptions. It's been a long time since I've sat at the piano or had a guitar in my hands, let alone played either."

"It's about time you did, then," said Tom. "Get over here."

She walked slowly across the room to the piano, the walnut floor creaking in its usual spot, just after the rug's edge. She slid onto the piano bench next to her brother.

"You play," said Kate. "I'll sing along."

He frowned at her, but turned to the piano and began the opening bars of the song. Phil, her dad, and Stokey began to pick out some back-up riffs, eventually joined by Ethan. She began the song, feeling her way into it, her voice a little uncertain, the vocal cords opening up from a long sleep. She could feel she was a little rusty, the harmonizing she'd done so far, however faintly, had helped, but she would have carried the main tune more strongly in the past. Tom was there beside her, playing the keys, softly supporting until they got the chorus. By then her confidence was there, at least enough that she could belt out the words she always sang with Tom that reflected *their* house that had one dog in the yard, instead of two cats. She glanced over at her dad. His eyes were glittering with emotion. She forced a grin. This was a happy, cheery song. They must be happy, cheery. Every memory that made this painful for her must be banished in the face of this song.

Tom nudged her, and she sang the second verse with more gusto and found herself swaying side to side with Tom. By the time the chorus was reached this time, it was filled with outrageous harmonies and descants by the rest of them, Ethan offering the most extreme, and Kate found herself laughing. If Tamzin had added her voice to the group, the sound had been drowned out by the others. It didn't matter, in the end, because much to Kate's surprise, she'd had fun.

The song ended with a "whoo hoo" flourish by Tom, a hoot from Phil and an "all right," from her father.

"I liked that version," said Ethan.

"That was great," said Simon. "Just like old times."

Kate nodded her agreement. The old times that had been good.

"Kate," said Phil, rising and moving over to pick up Tom's guitar. "Play one of yours," he said. He walked over and handed her Tom's guitar.

"Hey," said Ethan. He stood, unwound her guitar strap from around his neck and carried it to her. "Give me Tom's, and you have yours."

She opened her mouth to protest, but closed it after a moment. She didn't have the strength to argue or protest. And besides, it was her dad's night, and she didn't want to spoil it.

"Play 'Midnight,'" said Stokey. "Tom can do Missy's part."

She froze a moment, paling. She wouldn't be doing that song.

"'Midnight'?" asked Ethan.

"Yeah," said Phil. "It's a song she wrote years ago. She used to perform it with a friend of hers. It's one of her best."

She looked down the guitar, her hand still clutching it by the neck, and felt Ethan's penetrating gaze on her.

Kate studied the keys of the practice room piano. She could hear Carter next door sawing away on the Bach partita. It had been the wrong time to come. There was something off with the chords, it just wasn't working, and the noise next door wasn't helping. She was just about to stand when the playing stopped, and she could hear the shuffling of Carter packing away his violin. Great.

A moment later, she started the song from the beginning, clearing her mind. She sang along this time, hoping that would help her pinpoint what she was missing.

> I don't know, I don't know,
> Why you touched me so,
> When I heard you sing that night.
> Was it the song, was it your voice?
> Or that you caught me in your sight?
>
> It was only at midnight, only at midnight
> I'd admit you were the one
> Only at midnight, it was only at midnight
> I'd hope that you would come.

The words flowed and the music with it, and somehow the chord became a perfect seventh, creating a finish she knew was right.

Before she reached the last verse, the door opened. She halted, turned, and saw Ethan standing there.

"Sorry," said Kate, rising, gathering her things. "I didn't know this room was booked. I just came in on the off chance."

"No, no, it's fine." He placed a hand on her arm when she reached the door. "That's really good. I didn't know you could sing."

Kate reddened, surprised and flustered by his intense scrutiny. She remained paralyzed by his gaze for a moment, certain her emotions were written on her face. "Thanks," she eventually managed to mumble and hurried out the door before he could say another word.

Now, Kate could feel the weight of Ethan's unasked questions pressing down on her. Beside her, Tom sighed softly. She swung her legs around to the side of the piano bench and perched her guitar on her lap. She knew her father must be studying her too. They'd been so careful to avoid any mention of Missy and anything connected with her in the few times she had been home, so it didn't take any special powers to know they were aware of the slightest bit of a reaction from her.

She took a deep breath and fiddled with the pegs, plucked the strings, pretending that it required a slight adjustment, even though she knew that Ethan would have ensured it was perfect. Her calluses were long gone and her touch was off. Even now, without playing a note, she knew. It was going to hurt. She forced herself to stop the adjustments and strike up a chord. Any chord. A chord that would give her time to think. She didn't know why she couldn't think of a song. And then the "why" struck a memory. She smiled slowly and looked up.

She glanced at her father and began the riff. Slowly, a soft smile broke out on his face. It was one of the first songs her parents had encouraged her to sing, initially with the CD and then on her guitar. She began to sing, the words of Shawn Colvin's song "I Don't Know Why" coming out, the chosen key and register still easy and satisfying for her to sing. The group listened to her, her voice finding the familiar notes, the words something her parents had said reflected her own inquisitiveness and ultimately, her loyalty. Though the words might not apply now, she knew it would please her father and avoid any insistence on any other song that might call up memories she didn't want. Her fingers felt awkward, her fingertips already sore.

As she began the second verse, she heard another guitar over to her right. It could only be Ethan. A moment later his soft harmony joined her voice, and they were singing, just the two of them, the words coming effortlessly from his mouth. She shouldn't be surprised that he knew the song, and the fact that he did created a warmth that spread through her, lifting her spirits. She turned to him, his eyes catching hers, reflecting the emotions that flowed and eddied in her. The words took on a different meaning for a moment. Singing about if there were no music, laying down a life for that person, and though someone will make her cry, the singer would get her by.

Kate had to look away.

The song finished, Ethan giving it some lingering chords and an improvised riff. She was grateful for it. It gave her time to collect herself once again. At its finish she handed off the guitar to Tom and stood.

"Sorry, no calluses, so that's me done for the night." She put a grin on her face and made her way back to the occasional chair in the corner amid words of praise and thanks from the group. A soft, "that was really good, Kate," came from Ethan, but she didn't acknowledge it with anything more than a nod.

FIVE

Kate scanned the vast arrivals area of Leonardo Da Vinci airport, peering around clusters of families surrounded by baggage embracing, to the small number of drivers who held up signs hopefully to the tired stragglers emerging from customs door, wheeling large suitcases. The PA system blared out another message in rapid Italian, causing Kate to wince. A young man raced by, heading toward the door, his messenger bag flapping against his jean-clad leg. The outside door opened, and she looked over hopefully, but it was an older, gray-haired couple.

She leaned back against her perch on the wall nearest the customs door. Still no signs of Giancarlo. It had been a half-hour already. There had been no messages before she boarded the plane, when she'd texted him to tell him that the flight was about to leave. Was he annoyed that since she'd left Italy she'd only contacted him once, with a brief message to say that she'd arrived in the US? She checked her phone again and saw a missed call from him. In the noise of the airport she must not have heard it. She pressed the return call icon and listened. It connected almost immediately.

"Katerina? Where are you? Why didn't you answer your phone?" he said in clipped Italian.

She fought through the fog of fatigue to unravel the meaning of his words. It took her a few moments to understand and another to calm the spike of impatience.

"I'm at the airport, where do you think I am?" she said in English. She just didn't have it in her to phrase the answer in Italian. "I've been waiting for you for a half-hour." She paused again, trying to collect herself. "Have you been delayed in traffic?"

"No. That's why I phoned you. I can't pick you up. Mamma needed me at the lawyers to solve some important issues that have arisen." This time he spoke in English, as if he knew her expired patience and his transgression required it.

Of course, thought Kate. It could be for no other reason than Mamma needed him, to keep him from making the journey. But it seemed his mother always had an emergency.

"Fine. I'll catch the train."

"No, no," said Giancarlo. "Take a taxi."

"I can't afford a taxi all the way to Rome, you know that."

"I insist on paying," he said. "After all, it was my fault you have to make your own way here."

She sighed. It was bad enough that he'd paid for her flight to New York, and now he wanted to add the taxi too. "It's fine, Giancarlo. I'd better go now. Will you be there when I arrive?"

"I should be," he said and paused. "I'll try."

She understood the meaning of his words, the hidden reality of its dependence on his mother. "Okay," she said. "*Ciao.*"

"*Ciao, bella.*"

She ended the call and slipped her phone into her bag. It seemed heavier now, the laptop feeling more like Sisyphus's boulder, only instead of rolling it up a hill, it was on her shoulder. She shifted the bag to the other shoulder and headed toward the train station.

Kate sank gratefully into her seat and glanced out of the train window. Outside, people still crowded the entrances, struggling to board the train, lumbered down as they were with all manner of suitcases and bags. She closed her eyes against the mayhem, her body seizing the respite automatically. She was beyond tired. The journey and the tension of her visit, only made worse by drinking, had combined with the late nights, to leave her wrung out. Last night, especially. Though she hadn't sung any more songs on her own after the Shawn Colvin rendition, the night had continued with offerings by Ethan, Tom, and even Simon. She'd finally crawled into bed sometime past three, only to wake again a few hours later to ensure she caught her train to New York to make the early evening flight.

Now, it wasn't only her suit that was crumpled. She was crumpled all over, inside and out. *My God*, she thought, and the visit had only been a few days. She couldn't imagine what she would feel like if she had extended it to a week as her father had requested. The strain of the old life. The old self. A self she'd managed to put away, even forget at times. Now it clung to her, just like the hangover that had raged yesterday and was subdued to a dull throb this morning. She leaned over and retrieved the bottled water she'd bought at a kiosk in the train station and, uncapping it, drank deeply from it.

The water tasted good, but it did nothing to stop the jumbled memories from the weekend crowding her overtired mind. She tried to put her tearfulness and confusion down to her fatigue, but that didn't make it any easier to cope with the feeling of alienation and loss that she hadn't been able to shake since she'd arrived at Somerton Lake. The strange interaction with Ethan at O'Connor's and her father's odd friendship with him, not to mention her brother's relationship with Tamzin and Tamzin herself. Tom had always been easy going growing up, even a bit of a dreamer, despite the moments he'd tormented and teased her, but it had always been with a good humor and an undercurrent of brotherly affection. But this Tom, the Tom who ran the furniture shop, who crafted the beautiful dining room set, this was a Tom who didn't fit into her idea of him. Even his interaction with her was different. Less indulgent brother and more...she struggled to find the words and abandoned the search in the end. She was just too tired. She dug out her phone and earbuds, automatically selecting *La Boheme,* one of the operas Giancarlo had put on the playlist they shared. They were going to see it in Verona soon, and it wouldn't hurt to refresh her memory.

The opening notes of the first aria played, and Kate felt her eyes close.

———

Kate put down her Fendi tote on the small, elegant antique table by the apartment door. Light from the French doors in the living room ahead spilled into the small foyer where a few tiny dust motes danced in the air. Against the far wall of the living room, she could see that the nineteenth-century inlaid walnut dresser held a large vase of calla lilies. Were they for her? The arrangement was expensive, the vase unfamiliar. She smoothed a wayward strand of hair from her face. She'd tried her best to tidy it up on the train, but the lack of styling tools had defeated her in the end. At this point she was too tired to care how she looked, really. She sniffed. Espresso. Giancarlo always had an espresso at nine and another around noon. Was it noon already?

Giancarlo emerged from the small study next to the living room, his dark hair exquisitely cut and styled as always, his casual shirt and pants still elegant yet understated, again, as always. His lips, full and sensuous, broke into a smile.

"*Tesoro*," he said, pulling her into an embrace and kissing her.

She slid her arms around his neck and sank into his kiss, his welcome a comfort after so much travel. He deepened the kiss, his hand moving to cup her head, his other hand sliding farther down, pulling her closer into him. His desire was evident, and for a moment she could imagine responding, but fatigue washed over her. She pulled back.

"Sorry," she said in English, smiling feebly. "I'm exhausted. Do you mind if I lie down for a little while?"

He stroked her hair. "Of course. And I apologize for not collecting you from the airport."

She nodded. The gist of the words, spoken in Italian, had filtered through. He took her hand and led her toward the bedroom. At the door, he kissed the top of her head. "Go, lie down. I'll make us a light lunch." He kept speaking, the words faint against her head, the Italian rapid.

She nodded, made her way over to the bed, kicked off her shoes will and lay back on the bed. It was only a few moments later that she made sense of the words he'd spoken after he'd told her he'd make lunch. He would take her to the gallery so she could see the exhibition space. She knew there was a reason she should question that, but she dozed off before she could discern it.

———

Kate stepped back from the wall, creating even more distance from her work than she would if she hadn't had to keep her emotions in check. Beside her, Giancarlo talked intensely with Francesco, the stout, swarthy gallery manager. She was grateful that the two were so deeply engaged, because it gave her time to look at the exhibition on her own.

He'd told her months ago he would let her hang her art pieces. The thought kept echoing in her head as she moved around the mostly white space along the panels that discreetly signaled to the left and eventually to the right in the exhibition journey. Carefully, she examined the images on the white walls surrounding her, the spotlights tastefully and professionally directed to show the details of each framed image on display. It took a few moments for her annoyance to clear, but in the end, after reviewing Giancarlo's arrangement, Kate had to concede it was good. She should trust him to know. It was his job, his craft, after all. And, she reminded herself, it was his space, too, connected to his auction house. She took in the images one by one, evaluating them yet again.

The frames were sleek, modern, set off by pristine white mats. Kate still felt that the framing and mat choices might be at odds with her work, but Giancarlo insisted they were perfect for the tone and message of her art. Simple, expensive, yet still beautiful. Old world yet modern. Perfect for Rome. Her instinct had been to create special frames with herbs and vines carved into them, to highlight the narrative contained in the various photographs she'd taken of Messina, overexposed, tinted in magenta tones and printed on artist rough rag paper with fragments of Boccaccio's story of Lorenzo and Isabella contained in the *Decameron,* written in her careful calligraphy in the work's original Tuscan. And she would have begun with the image of the herb pot, to set the story front and center, instead of Giancarlo's choice of the ruins of Messina, which really didn't have anything to do with the story, but Giancarlo had argued it was such a significant identifier of Messina it was important to include it. And it would sell quickly for the high price he'd set.

She'd come up with the kernel of the idea several years ago, when she'd studied photography at the Arts and Culture School in Paris. It had prompted her to take some art classes, along with mastering calligraphy well enough to execute the project. The project had been put on the back burner by the need to support herself while she'd finished art school, and afterwards, when she'd decided to stay on in Paris. It had been difficult and the apartment she'd shared with a motley crew of other American girls looking for ways to remain in Paris had helped her eke out the money for a few years. Until she met Giancarlo.

He'd been attending one of the school's exhibitions to scout out potential new artists and happened to overhear her comments to one of her friends explaining one of the techniques used in a particular piece. His manner, as he inquired whether she was one of the professors in his accented English, was elegant, easily charming, and she'd felt herself incapable of resistance. The dark sultry eyes studying her intensely as she answered his questions, along with the high cheekbones, long aquiline nose, full lips, evoked a response that she instantly understood was more than an artist's appreciation of good looks.

It had been an understanding that he'd shared and had become a relationship by the end of his week-long stay and had her following him back to his home in Rome to live with him and develop her art under his patronage. To call it something as trivial as "help" didn't seem to encompass all that he was doing for her. Even the work she occasionally managed to secure as a photographer was through his connections, and they were limited to the occasional wedding or birthday event that didn't earn her enough to afford the lifestyle that she now lived. She owed Giancarlo everything.

Giancarlo came up behind her and rested his hand on her shoulder.

"Well, what do you think?" he asked her in Italian.

She turned and smiled at him. "*Bellisimo. Mille grazie*, Giancarlo." Or was it *bellisma*? Was exhibition feminine or masculine, or was that even how it was calculated in this case? She was just too tired to remember, if she did know.

Giancarlo kissed her lightly on the neck. "Good. I'm glad you like it. See, you didn't need to be here. We managed perfectly. And now you don't have to worry about it. You can relax until Friday."

She forced a smile, relieved that he hadn't found the few words she'd voiced lacking. At least it seemed so. "*Si, grazie.*

She felt another small surge of anger and she pushed it back down. She was tired, jet lagged. Her emotions were all over the place. The short nap she'd managed to take before a quick lunch now seemed too distant to remember.

"So," said Francisco. "Did the gallery in New York express any interest in Katerina's work?"

"*Si*, of course," said Giancarlo. "Cassidy Grady is very interested in our work and wants to offer us an exhibition, just as I predicted."

"She said she was interested and *possibly* could offer us a slot in January," said Kate.

Giancarlo gave a very Italian shrug. "It's only a formality."

"Let's hope so," said Kate.

"Of course it's only a formality," said Francisco. "Especially after she hears what a success this exhibition is."

Kate nodded, trying to appreciate Francisco's tone and words as enthusiasm rather than the obsequious toadying she sometimes felt it was. There was no doubt that Francisco was aware that his employment as Giancarlo's gallery manager gave him access to Giancarlo's connections and cachet as one of the prominent members of Rome's unofficial old nobility that their ancient pedigree and wealth guaranteed.

"You can do the Italian classics for Signora Grady. Keep to your theme, your brand. It's how we will make you famous, Katerina," said Giancarlo.

She looked over at Giancarlo and gave a startled laugh. "Fame?" she said in English. "I don't think so. I'd just be satisfied if I just sold a few of my works."

Giancarlo leaned over and whispered, "*Italiano, bella. Italiano.*" He put his arm around her. "Nonsense, we will make your name known among the art world. Everyone will want to have one of your pieces. I know these things. This is what I do. " He pulled her in closer and kissed her cheek.

"With one of the most ancient families of Rome behind you there can be no other result," said Francisco. "Every time you have appeared at his side, Rome has taken note. Soon, it will be all of Italy."

It took Kate a while for her fogged brain to translate his words, but when she did, she looked away, unwilling for Giancarlo to see how unsettling she found that remark.

Six

Kate pressed the thick linen napkin to her mouth in an effort to stifle a yawn. She blinked a few times and took a sip of the water from the delicate goblet of Murano glass. She replaced the glass carefully on the table, conscious that it had probably been in the family for generations. The glass beside it, filled with red wine, no doubt from their vineyard in the Tuscany hills, she was nearly too terrified to touch. Gold-rimmed and etched, its value seemed in regions that would mean it was better placed in a museum. But then the contents of the whole apartment belonged in a museum. The thought that Giancarlo's mother might be best placed in a museum, too, crossed her mind. But no. Though her manner of dress was timeless and classic, Paloma Fabrizi was very much aware of the world she inhabited, dominating it with the subtle iron touch that gave no hint of fragility.

Even now she sat at the head of the large, gracious table, with Giancarlo on her right, Kate on his other side, and the priest on Paloma's left. Or was the priest a deacon? Were deacons priests? He couldn't be a cardinal. Didn't they wear red? Purple, she knew, was the pope's color. His name that might have included a title had been lost in the rapid-fire introductions in Italian Paloma had given when she and Giancarlo had first arrived for luncheon at his mother's apartment. When Giancarlo had reminded her of it this morning, she'd had to stop herself from groaning. She was still jet lagged from the day before, but she knew better than to object. She'd just nodded and donned the pale yellow Dior sheath dress and matching shoes Giancarlo had selected. She'd grabbed the quilted powder-blue Chanel bag with the chain shoulder strap in the hopes that spoke "classic" enough for his mother, but she knew as soon as his mother had spotted it, she'd made a mistake. There had been no comment, no frown. It was just a glance at the bag and a fractional arch of her brow, and that had communicated volumes to Kate. Thankfully, Giancarlo hadn't noticed. He'd been too busy presenting Paloma with the vase of calla lilies, the flowers she'd seen upon her arrival the day before. The vase apparently was an antique purchased for Paloma at great expense and difficulty from one of Giancarlo's connections in Geneva. And what better way to present it than to fill it full of one of his mother's favorite flowers?

The vase now stood on the table, the flowers inside it statuesquely overlooking them as they ate. Or rather as Kate endlessly pushed the risotto around her gold-edged china plate. Her stomach really couldn't fathom eating very much. The travel, lack of sleep, and odd eating patterns seemed to have affected her appetite.

"Is there something wrong with your risotto?" asked Paloma, cutting into Giancarlo's discussion of Kate's forthcoming exhibition arrangements.

Kate looked up, startled. It took a moment for her to process Paloma's words, thrown out with a speed that Kate was certain few could match.

She put on her most reassuring smile. "There's nothing

wrong with it at all. It's delicious. I just don't have much of an appetite, that's all." She spoke slowly, trying to ensure that her Italian was perfect. "The trip home to America. I'm still feeling the effects."

Paloma's dark eyes focused on Kate intently. "Home? Is not Rome your home? You have said so frequently."

Kate flushed and tried to suppress the desire to pull every one of the black hairs of Paloma's perfectly coiffed bob from her head.

Giancarlo reached over and took Kate's hand and kissed the back of it. "She does of course think of Rome as her home. She meant to say 'old home,' but her Italian, it is not always perfect."

Kate gave Paloma a weak smile. "Of course I think of Rome as my home. It has given me everything." She squeezed Giancarlo's hand. "And Giancarlo. I think of Giancarlo as my home."

Paloma gave her a peculiar look. Had Kate expressed herself incorrectly?

She decided a fresh subject was needed. "I'm looking forward to the exhibition," said Kate. She looked over at the priest. "Will you be attending?" All Kate knew of the guest list was that it was extensive and filled with highly connected people.

Paloma gave a wave of dismissal. "Monsignor Carducci is far too busy with Vatican matters."

"Oh," said Kate, giving the monsignor an apologetic look. "I'm sorry, of course."

The monsignor smiled, his kind dark eyes twinkling, his thin mouth twitching with amusement. "It is of no consequence. I only wish I could. I understand from Giancarlo that you have much talent. How long will your works be on display at Giancarlo's gallery? Perhaps I might find some time to view them."

She glanced at Giancarlo. Back when they first planned the exhibition, he'd told her the exhibition would be at least until mid-November and possibly longer, depending on the response, but she knew he'd received inquiries about the use of the gallery all the time.

Giancarlo smiled warmly at the monsignor. "I would be honored if you were to attend the gallery, and I can arrange for a private showing at any time, if you so wish. It will be there until the end of next month."

"That's most kind of you," said the monsignor. "Perhaps it will be possible."

Paloma gave the monsignor a beatific smile. "You are good to spare a thought for Giancarlo's gallery, and you know we will accommodate you in any way possible."

Kate witnessed the exchange, translating the words slowly in her sluggish brain. It seemed benign enough, but instinct told her there was something subtle Paloma communicated to the monsignor. Perhaps it was the momentary trace of smugness on Paloma's face. She looked at Giancarlo again, studying his expression, but could find nothing there. She sighed inwardly. She was in no fit state to dissect this now, and if it was some unconscious transgression she'd made, she'd just have to make more of an effort with Paloma.

She reached up and fingered one of the pearl earrings she wore. They matched the pearl necklace around her neck. Timeless, classic, and expensive. Another gift from Giancarlo and one that Kate thought would have been a safe choice for today as well as a subtle signal to Paloma of Giancarlo's deep feelings for Kate.

The gesture caught Paloma's attention briefly as her eyes flicked toward Kate, but there was no other sign she'd noticed. Kate turned her attention back to the risotto. It was best to let the others carry on the conversation.

Thankfully, the meal held no more barbs, subtle or otherwise, and Kate's tension eased as they rose from the table. The monsignor said his goodbyes so that it only remained for Giancarlo and Kate to do the same. Soon, she'd be back at Giancarlo's apartment, where she could retreat to the comfort of her small studio, or at least attempt a short nap.

"Come through to the blue room," said Paloma. "There are one or two things I wanted to discuss."

Giancarlo looked surprised, but not alarmed. The tension that had been easing inside Kate started to rise again. They followed Paloma to the small private salon at the far end of the hall. Kate had been to this room only a few times and still found it almost as intimidating as the elaborate furnished dining room they'd just vacated. Though the space was smaller, the furniture was antique, with two facing sofas covered in expensive watered silk, an eighteenth-century maple escritoire, an occasional table containing a Chinese vase that undoubtedly was from a dynasty that made it expensive, and a few seventeenth-century paintings that were most likely contemporaries of Artemisia Gentileschi, a woman painter, and one of Kate's particular favorite artists of the time period.

Kate took a seat on the sofa beside Giancarlo, Paloma taking the sofa opposite them. She picked up a magazine on the small table next to her.

"I see you were in *Grazia* again, Giancarlo," said Paloma, flipping through it.

Giancarlo shrugged. "It was the sale of that painting."

"Yes, it was good for the auction house and you." She stopped at a page in the magazine and held it out to him. "However, this photograph of the two of you attending the Bertoli gala was not so positive. The caption suggests that you'd both had too much champagne, and I must say the photograph only supports that idea. And Katerina's gown..." Paloma gave a mew of distaste. "Giancarlo, you know better than to drink excessive amounts of champagne at events like these. For this exact reason. The family name is much too important."

Kate peered at the photograph over Giancarlo's shoulder and cringed inwardly. It wasn't the most flattering of shots, she had to admit. Her Valentino halter dress, while a lovely shade of deep blue, had been much too daring for Kate, and this photograph proved it. In the course of wearing the ridiculously high Manolo Blahnik shoes she'd stupidly selected because she'd been in a rush, she'd stumbled at the gala and her dress had shifted, revealing far too much of Kate's left breast for her liking. And Giancarlo, startled by her stumble, had managed to spill his drink on his Armani suit before he slipped his arm around her to steady her. It had been that moment the photographer had captured. A moment now a permanent and public reminder that Kate knew would follow her around for some time.

"Oh, Mamma," said Giancarlo, in a soothing tone. "You know these things are never how they appear. Kate merely tripped and I assisted her. It was nothing."

"Though it may have been 'nothing,' as you say, it now had become 'something.'" Paloma turned her gaze to Kate. "And the gown? It's clear that you have no understanding how a gown like that must be worn." Paloma closed her eyes for a moment. "I'll send Bibi to you. She can explain how to prevent such occurrences in gowns of that type."

"That's most kind of you," said Kate, conscious she was flushing hard. Though she stumbled over the words, she tried to infuse them with firmness. "But really, it's not necessary. It was the shoes and nothing more."

"Yes," said Paloma. "Those shoes. An unfortunate choice. Perhaps Bibi could help you there, as well."

Giancarlo reached for Kate's hand and squeezed it. "It's very generous of you to offer Bibi's services, Mamma. Any guidance you would give Kate will be invaluable." He stood, pulling Kate up with him. "Now if there's nothing else, we have to go. I have to get back to the gallery."

Paloma gave a small nod of acknowledgment and offered up her cheek for a kiss. Giancarlo leaned over and kissed her on alternate cheeks the requisite three times. For Kate, Paloma reserved a brief handshake.

Seven

The noise surrounded Kate, nearly stifling her with its intensity. A babel of sound in a language that Kate could hardly make sense of in the midst of the dull roar. The heavy heat of all the bodies pressed into what now seemed a small exhibition space spoke to Kate not of success, but a school of lemmings gathering for a jump: urgent, tense, and filled with expectation.

Kate sipped from her wine glass, hardly tasting its contents. The action gave her something to do other than stare at the people who milled around this very crowded room, and it also allowed her a breathing space from speaking to the numerous people who approached Giancarlo and in turn, her, after the introductions were made. The occasional flash of a photographer taking shots of people as they arrived could be seen to the right, in the reception area. The people now crammed into the exhibition space seemed more intent on meeting and speaking with each other than looking at the walls that housed her exhibition. Not that they would be able to see it if they bothered to look toward it. Though the images had script written on them, the little cards to the bottom right had a title, and the catalog gave the description, the art was something that should be taken in its entirety, both as individual pieces and as a whole.

She was conscious of the beads of sweat that gathered on her upper lip and trickled between her breasts. She only hoped that no traces of sweat were evident anywhere on the very expensive Dior dress she wore. Giancarlo had bought it on the advice of his mother, especially for the event. The chiffon draped effect with ribbon banding and straps exuded a suggestion of Renaissance mixed with classical Roman undertones. The suggestion was enhanced by her artfully styled auburn cascading curls and braids that seemingly escaped a cunningly woven ribbon. Antique Renaissance earrings from Paloma's personal collection adorned her ears along with a matching necklace at her throat, all of which seemed to accentuate the paleness of her skin. The jewels, priceless and irreplaceable, were an extra burden of responsibility Kate could do without tonight, but Paloma had insisted.

A balding, middle-aged man in an expensive navy suit approached Giancarlo, giving Kate a sidelong glance. The two exchanged greetings in rapid Italian and made a few comments that caused them both to laugh. Kate gave a smile that she hoped was appreciative. The heat was giving her a headache and causing her concentration to slip.

The man turned to her and Giancarlo introduced him. Kate nodded and held out her hand, but the man leaned forward and gave her the customary three kisses on alternate cheeks, taking her by surprise. Though there had been a few of those from people she knew were friends of Giancarlo's. She didn't recognize this man, and his name hadn't registered with her.

He placed his hands on her shoulders, looked into her eyes, and spoke. She tried to concentrate and managed to make out that he was praising her work. His eyes, however, seemed to hold more than appreciation for just her work, and she gave him an uncomfortable smile.

"*Grazie*," Kate said.

She felt Giancarlo slip an arm around her waist protectively, but the words he spoke and the tone he used were friendly. He must dine with them soon, were Giancarlo's closing words. She echoed his statement with a nod, though her eyes were focused over the man's shoulder. He departed soon after, and Kate gave a sigh of relief. Before she could ask Giancarlo about the man, he was greeting someone else and falling into another easy conversation.

She felt suffocated again, the heat, the press of the crowd, and her growing headache all contributing to the feeling. She leaned up toward Giancarlo. "I'll be back soon," she said in Italian after assembling the phrase in her head. "I'm just going to get a breath of air."

She moved away before he could object and slowly weaved her way through the tight clusters of people. Once outside the gallery, she breathed the night air gratefully. The darkness was calming and the noise inside the gallery was muted. Looking up, she could make out the stars, even amid the glare from the lights of various restaurants that lined this main road of the Trastevere area of Rome, and tried to pick out the familiar pattern of the Big Dipper, Orion's Belt, and Polaris. At Somerton Lake, she would have had no problem, its familiar placings at different times of the year so well known to her. Here, she was more tentative and struggled a bit before she located Orion's Belt, recalling Shawn Colvin's song. The song drifted through her head, and she found herself humming it, swaying a little to its rhythm.

The stars reflected overhead, the words taking her to the sky of the song's southern hemisphere and the seven sisters in that sky. "The song mentioned "the dreaming time." Fragments of the Australian indigenous community's creation myth floated through her mind, linking to images containing the swirls and patterns of that culture that bled into the images of early Anasazi drawings in the American Southwest and from that, the loose shape of an idea that caught fire in her imagination. And suddenly, it wasn't Shawn Colvin's lyrics going through her mind, but others. Fragments, a string of words emerging from a part of her mind she'd shut off long ago. "The skies above you with stories to be told...." The words to the next phrase were just shaping in her mind when she realized what she was doing and shut it down. Those days were gone. She wasn't that person anymore. With deliberate care she returned to Shawn Colvin's lyrics and conjured up photographic images of stars with creation stories attached that would transform into art pieces to convey the ideas. Would she use those stories? Or maybe fragments of her beloved Romantic poets? She searched her memory of the English literature classes that had opened her eyes to such a wealth of beauty and meaning and fostered the deep love she held now for so many of the nineteenth-century poets.

"There you are," said a voice in Italian. Giancarlo emerged from the gallery. He took her hand and pulled her toward the entrance. "Come back in. It's time for my welcome speech."

She followed him inside to the small reception area. Groups of people spilled out from the exhibition area toward the reception desk. Giancarlo led her to the desk, nodding to one or two guests who greeted him. He picked up a sheet and showed it to her.

"See, *tesoro*, you are a success." He leaned over and kissed her cheek.

Kate took the sheet from him and saw a sea of red dots. It was the master copy listing her art pieces and beside all but two of the twenty pieces was a red dot. Sold. She'd sold eighteen pieces before the end of the night. She looked up at Giancarlo in disbelief. His dark eyes were alight with joy, his mouth curved into a wide smile.

She grinned. "I sold all these pieces? My first solo exhibition, and I sold nearly all my artwork?" On impulse she gave him a big hug, squeezing him tightly while issuing profuse thanks.

After a brief moment he pulled her arms away and placed them at her sides. "Careful, you don't want to get the earrings entangled in my clothes."

She moved back in horror, a hand to her mouth. "Oh, Giancarlo, I'm so sorry. I didn't think."

"It's of no matter," he told her. "No harm was done."

He took her hand again and led her through to the exhibition room, toward the first piece, to the little area they'd roped off in the corner where a small podium with a microphone had been placed. He took up his place behind it, positioning her next to him. He rested his graceful long hands on each side of the podium and leaned toward the microphone a fraction.

"*Attenzione, per favore*," he said in a formal manner. He began his speech by welcoming the guests and outlining the gallery's pedigree before continuing with a brief biography of Kate, describing her origins in America only briefly, and then moving on to her studies in Paris. He built her an impressive pedigree, too, in the process, to mirror the glamorous one of the gallery. The speech wasn't entirely unfamiliar to her, because he'd given her the gist of it to check he'd made no glaring errors, but the slight embellishments now made her blush a little.

Instinct caused her to step back a little, as if the movement would disassociate her from the words. She scanned the polite faces turned toward Giancarlo and reassured herself that these people would hardly remember anything that was said. For them it was about who was present and that they should be seen to be there among these elite art collectors and aficionados. And the photographers. They were in the front, just before her, taking photographs of Giancarlo and her, making her blink when the flash was used. She adjusted her stance, remembering the coaching Bibi had given her to achieve the most flattering angle for the camera.

Polite clapping ensued as she realized Giancarlo had brought his speech to a close, his hand squeezing hers. He pulled her slightly to the side of the podium, turning to her. She gave him a puzzled look, conscious once again that her dress had twisted slightly in the movement. Did she have too much skin on display? Giancarlo lifted her hand to his lips and kissed the back of her left hand. He began to speak again to the assembled group, but Kate was too aware that her arm had lifted to such an extent she might be revealing more than she was covering on that side of her chest. She tried to shift to face the gathered group more, but Giancarlo held her firmly and continued to speak. She tried to concentrate on his words, but only small groups of words filtered in like "fate" and "heart," and all the while her urge to pull her hand away became stronger.

She scanned the group standing in front of her for evidence that her fears had been realized, but all she could see were faces filled with polite interest, a few indulgent amusement and others boredom. Thankfully, Paloma had chosen to leave after the first few minutes, staying only long enough for photographs. Her work had finished.

Kate felt Giancarlo take hold of the third finger and she looked over at him, puzzled. He slipped his other hand into his suit pocket and withdrew it a moment later holding something. That something was slipped on her finger and transformed into a large antique ruby and diamond ring. Stunned, Kate looked up at Giancarlo unable to speak. His eyes were filled with love, joy and triumph, all the emotions that she seemed to lack at this very moment.

He gave her an amused look, leaned over to her, kissed her cheek and murmured, "Say *si*, my darling."

"*Si*," she said, as instructed.

More cameras flashed, the assembled group clapped loudly. Kate fought the urge to close her eyes and cover her ears.

EIGHT

Light shone through the window beside her to the Persian carpet that covered the heavily varnished walnut wood floor. Even in the middle of October, the sun still had enough strength to feel like summer in Rome, especially now, in Paloma's apartment, with the French doors firmly closed and only a small gap in one of the other windows allowed for fresh air.

Kate resisted the urge to wave her hand to cool her face, putting the wine glass on the small table beside her instead and folding her hands in her lap. Left hand on top. It was unplanned, but she refused to read anything into it, just that it helped settle her, to calm her mind and get through this conversation with Paloma. Still, underneath her left hand, she could feel the bite of the ring against her palm.

As if sensing her nerves, Giancarlo reached over from his place next to her on the sofa and squeezed her hands.

"So much to celebrate," said Giancarlo.

"Yes," said Paloma. "The exhibition was quite a success. All but two pieces sold. You are to be congratulated, Giancarlo. You have established your prominence in the art world, without a doubt. We must consider the subject of the next exhibition."

"I was thinking that we should build on the success of this one," he said, his eyes alight. "A similar series, only with a subject strongly connected to Rome. Using Dante perhaps."

"Or Virgil. *The Aeneid*," said Paloma.

"Yes!" said Giancarlo, smiling at his mother. "*The Aeneid* would be perfect. There are so many sites that Katerina could photograph."

Oh, so they hadn't forgotten her role in the process, thought Kate wryly.

"I had an idea already," said Kate. "I might explore the concept of the stars and the cultural tales surrounding them. For instance, the Native American tales, like Star Boy, or even the Roman and Greek tales. Orion, for example.

"Orion is a Greek tale," said Paloma tightly.

"It doesn't have to be Orion," said Kate. She made herself smile. "It was just an example."

Giancarlo took her right hand and lifted it to his lips for a kiss. "I'm glad you are excited and are filled with ideas, *tesoro*. And I like the idea of the stars, but perhaps we can put that aside for now and focus on *The Aeneid*, which is a natural follow-on from the style and form of your first exhibition. It's a time to establish your brand. Your unique selling point that is your signature art form."

His words were filled with reason, and Kate could appreciate all the points he made, but her heart and her art were taking her elsewhere. Surely he could understand that the inspiration, the desire that led her to create, couldn't be governed so purposefully by a brand or a unique selling point?

"Give my thoughts some consideration before you make your decision, Katerina."

"Yes," said Paloma. "Giancarlo is the expert. You should listen to him."

Paloma smoothed her immaculately styled Schiaparelli gown in jeweled colors. She was attending a dinner following this discussion. Giancarlo had persuaded Kate that this visit was an informal celebratory drink to celebrate the success of the exhibition and their engagement. The engagement had yet to be mentioned or acknowledged in any way.

"I promise to give it some thought," said Kate, looking at Giancarlo.

He smiled back at her, his eyes bright and filled with confidence. "I'm glad to hear it. I don't do this for me, *tesoro mio*, but for you. Because I want you to be a success."

She nodded. It was true, every word that he spoke. He'd proved it over and over again during the past two years since they'd met. He'd supported her every step of the way, helping her build this new life, forge the path into the art world. Showing her the way, guiding her.

She picked up her wine glass from the table at her side. Her elbow knocked the arm on the journey back and a small bit of wine spilled from the glass onto the cloth of the sofa. She cursed softly, forgetting for a moment where she was, who was with her. At least the wine was white. She glanced over at Paloma quickly and saw a flicker of disdain pass through her eyes.

Kate put her glass back down on the table and rose. "I'm so sorry. I'll just get a cloth."

"Nonsense," said Paloma in clipped tones. She looked at her son. "Giancarlo, call for Sofia."

Giancarlo rose and made his way to the door. Once there, he opened it, and Sofia appeared a moment later, as if she'd been waiting for a summons. Giancarlo returned to his seat while Paloma issued swift instructions about the spill.

Kate rose to make way for Sofia and watched as the maid assessed the spill, left the room and returned a short while later with a damp cloth that was applied to the spot with such delicate care that the flush spreading across Kate's face and down her neck to her chest deepened. No words were spoken. The whole procedure was carried out in tense silence, a further source of humiliation for Kate.

Once Sofia left, Kate returned to the sofa and took up a position a little closer to Giancarlo, away from the stain. She placed her hands once again in her lap, noticing that a small drop of wine had found its way onto the skirt of her dress. She resisted the urge to tuck it under her, away from Paloma's eagle eye. She'd probably seen it already anyway.

"I wanted to ask you about the wedding, Mamma," said Giancarlo. He smiled over at Kate before returning his gaze to his mother. "We of course want to consult with you on all things, since you know the best how these things must be approached. When would be the best time for the wedding itself?"

"We should wait until the spring," said Paloma.

Giancarlo nodded. "Yes, that would time it nicely after Kate's winter exhibition in New York."

"That's not confirmed yet, though," Kate managed to say.

She knew she shouldn't be surprised that nothing more was said on the matter of the spill, or even a reassurance that it would be fine. And Kate felt somehow an offer to pay for it to be cleaned wouldn't be appreciated.

"It's only a formality," said Giancarlo. "If your two pieces aren't sold, we can put those in for that exhibition and you can just produce more in a similar theme. Perhaps a different photograph, but using similar phrases to the phrases used in the original series."

Kate blinked. "That's a lot to do between now and the exhibition, which might even happen as soon as January. Or it could be in the spring. She didn't commit to a definite date. She just said sometime early in the New Year."

"But it's not as many pieces as the series here," said Paloma.

Kate looked over at Paloma, opened her mouth, and shut it. "No," she said finally. "She said fifteen pieces. So that would mean thirteen more. Creating just over four a month. That's what will be difficult to manage."

"That's just one a week," said Paloma. She tapped her nail against the wine glass she had in her hand. "Surely you can manage that, given the reason."

Kate looked over at Giancarlo who smiled at his mother indulgently. "Oh, Mamma, you shouldn't tease Katerina in such a manner. And you should go easy on her for now." He looked at Katerina, humor in his eyes. "You must get used to Mamma's humor. It is one of the little wicked mannerisms she loves to use." He placed an arm around her. "After all, you are to be one of the family soon."

Paloma smiled, but it didn't reach her eyes. "Of course, Giancarlo." She drained her wine glass. "Since you have mentioned it, perhaps we should set things in motion. There is much to be done. I will of course consult with the monsignor, and I'm sure we can secure the basilica for the wedding. The reception, I feel, must be at the Villa Borghese. We can limit the guests to 350. Once we secure those details, we can ensure the attendance of those who should be there."

The words washed over Kate and hardly registered, not just from the speed of their delivery in Italian, but because she was too astonished at their audacity. In theory, she couldn't argue with the choices. She should be thrilled to be married at one of the oldest churches in Rome, and to have a reception at a location like the magical Villa Borghese would be anyone's dream. She just wasn't certain it was hers.

"That all does sound lovely," Kate said eventually. "But I would want to check with my family and give it some thought before any final plans are made. After all, there is no rush."

Giancarlo gave her a reassuring smile. "There is no rush of course, Katerina. But Mamma is naturally excited and she is correct to want to get arrangements underway, even if we can only speak in rough terms of a date. There is much involved in planning a wedding for a family as prominent as ours."

The last words echoed in Kate's mind. How would she be able to involve her family in the wedding when her fiancé was from a prominent family in Rome? It was difficult to imagine.

———

Kate blinked her eyes a few times to regain her focus. She put the calligraphy pen down and stretched out her arms. The current art piece, a scene of one of the pillars of Medina ruins printed in sepia on thin rag paper, was stretched out before her on the artist table. The large window in front of her showed the small piazza below empty of anything but a few stray leaves whirling in circles on the cobbles. Late afternoon sun cast shadows on the buildings across from her. A tabby cat padded out from the side of one of the buildings, stretched, and carried on its way. She smiled at the sight, reminded of Max, suddenly, when he would stretch on the back porch before going down the steps to the yard. He was such a soppy old soul, really, not a fierce bone in his body, and loyal to the core. She thought of how he'd slept at the end of her bed when she was home. Just like old times. As if she hadn't been away. His presence had meant a lot to her, she realized. And had gone a long way to helping her cope with what had changed and what hadn't been said, but hung in the air like bad cologne.

She turned away, pushing those thoughts out of her mind

and returned her focus to the art piece in front of her. She had only started the calligraphy, conscious that she had a deadline of sorts pushing her on. It made her feel uncomfortable, the joy of the process and creation of the work somehow now muted with that worry lurking in the background. She studied the piece, second guessing the phrase she'd selected for it. It was in the original Tuscan, not only because it was part of the remarkable nature of Boccaccio's foray into writing in the vernacular at a time when it wasn't the norm, but because the words and letters worked with the image. Perhaps the place was wrong, though? But she didn't have time to go through the process of printing another image. She'd carefully allocated the amount of paper for this project, and she was using the spare sheets already for this next exhibition that only might take place.

She sighed. She shouldn't worry about the cost of the supplies. After all, she'd made a tidy sum from the sale of the pieces last week. But she couldn't help but feel that the profit really should go to Giancarlo, because he had invested untold amounts in her already. And not just the art side. She tried to promise herself that she would pay him back for all of it and that she was holding true to that promise.

She took up the pen and continued forming the letter, dipping the pen into the ink when necessary. She'd managed two more words when her phone rang. She ignored the first few rings, thinking it was Giancarlo asking when she'd be finished. She'd already told him she wouldn't be back until the evening. She had too much work to do. It wasn't until she caught sight of Tom's name on her phone that she put down her pen and picked it up, swiping it quickly to answer the call.

"Tom?" She could hear the anxiety underlying the questioning tone of her voice. She found herself toying with her engagement ring, pushing it around and around on her finger. She stopped, hearing the hitch in Tom's voice.

"It's Dad," he said. "He's in the hospital."

"The hospital? How? When?" Her anxiety had turned to alarm. She stood up and began to walk around the room.

"He collapsed. Ethan found him on the living room floor this morning when he stopped by." He took a deep breath. "He's in Somerton Memorial. I don't know anything yet. They're doing tests."

"Where are you?"

"Here, at the hospital."

She nodded, even though she knew he couldn't see her. "What sort of tests?"

"I don't know, Kate. Tests." His tone was sharp, stressed.

She took a deep breath. Tom was upset, she understood that, but she also needed to know more.

"When will you know anything? Did they say? Is he still in the Emergency Room or have they admitted him?"

"He's still here in Emergency, but the doctors are with him now."

Kate looked at her watch. It was after five. That would make just it after eleven in the morning in Somerton.

"How is he now? Has he regained consciousness?" she asked. The questions were just delaying what she knew she would do, but she needed to know. She had to know.

"He's conscious, at least when they admitted him, about an hour ago. I've been out in the waiting room since then. Ethan called the ambulance and then called me. I met them here at the hospital."

His breathing was more even now and he seemed calmer, but that made no difference to her at this point. She'd decided, though in truth she'd decided the moment Tom told her that her father had collapsed.

"I'm coming over. I'll book a plane and let you know the details," she said.

"Good," he said. "You should."

It might have been the tone of his words or the words themselves, but her uneasiness increased and suddenly her eyes filled with tears. She brushed them away. There was much to do if she was going to fly out tonight.

NINE

Kate took her suitcase from the rack above, picked up her handbag from the seat and made her way to the end of the train to disembark onto the platform. It had been a long day, and the late afternoon sun was already sinking toward the horizon, casting long shadows along the platform. Dust hung in the air, stirred by the small dirt lot that was beside the station. It had been a small goods yard many decades before, during the railroad's heyday, but now it only sported weeds and an occasional hopeful poster about local plans for its use. Plans that warring local factions apparently never allowed to come to fruition.

Kate didn't mind, though. It was old and familiar, and she wasn't going to argue with that as she stepped onto the platform. People shuffled around her, some commuters and others returning from a day's shopping in New York City. She walked toward the station, wheeling her suitcase behind her, looking for some sign of Tom. She'd told him she'd take a taxi, but he had insisted on picking her up. She sighed. He was probably delayed.

A hand grabbed the handle of her suitcase and she stopped, startled.

"Ethan?"

"Hi. Tom sent me to pick you up. He's at the hospital."

He stood over her, his tall frame filling the leather jacket and jeans he wore, his black boots scuffed. His hair was stuffed under another ball cap, and he wore sunglasses. No wonder she hadn't noticed him. And it just seemed incongruous for him to be here now. But the whole experience since the phone call had been out of the norm, so she shouldn't be surprised.

He leaned over and gave her an awkward kiss on the cheek, the brim of his hat catching her ear. Her hair was pulled back in its usual chignon, but much of it had come adrift in the journey, a large amount from her own absentminded toying.

"Hi," she said, gazing at him, off balance. She could hear her heart starting to race. The dark glasses prevented her from seeing his eyes. "How's my father doing?"

He gave her a reassuring smile as they headed through the now relatively quiet station to the parking lot. "Much better. At least that's what Tom says. I haven't been to the hospital since yesterday. I saw Tom briefly this morning at your dad's place and that's what he said." He glanced over at her. "I wanted to check on Max, because I wasn't sure Tom would make it over there. He was there after I'd taken Max for a walk."

She nodded, trying to take in everything he'd said. Some of it registered with her, but she knew she'd probably be asking the same questions later. They reached the truck. She was surprised to see that it was her father's own truck, and Ethan, as if sensing her question, gave her an apologetic look.

"Tom told me to take your dad's truck. I only have my motorcycle."

She nodded as she opened the passenger door and slid inside. It made sense. It just felt strange to be in the truck with

Ethan driving, his presence filling it. She buckled her belt, leaned back and sighed, suddenly tearful. With another deep breath, she forced the tears away. There was no time for that, really. Strength was what was needed now.

She watched as he exited the parking lot onto the road, noting his confident yet careful manner. At least she didn't have to worry about a motorcycle racing mentality behind the road.

Once they were under way, she turned to Ethan. "How did it happen?" she asked.

"You mean his collapse?"

She nodded.

"I'm not sure. When I stopped by, he was there on the living room floor."

"He hadn't stumbled and fallen?"

Ethan shook his head. No. He was in the middle of the floor. I rushed over to him and tried to rouse him. Then I called 911. And after that Tom. I stayed there until the paramedics came and went with them to the hospital."

Tom had told her something similar, but still, she wanted to hear it again from Ethan. She didn't know if it made it seem more real, but she just felt she had to ask the same questions.

"And you don't know anything more? What tests he had? Why it happened?"

He gave her a patient look and shook his head. "Sorry, I don't. But we can head straight to the hospital if you like."

"Yes, thanks. I'd prefer that." She thought a moment. "Unless you need to get back. You can drive to the house, and I'll drive from there."

"No, no," said Ethan. "It's fine. I'd planned on going there anyway."

She nodded and sank into thought. She'd tried to think of several different reasons that could have caused her father to collapse. But he'd been so healthy, a fact that she could confirm from her visit that had been so recent it didn't seem possible that he could be ill now. She'd said as much to Giancarlo when he'd asked her after she'd explained the situation. He'd been immediately sympathetic and insisted he would book her on the next plane to New York. He'd told her she must do what she needed to do for her family and to let him know what the situation was. His reassurances had helped as she flung clothes into her suitcase and loaded her laptop into the Fendi handbag once again. Without any extra thought she'd worn the same suit as before, though she knew Giancarlo would no doubt disapprove, thinking it should have been cleaned first, but she'd decided that it was better to wear something that was already wrinkled rather than get another suit in the same condition.

At least she'd remembered to slip on her engagement ring before returning to the apartment, so that when she dashed around it was on her finger ready for his scrutiny. She'd noticed he checked for it when he saw her, as if he couldn't quite believe that they were engaged. Or perhaps that was her own sentiment projected on him. She certainly couldn't believe it. And now, with everything that had happened, it seemed surreal, like an otherworldly image ready for some phrase of poetry in a language she couldn't understand. It might have been that which had prompted her to remove the ring once she'd boarded the flight, though she told herself it would be safer for a ring so valuable. It was definitely out of place here, now, in this truck, on the way to the hospital.

———

Kate followed Tom down the corridor, Ethan trailing behind her, the endless green linoleum floor and beige walls of the different corridors running into each other. Muted footsteps and muffled voices reached her from various turns and corridor offshoots. She tried to read the signs so she could remember the way. She'd texted Tom when they were pulling into the hospital parking lot, and he'd messaged back to say that he'd meet them down in the lobby. After a brief hug, he'd led them up there, saying they would talk in a moment. She could see why now. It wasn't easy to reach. He led her through some double doors, and they walked by a nurses' station. Tom nodded to one of the people standing at the desk.

"Tom," she said, pulling on his arm to slow him down. "What's going on? Tell me what you know."

He gave her an impatient look. "I will. I'm just taking you to the visitor's room."

She released his arm and let him lead again, glancing back at Ethan for a moment. He gave her a cryptic look and looked to his left, over at the nurses' station. It was then that she saw the large sign on the wall behind them.

Oncology Department.

Her mind froze. Was this a mistake? Maybe they didn't have a bed available for him on a regular floor. Surely that was it. With growing anxiety, she followed her brother into a small carpeted room off the corridor. Pictures in soothing colors hung on the walls and two cozy sofas and a couple of armchairs were arranged around the room. One corner held a small child's play center and a box of soft toys. Magazines and books were piled on a side table, but the coffee between the two sofas held one thing only. A box of tissues.

Tom closed the door behind her and dropped into one of the arm chairs, head down, running a hand through his hair. She felt Ethan's presence behind her, a ghost of a hand on her back. Reassurance. She looked over at Tom.

"Cancer, right?" she asked. "Isn't that what you're going to tell me?"

Tom looked up at her, his eyes filled with agony. "Pancreatic."

"Pancreatic?" she mimicked dumbly. She dropped onto the sofa. She knew that was an awful diagnosis. Tears filled her eyes and she tried to brush them away, but it was useless; they continued to flow. "How long?" she asked in a hoarse whisper?"

Tom shook his head his mouth firmly closed.

"Has he had a second opinion?" asked Ethan.

She glanced at Ethan who took a seat on the sofa beside her.

Tom shook his head. "No, I don't know. Apparently, he got the diagnosis a month ago."

Shock rushed through her. A month? He'd known for a month? Why hadn't he said? "Did you know about this? Why didn't you tell me?" She could hear the shrill note in her voice, and she fought to control herself.

Tom shrugged. "The doctors were surprised when I didn't know. They'd assumed Dad had told me."

"You didn't know, either?"

Tom shook his head. "You think I would have kept this from you?" There was a hitch in his voice. "I would have insisted he tell you. You had a right to know. We both had a right to know."

"Did he say why he didn't tell you?" asked Ethan.

Tom gave him a pained look and shook his head. "I haven't asked. It's been...well, it's been frantic. The doctor explained the situation to me only this morning. He's the specialist. Dr. Morrison. He said that at the moment they've been focusing on pain management. Hospice care. He's had radiation therapy, apparently. But he won't have any more treatment, other than what he's had."

"Hospice care?" Denial echoed through her mind. "Did you talk to Dad at all?"

It was still difficult for her to take in. Questions crowded her mind, but she found it difficult to sort through them.

"Yeah, for as much as I could get out of him. He's the one who told me he'd had treatment, and that was that. There was nothing more to be done. And then he told me he didn't want to talk about it."

She opened her mouth to protest, but shut it. It wasn't Tom's fault her father was showing his stubborn streak.

"Does he know I'm here?"

Tom nodded. "I told him last night when I managed to get up here for a few minutes to see him before they shooed me out. He said he was glad."

"Did the doctor say what the plan is?" asked Ethan in a quiet voice. "Will he have to stay in the hospital now?"

"How long has he got?" She asked. "Weeks? Months? Days?"

Tom's eyes filled. He shrugged. "I don't know," he said hoarsely. "The doctor said it's impossible to be specific, but he said it could be months. Maybe three, maybe four. The radiation has helped."

"Has it spread anywhere else?" asked Ethan.

Tom looked at Ethan, panic on his face. "What? No. I mean I don't know. I didn't ask."

"That's okay," said Ethan. "I wouldn't have changed what the doctor said anyway. He'd have taken that into account when he was telling you how long to expect."

The words washed into Kate, a few lodging, stuck in her mind, while the rest flowed away. She tried to focus on her breathing. She wanted to be strong, capable when she met her father. After all, she wasn't the one who was facing death. Her mind hitched on that thought, and she skittered away. One thing at a time. Go greet her father. See what he needs. Find out if he's staying. The list of tasks lined up, giving her a tether for her to grasp and pull her forward.

She gave a nod that might have been directed at Tom, but was more likely to herself. "Thanks, Tom." She rose, took a deep breath. "I guess it's time to see Dad."

In her handbag slung over her shoulder, she heard her phone ring. Giancarlo. She fished it out of her bag, confirmed he was the caller, and rejected the call. She couldn't talk now. He'd have to wait.

———

Kate stroked Max's head, her hand pausing to play with his ear, rubbing the tip. He pushed his head against her hand signaling his need for more. He'd always liked his ears stroked. It made her smile. Just for a moment. From her perch on the living room sofa, she watched Tom through the arched entrance to the dining room, calling out measurements to Ethan. With phone in hand, Ethan made notes of the numbers.

Tom was disheveled, his T-shirt half tucked in his jeans. Strain showed around his eyes and his whole air was anxious, in contrast to Ethan, who exuded a quiet calm. A calm that reached Kate in the living room. Ethan's voice, even when repeating the mundane numbers as he noted them down, was reassuring and his body language exuded strength. Regardless of his undeniably handsome looks Kate would still find her gaze gravitating toward him for that reassuring air.

The afternoon light poured in through the windows, filling the dining room with light and creating a warmth that only fall could bring to this room. Cozy. Familiar. The bookcases, spines faded in the strength of the light that shone in during this season and late summer, somehow reassured her too. The dining room was the best. Her father would feel that same comfort. He'd be able to look out of the window in the evening. Eventually. For now, it just made sense. Fewer stairs. The downstairs bathroom, though lacking a tub or shower, could still work.

Tamzin stood at the kitchen entrance off of the dining room, leaning against the wall, her arms folded, frowning. She'd arrived about ten minutes before, not long after they'd arrived from the hospital.

"Are you sure about this, Tom?" she asked. "Surely he'd be better at a hospice, where they have all the equipment."

"It's decided," said Kate. "And we'll get the equipment."

Tamzin gave her a dark look. Max had crawled up onto the sofa. Somehow Kate couldn't bring herself to order him off.

"But you have a life in Rome," said Tamzin. "It will all be on Tom's shoulders. And that's too much."

Tom called out another measurement to Ethan and then fixed his gaze on Tamzin. "Tamzin," he said, his voice firm. "It's been decided. End of story."

"I'm staying," said Kate.

Tom looked over at her. "What?"

"I'm staying. I'll look after Dad."

She'd thought about it on the way home from the hospital, even after Tom had explained what he thought should happen. Even after her dad said he'd be fine, that he didn't need anyone looking after him yet. The collapse had been nothing. A blip. But to her it had been a warning. A signal that time was running out. And she wanted to spend that time, whatever was left, with her father.

"No, Kate. It's fine. I can do it," said Tom. "But if you want to stay a few days while we set up the bed, and all that and be here for him when he gets home, that's fine."

She shook her head. "It's my choice. I'm not going to change my mind."

"She's right, Tom," said Tamzin. "It makes sense. And besides, you have enough going on looking after the store and preparing for your own show."

Tom frowned at Tamzin. "The show doesn't matter, Tamzin. None of that matters."

"I can help out, too," said Ethan. "Look after the store a few hours even, if you want. Or do grocery shopping, prescription runs, or just be here at the house when Kate can't."

Kate gave Ethan a grateful look. His eyes were filled with kindness and compassion. And something else. Sorrow. "Thanks, Ethan. You don't have to, but we appreciate it."

"Yeah, man. That's really decent of you," said Tom. He looked over at Tamzin. "Tam, it'll be fine. We'll get through this. And if the show doesn't happen, well, it doesn't happen."

"But Tom," she began, but Tom held up a hand and shook his head.

"Not now, Tam," he said with a sigh.

On the side table beside her, Kate's phone rang. She glanced at it and could see Giancarlo's name come up. She picked it up, rejected the call, and replaced it on the side table. She'd have to call him later. After she'd showered and maybe had something to eat. Suddenly, the most appealing thing in the world was the thought of curling up on the sofa with a bowl of cereal watching a mindless film.

Ten

Kate stared at the phone, taking deep breaths. The house was quiet, with just the sound of Max's faint snore as he lay curled up beside her on the bed. Outside she could hear a distant leaf blower, an ordinary sound that somehow seemed both wrong and comforting at the same time. The words she'd rehearsed early this morning seemed to blend with the whine of the leaf blower. She braced herself and hit the phone icon below Giancarlo's name on her phone.

Giancarlo picked up on the first ring. She didn't even have time for a sip of her coffee before he was launching into a stream of Italian, expressing his concern that something had happened to her. Hadn't he received her brief text last night, she wanted to ask him. She admitted to herself it was a bit cowardly to send it after she was sure he'd gone to bed, but she didn't want him to phone her immediately. She hadn't had the words. She'd wanted to just put everything aside for a few hours, to let her brain catch up, to allow her mind to settle down.

"I'm fine, Giancarlo," she said soothingly. "There's a lot going on. I didn't have time to phone. I think I said that in my text. Did you get my text?" She spoke in English. She just couldn't muster up the energy to speak in Italian. Not now.

"Yes, yes," he said, switching to English. Maybe he could sense her mental state. Her inability to cope with much. "But you didn't say anything more. How is your father? What happened with him?"

She took a deep breath and explained as calmly as she could what had happened. Laid out the facts. She'd rehearsed it in her head beforehand, hoping he wouldn't interrupt her, because his sympathy would undo her, and she wasn't ready for that.

He didn't interrupt her. He let her finish, but that was when his sympathy emerged.

"Oh, *tesoro*, I am so sorry. That is so difficult."

She cut him off, feeling the tricks pricking her eyes already. "It's fine. Don't worry. We're doing what we can for him."

"Of course you are. He is your father."

The statement irritated her for some reason, but she pushed it aside. Her emotions were all over the place.

"What can I do?" he asked. "Do you need some financial help?"

"No," she said sharply and then softened her tone. "No, but thank you, Giancarlo. It's fine, really. All taken care of. We're moving him back here, to the house, today. I'm going to look after him. I'm going to stay...as long as necessary." She didn't want to even try to put a deadline to the amount of time she would be here. She couldn't think about it.

"You are going to nurse him? Can you hire one instead? I'd be happy to arrange it."

"No, no," she said, the sharp tone returning. She understood he wanted to pay for it, but it seemed out of the question. It wasn't his responsibility. "He's my father, Giancarlo. I want to take care of him myself."

"But it will be difficult for you, darling. You are not a nurse, and surely it would be best to have someone with the expertise, for both your sakes."

Another flash of irritation rose. This time it lingered for a few moments until she forced it away.

"No, there's no need. I'll do it. It'll be fine. Tom and I can organize it if we need to."

"Of course. I didn't mean to say that you wouldn't help as well. I just wanted to make it easier for you."

She felt herself soften, guilty for her tone. "I'm sorry, Giancarlo. It's all just a shock at the moment. I'm still trying to take it in."

"No need to apologize," he said. "It is overwhelming, I'm sure. Can I send you anything, then? Do you have enough clothes? Buy what you need, my darling. Use the card I gave you."

She thought of the credit card he'd given her months before, now tucked up in a drawer back in Rome. Not that she would have used it. In some ways she was glad it was there, safe. Unused.

"I'm fine," she told him. "I have plenty of clothes."

"Do you have anything suitable for the New York gallery? You could go meet with Cassidy there, finalize arrangements."

She bit back the remark that came to her. The gallery and her possible show was the last thing she wanted to think about. Giancarlo had continued to speak, waxing lyrical about the success of her current exhibition in Rome, which had been prompted by the recent sale of the remaining two works she'd had in the exhibition.

"I'm glad the works sold," she forced herself to say. Really all it meant to her now was more pieces she'd have to complete if she did get the exhibition in New York. It might be better to forgo the whole thing. "Giancarlo, given everything, it might be best to withdraw the exhibition proposal from the New York gallery."

Silence hung in the air between them for a moment. "Katerina, *tesoro,* I understand why it might be difficult for you to think long term, but it will do no one any good if you make decisions quickly. Give it a few days, and we will talk again. You'll have had some time to think, consider everything and have a clearer picture of what to expect in the next few months."

And that's when she found herself agreeing. Anything to finish the conversation, move it on to a point where she could end the call, and turn her mind to matters that were much more important.

———

Kate heard the rumble of the motorcycle's engine before she saw it. Not that she was looking out the window, waiting. But from her perch on the armchair, putting on her old Converse sneakers, she could easily see the motorcycle pull up in front of the house when it did appear. The sound alone sent her heart beating faster, something she argued with herself to assign to the impending visit to the hospital to see her father.

She watched Ethan dismount the bike, remove his gloves and make his way to the house, the pavement ringing with the sound of his boots that only grew as he mounted the wooden stairs to the porch. It was only then he took off his helmet, leaving his shaggy dark hair a disheveled mess. But with the weathered brown leather jacket, the dark jeans tucked into his boots, it was a look that was effortless, not from trying, but from a natural, unconscious approach. It was a look she remembered well, a look that had appealed to her from the first time she saw him. So easy, so comfortable in himself that everyone was drawn to him. And that charisma was still there, reeling her in even now. She sighed. This wasn't the time.

She heard the knock on the door, and she saw him standing there, fist raised, his back holding the screen door open. The doorbell had long ceased to work, and now it made her laugh to think about the years her father promised himself he would fix it. But what need, when everyone just tapped on the door and opened it, shouting their "hellos" before going through to the kitchen or backyard, where her father was most likely to be. If the door was locked, then everyone knew Frank wasn't home, and they should return later.

Before she reached the door, it opened, and Ethan walked through after calling out a brief hello, only to stop short, startled to see her in the living room.

"Oh, hey," he said, his eyes bright blue in the light. He broke into a grin. "I wasn't expecting you to be right here."

She smiled, unable to resist the grin. "Just putting on my sneakers." She looked down at her feet, frowning. "Not sure how good these will be, but it's all I could find among the spoils of the past."

She'd paired the Converse with her mother's old jeans, unable to bring herself to even attempt to try on her old hipsters. The top she'd settled on was an old Henley with her mother's mottled green suede jacket. It was worn bare in places, but she liked that about it, along with traces of her mother's perfume that still clung to it. She'd opted for this combination after discarding the Dior cashmere sweater and soft casual pants that she'd brought with her. The decision to abandon most of the clothes she'd brought with her had prompted a visit to the attic, where she'd found some of her mother's old clothes as well as hers.

Ethan surveyed the sneakers and then the rest of her, his brows raising slightly. "It all works," he said. "At least I like it."

She made a face. "Really? My mother was a bit boho. Indie folk chick. At least that's what Dad said. She died when I was ten, and I don't remember that much. Well, this jacket, I remember this jacket."

Ethan nodded. "It's a good jacket. And it looks good on you."

She felt a flush of pleasure. "Thanks." Somehow, his reassuring words made her feel better. She felt herself relax a little.

"Ready then?"

She nodded and, picking up the keys on the little table, threw them to him. "You may as well drive."

He caught the keys and nodded. "No problem."

———

The hospital, when they arrived, was busy with staff and others intent on their various tasks and destinations, an almost stark reminder that life was continuing on, moving forward, that the seismic shift in her world created no obstacle for the rest of the world from functioning as normal. It could be seen as reassuring, and in a way it was, but the reality of the hospital for her only brought home the nature of her father's condition, and her heart, which had been brought under control back at the house, now increased its pace.

As if sensing her anxiety, Ethan reached for her hand and squeezed it as they made their way to the elevators and pressed the button to summon it. The elevator doors opened, and Ethan, still holding her hand, led her on to it and selected the third floor. The idea of lucky number three passed through her mind and she wanted to label it the lie that it was. She dropped his hand, suddenly self-conscious and very aware of how good it felt.

"You okay?" he asked.

She nodded and looked away, suddenly knowing she needed to breathe deeply or she would be crying before she reached the third floor.

"Do you need any groceries, or anything?" Ethan asked. "We can stop by the supermarket on the way back. Maybe some grapes? Isn't that what you bring sick people?"

"Grapes?" She asked him in disbelief. "Dad hates grapes."

"Your dad hates grapes? Who hates grapes? Grapes are the boss."

"The boss? Really?" She shook her head, amusement flowing through her. "Where did you pick up that phrase?"

He shrugged. "I pick up stuff. I'm cool. My bros are cool."

She laughed. "Your bros are cool," she mimicked. "See now, I'd expect this from Tom, because I know Tom is lame, but I thought you hung out in New York City. Not Mr. Roger's neighborhood."

He crossed his arms. "I stand on my coolness."

The doors opened. Third floor. Ethan grabbed her hand and pulled her forward. "Come on. We'll ask your dad for an impartial judgment."

"My dad? Are you serious?"

She smiled at him, willing to play along with what was an overall lame exchange, let alone the words he used to affect a cool attitude. It helped. Stupid and silly as it was, it helped.

A nurse emerged from her father's room when they reached the door. She smiled brightly at Ethan. "You can go on in. I was just doing a few things."

"Has the doctor seen him this morning?" Ethan asked.

The nurse nodded, her gaze slowly taking in the rest of him. He'd put his ball cap on, and he was wearing his glasses, but that didn't deter her flirtatious smile. "He's around somewhere. Did you want to speak with him?"

Ethan glanced at Kate who nodded. "Yes, if he wouldn't mind. Unless he's spoken with Tom."

"My brother, Tom," Kate added.

The nurse looked over at her, tearing her eyes away from Ethan. "Oh, right. Frank Wilson's son. No, the doctor hasn't spoken to any of the family this morning, as far as I know."

She left, giving Ethan lingering glances, but he ignored them, looking at Kate.

"You ready to go in?" he asked.

She nodded. It could be no worse than yesterday. Yesterday, when her father been hooked up to monitors and a drip, he looked so pasty lying in the bed. Even his voice had been weak, feeble, though the reassurances that he spoke tried to convey the opposite.

She felt Ethan's hand on her back, a repeated small gesture of reassurance, she knew, but her body tried to argue differently. It was all nerves, she reminded herself. She was all over the place, and this was a reminder. She entered the room, taking in the empty bed next to her father, now vacated of its surly occupant who'd been there the day before. Not someone she would wish on anyone, let alone her father in such a state of ill health. Today, though, her father was sitting out in a chair, the monitors gone, the drip removed, and color returned to his cheeks. His dark brown eyes were bright enough, though she suspected he was taking something to keep the pain from clouding them. And his once big frame that would ordinarily fill the room somehow seemed less, shrunken to a size that didn't seem like the dad she knew. He looked up from the newspaper he was reading and smiled.

"Katydid," he said, his voice full and warm. "Come give me a hug. I didn't get to welcome you properly yesterday."

He opened his arms and took her in when she reached him and leaned down. His embrace felt good, real and comforting with its strength.

She pulled back and took a seat on the bed beside him. "I'm so glad to see you looking better, Dad."

"I'm fine now. Just a little blip."

"Well, not quite a blip," she said. She opened her mouth to continue, but her father spoke first.

"Ethan, hello. Thanks for coming. And bringing my special girl."

Ethan grinned at him and grabbed a chair from the wall, pulling it closer to the two of them. "Of course. I knew you'd need to see your special girl. How are you feeling? You look better than you did."

"I'm good. Feeling much better. I'll probably go home today. Don't want to overstay my welcome."

"The doctor said you could go home today?" asked Kate.

Her father shrugged. "I'm sure he will. There's nothing to keep me here."

"How about the fact that you have cancer and need monitoring? That collapse didn't happen for nothing."

"The collapse was because I over did it. I know better now."

There was a stubborn tone to his voice. A tone that she knew meant he would not be budged. She sighed. He would do what he wanted, she knew that.

"Well, let's wait and hear what the doctor says before you go making plans," she said.

Tom entered at that moment, his face filled with concern. "What plans are you making?" he asked his father. Tom nodded to Ethan and walked to his father's side. "You're not thinking of going home today, are you? Because you can think again. You're not ready yet."

"So you're the doctor now, are you?" her father said, humor in his voice.

"No, but given everything, there's no way the doctor will let you go home today."

"Again I say, you're the doctor now, are you?"

Tom folded his arms. "Dad." His tone was firm, no nonsense. Stubborn meeting stubborn.

"Look, son," said her father. "It's not up to you to decide. I was talking with the nurses, and they thought it might be possible."

"Possible," said Tom. "But not guaranteed. Besides, we haven't gotten everything in place yet."

Her father narrowed his eyes. "What do you mean everything in place?"

Tom looked at him. "You can't expect to come home and have everything the way it was before. Things have changed. And we're dealing with it."

"Tom," her father's voice was sharp, firm. "I am not invalid. I am fully functioning mentally. I am going home and living my life the best that I can."

Tom nodded. "Of course. But we've got things in place to help you. We're putting a bed downstairs in the dining room. That way you don't have to worry about the stairs."

Her father's eyes narrowed. "You did this without talking to me?"

"Dad, look. We had to make decisions. And so we did."

"It's only for when or if you'll need it," said Kate, cutting in before it got worse. Tom was never diplomatic. "In the meantime I'm here, in case you need help."

Her father looked at her, his eyes alight with hope. "You mean you're staying?"

She nodded. "As long as you need me." She didn't want to say the words that hung in the air. She couldn't.

"But what about Giancarlo? Don't you have things you need to do there?"

She shrugged. "It's fine. You're more important than anything I have waiting in Rome."

She took his hand and squeezed it, meaning the words in so many ways she couldn't articulate.

ELEVEN

The shades of golds, amber, and crimson were too much to resist. It was almost without thinking that she grabbed her camera and headed out the door, heading toward the riotous color at the end of the block where an old Victorian house lay hidden behind a thick forest of trees so lush with leaves, it was only the house's small turret roof that was visible. Kate remembered that house from her childhood, the trick-or-treat visits that seemed all the spookier because Professor Emerson always sat on the porch dressed as an motionless zombie, complete with pale makeup and dark-ringed eyes, green nails, and dirty clothes, only to rise up unexpectedly as soon as their backs were turned and scare them in the most deliciously wicked way. Back then, the trees had been moderately high and the house clearly visible. Now, the trees were just begging to be photographed, a collage of shapes and colors.

Kate walked toward it, scanning the other houses, the street and everything else about the neighborhood she hadn't taken in since she'd arrived. Or for a long time before that, when it came down to it. The houses were for the most part in good condition, only some a little tired at the edges. The inhabitants reflected the odd mixture of houses. Spacious old Victorians toward one end of the street with the more modest Cape Cod and Sears craft houses at the other end. The Victorian houses were occupied by the academics and the Cape Cod and craft houses by the local townspeople who worked in a variety of occupations. The townies, as the college students called them. And as odd and seemingly idyllic it might appear, it was when the children came into it that anything laudable disappeared and the usual lines were drawn. How could you make friends with someone who was away at boarding school or at best went to a private school? Still, Professor Emerson and his wife, also a professor, had always been nice to her, even if their son, five years older, hadn't.

She stood a few feet away from the Emerson place, lifted her camera and began to click, pausing every few seconds for adjustments for focus and depth, trying different angles, becoming completely lost in the process. Instinct told her that this would be good for a project. She wasn't certain what yet, but that didn't matter. She walked around the trees, catching different angles. She moved closer and caught more glimpses of the house. She photographed the small sections of the muted, pale gray wood with the navy trim that peeped out and liked the contrast the wood hues played against the colors of the trees. She was also taken by the wrought-iron trim that featured in places. The fine Victorian accents caught her eye, and she found herself photographing sections of them. They all sang potential to her and she found herself humming a tune, words drifting around in her head. This time she let it play out and just enjoyed the moment and the moment that came after it, savoring it all, because she hadn't felt this kind of joyous inspiration in a long time. Not since her initial trip to Medina. But even then, there had been constraints driven by Giancarlo's expectations and her desire to meet them. This time, in contrast she just felt the pure joy and instinct combined with no real goal or understanding of what it might become. And no need to know yet. Fluid, dynamic. Just filled with possibilities.

She continued taking pictures, moving angles, positions, and using a few different lenses. She might come back at a different time of day. Maybe late afternoon, just before sunset, when the angles and light were different from this early morning light. She checked her watch and drew in her breath when she saw how late it was. She needed to get back for her father. He was probably up by now.

Ever since he'd come home from the hospital, he'd been determined to prove to everyone he was fine, that he didn't need any extra help. He'd even made Tom cancel the order for the hospital bed and refused to even entertain moving his own bed downstairs. Every evening since his return the week before, he'd made the trip up and downstairs, his steps firm and even. He'd also made a point of making his usual meals, though Kate had noticed that Max had taken to sitting beside him at the table, fostering the speculation that Max had some involvement in the clean plate he presented to her when she went to do the dishes. He had expressed gratitude for her presence and the various ways she tried to make his life easier. He'd never been one for doing regular laundry, or vacuuming. Those had been her chores from the moment her mother had died. And his cooking had only been sufficient for basic meals. Now she took over all of it, and was glad to do it. It kept her mind and body busy while she fought off unwanted thoughts.

As she neared the house, she thought she could hear faint sounds of music leaking out from inside. Was her father playing a CD or an LP? He hadn't quite been won over to Spotify, despite Tom's best efforts, insisting he'd rather look at cover art and read the lyrics to gain the full experience of the artist's work. She made her way up the wooden steps, pausing to note the cushions that had been left out on the porch swing. Something she'd forgotten last night. She hadn't quite created a routine that would allow her to remember it without thinking. Maybe a list would do it. Daily tasks. All these little details had slipped out of her world in the last ten years.

She opened the door and saw her father and Ethan seated on the sofa and armchair, guitars in their laps, picking out a melody. Max was laid out on the floor, head on his front paws, content, while the melody they picked out ambled and wandered around him like a lazy old day. Ethan was in his usual casual clothes, a flannel shirt flung over the ribbed shirt, hair its usual shaggy mess. His face looked bared, open, with no glasses or ball cap to shield it from scrutiny. Both he and her father had relaxed grins on their faces, eyeing each other occasionally as the music progressed. Kate paused, taking in the scene. She found herself smiling.

Max rose from his place and made his way over to her for a head pat. Her father looked up, his face brightening. "Oh, there you are. I was wondering where you'd gone."

She held up her camera, the strap hanging around her neck. "I was out taking pictures. The trees are gorgeous right now and I couldn't resist."

Her father nodded. "Yeah, they're something, aren't they?"

"Where did you go?" asked Ethan.

He set the guitar down, next to the sofa. She saw it was hers and surprised herself that she was pleased he felt he could borrow it.

"Just down the street. To the house at the end. The Emersons'."

"Professor Emerson?" he asked.

She nodded. "Did you have him for biology?"

He shook his head. "I had her for Microeconomics 201. Brutal."

"She was brutal?"

He laughed. "No, but microeconomics was."

"You took micro economics?" she asked, disbelief in her voice. She couldn't imagine him being that interested in any kind of economics. "I didn't think you majored in business. I thought it was English." She flushed a moment, realizing she'd given herself away. She shrugged, adding, "At least that was what I heard."

He gave her a speculative look. "I didn't major in business. But my father wanted me to, so I compromised and promised to take some of the courses, if only to prove that I wasn't suited to it, like he hoped I would be. He wanted me to take over the family business."

"I thought he was in politics?" she asked.

"He is, but the family has a company up in Boston. Well, near Boston. Aviation parts." He grimaced.

"And you don't find that fascinating?" asked her father, humor in his voice.

Ethan shook his head and snorted. "God, no. My dad can wax lyrical about it, but it just leaves me numb with boredom."

She gave him a sympathetic smile.

"That must be tough. For both of you," said her father, suddenly serious.

Ethan stared down at his hands and bobbed his head slightly. "Yeah, it was. Is."

She looked over at her father, and saw his face was filled with compassion. He knew what that was like, his own father having disapproved of his music career, wanting him to put the furniture store first. Her father had taken it on eventually, after Kate came on the scene and it was no longer practical to take Tom and her along for gigs, or leave them with babysitters. Had he regretted that? But she knew deep down, he hadn't. Still, it must have been difficult for him to bear his father's disapproval and the guilt that had probably come along with it. It was something she hadn't spent time considering. Questions came to her mind. Things she wanted to ask him soon. The reason for the need to act she pushed away.

"Did you get some good pictures?" asked Ethan, his head still lowered.

She understood he wanted to change the subject. "Yes, I got some great ones. Do you want to see?"

He lifted his head and smiled, his eyes clearing. She moved over to the sofa and took a seat next to him. With a few deft clicks she pulled up the images on the screen of the camera and passed it over to him, conscious of the warmth of his thigh next to hers.

He took the camera from her and began to scroll through them. "These are amazing," he said. He looked over at her, his eyes filled with admiration. "You're really talented. I wish I could have seen your exhibition. Do you have photos of it?"

She reddened at his words, pleasure spreading through her. "Thanks. I do have some, on my laptop. I'll show you sometime if you want."

Ethan finished scrolling and passed the camera to her father, who took it. "She's very talented, my girl. Always has been. First music, and now this." He began scrolling through the images, smiling and nodding. When he'd finished he handed the camera back to her. "You've got some really pretty scenes there, Katydid."

She nodded, thrilled that both of them had liked her work, even though some, she knew, were just experimental shots that would probably be discarded.

"Have you been to the lake at all?" Ethan asked. "The woods around it are amazing at the moment. The trees"—he shook his head—"thick with color. The maples just have a magic of their own, don't they? The way they mix the crimson, fire red, sometimes almost orange, the blood red, and an almost purple red..." His eyes were filled with warmth from the memory.

His words echoed in her head, *thick with color*. All the reds. Something prickled at the back of her mind, more than a creative urge, an inspiration. She paused for a moment, still staring at Ethan trying to catch hold of it.

"Do you want to go see them now?" Ethan asked, studying her. "I can take you on the bike. I've an extra helmet. Unless you have something else to do."

His words pulled her out of her reverie. She glanced at her father. "No, no. I should stay here. Besides, I need to do some work."

"Nonsense," said her father. "Go with Ethan. Take the truck so Max can go along with you. He'll love it. And no arguments. Don't think I don't know you're just saying you should stay for me. I'm fine." The last words he pronounced firmly. "And besides, this is still work, isn't it? You're researching potential pictures."

She laughed at the thought. She supposed he was right. It would be work. She looked down at the old sweatpants she was wearing, which she'd paired with an overly large NYU sweatshirt that had been Tom's, the Converse on her feet. The sweatpants were hers, but worn and hip-hugging. Good for a quick walk on a morning not particularly cold, but not for a ride on a motorcycle to a lake that could very well have cool breezes blowing from it.

She smiled at Ethan. "Fine, great. Thanks. Let me just change a minute."

TWELVE

Ethan was right. The colors were vibrant and alive, making the leaves dance, creating mosaics of patterns in the late morning light, both overhead and underfoot. She raised her camera time and time again, clicking away, until finally, she was just looking through the camera, stopping only to change F-stops. This time she also panned a shot at a slow shutter speed, to create a blurred effect. Max raced on ahead, sometimes doubling back as if he was wondering what was taking them so long.

Behind her, Ethan followed her silently, allowing her full rein on her creativity. The wind meandered through the trees, rustling, stirring the leaves to flutter and flirt, as if posing for the camera. Phrases drifted through her head, scattered words like *tapestry of color weaving a song, the music of leaves.* It fed the images, and she reached for a poem, but the words eluded her, the phrases that she'd just created overriding anything else. Never mind, it would come.

Ethan placed a hand on her shoulder. "Look, there," he said. He pointed through the trees to her left with his other hand.

"See, through the trees. You can see glimpses of the lake and with the light just so it's twinkling. Like diamonds."

Kate looked through the area where he'd pointed and studied it. It was a tricky but a very good shot. One she could do much with if she got it right. Slowly, she lifted her camera, conscious that his hand was still on her shoulder, warm and very real. Steadying. She narrowed her eyes, trying to focus on the shot, adjusting the lens, considering a filter, but in the end she decided she'd just make a few more adjustments and try another approach, maybe an overexposure. She clicked a few times, angling the camera slightly differently each time, then besides selecting different F-stops, she also changed shutter speeds to create a different kind of motion effect, making small adjustments for each shot. She was excited. More phrases came to her mind. *Light weaves through the leaves, creating patterns among the shadows.* No, too ordinary.

Above her, the crimson and green canopy nearly encapsulated them, and it was as though they were in their own little world, wandering through the woods. Ethan's hand had left her shoulder, and it was now sunken into the pockets of his jeans, his flannel shirt open to the breeze that stirred around them still.

"Do you remember 'The Song of Wandering Aengus'?" she asked him on impulse. That poem was about wandering in the woods.

"You mean the Yeats poem? Of course I do. I was an English major, remember? But weren't you too?"

She grimaced. "Yeah, I was. Much good it does me."

"What do you mean? Your dad says your art incorporates literature in the images."

She shrugged. "Yes, true."

He spoke the words of the poem slowly, and she stood

there, letting them infuse her with the deep, rich intonation of voice.

I went out to the hazel wood
Because a fire was in my head
And cut and peeled a hazel wand

His voice was resonant and the words threaded their way through her and lifted her up. It was a magical poem, perhaps overdone, but it held a lot about dreams and wisdom.

He stopped a moment, half way through the second verse, as if he was searching for the words. She picked them up, half remembering.

And someone called me by name:
It and become a glimmering girl
With apple blossom in her hair
Who called me by my name and ran
And faded through the brightening air

He grinned at Kate. "Ah, so you do remember too." He reached up and plucked a maple leaf from her hair. "Not quite an apple blossom."

Kate smiled at him and gave a small laugh. "No, not quite."

He held the leaf, stared down at it.

Though I am old with wandering
Through hollow lands and hilly lands,
I will find where she has gone,
And kiss her lips and take her hands;
And walk among long dappled grass,
And pluck till time and times are done,

The silver apples of the moon,
The golden apples of the sun.

Kate stood motionless, watching him hold the leaf, speaking to it, as if it were the glimmering girl. She wanted to capture the moment, the voice, the image, the scent of the leaves, of fall that held so many memories. She started to raise her camera, but abandoned the idea. Nothing would capture this moment except what she could conjure up in her mind. The poem. Him, standing there in the filtered light that picked hidden glints in his dark hair, sculpted his face and accented the thick lashes, half-closed as he studied the leaf and spoke the final words of the poem.

He looked up at her and gave her a slow smile and held out the leaf to her. "My lady," he said. "Though it be not an apple blossom, it is the crowning glory of this wood."

Kate grinned at him, enjoying the moment. She took the leaf and curtseyed. "Why thank you, kind sir."

They continued on their walk, Kate tucking the leaf in her camera bag. She scanned the area for more shots as they headed toward the end of the path that opened up onto the lake, about a quarter around the lake, and where they'd parked beside the cabin where Ethan was staying.

Max took that moment to appear out of the woods and race to Kate. She gave him a few pats, and he sat down next to her, his tongue hanging out until she and Ethan continued their walk and he tagged along after them.

"What made you think of the poem?" asked Ethan, coming up beside her. "Besides the obvious." He gestured around them. "Wood, wandering."

She gave a nervous laugh. "Well I had a few ideas about my next project. Maybe using Irish poets this time. 'The Song of Wandering Aengus' came to me." She bit her lip. "I mean, I know this isn't a hazel wood, and I'm not really sure where I'd find one near here."

"I guess there aren't any hazel woods in Italy, either," he said.

She snorted. "No, probably not. Which is just as well, because Giancarlo wants me to do another project with Italian literary figures." She made a face. "Like Dante."

Ethan looked up sharply and laughed. "Dante. You're joking. How would you capture that in images, or does he want to insinuate that Rome is one of the circles of hell?"

She laughed. "Pompeii. An inferno of a different sort. I could photograph Mount Vesuvius."

He joined her laughter. "Wait for it to erupt, and you can get all that molten lava. What a photograph."

She gave him a serious look. "Hmm. Maybe. I mean the shots would be amazing. And I could do so much with them. Create a series. Yeah, I think it could work. Thanks, Ethan."

"What?" said Ethan, his expression filled with surprise. "You're not serious, I hope."

She elbowed him. "No, of course I wasn't serious. Though don't say a word to Giancarlo. He might like the idea and try to arrange for the volcano to spout off a bit of molten lava."

Ethan frowned. "Really? He'd do that?"

She shrugged. "I don't know. Probably not. His family is very influential, though. He might think it possible to get someone to seed it, or figure out a way. Or at least look into the timing of the next small eruption."

"Wow." Ethan was silent for a moment. "Your dad says that it's serious between you two."

"Yes," she said. "I suppose." The words of doubt slipped out before she could halt them. Was there a "suppose" about it? "I mean, we've been going out for a while."

"Your dad says you share an apartment now. That seems pretty serious."

She shrugged. "Yes, you could say that."

"But you don't? Say that?"

She bit her lip. "Yes," she said, forcing a firm tone. "Yes. I do say that."

"So, you're happy." His voice was soft, his eyes, searching.

She looked over to the lake just emerging as they reached the end of the path, the trees thinning to nothing. She took a deep breath, putting away the memory. It was only a lake. A narrow rocky shoreline was between them and the lake. She climbed onto one of the rocks that jutted out into the water, and from her new perch the expanse of the lake stretched out before her. It glittered in the sun, now at noon height, not quite overhead. She heard the soft lap of the water against the shoreline and let the sound soothe her for a moment. Max came up beside the rock and sat down, leaning his weight against her legs. Comfort. Reassurance.

She turned and looked down at Ethan. "Yes, I am. I owe Giancarlo so much. He's helped me more than I can ever repay. My career would be nothing without him. He's shown me so much. Taught me so much."

Ethan nodded. "Good."

The word was simple and seemed to imply approval, but it left Kate unsatisfied. She didn't want to say anything more, though, because there was so much she hadn't said. And the omissions hung in the air. She didn't know why she hadn't said the words that would confirm their commitment, their love. She was conscious, too, of the finger on her left hand that was still bare of Giancarlo's ring.

"Are you in a relationship?" she asked. The words had come out, perhaps from a defensiveness, or perhaps something else, something she'd rather not consider.

"Me?" said Ethan. He shook his head. "I don't have time for a relationship. I'm too busy."

"Busy? Busy with what?" She gestured around her. "You don't seem busy. Aren't you a songwriter for a few bands?"

He frowned at her. "My work keeps me very busy. The band I write for takes up a lot of time. Studio and other things."

"You only work for one band? Surely you have time to at least date."

He shrugged. "I'm doing other things." He cleared his throat and looked out to the lake, avoiding her scrutiny. "I'm writing a novel, if you must know. Well, trying to write a novel."

She jumped down from the rock. "Really?" she said, placing her hand on his arm. "That's great, Ethan." She squeezed his arm and grinned. "See, you're making much better use of your degree than I am. Writing lyrics and a novel. You even get the music too. Your degree major and minor."

He looked down at her, a wry smile on his face. "Yeah, I guess." He studied her face a moment. "Why didn't you minor in music, Kate?"

The grin froze on her face. "Why would I have done that?" she asked stiffly. She turned from him and started to retrace their steps through the woods back to the house.

Ethan, grasped her arm gently, holding her back. "Kate. I'm not sure why that question made you angry, but I'm sorry. I just know that you're extremely talented, have an amazing voice, and you obviously love music."

She forced her anger back down. It wasn't his fault. He knew some things, but not everything. She forced a neutral expression on her face. "No, it's okay. I shouldn't have lashed out that way." She took a deep breath. "It's a long time ago, Ethan. It's just what happened. I don't really play music anymore." He raised his brows. "Well," she amended, "I don't normally play music. I have other things in my life. It's just now, for Dad. I know he likes it."

Ethan smiled. "I'd say it's more than just your dad who likes it."

She shrugged. "Maybe."

"I like it. You're good."

She let the remark pass her by. "My dad thinks you're good, you know. I mean, you are, but he really admires you, I can tell. And that's no small thing, really."

"I know," he said, his tone serious. "I really appreciate it. I'm a big fan of his music. I have one of his CDs. I got it years ago, when I first heard someone play their music on the radio. I think I must have been about twelve."

"Twelve?" she asked, startled. "You were twelve when you heard an American Sky song?"

He nodded and laughed. "Yeah, it made an impact."

She blinked. She knew Ethan was under a year older than her. So that must have been right after her mother died. Of course, some local DJ would have played one of their songs.

"Which song was it, do you remember?"

"'Rossetti Girl,'" he said.

She flushed with pleasure. She loved that song, and she knew her mother had too. "My dad wrote that about my mother because he thought she looked like she was something from the Pre-Raphaelite period. When my mother sang that song, she used to dress the part. You know, hair loose, flowing gown, big eyes."

"I can picture it," Ethan said, smiling at her. "You look like that too, sometimes. Like now."

He reached out and touched her hair, which was loosely gathered into a braid. It hadn't seen her straightener since she'd arrived.

She laughed, aware of his hand still hovering over her hair.

"You're kidding, I know. I look like I've been dragged backward through a hedge."

He dropped his hand and looked away. "You look fine. It suits you. And what you're wearing. It's more like the Kate I remember."

Her heart stuttered at his words. There was so much in those words that confused, troubled, and angered her, but she knew it was best if she just left it all alone.

"I'm not that girl anymore," she said firmly.

He looked at her and nodded. Beside her, the dog nudged her hand, wanting a quick pet as they continued to the house.

Thirteen

The supermarket was busy enough, and Kate was glad for her list. She wasn't certain she would have been able to get everything that was needed if she had to just walk around and think of it between the number of people shopping and the store's new arrangement. Well, new to her. This was the second time she'd come, and she was still getting used to it. She pushed the cart toward the vegetables, consulting her list. The cancer counselor had given her a list of foods and a few brochures with recipes that would help her father with his digestion, and she was determined to do everything she could. It still felt surreal to be thinking in terms of advice from a cancer counselor.

The assortment of colors in the vegetable display caught her eye, and she smiled at the thought of photographing them. She'd taken pictures of the market at Piazza Navona in Rome many times and loved the play of color and shapes, the red peppers hanging down from a stall, the displays of reds, purples, yellows, and greens so vibrant against the white of the vendor's apron and olive skin tone. This was different, more orderly, the inside UV light giving it a different tinge that she could exploit on the computer. She tucked away the thought for another time, when it was less crowded.

"Kate?"

The voice came from behind and startled her. She turned. Mark. He was older, his face sharper, more defined and his frame had filled out, becoming muscular. The blue eyes were the same, though. There was no mistaking them or the light of recognition in his eyes. The pleasure.

The harmonies were perfect tonight. Missy crooned into the mike beside Kate, their eyes locked, their voices in perfect sync. It was the best performance they'd ever given, and they both knew it. Missy was rocking it in jeans and Doc Martens, her long hair swinging in time to the fringes of her jacket and it made Kate smile. The little variations on the guitar Kate had added had made Missy laugh and answer with her own flourishes on her guitar. They were on fire. She looked out into the audience and could see Mark there, his fingers forming a chef's kiss on his lips. He knew it, too, and was sharing the joy of it with them. The best night. The best night of their lives.

She stiffened at his smile. "Mark. How are you?" She kept her tone civil but distant. She didn't want to encourage conversation. She would exchange the basic pleasantries and excuse herself.

Mark moved nearer and took her into a big hug. He still had his boyish smile and the sandy dark hair, although now it was tamed into a more conventional cut. "It's so good to see you."

She remained still, unable to bring herself to return the embrace.

"When did you arrive?" he asked, his tone warm, eager. "I'd heard you were in Italy or something."

She nodded. "I've only been here a short while."

"Are you here for good, then? Have the charms of Italy worn off?"

Kate gave him a wan smile. "No. I still live there. I'm only here for a visit."

"You'll have to come over so we can catch up."

"Mark?" A woman came alongside Mark, sliding her arm through his.

It took Kate only a few moments to recognize her. Though her hair was shorter and no longer gathered up into a ponytail, she still had the same petite, slim athletic body that earned her the captaincy of the cheerleading squad back in high school. Belinda Masterson. Or Bunny, as she was known back then.

"Oh, Kate," she said. "It's you. Didn't recognize you at first." She waved her hand up and down toward Kate. "Your, um, clothes. They're kind of unusual."

If Kate had any question about the identity of the woman standing in front of her, the words and condescending tone gave all the confirmation she needed. She looked down at her mother's belted-in jeans, her mother's peasant blouse Kate had worn on impulse, and the old corduroy suit jacket that had been either her father or grandfather's, which she had paired with a dark wool scarf for good measure.

She looked up and grinned. "Paris fashion, Bunny. Sorry if you didn't understand that."

Bunny blinked, looked Kate up and down, her brow furrowed a moment, before she glared at Kate. Kate gave her a fake smile.

"I was just saying to Kate that we should catch up with her," said Mark. "Maybe invite her to dinner."

Bunny looked up at him, clutching his arm tighter. "Kate might not have the time, babe."

Kate stared at Mark who turned to her, a smile lighting his face. "Sure, you can make time for old friends, can't you Kate? It's been so long, and we'd love to have you over."

We? Since when had they become a "we"? She glanced at Bunny's left hand, where a wedding ring and an accompanying diamond ring rested. Kate's heart lurched at the betrayal. How could he? Though Mark had played football, she, Mark, and Missy had avoided Bunny at all costs. Kate gave him a look that she thought communicated all the disbelief and utter betrayal she felt.

"Please say you'll come," said Mark, the plea in his eyes as well as his voice.

She looked down at her feet, to hide the anger and hurt that were raging through her now. "I don't know. I'm pretty tied up with my father. He hasn't been well."

"Your dad?" said Mark. "I'm sorry, Kate, I hadn't heard. I hope it's not serious."

She forced a smile. "Thanks. I can't tell yet what the situation will be."

"Well, why don't you give me a call when you know more?" said Mark. He dug his phone out of his pocket and handed it to her. "Here, put your number in there, and I'll text you."

Kate took the phone reluctantly, unable to think of a reason to refuse. She was conscious of Bunny's sullen glare, and perhaps it was that which made her give her a smile and say, "Thanks so much for the invitation. I'll be sure to let you know."

———

Kate walked into the kitchen and set the grocery bags on the kitchen counter, Tom following close behind her. She'd refused his help to carry them in, suppressing her annoyance that he felt she couldn't manage, because she knew it was her own distress that was causing such a ridiculous reaction to his offer of help.

"You okay, Kate?" he asked, his face filled with concern. "Are you worried about Dad?"

She looked at him and shook her head and tried to put the meeting with Mark and Bunny out of her head. She'd didn't have to ever see them again. "No, I'm fine. Just a little tired, is all. You know, adjusting to the time zone and all that."

He studied her a moment and then nodded. "Yeah, I can imagine. You've had a lot going on since you arrived, and not really much time to just relax and get over the jet lag."

She gave him a grateful smile. "Exactly." She turned to the groceries and began to unpack them. "Have you been here long?"

Tom shook his head. "No, not long. Ethan was here when I arrived, but he's gone now. Said he had a few things to do."

"He was?"

She didn't know why she was surprised. He'd come the last few days, usually in the morning, to chat or play music with her father. She'd started to look forward to it, really, hearing the two of them talk about everything and nothing, but mostly about music. Yesterday she'd found herself sitting there and participating, singing along the one time they'd played one of her father's songs.

"Yeah. He and Dad really get along. I'm glad Ethan doesn't mind spending time with him. Phil and Stokey have said they'll come every weekend they can, but it's nice for Dad to have someone there during the week."

She nodded, agreeing wholeheartedly. Ethan was good to visit. He'd been more than good.

"Oh, you have a package, by the way. I caught the UPS guy when I arrived as he was walking up the path to the house."

"A package?"

"Yeah. It's on the dining room table. Biggish. From New York by the looks of it."

She gave him a puzzled frown. Was it from the gallery? But why would they send her something? "Thanks, Tom. I'll have a look after I put away the groceries."

"I can do it for you."

"Aren't you supposed to be at the furniture store?" she asked, suddenly remembering.

He shook his head. "Fred's there today. He's still part time. Usually I take that opportunity to work in the back in my workshop, but I thought I would come and see Dad instead."

She nodded. "He's still doing well. A little tired maybe. The stairs can be a bit much, but of course he'd never tell you that."

Tom snorted. "Yeah. He just told me he's fine. No problems."

She rolled her eyes. "You know him."

Tom squeezed her shoulder. "I'm glad you're home, Kate. And that you're here, keeping an eye on him."

Tears gathered in her eyes at his comment. "Me, too," she said softly.

He squeezed her shoulder again. "All right. I'm off now, if you don't mind. I'm going to try and get a few hours in at the workshop so Tamzin won't kill me the next time she sees me."

Kate raised her brows. "Really?"

Tom laughed. "Well, she's a real taskmaster. She wants me to have more pieces done. Not furniture commissions, but real art, as she calls it."

"Tom, all your work is art. There's nothing wrong if it's functional." She tried to keep her voice light, because she knew he could get prickly if he wanted.

He shrugged. "Yeah, whatever. Tamzin may disagree, and I don't want to renege on the commitment I made for the show."

She thought of her own promises she'd made to Giancarlo. "I know. It can be tough."

He smiled. "I suppose you do." He leaned over and kissed the top of her head. "See you." He walked out of the kitchen and after a brief farewell to her dad, he left, leaving her to mull over the unusual departing gesture.

"What's in the package?" shouted her dad from the living room.

She could hear him rustling around, rising from his armchair that had started to become his daily spot. From there he could look out the window, read his book, or play his guitar.

Half of the groceries were still sitting on the kitchen counter, but the cold items were now safely stored in the fridge. She wiped her hands on her jeans, and still wearing the corduroy jacket that Bunny had disapproved of, moved into the dining room. She thought of them again, still disbelieving the possibility of Bunny and Mark married. A short sharp pain seared her chest and she rubbed it unconsciously. She swallowed, took a deep breath and shoved the image of those two aside.

She glanced over at the dining room table. There, lying on Tom's beautiful table, was a large box. Her father joined her there a moment later and offered his pocket knife, a tool that had been by his side for as long as she could remember. She took it gratefully and used it to slit the tapes. The only label on the package was too blurred for her to really guess the contents of the box, but as she pulled back the packaging, she knew. Art supplies. Art supplies that she used back in Italy. The inks, calligraphy pens, the rag paper and all the other bits that she needed for her art. And a message stating that a printer enlarger was on its way in a separate delivery and a short note that indicated Giancarlo had placed the order.

Kate paused and stared down at it, not knowing whether to be overjoyed or deeply annoyed. There was an unsubtle message there from Giancarlo, without a doubt, but at the same time, she had more than enough time on her hands that refusing to use the supplies seemed ridiculous. Petty. And perhaps she might have the time to explore some of the new images she'd taken recently. Joy. She would decide on feeling joy at his thoughtfulness.

———

Max nudged her hand with his nose, signaling his need for her to pet him. She understood that sentiment all too well, because now, as she sat on her bed, she felt the same. The thought of Giancarlo taking her in his arms seemed all too desirable, a need that was so strong, she had to take a deep breath before she pressed the icon on her phone to initiate the video call. She hoped he'd pick up. She wanted to see his face, to feel reassured by his presence, even if it was virtual.

A rapid stream of Italian issued from the phone as soon as the call connected. She struggled to hear, trying to make sense of the words.

"Speak English, Giancarlo," she said, suddenly tired. "I-I can't understand you, I'm sorry."

"I am sorry, my darling. I was just about to phone you with some wonderful news, and I got carried away. You are well? How is your father?"

She smiled at the excitement in his voice. "I'm okay. It's good to hear your voice, Giancarlo. I've missed you." She took a deep breath. "My father is doing well enough, considering everything, but I can see he's getting weaker."

It was the first time she'd given voice to what she'd been observing, and it brought tears to her eyes. She swallowed and tried to clear her mind of all the implications of her words. "What's your wonderful news, then? I could do with some of that."

"This will bring joy to your heart," he said. "I have just spoken with your gallery owner in New York, and she has confirmed she will have an exhibition of your work. The dates she offered were the first week of February. I agreed immediately. We don't want this opportunity to slip through our fingers. She'll meet with you the day after tomorrow at her gallery to discuss specifics."

"What? No, I mean, I can't, Giancarlo. It's too soon. And I can't meet with her, then. I have to be here for my father."

"Oh, no need to worry about that, darling. I've arranged everything. That was my other surprise. A nurse will be there to stay with your father for the day so that you can attend the meeting without worrying about him."

His words stunned her to silence. "Giancarlo," she finally managed. "I appreciate your thoughtfulness, but it's unnecessary. I can make my own arrangements."

"I wanted to make it easier for you. You have so many other things to manage. Let me do this for you."

She shook her head, more for herself, to clear her mind, but the intent was there for him, too. "No," she said sharply. "No," she said again, this time softening her tone. "There's no need, really. I can have Tom or Ethan stay with him."

"Ethan? Who's Ethan?"

"What?" She caught herself. "Oh, Ethan. He's a friend of my father's. He's been visiting him regularly."

"Ah, I see. How nice."

Giancarlo continued on, explaining the specifics of the exhibition, but the words washed over her. All she could think was that the pressure to produce the works on time had become reality. She bit her lip and noticed the bare finger on her left hand. The ring was now safely tucked up in the top drawer of her dresser. She still hadn't put it on. It just seemed out of place here and, she told herself, liable to get easily caught or damaged in the mundane tasks she did every day now. Max, as if sensing her distress, licked her hand.

"You will tell her this, my darling?" Giancarlo was saying.

She caught herself. "Yes, yes of course."

"And you have the Versace suit with you, right? That has an edgy tone. Wear that."

The Versace. Which was that? The dark blue with the gold thread? "Uh, no. I don't have that one with me. I have the Chanel." She thought of the suit she'd worn. It was creased, she was certain, the journey from Italy ensuring that. She hadn't bothered to get it dry cleaned.

"The Chanel. Yes, good. Wear that, then. It's not quite as artistic looking, but it will speak your worth."

Speak her worth. Would it though? Was her worth in that suit, and would it explain the nature of her artwork?

"Yes, fine. I'll wear that."

"Did you get the package I sent?" Giancarlo asked.

"What? Oh, yes. That's why I phoned. Thank you for sending it."

"Oh, good. I'm glad it's arrived. Now, my darling, you have no reason to worry. You can work there on your art. You have everything you need, and if you need anything more, let me know. I will ensure you get it."

She heard his words and knew they were well meant, but they made her tired. She knew she would be appreciative that all her supplies were here at some point, but now it felt like too much. Now, all she could think was she needed a quiet place, a quiet moment with no pressure and nothing to think about.

Fourteen

The lighting even in this small office was carefully calibrated for its ambience, the air subtly scented with an expensive diffuser. Original modern abstract and representational paintings hung on the walls in an eclectic mix that pointed clearly to the owner's knowledge and expert eye. Kate had absorbed all these details of the gallery on her first visit, but now it felt as if she could study them. And so far, she liked what she saw.

Kate pointed to the images arrayed in a grid on her laptop and turned to Cassidy, the gallery owner. "These are some of the photos for my new project, but you get the idea for the theme and approach. It will be similar to the other exhibition in Rome, only the words of the poem fragments will be from the Yeats poem, 'Wandering Aengus,' weaving through the branches, like leaves. It will be the words wandering," she added, smiling.

Cassidy nodded, her dark eyes alive with excitement. Her hair was wrapped in a brightly printed scarf with braids woven through them, setting off her dark skin. It was a bold look that only reinforced Kate's impression of this confident woman.

Cassidy clicked on the first image and enlarged it. "Wow."

"I'm thinking I'd use that image with the opening phrase of the poem," Kate said. "I might also do 'The Two Trees,' as well. There's an image further on that would suit that. A few of them, really."

Cassidy clicked through the other images slowly, while Kate commented and described how she would approach the artwork she'd create from them. Cassidy nodded, asked a few questions, but gave Kate very little idea about her thoughts on the concept as a whole, now that she was explaining the details. Kate had only broached the subject of this other project after Cassidy had seen every slide from the pieces of the other exhibition in Giancarlo's gallery and some test images she had for his ideas for the one in New York. Cassidy had nodded and seemed to approve, but then she'd asked Kate what other works she might have underway in case the gallery decided to go in a slightly different direction. It was only after Cassidy's question that Kate had mentioned her idea about the use of Yeats's poems and the dynamic she would create from them. And now, the more Kate talked about it, the more she found she was excited to create it. To bring the image of the finished piece in her head into being.

After Kate finished describing the images, Cassidy went through them again, studying each picture carefully while she murmured to herself. Kate looked up and took in again the very chic office space with the large glass divider that separated it from the rest of the gallery. Through the glass she could see the current exhibition, an array of large canvases filled with dynamic impasto swirls of magenta and purple suggesting mountains, deserts and seas. The stark minimalist white walls with discreet lighting and bare walnut wood floor set it off perfectly. The works were eye catching and stunning, and for a moment Kate wished she could manage something so beautiful.

When Cassidy finished viewing the images, she looked up at Kate and beamed a smile at her. "I love it. I think we should go with this idea, instead."

Kate startled. "You mean instead of the Italian concept?"

Cassidy scrunched up her nose. "Though the Italian concept might be dramatic, I'm not sure you can marry phrases of Dante's *Inferno* to images successfully. And of course I think you'd mentioned you would use the original Italian. And I understand the reason. It is symbolic as one of the first works to be published in the vernacular."

Kate wasn't certain how to answer that. She wasn't even certain that *Inferno* was the first work to be written and published in the vernacular. She had a feeling it might have been one of Dante's other works. But Cassidy's sentiments matched her own, and though she hadn't really voiced those concerns enough to Giancarlo, it had probably factored in her lack of enthusiasm for the project.

"On the other hand," said Cassidy. "Using English poems and poets that link so directly to the landscape like this is pure genius." Cassidy tapped a purple-tipped fingernail against her lip. "Would you just use Yeats or would you use others? Or maybe just Irish poets? They would go over big here."

"I-I'm not really sure. I mean, Yeats just sprang to mind when I was looking at some trees. But they aren't hazel, so I may limit it to the 'Two Trees' theme and maybe other poets who talk about trees. Or relate to other aspects of nature."

She could feel the excitement building again. The ideas were flooding her mind, making her itchy to get started as soon as she could. The need to create, get lost in the process and the world of the image and the words that expressed it. If only she could weave in the music, she thought, it would be a perfect array of how the words, images, and sounds all linked for her when she thought of her art. It was a notion that surprised her as she thought it, startled her. She'd spent a long time suppressing that musical side and it just kept leaking out recently, a situation that disquieted her. She took a deep breath. She would do best leaving that aspect aside. Her artwork was enough.

"Is that settled then?" Cassidy was saying. "If so, I'll have the contracts drawn up and sent off to you. Do you have an agent? Giancarlo, is he your agent?"

Kate blinked at her, wondering what to say. "Well, I suppose he is. I mean he acts on my behalf, really."

She nodded. "I'll get them off to Giancarlo, then."

Cassidy stood and Kate shut down her laptop, stuffing it in her bag. She'd opted for her old leather messenger bag she'd used in college. Somehow her Fendi bag didn't match the clothes she was wearing. After donning the Chanel, she'd decided it was much too wrinkled to pass muster and ended up with her mother's rust wool skirt, her father's Aran sweater that she'd pulled in with a leather belt. On her feet she wore not the expensive Ferragamo pumps, but her mother's old black leather ankle boots, over some ancient dark-blue tights. Her hair, untouched by a straightener, was in all its full-volume glory, only loosely tied back with a navy ribbon she'd found at the last minute. The effect was far from sleek and polished, but it seemed to reflect how she felt at the moment. It was neither her old self back in college, nor her new self in Italy. It was different. Interim. Or maybe limbo.

She stuck out her hand to Cassidy. "Thanks, Cassidy. For everything."

"I should thank you," said Cassidy. She smiled. "I have a feeling this is going to be the rage this winter." She gestured to her. "And your look you've got going on there. You're really rocking the artwork, there, girl."

Kate looked down at herself and laughed. It all seemed

absurd suddenly. Her. Rocking a look that was her artwork. It was all too strange.

———

A cool wind-tunnel breeze caught Kate as she exited the gallery, catching up her hair and blowing it all around her, despite the tie that held it back. Kate greeted the sensation with a delighted smile, her mood excited and even joyful. The meeting had given her a real creative boost, and she reveled in the experience, realizing she hadn't felt this inspired in a long while. Her mind was already crowded with ideas and avenues to explore as so many possibilities opened up for her. She was itching to get started. She would set up a studio the first thing tomorrow. She was torn, though. The basement seemed ideal except for the fact that the natural light was limited to two windows at the back that were nearly ceiling height and very narrow. It might have to be Tom's room for now, or the small attic. You could just about stand there, and the fan window was low down, but it might work with a little juggling.

She was musing on the positives and negatives of each space when a familiar figure caught her eye emerging from a building down the street. Ethan? Was it really him? He was walking down the street away from her, wearing jeans, his usual boots and brown leather jacket, his shaggy hair covered by a ball cap.

She called his name, but he didn't turn. She quickened her pace, calling his name again above the New York traffic and other city noises that made hailing someone difficult. He paused, turned and she waved at him. He stopped, ducked into a store entrance, out of the way of the other people who were trying to make their way along the sidewalk. She caught up with him a moment later.

"Kate," he said, smiling down at her. "What are you doing here?"

He was wearing sunglasses, despite the overcast sky, and for a moment she wondered if he had a problem with his eyes before discounting it.

"I could ask you the same thing," she said, grinning. "I was meeting with Cassidy Grady. She owns the gallery over there." Kate pointed back to the direction she'd come from. "She wants me to do a show the first week of February."

"That's amazing, Kate," said Ethan. He pulled her in for a hug, and she allowed herself a moment to enjoy it, the feel of his arms around her, the strength of his embrace. "We should celebrate," he said. He looked around and pointed down the street farther. "There. A bar. I think a glass of champagne is in order."

She laughed. "No, really. No champagne. A cup of coffee would be good though."

"You sure?"

She nodded. "Absolutely sure. I have a train to catch, and if I have a glass of champagne, it might lead to more than that, and I'd end up finding a hotel." She widened her eyes and covered her mouth for a moment. "Did I just say that? I did not say that. Please ignore it."

Ethan gave a long laugh. It was a sound so genuine and warm that Kate flushed with pleasure at it.

"Don't worry. Honestly, I knew what you meant." He gestured next door to the entrance where they stood. "Coffee it is. How about there? It's a small coffee shop, and the cakes and muffins look homemade, so it can't be half bad."

Kate nodded. "Sounds good. A cupcake might be the best way for me to celebrate. I haven't had one of those in a long time."

"No cupcakes in Rome?"

She chuckled. "No, not really. It does have other things to offset cupcakes."

"I can imagine it must, especially if it's kept you there all this time."

He ushered her to the coffee shop, opening the door for her so she could enter, and all the while she was contemplating his last remark. By the time they'd ordered their coffee and a cupcake each, Kate had decided that she was overthinking it.

The aroma of freshly ground coffee filled the small shop, making it a perfect complement to the baked goods in the display case beside the counter. A few muffins were on a plate under a glass cover by the cash register. But the cupcakes had looked too good.

Ethan led them to the small table to the side, rather than the vacant one by the window. Granted, it was steamed up from the warm, moist air inside, so maybe not as attractive as it might have been. Ethan took the seat with his back to the window, and she sat opposite him, sliding her messenger bag onto the floor.

"Is your laptop in there?" he asked her, removing his sunglasses and shoving them in his jacket pocket. He took a sip of his coffee and focused his deep blue eyes on her.

She nodded. She'd noticed he had it black, like her. Somehow in her transition from the US to Paris to Rome she'd become accustomed to strong black coffee that morphed into espresso.

"I have images of my artwork on there. To show the gallery owner."

"I don't suppose you have the exhibition you did in Rome on there, too, and would care to show me right now."

She frowned. "Maybe later. Back in Somerton Lake. It's a bit awkward here."

"Of course. Sorry, I was really curious, but I can wait. But I'll hold you to that."

"Okay."

She was surprised at how glad she felt at his interest, but that interest also set off a small bout of nerves. The nerves were so familiar she discounted them immediately. He probably wouldn't remember anyway, and she certainly wouldn't offer.

"So," she said. "That's me explained. Why are you here?"

He took a big bite of his cupcake, chewed a little, and washed it down with another mouthful of coffee. "Needed that," he said. "It's been a long day. I was in meetings with the band I write music for. Admin stuff, mostly."

"Really? That sounds interesting."

He shook his head. "Believe me, it's not."

"What exactly does it entail?"

He shrugged. "Stuff. Sound and production checks on things already recorded. Discussion of new songs."

Kate raised her brows. "Ooh. New songs? Did you have some to give them?"

Ethan grimaced, avoiding her gaze. "Uh, no. Not really."

She studied him, noticing the slight tension around his eyes and mouth. "Not really? Is that another phrase for 'no'?"

"I'm kind of stuck."

She nodded, put a hand over his. "I'm sorry. I know that's not easy, and not everyone understands."

He snorted. "No, not everyone understands. Especially the label when they've lined up the band's next tour."

"Shit," she said. "Really? Do they have to record an album before they tour?"

He nodded. "There's a couple of songs in the bag. But that's all."

"How many do you need?"

He shrugged. "More than that."

"But can't any of the band members write some? Or at least help? You know, bounce ideas off each other."

He laughed. "Yeah, you would think so, but it's mainly me."

"What's the band's name?"

He gave her a sidelong look. "Are you telling me you're thinking you might recognize it?" His tone was teasing all of the sudden and it made her grin.

"I might. I haven't exactly been living on another planet, you know."

He folded his arms and gave her a wry look. "Tell me the names of bands you've listened to lately."

Kate bit her lip and gave him a defiant look. "I've heard of Beyoncé, Coldplay..." She trailed off, searching her mind. "Adele!" she added with a note of triumph.

He threw back his head and laughed. "So, we have Beyoncé, Coldplay, and Adele as options. Anyone else before you admit that you have no idea about the music scene today?"

"Paper Kites," Kate said, her tone smug. "They're still around." At least she thought they were, though the last time she'd listened to them, well, she couldn't remember. They would probably still be on her iPod if she could find that. She decided on a nonchalant approach and gave her best imitation of a Gallic shrug. "I don't really listen to contemporary music, much."

She started to say she listened to opera and classical, because those were the concerts that Giancarlo took her to, but decided against it. It would probably sound as pretentious as Giancarlo sometimes made it. Not to say that she didn't like classical or some of the operas, well, a few of them, but sometimes there seemed more performance surrounding the attendance than the actual music itself. She knew Giancarlo had to endure it because of his business, but he was so natural at it, so much better at it than she was,

"What do you listen to, then?" He tilted his head. "Let me guess. Classical?"

She flushed and nodded a moment later.

"Nothing wrong with classical," said Ethan. "I can always learn something listening to them." He tapped her hand. "And you're right. Paper Kites are still around. And so are the others."

"But none of them are the band you're writing songs for, I take it."

He laughed again. "God no. Paper Kites and Coldplay do well enough on their own."

"So who is it, then?"

He looked at her and sighed. "Prometheus Bound."

She repeated the name. "Really?"

He nodded. "Have you heard of them?"

She shook her head. "No, sorry."

He snorted. "No need to apologize. I didn't think you had."

She shoved his arm. "Hey. You were doing so well there. Classical, remember? Anyway. I'd like to hear some of their songs. Well, your songs. What kind of music do they play?"

He scrunched his nose. "Kind of grunge meets indie rock."

She nodded. "Right. Okay. And you write those songs."

He sighed. "Yeah, for my sins."

She grinned. "Sinful enough to have your liver pecked at?" she asked, alluding to the band, who obviously took its name from the Greek myth.

He chuckled. "Yeah, it's a bit like being chained to a rock and having my liver pecked at, to tell you the honest truth."

"And all for giving mankind fire. You naughty boy." She noted the joke had lightened his expression, the dark, grim look that had shadowed him since he'd appeared, now gone. "How long have you been writing songs for them?"

He frowned. "Long enough."

"Waiting for the chains to be broken? Waiting to get off that rock?"

He toyed with the crumbs that were the only remains of his

cupcake. Her own was only half-eaten. "Yeah," he said finally. "Something like that."

She'd been joking, her tone lighthearted enough, but his answer wasn't, not so much for what he said, but for what he didn't say. She could understand that. Her own chains, invisible like his, weren't attached to a boulder of a different kind, it seemed sometimes, and though no eagle was pecking at her liver, she did feel like she was dragging that boulder around with her wherever she went. Only occasionally had it released her, and even then it would reclaim her unexpectedly. Like the other day with Mark. For now, though, she would enjoy her cupcake and try and forget about those chains.

FIFTEEN

Kate yawned and stretched, staring out of the living room window. It was nine, and she needed breakfast. She hadn't slept well, her mind crowded with ideas for her art pieces. Outside, she could see Tom wielding a rake with determination against the carpet of leaves that covered the front lawn. She had planned to do it the next day, but Tom had beaten her to it. It was strange to see Tom raking the leaves when all her memories had her father doing it, especially when they were young. Then, he'd made it into a kind of game with the two of them helping him gather great piles of leaves, Max's predecessor, Butterscotch, barking and snapping at any stray ones drifting down from a tree. It was a kind of a race for her and Tom, so that they could jump in the piles before Butterscotch created his own chaos with them. Now, seeing Tom on his own, her father upstairs still in bed, she felt tears well, another small piece of evidence of the changes that were coming. How was she going to manage?

She was just about to put on her shoes to join Tom when she saw a figure emerge from a tired old van. Tamzin. Kate watched Tamzin stride over to Tom, her cluster of long braids swinging free from the binding she usually wore, and her patterned Doc Martens would seem odd, paired as they were with the baggy pants and the loose sweater that hung off one shoulder, but for some reason it worked on Tamzin. She was forced to admire Tamzin's style, though Kate's own style recently would fall more under the heading of "what was available and close to her size."

Tom looked up as Tamzin approached him. He nodded to her, leaned his rake against a nearby tree, and she threw her arms around him, giving him a big hug and kiss. He returned the hug while seeming only to endure the kiss, and a moment later put her to one side and took up his rake again. She stood there, talking, while he continued, gathering the leaves in an ever growing pile. After a few minutes she gave up and started heading toward the house. Kate stepped away instinctively, feeling guilty for intruding on what seemed a private enough moment.

Kate heard the door open by the time she was in the kitchen making her much-needed coffee.

"Oh, great," said Tamzin. "I'll have some of that, too, when it's done."

Kate looked up and nodded. "Sure, of course."

"Do you mind giving me a hand?" asked Tamzin. "I've brought some things for the game this afternoon."

"Game?"

Tamzin frowned. "The football game. Dallas and Pittsburgh?"

"A football game on TV?"

Tamzin nodded, looking at her curiously. "Yeah, you know. Passing a ball around and running with it?"

Kate fought the urge to roll her eyes. "Yes, I know what a football game is. I just didn't know that there was one on this afternoon and you and Tom were watching it." Why hadn't she known? Had it been a last minute thing, decided while she was in New York? Admittedly, by the time she'd returned Friday night, her father had been in bed and Tom anxious to get off home. But there had been all day Saturday. A Saturday she'd spent organizing her art studio up in the attic.

"Well, it was your dad's idea, from what I understand," said Tamzin, her tone slightly annoyed. "If I had my way, I'd be with Tom in his workshop helping him with his pieces for his show."

In Kate's view, there were so many problems with that statement, she didn't even know where to begin. "Well I'm sure my dad will really appreciate Tom spending time with him," she said stiffly.

"Yes, I know," said Tamzin. "I get it. And that's why I offered to come and be here this afternoon. Bring food. Serve the males in their ritual and all that."

Kate gave her a tight smile. "That's very good of you."

Tamzin shrugged. "You sticking around for it, too? It might be nice to have another female amongst all that testosterone."

"All the testosterone?" Kate asked, bemused. "Hardly overwhelming with the two of them."

"And Simon. And I think Ethan. Maybe Stokey, if he can make it. Phil can't."

Kate felt a small gut punch hearing Tamzin speak all those names casually. Especially Phil and Stokey's. They were her people, and the thought that Tamzin might have any claim on them left her feeling off balance. She knew it was petty, and that she had no right to feel that way. And Ethan. For some reason that bothered her too. Perhaps even more. She hadn't seen Ethan since they'd met and parted at the coffee shop in New York.

She tried to get these feelings under control and managed a smile. "That many men? I guess I'll have to stick around and help even things out." She took a deep breath. "All right. You need help, you said?"

Kate watched Simon dip a carrot stick in the small ceramic bowl filled with vegan dip and suppressed amusement as he put it in his mouth and nearly gagged. It was some kind of chickpea hummus concoction with spice. Tamzin had taken full charge of snacks, pointing out her healthy approach was the best thing to have, especially for her father. Her father had gamely attempted a few of her self-declared wholesome snacks and after a few bits had politely left the remainder on the plate on the small table beside him, in full view of Max. Max, however, had refused to cooperate and kept himself well out of reach of the snacks or her father's wiggling fingers to summon him over. Max was currently sprawled out on the floor by Ethan, who was sitting on the sofa end by the window, and showing no inclination to feed him. Tom, meanwhile, sat in ignorant bliss at the other end of the sofa, beside Simon. Tamzin was curled up on the floor at his feet, not quite in imitation of the dog, thought Kate wryly.

The game had started a short while before, just after Ethan had arrived, with Simon in his wake. The two had swept in, Max barking a welcome and Tamzin bustling in with her bowls of snacks. It was then her father had descended the stairs, giving everyone a hearty welcome, though Kate noticed the tightness around the mouth, and what was a gray tinge to his skin in some lights now had a yellow cast. He looked a little better now, ensconced in the armchair watching TV intently. She suddenly hoped that Stokey would make it. Her father could do with his friend.

"Anyone want something to drink?" she asked, rising. "Beer, soda, coffee?"

"I made a large smoothie," said Tamzin. "Would you like one, Mr. Wilson?"

Her father looked over at Tamzin. "Uh, maybe later."

Kate made her way to the kitchen, a deafening silence following her. She would bring in a selection of drinks and let people choose. That seemed the most diplomatic approach. She'd also use the opportunity to grab a bag of potato chips, or something that was a little more appealing to everyone else than the hummus and bits of peppers and celery. Once in the kitchen, she headed to the fridge and opened it, staring at the contents. The beer was there, two six packs in their cardboard holders, on the top shelf. Suddenly, seeing her father's familiar brand, she felt a wave of grief.

"Do you need a hand?"

She turned to find Ethan beside her, a sympathetic look on his face. She gave him a wan smile. "That would be nice, thanks. "Did you want a beer? Or soda? Or a smoothie?"

"Beer is fine, thanks."

He reached out over her shoulder and took two bottles from the carton, his arm brushing her shoulder. She felt the warmth of it, its touch reassuring and more, something that both comforted her and put her even more off balance. When he moved away to open the bottles, she felt the loss of him beside her. She shook her head. God, she was a mess.

She grabbed a beer for herself, took the opener from him after he was finished, and opened her own bottle, taking a deep swig. It was good, refreshing, she discovered. If Giancarlo could see her now, she could only imagine what he'd say.

She sniffed and looked over at Ethan. "Are both those beers for you?"

He shook his head. "No, I figured your father would want one. He usually does, right?"

She nodded, grateful that he understood. Something inside her shifted a little. An easing.

"And Simon too?" he asked.

"I don't know. I suppose. I don't really know Simon anymore." She opened the fridge again and took out two cans of soda. "I'll take a couple of these just in case." The knowledge that she didn't know Simon or anyone else in Somerton Lake struck her. How distant she felt from them. Even her brother.

Ethan cut into her thoughts. "I think there might be a bag of pretzels down in the left-hand cabinet by the fridge. And maybe some Fritos too."

"Really?" she said. She opened the cabinet and saw them. "Wow. I didn't know. I bought some potato chips the other day and put them over there." She gestured to the small basket that was on the counter across the room.

"Great. We'll add that to the pile."

"Dare we?" she asked, trying to add a bit of humor to her voice. "I mean, Tamzin has gone to all that trouble."

"Sure," he said. "Everyone has a choice then. That's what it's all about."

"Prometheus unbound, then."

He looked at her a moment and gave a slow, wry smile. "Maybe."

They took their haul through to the living room. She put the sodas on the table while Ethan placed the bags of pretzels, Fritos, and chips on the coffee table and handed one of the beers to her father. He took it silently, giving him a nod before turning his attention back to the football. She knew he usually got lost in it, but today there seemed an extra intensity about him. She looked over at Tom to see if he noticed. He was absorbed in the game, as well, though she could see a little twitch at the corner of his eye. She looked away, unable to watch his own struggle to create a sense of normality. Turning, she made her way back into the kitchen and grabbed the rest of the beers, picking up the opener as she passed the counter and retraced her steps back to the living room. Without a word, she opened one beer and handed it to Tom. He looked up at her, his eyes bleak and took it with a grateful nod. She opened another beer and handed it to Simon.

"Thanks," he said, his voice low. He made a small toast gesture and took a deep swig.

Kate glanced at Ethan, his eyes warm and knowing. He gave a slight nod. The nod said so much and had many possible interpretations, but she embraced them all as positive. She crossed the room to the spare armchair and resumed her seat. She could feel Tamzin looking at her. A moment later, Tamzin rose, made her way out to the kitchen, and a few minutes later returned with a glass filled with a smoothie. Kate had spotted it in the fridge. It had a slight green tinge to it and she knew it was probably extremely healthy, but probably not something she could drink.

"Did you play football in college or high school, Ethan?" asked Simon.

"Me?" said Ethan. "No, not really. I mean I wasn't on a team. I played soccer."

"Soccer?" said Tom. "Cool. Dad and I used to watch that too."

"I think your dad mentioned that once."

"You liked soccer, too, didn't you, Katydid?" said her dad. "You used to watch it during college when you weren't out doing your music thing with Missy."

"Missy?" said Tamzin, looking over at Kate. "Who's Missy?"

Kate froze, no words forming in her mind.

"Oh, that was Kate's best friend," said Tom. He took a swig of his beer. "They were inseparable. Even formed a band."

Her dad looked over at her. Without a word, he reached out and squeezed her hand. Kate held on to it, trying to get her emotions under control. She glanced at Ethan and he gave her a puzzled look, so many questions in his eyes. She looked away and caught Simon's gaze, his eyes filled with what seemed like pity. Pity was something she didn't want or deserve.

"What position did you play, Ethan?" asked her dad.

"Position?" said Ethan. "Oh. Wingback."

Her father nodded. "Impressive."

They chatted a little and she tried to calm down. She turned to the TV, but she could still feel Ethan's gaze.

"There you are."

Kate turned and saw Missy coming up behind her, her scuffed Vans and black jeans and jacket looking more Goth than ever, especially with her long black hair hanging loose except for the tiny braid on the left side of her face. Her eyes, rimmed with kohl, were flashing with annoyance.

"I knew you'd be here." Missy's tone was derisive, almost angry.

Kate turned her attention back to the soccer field, the long expanse of grass filled with players dressed in the college team's colors. She was standing at the far corner, in the shade, near the trees. Out of sight.

"It's not even a game. It's a practice," said Missy.

Kate shrugged. "I like soccer."

"You like Ethan. *Don't deny it. And I also know he plays music at O'Connor's." Missy snorted. "I can read you, Kate. Don't think I can't."*

Kate turned a puzzled face to Missy. "What exactly can you read?"

"You want to play music with him."

"What? No. Besides, he would never want to play with me. I'm nowhere near as good as he is."

Missy laughed bitterly. "Of course you're good. And I'm sure 'Mr. College Boy' knows it."

Kate moved away from Missy, giving her an angry look. "You don't know what you're talking about. Just go, will you?"

Missy glared at her. "Fine. But I know it's only a matter of time before you prove me right."

Sixteen

Her phone went off, the ring strident and shrill, interrupting her thoughts as she stood before the small table that was now her workspace in the makeshift studio in the attic. She'd piled the attic's contents at the far end, where the roof sloped almost to the floor. That space would be of little use to her, anyway. But here, at the apex of the roof, in front of the large fan window, she found she could sit at the folding table she'd dragged up there, and have enough room for her pens and inks and a large sheet of paper that would contain her art piece. Beside it, on a small bench, she'd set up her laptop, and on the floor beside that she'd put the printer enlarger that had been delivered that morning, grateful that there was at least one socket up there. The stack of paper and other supplies she'd arranged in tidy piles on the floor on the other side of the printer. It was basic, but it worked, and that was all she cared about. And now, after hours trying different exposures and filters on her laptop and finally being ready to print an image, the phone had rung.

She glanced over at it, thinking guiltily it might be Giancarlo, whose two phone calls this morning she hadn't bothered to answer, but wasn't him. It was Mark. She tensed, picked up her phone and, frowning, answered it, mustering a pleasant tone.

"Hi, Mark," she said. "How are you?"

"Good, good," came his voice. "Listen, I was just following up on that dinner invitation. Or even lunch, if that works better for you. How about Sunday? Tom would be around to look after your father then, wouldn't he?"

The silence hung in the air as she fought off the cold feeling that was spreading through her. Lunch. Could she do lunch?

"Please, Kate," he said softly.

And so she found herself saying yes. A yes that deep down she felt had no business coming from her mouth, because she knew she wouldn't be able to face it. A whole meal with Mark. A whole meal with Bunny scrutinizing every gesture, look, and word between them. She stared at the phone after it ended, thinking in the panic that followed her concession that she would call him back and tell him she couldn't make it after all.

She continued to stare at the phone, trying to work up the courage, when it rang again and Tom's name flashed up on the screen. She automatically pressed the connect button. "Tom? Is everything okay?"

"Where are you? Is Dad there?" She could hear the tension in his voice.

"I'm in the attic. By myself, working on my art projects. Why? What's wrong?"

"Nothing's wrong. I just wanted to talk. About Dad."

She heard his deep intake of breath and she felt herself brace. "What about him?" she said in a low voice.

"I-I think it might be time to move him downstairs. I mean...Sunday, you could see that was a struggle for him. He went to bed right after we had dinner. Didn't even finish his meal. And it took him ages to get up there. You saw that, right? I mean, it's time, don't you think? It would be easier on him."

She heard the words come tumbling out of him. Clearly they'd been assembled in his mind and piled one on top of the other to provide weight and certitude. To her. To him.

His voice wavered slightly on his next words. "You agree, right?"

She cleared her throat. Her mind told her that all his words made sense, and she should agree with him, support the decision, because of course he was right. Her heart didn't cooperate, though. Her heart found the idea repellent. Wrong.

"What about Dad?" she said tentatively.

"What about Dad?" His tone was defensive.

"I mean, shouldn't we ask him? He might say no."

Tom inhaled. "We have to convince him. It's for his own good."

She felt the tears come but she brushed them away and tried to find her voice. "Right," she said in a whisper.

"We'll tell him tonight," he said. "I'll come over there after I shut up the store. I'll bring pizza."

She nodded into the phone, unable to say a word. Tom ended the call, and she put it back on the table and stared out of the fan window. Below her, she could see leaves drifting and swirling in the light breeze, stirring them from the ground and bringing others loosened from branches to mingle with them in the lazy heat of the afternoon sun. She usually loved this time so much, but at the moment its beauty seemed out of place, a slap in the face to her current tumultuous emotions.

A beep sounded on her phone, signaling a text. She picked it up and saw it was from Giancarlo. *Please phone me, my darling*, it read in Italian.

It took her a moment to translate it, her skills out practice even after the few weeks she'd been here. She swiped the message aside and before she realized it she'd pressed the call button for Giancarlo. It connected almost immediately.

"Katerina," he said, his voice filled with relief. "You are well? Nothing has happened? Is your father well? I got so worried when you didn't answer my calls."

Fortunately, the fountain of words was spoken in English so she could grasp immediately the concern that his voice had only emphasized.

"Sorry," she said, her voice choking on the words. She paused to gather herself. "It's just been...a morning. Or afternoon. Busy?"

"What is it, *tesoro*? You sound upset."

"I-I'm okay," she said. She struggled to get herself under control, breathing slowly in and out. "I, I mean, Tom and I have been talking about my father, that's all."

"What about him? Have things become worse? My poor darling. Tell me what I can do."

"No, no. It's fine. Tom wants to move my father's bed downstairs, that's all."

"I see. Well if it makes it easier on him, then it's probably for the best. What do the doctors say?"

"The doctors? I don't know. I haven't talked to them. Maybe Tom has."

"Talk to them. They should know best."

She wanted to tell him that they didn't know best. That it was for her, Tom, and her dad to decide. Her dad most of all. "Thanks," she said in the end.

He talked on, catching her up on the news of his social circle in Rome, the new exhibitions coming to various galleries, and an upcoming auction he was dealing with. He also mentioned his mother and her wish that her regards be sent to Kate. And Kate listened to all of this with a growing dispassion, though his voice was calming, reassuring and despite the fact that she didn't care about any of the events and updates he shared, she felt to some degree soothed by his voice.

"We will talk soon," he said. "Tomorrow, *tesoro*. I will phone you then. Okay?"

"Okay," she said feebly.

He ended the call with several endearments and a final "I love you," in Italian. She repeated it after him, conscious of the still bare left-hand finger.

SEVENTEEN

Kate stood on the back porch, the moonlight revealing the big piles of leaves she'd created earlier. It seemed impossible that so many leaves had fallen since Tom had raked. She hadn't managed to pick them up and put them in the trash bags. It had been late afternoon before she'd begun the task, putting it off until she knew it would be a case of rushing around with the rake, gathering up the leaves in piles that Max couldn't resist scattering, so that it took twice as long. Even though the air had been cool, even with only Tom's NYU sweatshirt on, she'd been sweating hard at the end. The fall weather was starting to settle in with greater confidence now. She knew Tom would ridicule her halfhearted raking efforts, and she would probably have to start from scratch tomorrow, if the promised breezes picked up in the early morning.

Just as she was about to return to the kitchen, she felt her phone ring. She pulled it out of her pocket and saw Ethan's name appear. Surprised and a little curious, she answered the phone, a small bit of tension in her stomach. "Hello?"

"Kate, good. I've caught you. Can you come over now? There's something I have to show you."

"What? What do you mean? What do you have to show me?" Her mind couldn't even remotely conjure up anything that he might want to show her.

"It's nothing bad," he said. "You'll like it, I promise."

"Can't you tell me?"

"Can you come?"

She looked around. She thought of her father inside. He was already tucked up in bed, settled. And he'd seemed a little brighter today, despite the fact that the night before, Tom had talked to him about moving downstairs. It was set for tomorrow, Tom arranging for Fred, her father's assistant, to cover for him at the store.

"Yes, I guess I can come now."

"Great. As soon as you can. Meet me at the dock. And bring your camera and your lenses." He ended the call then, and she looked at her phone a moment, puzzled.

———

She got out of the car and, after retrieving her camera bag, headed from the gravel drive toward the dock. She could see Ethan there, the moonlight casting a glow on him, as he sat with his feet dangling over the side, staring out across the lake, his navy jacket and shaggy dark hair almost ethereal against the water and sky he was silhouetted against. A soft breeze disturbed his hair.

Without thinking, she withdrew her camera from the bag, and with the lens fixed, she lifted it to her eye and framed the shot. With the angle of the moonlight, the cloud, it was an extraordinary shot. She pressed the shutter, and changing the angle slightly, took several more shots. She moved forward stealthily, as though she were stalking a deer, bringing him closely into focus so that he almost filled the frame, the edges of the light playing against his shape. Even with the jacket, she could see how well built he was, the broad shoulders, the trim waist, the arms, bracing himself on either side.

She lowered her camera and moved closer, but this time he heard her and turned. A wide smile broke out on his face. He rose and came to meet her. There was no hat or glasses of any kind to obscure his face or the expression now filled with pleasure.

"You made it," he said.

She nodded. "How could I refuse a command like that?"

"You won't regret it." He reached out and took her free hand. "Come with me."

His grasp was warm, firm. Those hands, the long beautiful fingers she'd always admired when he played the guitar. Now they felt strong, confident, even safe.

He led her to the dock and positioned her so that she faced slightly off to the right. He stood behind her and reached over her shoulder with his left hand and pointed, his right hand resting on her shoulder. She felt his touch again, so strong, confident, warm. But this time it didn't feel as safe. Not safe at all. She made herself follow the direction of his finger.

"There," he said. "Can you see it?"

She took a deep breath and willed herself to look, pushing aside all the dark thoughts the lake brought back for her. She blinked a few times and then she saw it. A small gasp escaped her. The lake, glass-like in its stillness, reflected the sky and land-scape in almost perfect imitation. Clouds that drifted low across the sky also moved across the lake in mirrored action. But in an accident of angle and refraction, the house, Zig's cabin, stood half-tucked inside a misty cloud that seemed more magical than real.

"Wow," she said, staring for a moment.

She lifted her camera and began to take shots, pausing

momentarily for her usual adjustments in F-stops or lenses. Beside her, Ethan stood silently, his hands in his jacket pockets, watching her work.

When she was done, she turned to him, her face filled with joy. "That was amazing. Thank you."

He smiled. "Do you see it, though?"

She looked over at the reflection again, tilting her head. The clouds had shifted shape and the house had emerged, no longer half-obscured. The reflection had softened some of the house's weathered appearance she'd noticed the first time she'd been out here. The rotting end of one of the wooden plank steps, the peeling paint, the sagging porch. In the reflection it looked more well-loved than neglected. She wondered if Zig's family had used it recently, before Ethan had come.

"The House of Clouds,'" said Ethan.

"The House of Clouds,'" she said, repeating his words, trying to understand.

Ethan turned and looked at her, his eyes twinkling.

> *I would build a cloudy House*
> *For my thoughts to live in;*
> *When for earth too fancy-loose*
> *And too low for Heaven!*
> *Hush! I talk my dream aloud—*
> *I build it bright to see*
> *Build it on the moonlit cloud*
> *To which I looked with thee.*

The words of the poem he spoke infused her body, stripping away the years, the thick skin and all the walls she'd worked so hard on in the past several years. Elizabeth Barrett Browning. That poem. The poem that had opened her up to so many possibilities. Possibilities that ultimately led her to fall apart.

Could she do this? Should she do this? Unable to help herself, she stared at him, eyes wide.

"You do remember, don't you?" he'd said when he finished the first verse. "Elizabeth Barrett Browning. We studied that poem in class. You loved it, too, I seem to remember." His tone was warm, resonant, and excited. "I thought this view and the poem would make a perfect combination for one of your art projects."

She stared at him a moment, then looked out at the lake, to the reflection, her mind whirring. She found herself nodding slowly. It was unmistakable how perfect it was. She couldn't deny it, or how well it would fit in with her poet theme. Her creative side exploded again, running away with the applications, the uses the images she could work and weave with the words and what she had on her camera. She would have to do it. Her creative side wouldn't let her shut it down, it was too late.

Kate smiled, still staring at the lake. "Yes, it is perfect, isn't it?" She lifted the camera to her and this time she decided she would invert the image when she printed it, which would compel the viewer to look twice in an effort to discern which image was real and which was the reflection.

Eighteen

Kate stood in the kitchen, sipping a hot chocolate, her hands circling the mug, warming themselves. Ethan stirred the contents of his own mug and picked it up to face her, taking a large drink of the chocolate. He leaned against the counter a few feet from where she stood. It was an old Formica counter, full of cracks and stains, but scrubbed clean, she noted, like the stainless-steel sink and the side-by-side refrigerator in avocado green that stood guard at the end of the counter in all its faded glory. With the pine cabinets and linoleum flooring covered by a braided rag rug, it was a retro look in its purest form.

"Ah," he said after swallowing the chocolate. "That's better. You can really feel the cold off the lake."

She nodded. "I know. It's the kind that sneaks up on you."

The hot chocolate had been at Ethan's insistence as they walked the path back from the dock to the house. She couldn't deny her own toes were starting to feel numb and her fingers too. Standing there talking and taking pictures had given the wind and damp ample opportunity to find the gaps and vulnerable places in her clothing.

The house, or cabin, as Zig had called it, was warm, and she put her cup down a moment so she could shed her coat. Though it was really just a summer place, with the windows to prove it, Ethan had lit a fire in the big wood stove. It must have been burning a while, because the large open-plan room that comprised the kitchen, eating area, and living room had a toasty quality that made her want to curl up on the old colonial-style sofa and read.

Seeing no coatrack or closet, she put her coat on the back of one of the pine chairs drawn up to the kitchen table that served as the eating area. She caught sight of the laptop propped open on the table by the chair opposite the one where she'd slung her coat.

"Working hard on lyrics?" she asked, curious.

He snorted. "God, no. I do that with the piano or the guitar and a notebook."

"Oh? What's this, then?"

She'd meant the tone to be light, playful. Anything to get her mind off their previous conversation out at the lake. The poetry. It was still unnerving her. She knew he didn't have any idea what that poem meant to her. Or the journey it had taken her on and his part in it. Her mind told her that over and over as they walked toward the house. The House of Clouds. She shook her head.

"It's my novel," he said, his tone awkward. He shoved his free hand in his pocket and went over to stand in front of the laptop in an almost protective move.

Kate looked at him and raised her brows. "Your novel? Really?"

He looked down at the laptop, avoiding her gaze. He nodded.

"What's it about?" she asked, trying to keep her tone nonchalant.

She was so intrigued, part of her certain that anything Ethan touched would be gold, his talent in so many things self-evident, and the other part of her wanting to witness what this Ethan Peterson would do with words. His essays in college had always stunned her with their erudite quality, and she'd always felt intimidated by his ability to find such insights in the literature and speak about them so eloquently.

He shrugged. "Life. A life."

She laughed. "Very obscure and literary. Tells me everything I need to know."

He looked up at her and matched her laugh with his own. "I know. Pretentious. You don't have to tell me. I'm just messing around."

But something in his eyes told her he wasn't messing around. "Can I read a little of it?" she asked softly.

He studied her a moment. "Like I said, show me images of your exhibition, and I'll show you some of my novel."

She gave him a puzzled look, uncertain for a moment if he was serious. She made an impulsive decision. "Fine." She indicated the laptop. "Is that hooked up to the internet?"

He nodded.

"All right," she said, grabbing the chair nearest to the one in front of the laptop and sitting in it. "Get it up, and I'll show you some of the images that were posted on Giancarlo's gallery website. They should still be there."

It only took Ethan a few moments to bring up the internet after he sat down. He passed the computer to her and she took it, typed and clicked away until she found the right screen and passed it back to him.

"There," she said. "You can scroll through the images. They aren't all there, but most of them are."

She watched him as he slowly moved through the images, studying each one carefully, deftly zooming in when he could.

She could feel herself grow increasingly tense, waiting for any comments or questions as he silently examined her finished work. For some reason his opinion mattered greatly. And if she was honest, it mattered more than anyone else she'd shown it to. Not since her professors at art school. Even Cassidy hadn't evoked this kind of response. The realization unnerved her, not only for its surprise, but also that she didn't want to consider its reason.

He looked up from the computer, his eyes wide and filled with appreciation, wonder. "These are stunning, Kate. So talented. I love them. Boccaccio's *Lorenzo and Isabella*, right?"

She stared at him, too stunned to speak for a moment. That he would understand, make the connection, was more than she'd expected. She'd omitted explaining it to him, not because she thought he would understand, but because she'd been so flustered and anxious to get it over with and had forgotten.

"How did you know?" she asked. The question held more than one meaning, she realized.

"You mean how did I recognize it?" He shrugged. "I'm no expert on old Italian, or rather Tuscan, but I can recognize some of the words as Italian and the images, well, they confirmed it."

She gave him a surprised look. "You remember?"

He pulled back a little. "How could I forget? Professor Pickering would slay me alive."

"You had Pickering for Western Civ Lit?"

"I did. You did, too, obviously." He gestured at the images, now displayed on a grid on the computer.

"But when?" she asked. She had no idea why she'd asked the question.

He laughed. "I don't know. Senior year?"

"Oh. Of course." She barely remembered that year. She looked around, suddenly desperate to change the subject. She caught sight of some instrument cases lined up in the living room area, behind an armchair. "Are those your instruments? Can I have a look?"

She got up and walked toward them and caught sight of the piano on the wall opposite. "You have a piano too?"

Its quality was evident so that she could see without even questioning it that the piano was newly installed and not one that the Ziglers had left behind. She eyed the instrument cases. They were hard-shelled, some showing stickers so worn there was only a ghost of an outline of the word "fragile" on them. There were guitars and what was most likely a mandolin and another one she wasn't quite certain of. She picked it up, curious, and laid it across the armchair to open it.

Ethan came up behind her. "It's a Gold Tone GM6 mandolin guitar."

She looked up at him, surprised. "Really?"

He reached around her and picked it up from the case. "Have you ever played one?"

She shook her head. "No. I've heard someone play one once. A friend of Phil's came to one of our music gatherings. But I was pretty young, and I don't remember it that well."

He went over to the sofa and took a seat, holding the instrument. He strummed it lightly, twisted a few pegs for fine tuning. It had six strings like a guitar, a body shaped like a mandolin, but with a longer neck. Its sound was fascinating. Higher pitched than the guitar, but a little deeper than the mandolin. This particular one resonated beautifully as he began to pick out a tune, his fingers deftly moving about the strings. Kate watched, captivated by both the sound and the sight of him playing. His talent, his natural ear, and inner sense of rhythm were all so perfect, so inextricably linked, it made her sigh with the beauty of it. She could watch him play for hours, his body in tune and completely absorbed in the music he was creating. She knew what he was feeling, that lifting, that sense of being lost in a different plane.

Envy and longing took her over and a huge sense of loss. How much time had passed since she'd felt that? The perfect bliss of playing music? But the loss was part of her payment.

His fingers, they were mesmerizing. So beautifully formed, as if each gene knew it must create the perfect hand for him to create and play this music. It was more than that, though. Even with the fedora on his head, she could see how much the music filled him, took him over. The words, sung in deep, vibrant tones that hinted and played with the emotions of the song, filled her just as the music did, almost as if she was physically connected.

Seated at the back of O'Connor's at a table off to the side, her view of him was partially obscured. Here she could observe him carefully, marveling at the music he made, the words he wrote and the technique he used. At least that's what she told herself, even as she was drawn to his face, her eyes following its shape, the contours of his face.

"So, I'm here." Missy slid into the seat next to her. "Let's see what the big deal is."

Kate dragged her eyes away from Ethan and looked at Missy. "He's good. You'll enjoy it."

Missy grunted and shifted her gaze to Ethan. Kate returned her attention to Ethan, confident that his talent would convince Missy that it was the music that drew her here every Thursday night. It only took a moment to get caught up in his music, in his voice, and everything about his performance.

"So that's it," said Missy, her voice dark and knife edged. "You want to play music with him, don't you? Once you work up your wussy self to ask him. Here I was, thinking it was all a ruse so

that you could ask him to play music with us, *but you want him all to yourself."*

Kate looked at Missy in horror. She shook her head. "No, no. It's nothing like that. I just thought you would appreciate his music as much as I do."

Missy gave her a sour angry look. "Do you think I'm a fool? Just look at you. You're drooling over him, not his music. Him." She rose. "Forget this. I've been patient with you missing practice, putting your college friends ahead of me. Ahead of us. Our band. Fuck you, Kate. Just fuck you." Before Kate could stop her Missy shoved her way through the crowd to the door and left.

Seated on the sofa in the cabin, Ethan finished playing the mandolin and smiled at her. It was sweet, and she could see how much joy he'd derived just from that small amount of playing.

"Do you want to try it?" he asked, holding out the instrument.

She shook her head and rose. "Sorry, no. I should get going."

Nineteen

Kate looked at the selection of wines lined up on the shelves in front of her, their labels a variety of styles and designs. Should she get a bottle of Italian wine? The selection wasn't too bad, but she knew little enough, having always left the matter of choosing wine to Giancarlo. Perhaps a French or California wine would be better.

She sighed. Maybe she was better off taking a six pack of beer, like she would have done ten years before, when Mark drank only Coors. And Bunny, what would she drink? Cocktails? A Coors would have sufficed for her back then, too, because that's what all of the football team drank.

She thought of her brother and thought for a moment she might call him and ask him what he thought. He would have a better idea than she would, she was certain of that. Or maybe even her father, though the moment the thought entered her head she threw it out. He was getting weaker, she knew, and even though they'd moved him downstairs to a purpose-built hospital bed, he was needing his pain medication more and more often. She knew he didn't always sleep at night, either, though he would insist he was fine for her to go upstairs to her own bed rather than use the couch downstairs. But for her, sleep was fitful at best, and the few times she'd talked to Giancarlo she'd been testy and sharp with him.

She looked at the wine selection and sighed again. What did it matter if she took the wrong wine? She would get a wine she would enjoy, because she knew she'd need as much of it as possible if she was to get through this dinner.

———

Kate could hear the voices the moment she entered the kitchen, setting the bag of groceries on the counter beside the back door, along with her keys and wallet. She frowned, curious to know who'd come over to see her father. A few neighbors stopped by about once a week and Stokey and Phil called regularly. In fact, Phil had promised to come up this weekend. But it clearly wasn't a neighbor, or Phil or Stokey. And Tom was at the furniture store. But there was something familiar about the voice that filtered through to the kitchen. Something that made a tight knot form inside her.

She made her way out of the kitchen, her Converse sneakers squeaking a little on the wood floor that led down the short hallway to the archway that opened to the living room. Taking this path gave her time to collect herself and confirm what she knew, the louder and more distinct the voices became. She took a deep breath and entered the living room, a bright smile painted on her face.

"Giancarlo," she said, her voice breathless, surprised.

Giancarlo, seated on the faded dark sofa, near her father, rose. Neither his Armani suit nor the crisp white shirt beneath it showed any signs of the journey from Italy. His hair was immaculately styled, and there was only a shadow of his dark beard showing on his face. His dark eyes glittered as she moved toward him, around the scarred and stained coffee table. They exchanged the three kisses on opposing cheeks, a custom that now seemed almost alien to her. Their gazes locked a moment, and she saw the puzzlement on his face.

Max, suddenly aware of her presence, scrambled up from his place behind her father's chair, and came over to her, giving a small bark of hello. She leaned down and patted his head, conscious of Giancarlo stiffening beside her. She'd never seen him around dogs before and it never occurred to her Max would be a problem for him.

"Kate," her father said, his tone filled with false joviality. "I was just about to call you to see where you were. We've got quite the surprise here with Giancarlo turning up."

She gave him a weak smile, taking the seat beside Giancarlo on the sofa. He took her hand and held it on his lap. The dog resumed his place behind her father's chair.

"It's great to finally meet Giancarlo," her father continued. "And to have him deliver the wonderful news."

She stilled, understanding what was coming.

"You're engaged!" Her father studied her closely and she looked down, unable to meet his eyes. "He tells me that you were waiting for him so that you both could tell me together."

The words he didn't speak hung in the air. The words that made it a lie. It was clear she didn't know he was coming. No plan had been made to accommodate his arrival either in sleeping or meal arrangements.

She tried to smile as she glanced over at Giancarlo. His expression was closed, unreadable. But still, she was grateful that he'd invented the subterfuge, if only to save them both some level of embarrassment. It was all her fault, though. Why hadn't she worn her engagement ring? It wasn't that intrusive on her daily tasks, and there was no real risk, not really.

She jumped up and pasted a wide smile on her face. "I'll just go get the ring, Dad, now that you know. It's beautiful."

Her father gave her a close look. "Come, let your old man give you a hug first. And while you're getting the ring, we'll have a glass of champagne. Your fiancé was kind enough to bring a bottle. We can use your mother's glasses. They're in the top cabinet by the basement."

She nodded, rising, and made her way over to him. He leaned forward as she bent over him, circling him with her arms. His frame was nearly skeletal, so frail, and she fought the tears that rose at the back of her throat.

His lips were at her ear and she heard him whisper. "Are you okay? Is there something you want to talk about?"

Her breath caught at his words and the tears spilled over. She pulled away slowly, wiped the tears from her eyes and forced another smile on her face. "I'll be right back," she said.

———

"We will go to a hotel," said Giancarlo.

They were standing in her room, its size and decor suddenly pressing in on her. Her hastily made single bed, shoved up against a scuffed yellow wall, still clad in posters that dated from ten years ago, seemed incongruous against Giancarlo's custom-fit clothes, shoes, and perfectly styled hair. He followed her glance that was now caught by the faded old desk on the wall by the window that sported ink stains and digs from the many times she'd used it for her homework, not to mention the old laptop computer that still sat closed upon it. The sweatshirt and Henley she'd worn the day before were still draped across the back of the pine chair that was pushed into the desk. She resisted the impulse to grab them and shove them in the closet. A closet she would never let him see if she could help it.

The suitcase containing the designer clothes she'd brought with her from Italy was propped up by the chest next to the closet door. She'd long removed any of the items she wanted out of them and had zipped it up to better tuck it out of the way.

"A hotel?" she said, dumbly.

"Yes, it is easier, no?"

"But...I can't leave my father, not now," she said lamely.

"I will hire a nurse for the nights, so you don't have to worry." He moved closer to her and took her into his arms. "I am here to help, *tesoro*."

She felt his arms, strong, comforting and allowed his strength to seep into her. The guilt she felt over her what she could only think of now as deceit lurked at the back of her mind.

"I'm sorry," she said softly.

He pulled her back a little so that he could see her face. His dark eyes searched hers, his own containing traces of puzzlement and hurt.

"I don't know what I was thinking," she said. "I mean I wasn't thinking. Everything moved so quickly, I've hardly had any time to think."

He studied her, his desire to find truth in her words obvious. He picked up her hand and kissed the palm, turning it over to see the ring glinting on her finger in the late afternoon sunlight that poured through the window.

"Do you like it, Katerina? We can get a different one, a modern one, if it is what you prefer."

She widened her eyes. "No, no. It's beautiful."

She heard her father call her name. She gave Giancarlo an apologetic look and made her way out of the room to the top of the stairs, answering him self-consciously.

"Move into our bedroom," he shouted up to her.

She blinked. He'd always referred to his bedroom as "our

bedroom," as though her mother were still there, using the bedroom with him. She moved down the steps until she reached the bottom and looked in through the archway into the living room.

"Your bedroom?" she said, her voice quieter.

"Yeah," he said. "You two will never fit in your bed, and the bed in Tom's room isn't much bigger. It's best if you use our bedroom. It's a king-sized bed. You'll both feel more comfortable."

She went to open her mouth to object, but shut it. She'd rather stay here, for so many reasons, primarily because she didn't want to leave her father, nurse or not. But she was keenly aware of the tired furniture in her father's bedroom, most especially the old bed that he'd had since her mother was alive. That would make it around twenty years old, emphasis on old, rather than antique. And did she really want to be in bed with Giancarlo here, with her father sleeping downstairs?

She bit her lip and made her decision. "Thanks, Dad. I'll just go get it ready."

Twenty

Kate lifted her wine glass to her mouth and watched as Giancarlo took a sip from his glass and made an effort not to grimace. She knew it was awful, compared to his standards, but it was all she could get when she popped out to pick up a few things to cook dinner. A dinner that would be more to Giancarlo's taste, since she didn't think he would care for the meatloaf and mashed potatoes that she'd originally planned because it was easy. They'd been all sold out of the fresh pasta, though, so she'd resorted to dried.

She looked down at her blouse, checking for any splatters. It was the last thing she needed, getting red pasta sauce on her pale blue Balenciaga silk blouse. She would need to be careful. She'd decided to unearth her wardrobe from her suitcase in an effort to make Giancarlo feel more at home in what he called his leisure clothes, but anyone here would call "dressing up." Both of them were far too dressed up for squeezing around the kitchen table surrounded by the counters, stove, and a sink loaded with the detritus of her cooking.

"Nice, Katydid," said Tom, as he took a large bite of the

pasta. "You really upped your cooking skills in all your adventures."

Beside him, Tamzin toyed with her food, shoving it around the plate with her fork as though it was a mop on a floor. She put her fork down and took a sip of her water. She'd brought a large pack of bottled water, glass, not plastic, because that didn't decompose, or was it give off gasses into the water? Kate couldn't remember, or keep up.

Both Tom and Tamzin had turned up earlier that day after her father had called Tom to tell him about Giancarlo's arrival and Kate's engagement to him. Tom arrived with Tamzin in tow, since she was here on a weekend visit. When Tom met Giancarlo, he'd given him a hearty handshake and made a visible effort to be pleasant. It was only in the kitchen, later, when Kate was stirring the pasta sauce, that he'd come in on the excuse of stealing a cherry from the dessert cookies she was making that he gave her a puzzled look and asked her about the engagement.

"I'm surprised," he'd said.

"Surprised? Why? We've been together for a while."

He looked at her a moment, shook his head. "Nothing," he said. "Forget I said anything."

"What about you and Tamzin?" she'd asked on impulse.

"What about us?" he said, a slight edge to his voice.

"You've been together for a while."

He gave her a look. "Just drop it." He'd walked out then, leaving her to stare at his back.

Now, looking at Tamzin, her eyes somewhat steely, her mouth tight, Kate wondered what Tamzin thought about her relationship with Tom.

"Katydid?" Giancarlo asked her in a low voice, while her father chatted to her brother about the store.

She looked at him and frowned. "Sorry. It's a long story. I'll tell you later. It's just Tom."

"But I heard your father say it, too," he said.

She reddened. "Well, Tom started it, and it became a kind of a fond joke."

"Fond joke?" he said quizzically.

Kate shook her head. "Never mind."

"Are you going to Ethan's gig tonight?" her father asked. He sat at the end of the table, sipping his carton of specially fortified drink. She could see that he was trying to give some semblance of normality to this dinner, and she loved him for it.

"Ethan?" said Giancarlo. "Is this the Ethan who is your father's friend?"

Kate nodded and, turning to her father, shrugged. "No, I'll spend the evening with Giancarlo."

"Why don't you take him?" her father said. "He'd like O'Connor's."

She glanced at Giancarlo, searching for a reason that would put him and her father off. Her instinct told her it was a bad idea for many reasons. "We can stay home with you," she said. "I'm not sure it's Giancarlo's thing, anyway." She smiled at Giancarlo to ensure he understood there was no mean intent in her statement.

"On the contrary," said Giancarlo. "I think I would like to listen to some of the music you grew up with." He squeezed her hand. "You have only recently come to appreciate opera."

"Opera?" said Tom, disbelief in his voice. "Kate likes opera?"

"I like all music," said Kate. She could hear the defensive tone of her voice and sought to modulate it. "Opera is an important part of Western musical heritage."

Tom grinned at her. "Yeah, sure."

"I've never heard any opera," said Tamzin. "Not really. I mean, I'm aware of it, but I don't think I could name one."

Kate turned her gaze to Tamzin. The words had been delivered in a tone that only hinted at mockery, but as she'd said them she had looked at Tom, as if she wanted him to share the joke. A metaphorical elbow in his side that symbolized how much she thought Kate's interest was asinine.

"The four of us should go to Ethan's gig tonight," said Tom. He looked at his father. "That's okay, right? You can always call us if you need to. We'll only be gone for a couple of hours."

"Sure, sure," said her father. "Don't worry about me. I'll probably be fast asleep most of the time you're away."

She knew that wasn't true, that his pain meds didn't always help as much as they should, but she decided not to argue.

———

The pub was beginning to get crowded. They'd managed to secure a high table in the center and Kate felt a bit of relief at the thought they wouldn't be in the front, in plain view of Ethan. Here, in the middle, there was at least some chance she could obscure herself behind the couple who had the table in front of her.

She could see Tom at the bar getting the drinks, Tamzin at his side to help him bring them back. It was that same student tending the bar that had been here the first night she'd arrived for her father's birthday weekend. That night seemed years ago now, and she almost felt overwhelmed at how much had changed since then, and the wish that she could go back to that moment entered her mind. The student pressed one of the real ale taps forward, filling a glass, but still cast glances over to the stage where Ethan was tinkering a bit with the mike, oblivious to her gaze and every other woman's in the pub. It was still fifteen minutes before he was due to play. He was wearing his usual dark jeans, black boots, and Henley and flannel shirt combination. The fedora was laying on the stool, ready for him to pick up.

"He is much younger than I expected," Giancarlo said into her ear, startling her from her thoughts. "I thought you said he was your father's friend."

She tried to keep her expression casual, though she could feel herself redden. "He is," she said in an even tone. "They share a love of music. My father used to always come to gigs here. Ethan used to play gigs here, too, years ago."

"Your father played music?"

She widened her eyes. She'd never discussed her father's music with him before. Against his involvement and love of opera and classical music, it just seemed, well, something that wouldn't measure up. The realization brought her thoughts up short.

"Yes," she said, slowly, as she decided what she would say, confused by the feelings that had just run through her mind. "He was in a band. My mother too. They toured around Connecticut and a bit of New York before Tom and I were born."

"He was?" He searched her face and she fought the urge to look away.

She shrugged. "Sorry, I should have mentioned, but it was a while ago."

"What was a while ago?" asked Tom, placing a glass of chardonnay in front of her and the other one in front of Giancarlo. Not the bottle of champagne that Giancarlo had originally requested until she'd explained to him that he would be better off with a simple glass of wine.

"Katerina was explaining to me about your father's music career."

Tom brightened. "Yeah, my parents were really good. And so were the others in American Sky."

"American Sky?" said Giancarlo.

Tom nodded. "That was their name. Didn't Kate say?"

Giancarlo shook his head. "No."

"Kate's just as good too. Have you heard her play?"

"Hey guys," said Ethan, coming up to their table.

He'd put the fedora on, but he had it perched at the back of his head, so that Kate could see his eyes clearly as they found hers, a question at the back of his. Kate could feel Giancarlo's eyes on her, and knew that he had a thousand questions waiting to be asked.

"Hey, Ethan," said Tom, finishing off a "bro" hug. "How's it going?"

Ethan nodded. "Yeah, fine. Everything all right with you folks? How's your dad?"

Tom scrunched up his nose. "You know. 'Bout the same."

Ethan's eyes slid over to Kate, and this time she knew there was no question she was blushing. "Hi, Ethan," she said, forcing a big smile on her face. Suddenly she was conscious of the engagement ring on her finger.

Giancarlo extended his hand to Ethan, almost squaring up to him. "I am Giancarlo, Katerina's fiancé."

Ethan took his hand and gave it a shake. "Ethan."

"I look forward to hearing your music," said Giancarlo.

Ethan smiled, looking back over to her for a moment, a trace of amusement and question in his eyes, and Kate glanced away. Giancarlo leaned back in his chair and draped his arm across her shoulder. The language was clear, and Kate fought the urge to move forward, closer to the table.

"Ethan, can you play 'Rossetti Girl' sometime tonight? So Giancarlo can hear one of Dad's songs. That's if you have a bit of flexibility in your playlist. I know you have your fans, and it's all about pleasing them." His tone was teasing, but Kate felt there was some truth in the last remark, in any case.

Ethan laughed. "Of course I can, it's not a problem. And my fans, well they will just have to make an allowance this once."

Ethan's tone at the end of his words had been full of irony, but Tom still played on it. "You know you're a babe magnet. I see them lining up for your autograph after each set."

"Hardly, that. I've signed only a few autographs."

"Oooh," said Tamzin. "They'll be worth something some-day. I'd better line up and get mine."

Kate looked over at her. Something about her tone made Kate feel she might be half-serious.

Ethan pulled at his hat, lowering the brim. "Hardly that, I think. And besides, I'm not looking for fame."

"What are you looking for?" asked Giancarlo, studying him.

Ethan looked at him. "Just to write and play the music I like."

"And earn enough," added Tom with a chuckle. "Enough to eat."

Ethan nodded. "Exactly."

"Well," said Tom. "I think you have that one sealed. I hear that Pete O'Connor was talking to his brother who has an indie club in New York and he wants you to play there."

Ethan gave him a surprised look. "Really? Pete hasn't said anything to me."

Tom gave him a knowing nod. "He will."

Ethan's expression became unreadable. "Thanks for the head's up, man. I appreciate it." He lifted his Patek Phillippe watch. "I better go. Time to start."

He nodded to the others and made his way to the stage. Kate watched him go, somehow both glad and disappointed at his departure, the discomfort she'd felt over his interaction with Giancarlo so strong that it took all her effort to set it aside and enjoy the night. An effort that she knew was fruitless and her enjoyment only a pretense.

TWENTY-ONE

Clouds scudded along the sky, moving more quickly than the traffic Kate could see from the window of the hotel room. The Manhattan streets were thick with cars, buses, and even a few bicycles whose business it was to thread their way through the traffic on some urgent delivery. A late Friday afternoon meant that everyone was either desperate to get out for the weekend away from the city, or desperate to get into it for an evening's entertainment.

Kate felt Giancarlo come up behind her and slide his arms around her waist, pressing his lips against her neck in a sensuous kiss. They'd just arrived at the Four Seasons, Giancarlo making a weekend reservation the day before as a surprise to her after privately checking with her father and arranging for a nurse to come and spend the night. She found it impossible to protest, especially after he'd said that he'd spoken to Cassidy at the gallery and Cassidy had jumped at the chance to have lunch with the two of them on Saturday. And afterwards, he'd told her, they'd have dinner and a night at the Metropolitan Opera House. *Tosca* was playing, one of Giancarlo's favorites.

He turned her around to face him and cupped the back of

her head, giving her a deep kiss, the fingers of his other hand tracing her bare neck, her hair now straightened and carefully arranged into the chignon style he favored. She responded to his touch, knowing that he'd been waiting for this moment all day. He'd made love to her the night before, but it had been quick and more proprietorial than loving, dominating her with his body. But this morning when he'd asked her to wear the deep blue Dior shift dress, matching coat along with the impossible Louboutin heels, she knew he had something more prolonged in mind. The conclusion proved true on the train ride up. The seats in the more spacious business class gave him more room to slide his hand along the inside of her leg to her bare skin just above the edge of the stocking he'd also asked her to wear, and lean over and kiss her neck as he angled his back just enough to the aisle so that no one would see. It had been impossibly seductive, his finger brushing her thighs just enough so that although they were feather light, his intent was most definitely clear. Her reaction, though, was more self-conscious awareness of the public nature of their surroundings.

Now, he was picking up where he'd left off on the train, his hand reaching lower, hiking her dress and sliding his fingers along the edge of the stocking. He moaned into her mouth and pressed close. She could feel his erection through his suit pants. He'd removed his tie and jacket the moment they'd come in the door, and now he started on her, taking off her jacket coat and pulling down the zipper on the back of her dress to give him access. He inserted his hand inside the dress, his hand stroking her back, until he broke the embrace a moment later to allow her dress to fall to the floor, leaving her standing in her heels, stockings, and Italian lingerie.

She stepped out of the dress, feeling strange in the lingerie, shoes, and stockings. Though she knew it had been a little more than three weeks since she'd worn anything like this, it seemed alien on her body now.

Giancarlo didn't seem to notice any difference as he pulled her once again toward him, murmuring Italian endearments to her while he kissed her all over and skimmed his fingers along her body. She gave way to the moment, aware of her body lighting up to his sensuous touch. He led her over to the bed, and, quickly removing his own clothes, drew her down. She stopped and tried to remove the shoes, but he put his hand on her arm, murmuring to her to leave them on. And there, on the bed, he wooed her carefully and with all the sensuality that any woman could ask for. His touch was sure, experienced, and she followed his lead and tried to lose herself in the moment and in him.

———

Kate felt Giancarlo's eyes on her, studying her carefully. The coin-sized piece of turbot so beautifully arranged and delicately garnished on the white plate seemed too much a piece of art to disturb with something as mundane as a fork, and later, mastication. This exclusive little Italian restaurant tucked away in Tribeca was run by an up-and-coming chef vying for a Michelin star. Giancarlo's dish was no less a work of art with its three pieces of ravioli stuffed with something she couldn't pronounce, but Giancarlo assured her was a kind of truffle. The sauce was light, more like a foam reduction, or was it a jus? She was too tired really to take that much interest.

The day had been full and after a virtually sleepless night, she was exhausted. The first half of the night had been taken up with Giancarlo's lovemaking, an effort he'd begun again after pausing for dinner in the hotel, but later, after he'd fallen asleep, she'd found herself still awake, her mind too busy with thoughts of her father and Somerton Lake.

She'd risen finally, about an hour after dawn, the light peeking in through the crack in the long drapes that blocked out the city vista and only muted the sounds of traffic and everything else that made up the urban soundscape. She had no swimsuit, so she wasn't able to go for a swim, which might have gone a long way to clear her head, and she didn't have any interest in the workout room or any of the other amenities. As a consequence, when Giancarlo stirred a while later, she still felt restless, disquieted. It made her glad when he'd opted for breakfast out eventually, and they'd settled on a nearby diner that served espresso. Later, after returning to prepare for the meeting with Cassidy, she found herself once again in a pair of Louboutin shoes, only this time paired with a silver coat dress with an embroidered vine pattern on the hem. The stockings were also back, along with a different set of Italian lingerie, one of the gifts Giancarlo had brought with him. A gift that was more for him, she'd thought. Now, though they were in a formal setting, at least she could sit and ease her aching feet.

"Why didn't you tell me that you were changing the theme of the exhibition?" asked Giancarlo.

She sighed inwardly, her heart sinking. She'd known it was coming, even though Giancarlo had been pleasant and attentive throughout the lunch with Cassidy, who'd enthused about Kate's new direction for the exhibition and how successful it would be. Kate knew those reassurances wouldn't be enough for Giancarlo. He believed strongly in the original plan, felt that he was building a solid name and platform for her art career. For a little while after the lunch, when they'd taken a taxi to the MMA and viewed some of the art exhibitions there, she thought he might make nothing of it. But as they walked around the galleries, while she struggled not to groan with pain at the increasingly hobbling shoes, Giancarlo had fallen silent. At first she thought it might be that he was contemplating the various paintings and artworks, but when she found him frowning at her, his eyes distant, she couldn't fool herself any longer. He was angry at worst, annoyed at best. At her.

He continued to stew on his thoughts after they left the gallery, took a taxi back to the hotel for yet another change of clothes. She'd started to be glad that they would be attending the opera, where conversation was unnecessary. But it seemed he wanted answers now, before the opera.

"It just seemed to happen," she told him. "Cassidy and I were talking, going over my images from the exhibition at your gallery, and then I showed her a few potential images for the Dante while I explained to her what the finished pieces would look like. She seemed to like them, but she also asked me what other ideas I had."

"And you had these ideas, when?" he asked, his eyes narrowing. "I don't remember talking about them with you."

She shook her head. "It was recently, I promise. I had just been taking pictures of the trees with all their fall colors, and I started thinking that they reminded me of a particular poem."

"'Song of Wandering Aengus,' I think you said."

"Yes. It's a Yeats poem. I mean, the trees aren't hazel, like they are in the poem, but there's the 'Two Trees' poem, too. But it got me to thinking and then..." She trailed off, trying to decide how to explain what happened with Ethan and the house of clouds image that he'd pointed out for her. She knew she would keep his name out of it, but she had to formulate exactly what to say to Giancarlo so he could understand the beauty and synchronicity of the idea.

"And then?" Giancarlo arched a brow.

She smiled. "And then I was out at the lake one evening. The trees there are so full of color, it's like a painting in itself.

There was a light cloud like mist reflected in the lake right by a house. 'House of Clouds,' I thought. That's a poem by Elizabeth Barrett Browning about a place to build your dreams. Or a particular dream. I studied the poem in college and it came back to me, then."

She was rambling now and brought herself to a halt. She put down her fork and took a sip of the wine whose memorial year she'd forgotten, surprised again by the sight of her carefully manicured and painted nails. She couldn't remember a time when she'd done that before Italy. Giancarlo had insisted she have a manicure this morning, when she'd had her hair done, before the lunch, through one of the concierge services. Finely manicured nails were so impractical for an artist. But he'd told her it was a treat and had wanted her to have a pedicure as well, but she'd refused, citing that her shoes weren't open toed. Even now, her black silk evening shoes sported a dusting of crystals in a star pattern instead of an opening for her toes. They matched the three-quarter-length black bias-cut silk gown that also had tiny crystal star bursts artfully distributed across the torso. This gown, she knew, was a Schiaparelli. Giancarlo's mother had made certain Kate understood that when Giancarlo had taken his mother along to help choose an evening gown for her last month for one of the events approaching Christmas. But Giancarlo had brought it with him for her to wear in New York, because, as he told her, he wanted her to dazzle everyone there.

At the moment she felt far from dazzling under his intense stare.

"'House of Clouds?'" he said, his brows drawn together. "I do not know this poem." He muttered something in Italian that she didn't catch. A moment later he sighed. "Katerina. We made a plan. It was carefully thought out, and it was built on your work in Italy. It is a unique and important identity that you established in your show. Your name, the theme, the approach, it was what we agreed. It is good business. And it is you. Who you are as an artist." He waved his hand. "You cannot change it on a whim because you saw some pretty trees."

"It was more than trees," she said, her tone hard. "It was a feeling. An instinct."

He frowned at her, shaking his head. "Katerina, Katerina, I am sure you feel this strongly. You are an artist. Of course you do." He took her left hand and kissed the outside of it. "We will see what we can do to make this work. But next time, you must promise me you won't go wandering off course because of some momentary notion."

She shook her head. "I know you are upset, and I'm sorry I didn't say anything sooner, but it's what I want, Giancarlo. I want to do this exhibition. I feel inspired and my work so far, I think, shows it."

"You have done some pieces already?"

She nodded. "A couple. I set up a makeshift studio in our attic. The two pieces are a little experimental, because I wanted to try out a few different things. But I'm pleased with the results so far."

He nodded, serious. "You must show me then. When we return to your father's house." He squeezed her hand. "Now, we will talk of more exciting things. I have some news. I have spoken to Mamma while you were in the shower earlier and she has said that she has a date for Villa Borghese in April. And, the church has been arranged."

"April?" she said. She could hardly fathom anything in April. April was a different universe, one she just couldn't entertain.

"Yes, *tesoro*, isn't that wonderful? It's a perfect time. Your exhibition will have finished here, and Mamma says that it is almost certain that *Grazia* will ask for a whole spread about the wedding for their April or May issue. They will want to know about your art as well as my gallery."

She nodded, at a loss for words, her mind a blank slate. She looked down at her hand in his, with their carefully polished pale pink nails, carefully matched to the ruby engagement ring. It didn't seem possible that the hand he held belonged to her.

He gave it another squeeze and released it, pulling out his phone. "Oh, and even more exciting for you, Mamma asked me to show you this picture. It's the perfect wedding gown. Marcelo, her couturier at the Valentino atelier, recommended it to her after she showed him your photograph. She's arranged to put it aside until you can return and have it properly fitted. Mamma has been wonderful putting all this together. She knows that you have so much to do, so she thought she would help as much as she could."

He held out his phone and Kate took it, staring down at the image of a dark-haired model, hair pinned up, dressed in a sheer flowing gown embroidered with tiny red roses and dark vines all over the dress. It was artful and sophisticated, achingly beautiful, the train mid-length and almost suggesting medieval. Kate could only imagine its cost. Or perhaps not.

She looked up at Giancarlo. "I don't know what to say."

He covered her hand with his. "I understand. It's overwhelming. And your mind maybe has been on other things. You no doubt think of your father. And I have been considering that. Perhaps we could contact your priest and see if he would do a blessing. We could make a little ceremony of it while I am here. Hold it in your back garden, or even in the house, if you think your father wouldn't be able to manage anywhere else. Would you like that?"

She was hit by a moment of panic. A priest. A blessing. In her backyard. The idea of it seemed impossible.

Twenty-Two

Pockets of mist hovered over the lake, the trees arcing around them as though they were trying to contain them. Many of the leaves were brown now, especially the oak, and the vibrancy had muted to a soft maroon, umber, and sienna color, against the background of the green of the pine trees now emphasized by the overcast sky. Kate studied the scene, wondering if the memories would ever leave her. The lake seemed harmless, and it was, she reassured herself.

She hadn't bothered to lift her camera yet, having taken a seat on the edge of the dock, her feet dangling over the water. It was early, barely past dawn, and cold.

She pulled down the wool beanie she'd shoved on her tangled hair and pushed her hands in the pockets of her mother's old wool pea coat. She took deep breaths and made an effort to continue to observe the lake, the trees, and the mist in detail. Noted all the tiny movements, the way the mist curled over near the far shore, the stillness of the water, the distant splash of a fish and the scent of pine in the air.

It had been another night of little sleep, the third in a row.

Last night owed nothing to Giancarlo's amorousness. Even he seemed to have given into the exhaustion of the last few days' activities. No, it was her own mind, the turmoil, the unnamed restless desire to do something.

Her dad had sensed it. He'd even questioned her quietly when they'd had a moment alone, yesterday afternoon, when she and Giancarlo had returned from New York. He'd taken her hand as she leaned over to kiss him goodnight and looked into her eyes and asked her what was wrong. She'd shaken her head and denied that anything was wrong, but she'd given him an extra long hug that night, noting his jaundiced skin and that he was so frail now she might snap him in two.

That was part of it, she knew. The waiting. The knowing what was to come and being unable to stop it. Halloween had passed that weekend she and Giancarlo had been away, and no one had even remarked on it. She could imagine the darkened house and the nurse's quiet tread as she ignored anyone who'd attempted to knock the door for a treat.

Tom felt the waiting, too. She could see it in his stiff demeanor and false heartiness, along with the shadows in his eyes and his drawn face. He'd been there yesterday when she'd returned, frowning when he'd caught sight of her tamed hair and chic outfit. His only comment had focused on her shoes, a seemingly innocuous remark about slipping on her more comfortable Converses, but Kate heard and felt all the subtext. Tamzin hadn't been with him. Apparently she was in Boston and wouldn't be down for a while, She had too much to do. Tamzin obviously knew he wouldn't make the trip up to see her, not now, but surely Tamzin could see Tom would need support more than ever.

Kate sighed and lifted her camera, hoping she might get lost in the image through the lens. Think about its possibilities.

Possibilities that she knew deep down Giancarlo wouldn't approve.

"Penny for them?"

She turned, startled to find Ethan behind her wearing sweatpants, a sweatshirt, and running shoes, a beanie shoved on his head. He was breathing heavily, and she could see beads of sweat on his brow and upper lip. He swiped the beanie from his head, wiped his brow with the back of his arm and took a seat beside her. She could smell the sweat from his earlier efforts as it mixed with the scents of pine and wet mist from the lake.

She struggled to find words to say to him. They hadn't spoken since his gig at O'Connor's, and it seemed to hang over them now, despite his casual words.

"Careful, you don't want to cool down too quickly," she said finally, turning to face the lake again. His body heat created from his run began to penetrate her thick coat, heavy and quiet.

He shrugged, drew up his knees and rested his arms on top of them. "It's okay. I usually come and sit here for a while after my run."

"You run every day?" She kept her eyes resolutely fixed ahead.

"Most days. Well, here. It hasn't always been possible."

She could detect a trace of frustration and sadness in his voice. She started to ask him about it, but he interrupted her.

"How's your father? I stopped by on Saturday, but some strange woman told me he was asleep and couldn't be disturbed."

She bit her lip. That nurse. The woman had been incredibly efficient and, Kate was certain, highly qualified for the job, but there hadn't been much of a personal touch. Kate had been glad that Tom had let her go when he'd arrived Sunday morning. His disapproval over that hadn't been spoken either, but it was clear enough.

"Sorry. I-I was away with Giancarlo, and Tom couldn't manage the whole weekend, so Giancarlo arranged for the nurse."

"You could have asked me," he said quietly. "You know I would have stayed with him." His voice was distant, even a little cold, but underneath, she detected a trace of hurt.

She looked at him then, apology and more in her eyes. Her phone rang at that moment, and she tore her eyes away to look at her phone. Giancarlo. She pressed the connect icon and put the phone to her ear. "Yes?" she said hesitantly. She imagined he must be angry, because she'd left him still asleep without a word and her father tucked up in his bed in the darkened dining room, Max snoring on the floor beside him. Max had only looked up at her and put his feet back on his paws, uninterested in her early morning outing.

"Katerina?" His voice was urgent, sharp.

She winced. "Yes? Sorry, I left without saying anything, but—"

"You must come now."

"What?"

"Your father, you must come now. He has taken a turn for the worst."

She rose quickly, all other thoughts fleeing her mind. "When? How? What's happened?"

"Just come," he said and ended the call.

She looked wildly around, trying to collect herself.

"What is it? What's wrong?" asked Ethan, suddenly beside her, his hand clutching her shoulders.

She looked up at him, tears collecting in her eyes. "It's my father. I-I have to get home. Now."

"Let me take you," he said. "Give me your keys."

She stared at him, at a loss. "What?"

"Where are your keys, Kate?"

Keys. She dug her hand in her jacket and withdrew the truck keys. "Here."

He took them from her and led her to the truck while she tried to focus on what might be happening.

TWENTY-THREE

The noise was increasing as more mourners, clad in various shades of dark colors, came through the door of O'Connor's pub. From her place by the kitchen door, Kate recognized most of the faces, some that she hadn't seen since her teens. It gave her a strange comfort, though, to know so many people would turn up to pay tribute to her father. It showed how much he was part of the community, how much they appreciated him. He deserved to be appreciated. The thought brought the tears to her eyes and her throat to close again, so she focused her thoughts on the trays of food that were being set out on the bar. Pete O'Connor had insisted on providing food and his place for people to gather after the funeral, telling Kate that her father had brought enough custom and cheer to the place over the years through his music as well as his support. Kate had been grateful for his generosity and also the fact that it was one thing she didn't have to think about when she and Tom had made the funeral arrangements. Now, looking at all the plates of cold meats, cheeses, various salads, taco fixings, burritos, mashed potatoes, creamed corn, lasagna and other dishes, she realized that others had been involved in making food as well.

Phil came up to her, draped his arm around her and pulled her into his side. He kissed the top of her head. "You doing okay there, sweet girl?"

She gave him a tiny nod, and put her head on his shoulder.

"We'll give him the best send-off," said Stokey, joining them from the kitchen. She'd seen him bringing some boxes of pies donated from the local diner in through the kitchen back door.

"He'd break all the strings on my mandolin if we didn't," said Phil, giving him a grin that Kate noticed didn't reach his eyes.

"And kick in my drum set," said Stokey.

Kate gave a small laugh, grateful to them both.

Stokey smoothed her hair. "You hanging in there?"

She looked over at him and gave a shrug. "Trying to."

"Well, I can't ask for anything more," he said.

"Will you come up and play a few songs, darlin'?" asked Phil.

She gave him a wan smile. "I don't know."

He squeezed her shoulder. "No worries. You don't have to decide now."

"How about if you did 'Our House' with Tom?" asked Stokey. "He'd be there, and it would be a great one for the two of you."

She took a breath in. "Maybe. Yeah. I'll see."

She looked over to the stage and saw that her guitar case and Tom's were there among the other equipment and instruments. It would be something she knew her father would have liked. And she wanted to do it. For him.

"What does Tom say, or have you asked him yet?"

"He's all for it," said Stokey. "He said to check with you, though."

She searched the room for him. He had been near the door, chatting to people as they entered. She knew she wasn't ready to handle that. It had been hard enough at the church door, when people filed out after the service and shook her hand, offering their condolences. Giancarlo had sat with her in the front pew of the church on one side, dressed in his dark Armani suit, rubbing her shoulder and squeezing her right hand on occasion. Tom was on her other side, and it had been his hand she'd clutched and found comfort in through the whole of the service, except when he rose to give one of the readings. She had felt unable to do it. Ethan had sat behind them along with Phil in an old, ill-fitting suit and tie, Stokey in hastily gathered together jacket, tie, and slacks, and Stokey's wife in a dark trench coat that she kept tied. After the readings, Stokey had read the lyrics from one of her father's favorite songs, citing a funny story about how he misheard the lyrics and for years thought 'Duncan, I love you' was 'the dove above you,' infusing it with far more meaning than it deserved. Phil had given the formal eulogy, speaking about her mother and her father, the love they shared for music and each other. It was a story she hadn't heard in years and it made her laugh to think of it, because it was so much like her father.

She caught Tom's eye, and he gave her an inquisitive look. He glanced over to the other side of the entrance, where Giancarlo stood vigil, solemnly shaking people's hands. She'd abandoned him a few minutes before on the excuse to check the kitchen and see if anything was needed. He'd insisted that he would be fine, and Tom hadn't seemed to mind. Tamzin was there for a little while at the start, but had disappeared into the crowd. She'd sat in the back at the church service, arriving late, dressed in a yellow long-sleeved dress that had navy splashes of color, like something from a Jackson Pollock painting, and dark suede mid-length boots that laced up. Her braids were loose and swinging around her waist, and her nose sported a septum ring. Kate had also noticed a new tattoo on the back of her hand when they'd sat next to each other in the limousine on the way to the cemetery. She'd caught Tom's momentary frown, though she wasn't sure whether it was provoked by the outfit, her new additions, her lateness, or everything in general.

Tom started to thread his way through the clusters of people and tables heading toward her. As if on cue, Giancarlo broke away from a group he'd just greeted and followed Tom.

"There," said Ethan, coming up behind us. "That's the last of the equipment set up. And Jackie said she has enough plates now."

He'd gone over to the local restaurant at Pete's wife's request and asked if they'd be able to lend some to O'Connor's for the evening, offering to pay for any breakages. They'd agreed in the end, though Kate couldn't imagine how Ethan had convinced them. He'd been doing that, picking up the slack, noticing what was needed.

"Thanks, man," said Phil, pulling away from Kate and slapping Ethan on the back. "And you're sure you don't mind stepping in tonight?"

"You mean to play with you guys?" Ethan said. "It's an honor. I couldn't believe it when Tom asked me."

"Of course he would," Kate said. "Why wouldn't he? You're perfect for it."

Ethan looked down at her, running a hand through his hair. "Thank you," he said, his eyes warm and filled with emotion. "That means a lot to me."

Kate noticed his dark tie and jacket were long gone, and the top button of his dress shirt was undone, but he still looked good. Appropriate and good. She'd been surprised to see him in his beautifully cut but classic Tom Ford suit, so used as she was to his jeans and Henley shirt uniform he seemed to always wear.

She wouldn't have minded if he'd worn that either, knowing her dad would have only smiled at it.

Her own outfit was far from stylish. She'd decided to exchange it for the old black dress from some long ago high school dance after she'd returned from the funeral. Giancarlo's silent disapproval of both her wardrobe choices that day were clear. But it was this one, her mother's dark green crushed velvet dress, gathered just under the bust, with wide bell sleeves, that seemed to really have concerned him. Her mother had worn it often while performing, and somehow it seemed the best thing for today. Her hair was scooped up at the sides and gathered at the top, so that it flowed down, just as her mother had worn it on stage. She hadn't bothered to straighten it either, wanting it to be as close to her mother's look as possible.

"You'll be great," said Phil. "And we'll give you all the cues. You have the playlist?"

Ethan nodded. "Yeah, Stokey gave it to me. I was wondering, though, should we add 'Rossetti Girl'?"

Phil looked at Kate. "Is that okay with you, darlin'?"

"Don't worry about it," said Ethan, hastily. "I mean if you don't want us to do it. I just thought..."

She took his hand and squeezed it. "You thought right. Please. I would love it if you played it."

"Played what?" asked Giancarlo. He leaned over and kissed Kate on the lips. "*Va bene, tesoro?*" he whispered in her ear.

"Ethan is going to step in for my father when they play music later," she said. "And he was asking about playing a song my father wrote about my mother, 'Rossetti Girl.'"

"Your father wrote a song about your mother?" said Giancarlo. "This I must hear."

She forced a bright smile. "Well, you will. Ethan's going to sing it."

"Ethan?" Giancarlo eyed Ethan who held his gaze steadily. "Surely it would be Tom who would sing it."

"What would I sing?" asked Tom. His own tie hung loose around his neck, his shirt sleeves rolled up, his hands in his suit pants pockets.

"Wouldn't you want to sing your father's song?" asked Giancarlo. "Kate said you used to sing and play together."

"He means 'Rossetti Girl,'" said Stokey. "Ethan's going to do it."

"Yeah, he should," said Tom. "Ethan would do a much better job than I could. It's too low for me." He turned to Kate. "You should do Mom's part. You'd really rock it, especially the way you look right now."

"Definitely," said Stokey. He knocked fists with Tom. "Good thinking."

"Are you up for it?" asked Ethan. "Don't feel you have to."

Tom studied her carefully. He put a hand on her shoulder. "For Dad. And Mom. You can do it."

She shook her head, her stomach tightening. "I don't know. I haven't been up on stage for a long time. Not since..." She trailed off, unable to complete the sentence.

"I know," he said to her, holding her gaze. "I know. How about this—we'll do 'Our House' together. The two of us. We'll do it before 'Rossetti Girl.' And if that goes all right, do the chorus of 'Rossetti Girl' with Ethan. You won't be singing alone, and it won't be any of your old songs. Only stuff from before. When we were young."

"When we were young," she echoed, nodding. She bit her lip. "Okay. I'll try."

"No pressure," said Ethan, resting a hand lightly over hers. "You can bow out any time. I'll cover it. Don't worry."

She gave him a grateful look. "Okay," she said softly.

Giancarlo took her hand and pulled her forward, his arm

slipping around her waist. "This is wonderful. I look forward to hearing my *tesoro* sing."

She glanced over at Ethan and then Tom. Ethan's expression was unreadable, but Tom's held a hint of impatience. She looked away. Phil and Stokey were discussing the re-order of the set list and drew Ethan into the conversation. She was grateful for that. She would rather not be in the spotlight at the moment.

"I'm just going to freshen up," said Kate. She slipped from under Giancarlo's hold and made her way to the ladies' room.

The pile of food on her plate was random, and she honestly wasn't sure how half of its contents had arrived there. Kate knew she'd been distracted by people coming up to her and speaking, and also by a general distraction she seemed to be suffering from since Tom had talked to her about the set list.

Even now, as she wound her way through the tables toward the one by the window that contained Giancarlo, who was still wearing his jacket, talking politely to a woman who might have been in Tom's high school class. She was open and friendly, laughing a little, her short, dark, bobbed hair falling forward as she tried to manage her disintegrating taco.

Mrs. Cavatino grabbed Kate's arm as she passed by her table. "Hon, it's so good to see you. I'm so sorry about your dad. He was such a good man."

She nodded, trying to smile, the now familiar phrases echoing through her head.

"Sit a moment," said Mrs. Cavatino, pulling out the vacant chair next to her. "Don's just gone for a second helping, so he won't be back for ages."

It was difficult to refuse. Mrs. Cavatino had been her third grade-teacher and had always doted on Kate, even before that. She'd been in school with Kate's dad, and Kate had always suspected there'd been a secret crush in the past. Her dad had told her once she'd been in some kind of grunge band back in the late eighties, something Kate had found hard to believe then, let alone now, as she noted Mrs. Cavatino's tired blonde hair, plump cheeks, dark turtleneck. and pants.

Kate took a seat reluctantly. This had been the third time since she'd started her journey to the food spread at the bar. She was grateful, in a way, that people wanted to share memories of her father as well as personally offer their condolences, but she wished it wasn't today. Today she didn't feel able to manage it.

Mrs. Cavatino patted her hand. "Look at you in your mother's dress. You look so much like her. She was such a beauty."

"Thanks," said Kate looking down at her food, picking at the tortilla chips she'd spotted on her plate. She put one in her mouth and crunched down on it, the flavor filling her mouth. She was hungry, she realized.

"How are you?" asked Mrs. Cavatino, her eyes searching Kate's face, her expression filled with kindness. "I haven't seen you in so long. Every time I ran into your father, he had such exciting things to report. Imagine you, living in Italy. And an artist!"

Kate gave her a wan smile. "Yeah, I know."

"I was only there once, with Don. We were part of a tour. We went to the south, mostly, where Don's family is from. But we had a day in Rome and it was wonderful. All that history. You must love it."

"Yes, it's great." That world and that Kate seemed so far removed from her at this moment, she could hardly believe it herself.

"So, who's the handsome young man here with you? He looks Italian."

Kate glanced back over at Giancarlo, who was nodding to that same woman. His signet ring flashed in the light that poured in through the frosted window. It must be afternoon, she thought mildly, if the sun was pouring in.

She turned her attention back to Mrs. Cavatino, who was looking at her expectantly.

"Oh," said Kate. "Sorry. I was daydreaming. Yes, Giancarlo's Italian."

Mrs. Cavatino raised her brows. "Giancarlo? Oh, now that's a name to love. Have you known him long?"

"Two years or so," said Kate. Had it been that long? Really it seemed impossible, even now, when she totted up the time in her head.

"And is it serious? I presume you two are together, I mean, since he's here and all."

Kate found herself nodding. "Yes, yes, I suppose you could say that." She was suddenly conscious of the engagement ring on her finger, and she slipped her hand under the table. She picked up another chip.

"How's Mr. Cavatino doing? And Brody and Cheryl? They must be, what, in their thirties now?"

Mrs. Cavatino gave her a huge smile. "Everyone's great. Both of them are married. Brody's an accountant at a big firm over Hartfield, and he and his wife Merry have two boys. And Cheryl married Carson, you remember him? He has a construction business and they live in Waterbury. Cheryl's a housewife and hoping."

Hoping? What would she be hoping for? It was a puzzle that held her for a moment until Don returned and greeted her. She rose from her seat, grateful for the reprieve, and after answering Don's greeting, left.

By the time she reached Giancarlo she'd been stopped several more times by people giving their condolences. It wore her out, and for a brief moment wished for the concert to begin so that she could escape it for at least a while when she was on the stage.

"There you are, darling," said Giancarlo rising.

He pulled out the chair on his other side and took her plate from her while she sat down. She greeted the woman next to him, remembering suddenly that her name was Sunita.

"Sorry it took me so long," she said to Giancarlo. "A lot of people stopped me as I was getting food."

"Yes, of course," said Giancarlo. "I saw that. Sunita was kind enough to keep me company."

She could tell by his even tone and formal manner that it had been far from entertaining company in his view, but his smooth manners from years of socializing and networking for his business gave him the skills to hide it well. She realized perhaps that she did know him to judge that much.

"Sunita, how have you been?" Kate felt provoked to ask. "Did you head into law in the end? You went to Wheaton College, didn't you?"

Sunita nodded, beaming. "Yes, yes. I did and then on to Harvard. My father went to law school there, so he was determined that I would go there too."

"So no Columbia, then."

Sunita grinned. "Bite your tongue."

Kate picked up another taco chip and crunched down on it loudly. She could feel Giancarlo's disapproval, and it made her smile. He was so funny, she thought. "So, are you with a practice or did you set up on your own?"

"I was in Boston for a while at a criminal law firm, if you can believe it, but now I'm doing contract law in New York. I switched when I married my husband. We're at the same firm. He does patent law, though."

"That's great," said Kate. "Are you living here?"

Sunita nodded. "Well, not too far out of town. We built a house overlooking the lake on the north side. We're trying for a baby now, and we want a healthy environment for our children."

Kate nodded, trying to feign interest in something that seemed so alien to her. Sunita had moved here with her parents from Boston when she was young. Her mother had been an ethics professor at the college and her father had been a lawyer in New York. She'd spent her first two years of high school in Somerton Lake, if Kate remembered right, because her parents thought she was too frail to attend boarding school.

"Your parents are doing well?" Kate asked as soon as Sunita had finished citing the merits of her life.

Sunita nodded enthusiastically and began updating Kate on them, while Kate marveled that she had both parents and was starting her own family, and all Kate had was Tom. Her only other relative was an uncle that lived in Canada.

Giancarlo took her hand, as if sensing her thoughts. She fought the urge to withdraw it, just as she wanted to withdraw herself from this table and this room.

Stokey came up to the table and leaned over it to Kate. "You about ready to get up on stage so that we can do the final setup?"

Kate looked up at Stokey, his eyes searching hers, the questions, love, and compassion all there for her to see. His question held more than the words implied. And she realized at that moment that of course she had a family. And her family was about to go on stage.

She smiled at him. "Yes. I'm ready."

TWENTY-FOUR

Kate placed the guitar strap over her head and adjusted it to a comfortable position. It took a few moments to find that old place where the guitar neck was just slightly raised to the left and the body of the guitar was placed in front of her, so that her arm curved effortlessly and her hand could move across the strings with ease. She used to be able to find that place without thought, but now it took a few adjustments, a little strum, and a further adjustment of the strap at her neck.

She fiddled with the strings, plucking and twisting the tuning peg at the neck, until her ear was satisfied. Below, sitting at the tables, on chairs lining the walls and the stools up against the bar, were all the people who knew her father and wanted in some way to be part of the music and the honor everyone on stage was determined to pay him with. Formica boxes had been distributed around the room to receive donations for the local cancer charity. Already two boxes, one at either end of the bar, were filled with bills.

Tom was already sitting at the piano on the left of the stage, while on the opposite side Stokey sat at his drums. Phil and

Ethan were up front at the mikes with a spare for Tom, later. Kate positioned herself farther back, nearer the piano. Nearer Tom.

Ethan began tuning his own guitar, and Kate looked over to him, her back to the audience. He was wearing his fedora now, perched low on his head, his shirt sleeves rolled up, the top button still unbuttoned. It should have looked as incongruous as Phil and Stokey's own clothes, but it didn't. Somehow, he carried it off. He caught her glance and gave her a wink. She smiled, glad for the encouragement, until Tamzin's voice caught her attention. Tamzin mounted the stage and strode over to Tom, cutting in front of Kate to sit on the piano bench, next to Tom. Kate glanced at Ethan again and he arched his brow, a wry smile forming. She widened her eyes.

"Just wanted to wish you luck, babe," said Tamzin, leaning across to give Tom a kiss. "I'm just over there, if you want me to help out with the vocals or anything."

It took Kate a few seconds to realize that Tamzin had drunk more than a few beers, or whatever alcoholic beverage she'd decided wasn't poisonous to her body.

"No, we're good," said Tom tightly. "Just go sit down."

She put her arms around his shoulders and gave them a big squeeze. "Okay, babe. Just so you know, I'm here if you need me. You've been through so much."

Tom peeled her arms from around him. "Thanks. Now, just go. We're just doing the final sound check."

She bobbed her head in acknowledgment, rose and strode across the stage again, her long braids swinging wildly behind her. Kate looked at Tom and saw the anger in his eyes. She put her hand on his shoulder and gave it the slightest squeeze.

"You okay?" she asked softly.

He sighed and nodded. "Yeah. Let's get started. We're up first."

She nodded. Phil had mentioned it earlier, checking that she was okay with it. Her thought was to get it over with, and at that moment it still seemed the best plan. Kate took her place at the mike, angling it so that she could look at Tom while he played, but still have most of her body facing the audience. Phil, Stokey, and Ethan took their own places. Tom played the opening chord for "Our House" and the two of them sang, their eyes locked, the harmony still there.

She strummed her guitar, her fingers finding the position without thought, the words coming automatically. Tom's eyes continued to fix on hers, and she was only vaguely aware of Phil and Ethan lending their harmonies, joined by Stokey's subtle drum rhythms. It wasn't a long song, but after the opening phrases, she found she became lost to it, the music soaring through her, the joy of it awakening the familiar pleasure that was like nothing else.

Tom grinned at her, his eyes twinkling. He knew. He knew what it was like and what it did to her. She returned the grin and for those moments she felt the lightness, felt uplifted and free, as she followed Tom's lead. All too soon, the song ended, the last few guitar chords echoing as the words faded away.

She took a deep breath while around her the applause rang out, strong and loud. She gave a nod to the audience, not really looking at them or taking in anything about them. She could feel Tom's hand resting gently on her back, reassuring her.

Ethan looked over at her, the question in his eyes. She felt a small push on her back from Tom. The high from the previous song was still coursing through her, so she smiled at Ethan and gave a nod. He adjusted a peg on his guitar, grinned at her to signal he was starting. She placed her left hand on the guitar neck in readiness, and at his nod they began.

The opening fingerpicking came easily after the first few times, and the tension inside Kate eased a little, knowing that

Ethan would lead out, and all she had to do was come in with the counter phrases at the right time. It was a beautiful song, and as Ethan began the opening phrases, she knew that he understood her father's music. It was there in his tone, the guitar style and even his posture. She responded instantly and sang the counter phrase, her gaze locked with his. Perfect. Just like she'd thought it would be all those years ago when she first heard him singing. When she thought about how his voice was a match for hers, that his understanding of the music would, without a doubt, stretch to her own. If only there was an opportunity for it.

> *Out of nowhere she was there, with the fire in*
> *her hair*
> *With her eyes of green and gold, full of stories all*
> *untold*
> *And her flowing graceful air, she gave a smile oh*
> *so rare*
> *That Rossetti girl, that Rossetti girl, that Rossetti*
> *girl.*

> *Then she picks up her guitar, plays it boldly, plays*
> *it hard*
> *And the truths she sings out loud, she sings them*
> *slowly and uncowed*
> *She wins me fast, she wins me true, and I hoped*
> *she felt it too,*
> *That Rossetti girl, that Rossetti girl, that Rossetti*
> *girl.*

She glanced out into the audience and saw the nodding heads, a few with teary eyes, remembering, and some with big grins.

And then she saw Mrs. Markowsky, Missy's mother, her eyes fixed on Kate, her expression filled with sadness. Kate's voice faltered. It was the end of the second verse. She tried to continue, but her voice became soft, thready. Ethan gave her a puzzled glance but sang on, the words of her counter phrase issuing from him with perfect ease while everything Missy had said and she had denied ran through her mind. No, this wasn't the life for her. Hadn't she known that? This was evidence of the betrayal of the worst sort and with the highest price paid. Her father's song wandered through her, but it did nothing to drown out the other painful emotions inside her.

> *By the time she ends the song, there's only one*
> *place I belong*
> *She becomes my true North Star, so I pick up my*
> *guitar*
> *And with all my skills and art, I tell her all that's*
> *in my heart,*
> *Be my Rossetti girl, my Rossetti girl, my Rossetti*
> *girl.*
>
> *When the song comes to the end, I hope her look's*
> *not as a friend*
> *She lays her finger on my lips, with my heart now*
> *in her grip*
> *She whispers sweetly in my ear, I will always be*
> *right here,*
> *As your Rossetti girl, your Rossetti girl, your*
> *Rossetti girl.*

The song finished, Kate only pretending to play by the time the last lingering chord sounded. Phil had stepped in with the mandolin, and Tom had taken up his guitar to take some of the chorus and to lend a fuller sound to the song. Her dad hadn't ever intended such a sound, but it didn't matter now. It was her fault, and she realized that she was more a liability up there than an asset. When the song finished and the applause sounded, Phil came around from the drum set and picked up the mandolin, stepping up to the mike to share it with Tom. She used that opportunity to slip off the back of the stage and head toward the kitchen and the back door.

———

Tiny shards of broken glass glinted in the spotlight just by the back door and closer, near the steps, cigarette butts littered the area. Kate started to count them, noticing a few hadn't even been crushed, and a few still had tobacco spilling from their ends. She almost wished for a cigarette now. She'd never really smoked, unless you counted the clove cigarettes she'd tried in her sophomore year of college. Missy, a dedicated smoker of all things herbal, thought they were hilariously pretentious, and her ridicule had caused Kate to stop.

Behind her, the back door opened and someone came down the few steps to sit beside her on the last one. She didn't need to look across to know it was Ethan. His scent, his "Ethanness," greeted her, and spoke all the words she did and didn't want to hear. She realized there was no sound of music playing inside. Were they finished in there? Had she really been sitting there that long? She played with the ring on her finger for a moment and then dropped her hands so that they dangled off her knees.

They sat for a few moments in silence until Ethan nudged her. "You were good in there."

She snorted. "Did you lose your hearing? You were the one who was good."

"Kate," he said, "you *were* good. You *are* good. The fact that something happened to cause you to freeze doesn't mean you aren't good."

She shook her head and gave another snort. "I was good. A long time ago. But that was then, and I don't belong anywhere near a stage now." She said it with conviction and meaning that should convince her heart as well as Ethan.

"Are you sure? Because I have to disagree with you. And I'm not alone."

She looked over at him quickly. "What do you mean? You haven't been talking to the others about me, have you?"

"I didn't have to. I could tell, and the few remarks that Phil and Tom made only reinforced my own thoughts about your talent."

She frowned, looking away, not wanting to hear the words. "I can play music, sure. But loads of other people can, and it doesn't mean I should be up on a stage. I'm a different kind of artist now. That's where my real talent is."

"Does it only have to be one talent? One area?" he said after a few moments.

Something about the words, the tone, made Kate wonder for a moment if he was directing this question to her alone.

"Maybe not. But for now, my photographic artwork is where I'm devoting my energies."

"But you clearly love music so much. Can't you at least allow yourself to play it for your own enjoyment?"

She clasped her fingers together and rubbed her thumbs agitatedly. "You don't understand. Just leave it."

"What happened?" he asked softly. "Why did you stop? Was it Missy?"

She whipped her head around toward him. "What did they tell you?"

Ethan shrugged. "Tom just said that your best friend died,

and you haven't played music since then. Is that why you went to Paris?"

"It was an opportunity. Who wouldn't want to go to Paris?"

"And never come back?"

She scowled at him. "I've been back."

"Only for brief visits, according to Tom."

She looked away, forced a shrug. "Life changed direction. I got caught up in it and made a career overseas."

"A life that doesn't include something you love."

"I have music in my life," she said, trying to keep her tone even, desperate to keep out the defensiveness that she felt.

"Yeah?" he said, surprised. "What kind of music are you into nowadays?"

If he hadn't sounded so genuinely interested, she would have shut him down with impressive knowledge of Italian opera and classical music. But now, she just sighed. "Opera, mostly. Giancarlo and his mother like it."

"And you don't?"

"I do," she said, suddenly tired. "Some of it. I can't say that it's my passion now, but there are some beautiful arias."

"Like 'Visi d'arte'?" he asked, grinning.

She gave him a startled look. "You know that aria?"

He nodded. "Sure. My parents were into opera big time. It's beautiful."

"Yes," she said, sighing, "it is. And there's a lovely one in *La Bohème*, too, that I like, 'Si, mi chiamano Mimì.'"

"Yeah, I can get behind that."

"You know that one, too?"

"Kate, my parents wanted me to play classical music, not this trashy stuff."

She laughed. "No, I don't suppose this music would have fitted their image." She cocked her head, studying him. "But they are okay with you writing songs for that band, right? I mean not many can make it in the music business."

It was Ethan's time to study his hands. "It's not the Boston Symphony, though, is it?" His nostrils flared. "Or my father's business."

There was something in his voice that caught her attention. It was more than the obvious struggle to achieve success that his parents would approve.

The back door opened again. This time Kate looked around and saw Giancarlo appear, puzzlement and concern on his face.

"Katerina. You are here. Is something wrong? I have been looking for you for a while. I had no idea where you'd disappeared to. One moment you were up on stage, the next you were gone. I finally asked Tom if he had any idea, and he suggested here."

Kate and Ethan rose at the same time, turning to face Giancarlo. Ethan went up the steps, passing Giancarlo. "I'll just go and help with the equipment," he said, leaving the two of them alone.

Giancarlo moved down to her and took her in his arms. "Are you all right? You look pale."

She gave him a wan smile. "No, no, I'm fine," she said speaking into his chest. "I just felt overwhelmed, that's all. You know, the funeral and everything."

"Of course, *tesoro*," he said. "It is only natural. Let's get you back to your father's house. It's been a long day."

She nodded and allowed him to guide her up the steps, trying not to think what it would be like, sleeping in the house without her father there, only Max.

Twenty-Five

Giancarlo, dressed in camel-colored pants and a Missoni sweater, was seated at the kitchen table glancing at his phone when Kate entered, yawning, still in her old pajamas, Max trailing behind her, his nails clicking on the linoleum. Max went to the back door and waited patiently while she opened it for him, and she watched him amble out, closing the door after him. She looked over at Giancarlo, noting the name on the cardboard coffee cup beside him.

"You went out for coffee?" she asked, surprised. Since he'd arrived he'd been drinking the coffee produced by their twenty-year-old coffee maker.

"I finally found a place that sells espresso," he said. He took a sip and shrugged. "It's not bad."

She suddenly felt guilty. She should have thought of going out for coffee, or at least suggested it. She took a seat at the table opposite him and he reached into the paper bag beside him and withdrew another cup and pushed it to her. "I got you some as well."

Her guilt deepened as she took it, thanking him. "I'm sorry we didn't do this earlier," she said.

He reached out his hand and covered hers. "There is nothing to be sorry for. I understand."

She nodded and took a sip, stunned by its strength. She hadn't had an espresso since she'd left Italy. She needed to put something in her stomach to face the rest of it.

She rose and headed toward one of the cabinets. "Can I get you any breakfast? There's eggs, bread, or some cereal here, if you want it."

"No, thank you. I had a biscotti I bought at the same place I got the espresso."

"Oh, of course." She stared at the array of cereals and saw the big canister of Quaker Oats at the end. She'd had oatmeal a few times when she first arrived and her father was still eating regular food. It had been his breakfast of choice in the fall and winter. She reached for the canister, ignoring the rows of nutritional drink boxes that were lined up on the bottom shelf. It had been a week since the funeral, and they were still there. She just hadn't been able to do those mundane tasks she knew were there, just hanging over her.

She put the recommended amount of oats in a pot and added milk. She would make it by the old-fashioned method, on the stove, with milk, dumping a handful of raisins into it as she stirred. She could feel Giancarlo's eyes on her while she swirled the wooden spoon around the pot in a figure eight movement. It irritated her for some reason, and she knew it shouldn't. He'd been supportive and understanding in his way, since his arrival. He'd said nothing when she'd left their bed the first night after his funeral and found her way to her old bed, Max sleeping on the floor next to her, two lost souls. Max had been following her around ever since, and she found it reassuring and comforting. Odd that she preferred his company to Giancarlo, but there it was.

When the oatmeal was done, she spooned it into a bowl,

doused it in maple syrup and resumed her seat. Giancarlo gave her a curious look, but said nothing and resumed scrolling on his phone. A moment later he put it down.

"I've been checking flights," he said, quietly.

She looked up at him as he searched her face.

"It is time, Katerina. We must go home soon. Already there are things that I need to attend to. I cannot put it off any longer. Not to mention the wedding. There's much to be done for it. It will be here before we know it."

She stared at him, all words vanished from her mind. "The house," she said finally. "There's too much to do. Max. I can't leave Max." Her thoughts were fragmented, half formed.

"Surely Tom could handle the sale of the house. Or, if you like, I can arrange for a company to clear it out. And then I'll have someone handle the sale. It can be done quickly, without any effort." It may have been the look of surprise and panic on her face that caused him to add, "Or I could arrange to rent it out, put everything in storage for a while, until you and Tom are ready to sell it."

She shook her head back and forth both in denial and in confusion. She could no more imagine renting her childhood home to anyone than she could think they would ever sell it. It was where she grew up. It held so much of her mother and father. And Max. How would Max cope?

"Max," she said. "We couldn't do that to Max."

"Max? The dog?" His disbelief at her words was evident in his tone. "Surely Max will be fine living with Tom."

She shook her head again, knowing he didn't understand. How could he, when she didn't even understand what her own feelings were?

"I'll have to talk to Tom. It's for the both of us to decide." It wasn't Giancarlo's place. These unspoken words hung in the air.

Giancarlo squeezed her hand. "Katerina, I am only trying to help. I know that you are grieving, and I want to make it as easy as possible for you."

The guilt descended on her like a heavy weight, knowing that she should apologize. Kate knew that his manner of helping was to take action. Solve problems. Make a plan. She was being awful to him, and she didn't know why, except that she didn't want his plans, his actions, right now.

Her hand still in the grip of Giancarlo's, she felt the stone of her engagement ring bite into the finger next to it. She withdrew her hand to ease it and the stone glinted in the morning light.

"Giancarlo, I-I think you should go back to Italy on your own. I know you have put off so much of your business for my sake and I'm grateful, but I can't go just now. There is a lot that must be done. A lot to decide. And I'm not quite ready for any of it. I don't even know what Tom's thinking. All I know is that for now, I need to be here."

Giancarlo stared at her, his dismay written all over his face. "Katerina. *Tesoro.* I know you are upset. I know you haven't slept well, and that you are filled with grief. And it's for that reason I want to take care of you. To take you home where I can help you best. Here, it is too filled with memories. Back in Rome you will find it easier to become your old self again. Trust me."

Her old self. She studied his handsome face, the dark, chocolate eyes, sensuous mouth, fondly. She reached across to him and touched his arm.

"You are a good man, Giancarlo. And I know that it's what you feel is best for me, but for now, I know I need to be here." She looked at the ring on her finger and twisted it off, handing it out to him. "And for now, I can't think about a wedding, let alone making decisions about arranging it. I can't think beyond today, except to know for now I have to be here."

Giancarlo looked at her, a shocked expression on his face. "What? No, Katerina. No. Don't be hasty. Staying here for now doesn't mean that we can't be married in April."

Kate shook her head slowly. "I don't think it's fair to you to hold you to an engagement when I don't even know when a wedding would happen. Giancarlo, I don't know where I am anymore. Right now, I just feel afloat, drifting around, and the only thing that's anchoring me in any way is this house. And Max and Tom."

He closed her fingers over the ring, shaking his head. "No, no Katerina. I understand things are difficult for you, but it's not the time for hasty decisions. Keep the ring, please, and come home with me. We'll leave things as they are, come back again in January, in preparation for the exhibition."

The exhibition. She hadn't thought about the exhibition since her father died. She wasn't even certain she could create anything, let alone pieces worthy of an exhibition. She looked away, taking a few shaky breaths.

"I don't know if I can do the exhibition, Giancarlo."

He took both her hands, squeezing them tightly, the ring cutting in sharply against her right palm, where it had been pressed. "You must, Katerina. It's important. To you, to your career. And it will help you now. Give you something to focus on."

She looked at him, the irritation she'd felt before suddenly back. How did he know what would help her? How could he presume that?

"No," she said, placing the ring on the table in front of him. "I'm not going with you. I'm staying here. For now. And if I can, I will work on the art pieces, but at the moment, I can't focus enough. My mind and emotions are scattered God knows where. But I do know that Italy is one place I won't find them."

She rose, pushing back her chair, her half-finished bowl of oatmeal in her hand. "I'm going to get dressed now." She placed the bowl in the sink, resolving to deal with it later and left the kitchen, leaving Giancarlo gripping the ring, distraught. The silence echoed through the house as she climbed the stairs to her room, feeling numb.

TWENTY-SIX

Kneeling on the living room floor, Tom studied the violin case in front of him. He'd brought it down from their father's room to join the rest of the instruments that were spread out across the living room floor. The long drapes were pulled back from the window, letting in the light, as well as revealing the dust and general disorder of the room. The dining room was no different, and if anything, the yawning space in the middle of it where the hospital bed had been seemed to have gathered more dust and dirt than anywhere else. A spare drip stand still stood pushed up in the corner and the lamp and bed stand that they'd set up for their father was still there, the former lying on the floor and the latter still in the original position Tom had placed it.

"I have no idea where this violin came from," said Tom, shaking his head. "Do you, Kate?"

Kate shook her head from her place seated on the floor nearby, Max sprawled beside her, watching them all. "Could it have been Mom's?"

Tom shrugged his shoulders. "Maybe. There might be something inside to tell us whose it was."

Ethan, squatting on the floor next to Tom, spoke up. "Maybe there's something in one of your father's files. He insured these instruments, right? I mean some are pretty valuable."

Tom looked at Kate, the question in his eyes. She shook her head slowly. "I have no idea."

"I'll look in his desk upstairs," said Tom, rising. "Kate, you look inside the case and see if you can discover anything."

Kate nodded and Tom headed up the stairs. She looked at Ethan. "Thanks for coming. I mean, I don't know if it's a good idea to look at these instruments now, but Tom seemed to think so."

Ethan smiled at her, a lock of hair falling across his brow. His hair had grown enough now that it approached the way she remembered it from ten years ago. In fact, dressed in the sweatshirt and jeans as he was now, it could have been ten years ago. And in some ways, she wished it was. That she could have a chance to make those years better.

"Are you doing okay?" he asked.

He glanced down at her bare finger, concern in his face. She hadn't told him directly what had happened between her and Giancarlo and she didn't know if Tom had told him anything of what he knew, which was only that Giancarlo had gone back to Italy, and she was staying here for now. But Tom had noticed the absence of the ring and thankfully had chosen not to comment on it. Perhaps it was because she hadn't asked any questions about the status of his relationship with Tamzin, who Kate hadn't seen or heard from since the funeral.

"Yes, no," she said, shrugging. "I don't know." She gave him a weak smile.

"I can imagine," he said. "And this can't be easy," he said, indicating the array of instruments.

She sighed. "It's actually all right. I mean we aren't doing anything but looking at them. It's not like we're selling them, right? Just wanting to know what's there. And in a way, it's like being with my dad. Holding the guitars, or the mandolin, even. It even makes me feel like my mother's here."

She knew she was rambling, uttering random thoughts that were as scattered as she felt, but Ethan just nodded, an understanding expression on his face. She somehow knew he appreciated the instruments, not only objectively as a musical instrument but as a holder of memories, as something that had a personality with its quirks and sound, like a cat or dog who was a long-term family member. The mandolin had a slightly buzzy "E" string unless the peg was given a quarter turn upward before it was tuned. And one guitar had a fractionally wider neck than usual, so the fingers had to be positioned in a slightly different position, especially the third finger. But for all that trouble, it had a really deep rich sound.

"I'm glad you don't mind this," said Ethan. He ran his hand lovingly along the Gibson guitar he held. "It's certainly a privilege for me to be able to get a chance to see all the instruments and try them out. I knew your father had some good ones, and he let me play a few, but I didn't realize he had this many."

Kate laughed. "Yeah, he collected a few over the years. Couldn't help himself. His closet housed more instruments than clothes. Mostly guitars. And my mother's mandolin and guitar. He'd never get rid of them."

"Do you play mandolin?" Ethan asked.

"A little. I was more the guitar girl, though. And then piano for a while, like Tom."

"Did Tom play the mandolin at all?"

Kate shook her head. "No, he never bothered."

"And no one played the violin that you know of." He indicated the violin case on her lap.

Kate looked down at it. Max moved over and nudged her

hand, signaling she should pet him. Absentmindedly, she stroked his head while she flipped up the lid of the case and examined the inside of it.

Laid in its bed of deep blue velvet, the violin seemed old, the shellac that coated it faded, the wood scratched. Horsehair hung loose from the bow inserted in the lid. She lifted out the violin. The strings were loose and would most likely break if she tuned it, but still, there was something about it that seemed homely, comfortable. She handed it over to Ethan to examine while she explored the small compartment in the case. When she lifted its lid, she saw a desiccated block of rosin and a couple of spare strings in packets. Under the packets she found a woven silk bracelet of gold, green, and brown. She picked it up and held it for Ethan to see.

"What is it?" he asked.

"A friendship bracelet, I think?" she asked him.

Ethan grinned at her. "The violin definitely belonged to a girl, then."

Kate raised her brows, her eyes full of mischief. "Really? Maybe a girl gave it to a boy, and he carried it around in his violin."

He waggled his brows. "A love token," he said.

She laughed and he reached over and plucked it from her hand. "The colors are nice, though." He looked at her. "You should wear it. It goes well with your eyes." He fingered the bracelet, studying it and then her.

She blushed as he handed it back to her, feeling his eyes on her. "Maybe," she said. "It is nice."

"What's nice?" asked Tom coming down the stairs, a file in his hand.

She held up the bracelet. "I found this in the violin case. It's a friendship bracelet, I think."

Tom walked over to her, squinting at it. "Huh. I don't think I've ever seen that before. Do you think it was Mom's?"

Kate shrugged. "I don't know, maybe."

"I was just telling her she should wear it. The colors suit her."

Tom nodded. "Yeah, they do." He held out the file to Ethan. "The insurance stuff is in there. Can you have a look at it? See if it's enough for what we have here?"

Ethan nodded. "Sure, of course."

"Great. Thanks for doing this, man. I don't know that I could trust anyone else, except maybe Phil or Stokey, and I'm not sure they'd even know enough."

Ethan looked at him and nodded. "No problem. I'm not sure I have the expertise, either, but I can at least look it over and recommend someone."

"Thanks. You're in the music business, and I'm sure you have more contacts than any of us put together."

"Yes," said Ethan. "That's true." There was a hint of bitterness in the tone and it caused Kate to look up at him.

———

The air was cold, Kate's breath coming out in little puffs, and fallen leaves crackled under their feet as they made their way through the woods. She could hear Max up ahead of them bounding through the bushes. It was the first time he'd had a good walk since her father had died, Kate realized. She and Tom weren't the only ones benefiting from a time out from the house. It had been Ethan's suggestion, and now she was glad of it. If only they weren't headed to the one place she'd deliberately avoided since returning to Somerton Lake.

Up ahead, Tom strode through the trees purposely, moving

toward the rise, the one they used to go to when they were growing up. The one that led to the huge rock that jutted out above the lake. Anyone sitting on it had the whole countryside at his feet. At least it seemed that way. She and Tom used to play lookout up here when they were bicycle-riding age and Tom's friends didn't mind if she tagged along. Later, it became the place to sit and try out all things teen, from smoking to making out.

Behind her she heard Ethan curse. She turned, and he gave her an apologetic look. "Sorry," he said. "I tripped on a root. Wasn't paying attention."

She smiled. "Some hiker-explorer you are."

"Hey," he said, his tone filled with mock indignation. "I'll have you know I was an Eagle Scout."

"Really?" she said, surprised. She'd pictured him in country clubs or summers on Cape Cod. Eagle Scout didn't seem to fit.

"Yes, really," he said. "I'll build a fire for you, if you need convincing."

She laughed. "By rubbing two sticks together, you mean?"

"Of course," he said, grinning at her.

The woods opened out, and they veered off the path to climb the rise. She felt her heart rate increase, the dread starting to grow. She slipped on some scree and felt Ethan's hand on her back to steady her.

"Careful," he said.

"Eagle Scout to the rescue," she said, forcing a laugh.

"Hey, you two, hurry up," said Tom, standing on top of the rock. Max was beside him, wagging his tale.

It didn't take Kate long to reach the rock. Tom held out his hand to draw her up onto the rock, Ethan following on behind. When she reached his side Tom gave her an encouraging look. He knew what this was doing to her, and she wanted to throttle him for leading them here.

"Wow," said Ethan, taking in the view. "I had no idea. What a great place."

The three of them took a seat on the flat rock, Kate facing the two men rather than the view. She couldn't bring herself to look. To imagine things. She knew that below them, the lake spread out, the gray sky, green pine trees, and the brown of the bare deciduous trees reflected in it. She'd seen that view plenty of times.

Ethan gave Kate a curious look but said nothing. She drew her knees up against her chest and wrapped her arms around them.

"Do you see your cabin over there, Ethan?" Tom asked, pointing. "Or rather Zig's."

Ethan looked in the direction he'd indicated and nodded. "Yep. I see it now. It's a great place. So quiet, beautiful."

"Will you be sorry to leave come January?" she asked Ethan. "It is January you're leaving, right?"

Ethan nodded. "Sadly yes. Emphasis on 'sadly.'"

"You'll come back, though, right?" said Tom. "You'd be welcome at our place any time."

Ethan looked at Tom, the sadness increased. "Really, I wish I could promise I'll be back, but I have no idea if I can. It's dependent on a lot of things not entirely in my control."

Tom nodded. "I get that. I wish I could be sure of things, too. And where I'll be."

Kate looked at Tom. She'd heard all the unspoken pain, frustration, and confusion in his voice.

"Do you think you'll keep the store?" Ethan asked.

It was a question Kate had known had to be voiced, but she hadn't had the courage to speak it, let alone hear the answers. She was glad that Ethan had been the one to say it.

Tom sighed. "I don't know. I suppose I'll keep things as they have been. I'll probably have to cut back on my own projects, though. Dad did a lot of the general admin and the books. I searched out vendors and worked with them, monitored inventory, that kind of thing."

"Get someone to look after the books," said Kate. "Or maybe I could do it. I don't have experience, but I can take some online courses."

Tom gave her a quizzical look. "You're thinking of sticking around?"

She shrugged. "I'll pitch in as long as I'm here." It was an impulse to help. To keep things running as they had been so that there was as little change as possible. It was what her father would have wanted, wasn't it? She couldn't bear it if Tom decided they should sell the store.

"Have you thought about changing the direction of the store a little bit so that you can incorporate your own work more?" asked Ethan. "Also maybe taper off the general manufactured furniture and bring in other artists who design and craft furniture. Make it more bespoke. Go after the high-end clients. Market online more. You have a website, right?"

Kate looked at Tom, his face stunned with the ideas that Ethan had thrown out. She could see it had really sparked something inside of Tom, and even she felt excited by the thought of Ethan's suggestions.

"What's the website like, Tom?" she asked. "I haven't looked at it in years."

Tom shrugged. "It's still pretty basic. Dad would send updates to the guy he paid to set it up. Like sales, new arrivals, that kind of thing."

Ethan nodded. "For that type of store, that's fair enough. If you decide to go in a different direction, you could up the marketing outreach on that end."

Tom grinned. "Listen to you, finance guy."

"Ethan took business courses at college," said Kate,

knowing even that statement undersold the worth of the suggestions he'd made. She realized again that he'd led a life filled with so many unknown elements in the years since she'd seen him.

"Really?" said Tom. "Well, thanks. It certainly seems a lot handier than my own degree in plant biology."

"Biology?" asked Ethan.

Tom snorted. "Yeah, I had this idea I would be studying trees. You know, their composition. Find ways to help them survive disease at the cellular level. I ended up loving wood and creating things with it. Natural segue."

Ethan laughed. "Natural segue."

Kate took in Tom's words. She hadn't known how Tom had come to work in wood. Again, the years since college yawned between her and Tom. She perched her head on her knees, suddenly feeling sad.

"Thanks, Ethan," Tom said. "You've given me a lot to think about."

"No problem," said Ethan. "Glad to help."

Hearing Tom's hopeful tone, the trace of excitement still there, Kate found her sadness ease.

Twenty-Seven

The sound of the guitar was almost hypnotic as Tom played a well-known Doobie Brothers riff on Ethan's classic D'Acquisto archtop guitar. Kate hadn't ever seen one, let alone played it. The sound was bright and energetic, and she couldn't help but smile. It was a magnificent guitar, one she hadn't known he'd possessed, but the moment the three of them had arrived at Ethan's cabin Tom had prowled around and investigated all the instruments he could find. At Ethan's encouragement, he'd tried out each one, throwing out comments, praise, and admiration as he did. His favorite by far was what Ethan had told them was a 1928 parlor guitar similar to the one Joan Baez played. Tom had almost been afraid to touch it.

Kate had watched it all, silent in her place at the dining table, sipping the hot chocolate Ethan had made her earlier, just after they arrived. Tom's mug lay half-drunk on the table, long abandoned. Ethan was sitting next to her, smiling at Tom's delight and appreciation over his explorations. Max had found a place to curl up under the table between her feet and Ethan's, his head on her shoes and, she suspected, his rear on Ethan's.

The light in the room was starting to dim as the afternoon headed toward evening. This late in the fall, she knew it would be dark very soon.

She rose. "We should get back, I suppose."

Ethan put a hand on her arm. "Stay. I'll cook dinner. Zig's coming over a little later, so I'm cooking either way. It's no big deal to add a little extra."

"You're cooking?" she asked, her eyes widening.

He gave her a wry smile. "After a fashion. It's only spaghetti. But I do a mean spaghetti, I'll have you know."

"Yeah, cool," said Tom. "Count me in."

Kate laughed. "You'd do anything to be able to hang out with those guitars."

"Hey," he said. "It's not every day I'd get a chance to play one of these beauties, let alone all of them. You must have spent a fortune on these, Ethan."

Ethan shrugged. "I've been collecting them for a while. Some are ones I've always wanted, like the one you have there, or the parlor guitar you played earlier. Classic sounds."

"The songwriting business must pay well," said Tom, grinning. "Looks like I picked the wrong field."

"You're a really talented craftsman, Tom," said Ethan. "I'm sure it won't be long before your pieces are in high demand."

"I agree," said Kate "Don't let anyone tell you anything different. And if you need help with getting images together of your finished pieces, let me know. I'd be happy to take pictures of them."

Tom looked at her, his expression wide and happy. "Really? That'd be great. I'd like that."

Kate nodded. "Sure. I can do some tomorrow if you have any pieces ready."

"Give me another day, and then you have yourself a date."

"Fine," she said, matching his delight with her own smile.

She felt lighter, somehow. Pleased and already thinking about how she might approach the project without even having seen the pieces Tom had created.

Ethan rose. "You two carry on. Try out whatever guitars or whatever you want. I'm just going to start dinner a minute."

"Let me help," said Kate rising quickly. "I can be your sous chef."

Ethan laughed. "A sous chef for spaghetti? No, no, you're fine."

"Let me throw together a salad or something. Or peel onions, chop garlic and peppers."

"Okay," said Ethan. "Consider yourself head salad maker."

She headed for his fridge, glad for a task. The thought of trying out any one of the guitars was tempting, she realized, much to her surprise, but she wanted to help Ethan. It was the least she could do.

An hour later a delicious herby aroma filled the air as the marinara simmered on the stove. In the end Kate had chopped the garlic while Ethan had unearthed the tomato puree, peeled tomatoes and all the other secret ingredients he claimed came from a vague source who taught him cooking several years ago. She'd enjoyed it, the two of them working in comfortable silence while Tom strummed and finger picked his way around a few guitars, occasionally humming, occasionally singing. Once or twice Ethan pitched in singing along in a low voice, tempting her to join him. He'd grinned the first time she did and the second time it had been more of an exaggerated mime of a rock star, as she grabbed up a cucumber as a surrogate mike, singing soulfully to it. It was his laugh that had got her then, so joyful and full of mirth that his eyes had crinkled. She found herself laughing in response and she wanted to hug him, to keep that joy and hold it inside of her. In the end he put his arm around her and pulled her into his side, the laughter still in his face.

"You are definitely rock star material with that act," said Ethan.

He pecked her on her head and released her but she felt the contact linger, warming her.

"Hey you two," said Tom from the living room area. "Stop making fun of me."

"We're not," said Kate. "You're really good. I was just enhancing the performance by adding my vocals."

"Definitely enhancing," said Ethan. "I think we have a rock star in the making."

"Ha!" said Kate. "Never in a million years. Who would want that shit?"

Ethan fell silent, his face suddenly serious. "You have it in you, you know."

Kate gave him a doubtful look. "If you never made it, why would I? And besides, I haven't thought about that kind of thing in years. And making it big as a rock star was never my goal."

Ethan raised his brows. "No?"

She shook her head. "No, Missy and I, we just wanted to play music, do gigs like my dad and mom did, make enough to keep going and enjoy what we did. Now it's all changed anyway. Posting songs online, Spotify, Soundcloud, YouTube and all that. I wouldn't even know where to begin."

Ethan nodded slowly, his expression suddenly shuttered. "Yes, it has changed."

He turned around and started to stir the sauce again. Kate wasn't certain what had shifted the conversation, but she knew that Ethan had turned inward, becoming almost inaccessible.

It had been the knock on the door a few moments later and Zig's entrance that had shifted the atmosphere back to the easy one it had been before. And now, with the marinara ready, and

Zig juggling peppers, she was trying to cut for the salad, it was as if those few moments had never existed.

Tom picked out a tune on the piano, while Kate and Ethan sat sprawled on the sofa and Zig the armchair. All three drank beers, content to listen to Tom for the moment. The meal was finished, dishes done, thanks to Zig and Kate, and now they were just relaxing, their stomachs full of what Kate had to admit had been a delicious meal. Maybe it was his grandmother's recipe, or whomever he'd ascribed it to.

She'd enjoyed the lazy conversation that had gone with it, catching up with Zig who was fast becoming a key person in the software company he worked for, developing apps and other key pieces of software in the ever burgeoning area of the exercise and active life range of the company's boutique brand. His dream was to go out on his own, developing various apps around the music industry, and after talking to him, Kate had no doubt he would make it happen.

"Do you play an instrument?" Kate asked Zig.

Zig shook his head and grinned. "I am an appreciator of music. I design things that help make it happen."

"You should see his LP collection," said Ethan. "I'm sure it's worth a fortune."

Zig shrugged. "Probably. But it doesn't matter. I'm not getting rid of it."

Tom stopped his playing and turned around to face them. "What kind of music do you collect?"

"All types," said Zig. "Anything from Klesmer to hard rock, from jazz to ska."

"Classical?" asked Kate.

"Oh, well, no. Not really. I leave that to Ethan here. His collection is just as eclectic but in a slightly different direction."

Kate looked over at Ethan, surprised, even though she knew it wasn't unreasonable for him to have a collection of music. Of course he would.

"Not a Spotify fan?"

Ethan smiled. "I do Spotify. But there are some recordings I like to collect in LP form."

"Just like Dad," said Tom. "No wonder you two got along."

Ethan laughed. "Yeah, we did have that in common."

"I think you had a lot in common," said Kate quietly.

Tom nodded thoughtfully. "It's true."

It struck Kate that it was the first time their father had been mentioned since the walk, and it didn't immediately bring tears to her eyes. In fact, it had only made her feel warm inside to hear her dad mentioned in that context.

"Thanks," said Ethan, a surprised look on his face. "I see that as a real compliment."

"How's the songwriting coming?" asked Zig. "Still stuck?"

Kate glanced at Ethan, wondering what his response would be. Since he'd mentioned it to her, it had been in the back of her mind, tickling her every time she looked at one of her photographs or heard a tune wandering through her head.

Ethan rolled his eyes. "Thanks for the reminder."

"Look, man," said Zig. "I offered you one of my apps. It can write the song for you."

"Ha, ha," said Ethan. "As if it were that simple."

"It is. It is," said Zig, but Kate saw the twinkle in his eyes.

Ethan threw a cushion at him. "You blaspheme. My talent is precious. God given. It is beyond any computer software or app."

"Are you insulting my coding skills?" Zig folded his arms, his expression a mock glare.

Tom laughed and Kate had to smile.

"I'm afraid I'll have to side with Ethan on this one," said Tom.

"And me," echoed Kate.

Zig held up his hand. "Bah, you're musicians. You're all biased."

The words startled Kate. How long had it been since she thought of herself as a musician?

TWENTY-EIGHT

Kate studied the image on the table, squinting her eyes a little to get that distant, objective feel of her work so far. With a sigh, she rose, propped the image against a hastily cobbled prop from a small pile of old books found in the corner and a worn, carved wooden box that at one time had contained essential oils or something.

She moved farther away from the image, blinking against the light coming from the fan-shaped window behind the work. Not the best way to look at her image, but still. A slight chill took her, and she rubbed her arms. She'd been still for so long that she'd started to feel the cold that was creeping into the attic as the patchy sun shifted to the back of the house. She'd need to bring a space heater up soon. The weather was really starting to shift into winter. It would be Thanksgiving shortly, she realized. She felt a stab of pain. The first. The first of the "firsts" she knew she was facing. And what hurt more, she now knew that the "lasts" for so much—holidays, special occasions—were too many years ago. And she had no one to blame but herself.

She sat on the floor with a thud and let the tears come. For days and days now, she'd fought feeling sad, fought that overwhelming sorrow that threatened to overtake her, to drown her. And now, she didn't feel like fighting it, she just let it come. Max, who'd been curled up by the table, nudged her, and she hugged him, her sobs coming in great gulps.

She didn't know how long it was before a sound penetrated her grief. And then a shout. Her name. She wiped her face using the heels of her hand, wondering if she would just ignore the person in the hopes he would go away. Max started to bark, making his way over to the door.

If Max's barking hadn't decided it for her, the opening of the attic door was the final arbiter. She looked up to see Ethan standing in the entrance. She stared at him, sniffing, watching Max go to him and lick his hand. Ethan patted him absent-mindedly and frowned at Kate, his brows drawn into a question, until a moment later, when his expression flooded with understanding and compassion. He walked forward, lifted her up and folded her into his arms, rubbing her back. Kate felt the comfort and warmth of his embrace, the soothing rhythm of his hand against her back. They stood like that for countless moments, and Kate sank into it, wishing it would never end.

Eventually Ethan pulled back, checking her expression. "Bad moment?"

She nodded, and he put his arm across her shoulder.

"I wondered when I called and texted you and didn't hear anything. I thought that it was something like this, or you might be working." He nodded over to the table. "I see that both were true."

She gave a weak laugh. "Sorry. Yes, I was working." She looked around for her phone. "My phone must be downstairs."

Ethan squeezed her to his side. "Spoken like a true artist."

The smile she gave now had more of a genuine quality than her laugh. It was nice hearing him call her an artist.

"Can I see?" asked Ethan.

A small bout of butterflies rose in her stomach. Somehow, showing Ethan her raw work made her more nervous than any of the times she'd shown Giancarlo. She managed a small, indifferent shrug and gestured to the piece she was currently working on.

Ethan walked over to the table in front of the fan light, Max following and plonking down in his old spot. Ethan took up the piece there and turned it around so that the light shone on it. The seconds ticked by as he studied it, and Kate waited, unconsciously holding her breath.

Ethan looked up, shook his head and smiled widely. "Amazing. What you've done. You are so incredibly talented."

The basic image was the one she'd taken with him that time when he pointed out the reference to the poem "House of Clouds." She'd blurred the image a fraction, added a filter to increase the surreal quality. And now, using sepia gall ink, she'd threaded phrases of the poem in and around the clouds and through some of the trees, both in the image and in the reflection, a counterpoint of reality and mirage. She'd thought she still had a few more phrases to weave before she would consider it done, but now, looking at it with Ethan's words ringing in her ear, she wondered if she would just leave it as it was, with an uncertain ending. A suggestion or questioning of the existence of dreams and the places they're stored.

"This is beautiful, Kate," said Ethan, his eyes intense on hers.

She flushed under his praise. "Thanks," she said softly.

He placed the piece flat on the table. "Your gallery owner is going to be thrilled."

"I hope so. Though I'm not sure she'd be happy with my pace."

"How many pieces does she want?"

"Fifteen at least."

"How many have you done?"

She wrinkled her nose. "Five?"

"You're not sure?" he asked, grinning.

"Well, five counting this one. I mean, they all have to be framed."

He nodded. "So, you have two-and-a-half months before the exhibition."

"Well, I have to get them framed, and they have to be hung, so I have probably six weeks at worst and seven, eight weeks at best. Probably less. And there's Christmas in between. Plus I don't even have all the images I need, yet. And I probably could do with another poem."

He started laughing at her. "You sound like me. Worst case scenario, always. The song is crap. It will go nowhere. The music is cliché. And on it goes in my head."

She widened her eyes. "Really? But you're so good."

He shrugged. "You're so good."

"But you're experienced. You've been writing songs for a long while. All the time I've known you at least, and that's been ten years."

He looked at her silently, searching her face. "Doubt can still happen. I don't think it ever goes away. Just comes and goes."

"Is that what's giving you the problem, then? The doubt has come back?"

He sighed and looked away, toward the fan window. "Doubt, questioning and a bit of frustration."

"Frustration? Questioning?"

"Frustration with myself, mostly. Questioning if this is what I really want to do."

She gave him a puzzled look. "You don't want to write songs?"

"It's not that so much as who I'm writing for." He glanced at her and looked down. "It's complicated."

"Is this to do with your dad?" she asked softly.

He raised his head slowly, nodding a little. "In part. You could say that one of the reasons I'm here is for some self-examination."

"And is what you've found causing some of the songwriting block?"

He nodded slowly again. "Yes. Probably. I'm supposed to be writing songs I really don't want to. For a sound that really isn't me."

She gave him a sympathetic look, reminded of Giancarlo and Paloma's insistence she create pieces about Dante's *Inferno*. "I get that," she said, sighing.

He took her hand and squeezed it. "Thanks."

Twenty-Nine

The aroma of roasting chicken and herbs filled the air, making Kate's stomach grumble as she grasped her wine glass tightly and nervously played with the tassel on her blouse. The deep, soft sofa seemed to envelop her, and its oversized cushions and ornamental pillows that surrounded her increased the feeling. Even with her tall frame, her feet only just touched the floor. The matching loveseat didn't seem like a better proposition, and the small hairless cat curled up on the little lap blanket on one side had confirmed it.

Soft voices from the kitchen drifted into her and she wondered what Bunny and Mark were talking about. Her probably. The unlikely invitation had been reissued the day before, just after Ethan had left, and she had no excuse now to refuse it. In the end, she thought she would just get it over with and had offered to come that night if it was convenient. Mark had pounced on her offer, as if he thought he had to pin her down as soon as possible in case she got away.

Mark came through from the kitchen, a beer in his hand. He was wearing chinos and a button-down shirt under a tan crew-neck sweater. He gave her a big smile and took a seat beside the cat, who lifted his head and gave him a disdainful look, before resuming its position. The house was a recently remodeled ranch house, the lines now smooth and sleek on every bit of trim, wall colors full of slate grays, taupes, and eggshells, with the furniture to match. Over the dining table at the other end of the open room, she'd noted the angular chrome light fitting that had just that amount of bling that she knew exactly who'd picked it out.

"I'm sorry about your dad, by the way," he said. "We were at the funeral, but Bunny wasn't feeling well, so we went home right after."

She nodded and said, "Thanks," unsure what else to say.

"I used to see your dad in the hardware store all the time, these last few years. But I always liked him. He was so cool with us, considering all we got up to." He shook his head.

He meant what Missy got up to. What she inevitably dragged them into, her forcible personality and her love of pushing the boundaries a dangerous combination. Kate made herself smile. "He was cool, in his way."

"Remember that time..." His words were broken off by Bunny's entrance, a wine glass in her hand. "Everything all right, babe?" asked Mark.

Bunny's navy pants, paired with scooped pale blue shell under a cashmere wrap, seemed to suggest she'd moved onto to her mother's country club circle's shopping venues.

Bunny nodded to Mark, a neutral expression on her face. "Of course, it is."

She moved to the loveseat, picked up the cat, kissed his head and murmured a few endearments to him and sat down next to Mark, placing the cat on her lap. A cloud of Chanel No. 5 wafted over to Kate.

Bunny turned to Kate and gave her a stiff smile. "Dinner

will be ready in about twenty minutes. I'm sorry to keep you waiting. I only got home from work an hour ago."

Kate nodded, feeling at a loss. What did Bunny want her to say? They were the ones who had been pressing her to have dinner with them. Though to be fair, it was probably Mark. She looked over at him, her brow arching ever so slightly. It was almost automatic, this reaction to Bunny. The three of them had always shared this understanding, this silent mockery of the drama queen of all drama queens. A mean drama queen was the actual fact, one they labeled as the queen of the "Heathers."

"How are your parents, Mark?" asked Kate, searching for neutral territory.

"Good, thanks," he said, his blue eyes twinkling. "Dad's retired from the company now, busy being a bigwig in the Lions Club, and Mom is getting really active in the homeless charity project the country club is running." He patted Bunny's hand. "In fact, she's working with Bunny, who's the chairperson. Bunny's raised loads of money for worthy causes in the last few years."

His voice was full of pride, and Kate had to look away, studying the wine in her glass. *For Christ's sake,* she thought. *How can he sit there mouthing such platitudes to her, of all people?* She bit her lip, took a few deep breaths and looked up. "Great," she said, her tone flat.

"They're important causes. It makes a difference," said Bunny, her tone defensive, belligerent.

"I'm sure it does," said Kate. She made herself take another deep breath, resisting the urge to check her watch.

"I know you don't think much of the country club or anyone who goes there," said Bunny, her voice rising what seemed like an octave, "but it does some really good things for the community. It isn't all about pleasure."

"And golf," muttered Kate.

"What?" said Bunny, her eyes flashing.

"Kate," said Mark, frowning.

"Sorry," said Kate. "I didn't mean that." She shrugged. "You're right. It was never my thing. But who am I to say anything about what it's like now?"

Bunny pursed her lips. "It's always been involved in supporting community concerns." She smiled at Mark, her expression softening. "And it's a good opportunity for Mark to network." She glanced at Kate. "You know he works for Daddy now at his investment firm."

Kate gave Mark a stunned look. She hadn't known. She hadn't thought to ask Mark where he worked, or anything else about how he'd spent the time since she'd last seen him. She swallowed back the bile in her throat at the thought of what Missy would think about what he'd chosen to do, let alone where and with whom he'd chosen to do it. In the end, Kate nodded, resolving to do or say nothing beyond the basic pleasantries.

"You've done wonders with this house," said Kate. "It's lovely."

Bunny took a deep breath and launched into the description of the renovations she'd overseen in the year since they'd bought it, just after they'd married. Kate was grateful that Bunny's love of design and decor had her waxing lyrical about every minute detail, so that she could just nod occasionally and tune it out while she counted down the hours until she could leave. Two, she decided. She would give it two. Surely no one could fault her for that.

———

The distant sounds of road traffic reached Kate's ears, reminding Kate that though this house had a nicely proportioned gravel drive leading up to it, there was still a main road to greet everyone at the bottom of it. She sipped her wine glass, wishing for the tenth time that she hadn't been forced to nurse this glass of wine the whole night. A whiskey sounded perfect. A vodka and tonic. Anything that might take the edge off this awful evening she'd endured. Bunny had run out of steam about the house just before they sat down and Mark had tried to pick up the baton, talking about different changes in Somerton Lake and the prospects for the college football team moving up to a bigger conference. He'd never even attended Somerton Lake College, opting for a small state college a few towns over so that he could be near Missy when he didn't get a football scholarship at Somerton. Now, he'd been talking about it like it was really important.

All throughout, Kate had nodded, making little noises of interest, eating her chicken with its special herbs, done in some special gourmet style Kate was certain Bunny had either learned on a course or studied carefully and copied from one of the professional cooking shows. Kate had felt unable to eat the light-as-air mousse topped with a crackling spun sugar cage, but had forced it down anyway, issuing what she hoped were the right compliments and assurances of its quality.

A tiring day and brewing headache had sent Missy off to bed early, leaving Mark to insist she stay for a cup of coffee on the deck where an outdoor heater blazed away, keeping the evening's growing cold at bay. She sighed, wishing Mark would hurry with the coffee so she could drink it and be on her way.

Kate approached Missy as quietly as she could in the dark parking lot, aware of the gravel crunching noisily underfoot. Carefully, she avoided the smashed glass from a stray beer bottle and winced when she saw the used needle less than a foot away by the bar's back door. Sam's wasn't known for its quality facilities or its stellar customers. She could see Missy, though, leaning against a dumpster next to some emaciated guy, smoking a joint, her dark hair tangled and unkempt, her jeans and tank top nearly hanging off her. Why wasn't she freezing in this cold weather without a coat? But Kate knew. Though it had only been a month since Kate had last talked to her, a lot had happened in that month.

Something made Missy look across the parking lot, and catching sight of Kate, she straightened up and made her way over to her. Kate halted, a brief flicker of hope rising in her that was dashed a moment later when she saw the rage in Missy's eyes.

Missy flung her arm out wide. "Oh, no, oh no, you don't. You don't get to come here and talk to me."

"Missy," Kate said, trying to keep a reasonable tone. "I only want to talk."

"There's nothing to talk about."

Her voice was rising, getting louder, and Kate resisted the urge to tell her to lower it.

"I just want to know if you still want to do the Fowler gig, that's all. See when you want to rehearse."

"You must be joking. Why would I want to do a gig with you ever again? You blew me off, Kate. It's you who doesn't want to do this anymore."

"I'm sorry, Missy. Really sorry. I got caught up in something. I couldn't get away. I didn't mean to miss the gig. I've told you. I'll make it up to you, just like I said. I've got feelers out for several other gigs. My dad said he'd help us too."

"I don't want any part of your leavings!" She was screaming now. "Go off with your lame college boy you've been lusting after. See if he can give you what you want. You obviously don't want our dream anymore." Kate flinched as Missy flung those last words at her, each one cutting her like a lash.

. . .

The back door opened and Mark emerged, two steaming mugs in hand. He made his way to her, handed her one of the mugs, and took a chair next to her. They stared out into the night silently. The sky was dark, clouds crowding in so heavily that Kate wondered if snow was in the forecast.

"Well, you've obviously moved on," Kate found herself saying.

"And so did you." His tone was sharp, defensive.

So glared over at him. "Not as much as you may think. And I didn't become so chummy with someone who hated Missy that I married them." The words spilled out of her, full of all the pent up bile that had been inside her since first seeing Bunny and Mark together. "God knows what Missy would say if she saw you two now."

"What would you know?" snarled Mark. "You went abroad. And everyone you left behind had to pick up the pieces."

She snorted. "You know nothing."

"And neither do you," he said sharply. He took a deep breath. "It took me seven years, Kate. Seven long years to get to a point where I could face myself in the mirror. Seven years before I could even look at another woman. She broke me. And for a while, I thought it was for good."

"Apparently, it wasn't for good. Yay for you." Kate gripped her mug, trying but failing to keep control of her emotions.

Mark ran his hand through his hair, mussing what had been an immaculately arranged style. The gesture returned him to more of the image of Mark she remembered.

"Look," he said. "Bunny is a good person. You don't know her. You never really knew her. She wasn't like she appeared to be in high school. She had a lot of pressure at home and it made her insecure. She really struggled with it."

Kate gave him an incredulous look. "Bunny? Are we talking about the same person?"

"I know it's hard to believe, but she hid it well."

"Behind sarcasm, bullying and belittling." Kate shook her head. "You saw how she was with us. Or maybe you didn't, because if you were around, she was sickeningly sweet."

Mark nodded. "I know. And I know why she got the "Heather" label. But it was all an act, Kate. She was jealous of you, jealous of Missy. Especially Missy. You both knew who you were. You were both so confident, not giving a damn what people thought about you."

Kate stared at him. "What? We were both messes."

Mark shook his head. "No, you weren't. You had your music. The two of you shone up on stage. You were mesmerizing. Even I couldn't compete with that. I knew with Missy the music always came first."

Kate felt her tears well up. "Until it didn't. Until I decided that I needed to get Ethan's attention and play with him at the music department one night. The night of the gig at Seventh Heaven."

"It wasn't you, Kate. Sure, she was furious about that, but she was already starting to go off the rails."

"No. You're wrong. It is my fault. She knew how much I liked Ethan and also that I was dying to play music with him. She was scared she was going to lose me, and I didn't make her understand that it wasn't true."

Mark took her wrist. "We're not at fault. It took me years of therapy to realize that. Missy was a drug addict, in the end. And nothing would have changed what happened. It was her choice. All of it. You have to accept that."

The tears started to spill down her cheeks. "No, you're wrong." She dug her heels into her eyes trying to stop the flood.

She rose, placing her cup down on the table. "It's late. I'd better go. Thanks for a lovely evening. Please tell Bunny I appreciate it." She walked to the deck steps and made her way down them into the night.

———

Around her, the night air hung heavy with moisture. *Definitely snow in the air*, she thought. Staring out to the lake, she could almost imagine tiny flakes floating around in the sky, but realized a moment later it was the lights from a few of the houses on the opposite shore. The wooden dock beneath her shifted ever so slightly in the stiff breeze that made the currents. She shivered in her pea coat. Really, she needed to get herself a heavier coat.

The water lapped heavily against the posts below her. It wasn't a night to be admiring the lake, but she knew that wasn't what had drawn her here after leaving Mark's. She shook her head, trying to dispel the words that echoed in her head. Mark's words. And here she was pushing herself toward the punishment she knew she deserved. To negate Mark's words, no matter how tempting they were.

She stared at the water, trying to imagine Missy, desperate, grieving, hurt. Above her, clouds started to shift and for a few moments, it cleared enough so that the moon appeared, bright and confounding in its mirror image in the lake. And beside it, for just the briefest of moments, was Ethan's cabin, floating beside the shivering moon. She sniffed, smiling at its almost determined effort to appear and laughed at its fight with the clouds that warred overhead with the moon. The phrase from the "House of Clouds" drifted through her mind.

Build it on the moonlit cloud
To which I looked with thee.

She repeated the words, watching as slowly, the clouds took over again, and the house was engulfed by them. But the image lingered in her mind, and the phrases that went with them, all mingling together and becoming something more. Something with a melody that took root in her mind. She looked over at the cabin, a faint light still on downstairs. Should she go to him? What would she tell him? A few bars of music and an odd phase or two and his problems were solved. She snorted. She needed to solve her own problems first. All Ethan would probably see was that her life was a mess. And it would be the truth.

THIRTY

Kate blew on her plate, the heat from the melting cheese and sizzling tomato sauce prompting the move. Despite its high temperature, Kate inhaled the aroma of the herbs and tomatoes of Gino's pizza special, an old favorite. She'd been glad that at least this one thing hadn't changed in Somerton Lake. College students still crowded the table, with the odd scattering of townspeople and high schoolers in this late afternoon, only a week before Thanksgiving.

Opposite her, Zig picked up a piece of his pizza, taking a large bite out of it, and then waved his hand in front of his face, his mouth opening slightly, his eyes watering.

"All these years and you still haven't learned how to eat pizza?" asked Ethan, his voice filled with laughter.

Zig glared at him, downing a full glass of water before speaking. "Don't mock me. Waiting on a Gino's pizza is impossible."

"Yet Kate and I manage to do it." Ethan shook his head. "It's all about learning restraint. Maturity. Face it, you're no more mature now than you were as a college student. No wonder you're dating one."

Kate looked at Ethan beside her. She'd been glad to accept his invitation to join the two of them at Gino's, but she had been surprised when he'd slipped into the booth next to her and not Zig.

"Zig's dating a college student?" she said and turned to stare at him. "A Somerton College student?"

Zig frowned. "What's the problem? I'm not that much older than her. She's a senior."

Ethan laughed. "As I just said, you're just about the same in terms of emotional maturity."

"Doesn't it feel strange," said Kate, "dating someone from the college you left years ago and well, she's still there? Attending classes. Studying, taking exams. That seems so long ago for me."

Zig shrugged. "I like her. She's cool. We have things in common. She's a gamer. And she loves music. I've seen her collection. She knows her stuff."

Ethan looked at Kate, raising his brows.

"Is that code for something else?" asked Ethan. "Or have you shared Spotify lists?"

Kate laughed and Zig gave Ethan a mock glare. "I'm serious, man. She's cool. I want you to meet her, you'd like her."

Ethan's face shut down. "It's not that serious, Zig."

"No," said Zig. "Really. She's cool."

Ethan looked over at Zig, studying his face. "Fine," he said, eventually. "Bring her over sometime."

———

The cabin was more familiar now, and Kate took a seat in the armchair, any discomfort long vanished. Despite Ethan's earlier teasing, Zig was in a good mood. It had been his suggestion they go back to the cabin, and now he opened the fridge, pulled out a beer, and after removing the cap, took a swig. He gestured first to Kate, who nodded, and then Ethan who shrugged.

"Sure, why not?" he said. "But just one. I've got a full day of writing tomorrow."

After Zig delivered the beers, he took a seat next to Ethan on the sofa, Kate now seated in an armchair.

"You've moved past your song writing block?" Kate asked Ethan.

He gave her a sheepish look and shook his head. "The novel. I'm nearly finished with the first draft. I want to write while it's clear in my head."

She laughed. "Only you would skive off by writing a novel."

"Wait, wait," said Zig. "You're experiencing a song writing block? Why didn't you say, man?"

Ethan frowned. "Sorry. It just kind of happened. I have a lot on my mind and I thought it would go. That it wouldn't be a big deal."

Zig widened his eyes. "Wow. How many have you written?"

Ethan looked away. "A few."

"Do the guys know?" asked Zig.

Ethan gave him a dark look. "No. And I intend to keep it that way."

Zig gave him a sympathetic look, shaking his head. "Wow," he said. "Just wow."

"I was trying something new," said Ethan tensely. "Trying for a different voice, a different style."

Zig shook his head again. "They won't like that. You know they want to keep that gravy train running."

Ethan ran his hand through his hair and sighed. "I know. You're right. That's partly why I'm stuck. I mean I have a few ideas, but"—he shrugged—"they just don't gel. Not really. Not for that sound."

Zig cast a look in Kate's direction before returning to study Ethan. "You have to do it, you know that, don't you? You're bound by a contract."

"I know," said Ethan, his tone a little sharp. "You think I don't know that? That's why I'm here."

"No," said Zig. "It seems like you're here writing a novel. A novel for friggin' sake. Why?"

Ethan raised his eyes to the ceiling. "Because. It's something I have wanted to do for years."

"Do it after this album. Finish this album, fulfill the contract, and then you are free. Why mess it up?"

"Look, Zig. If the words, the music aren't there, they aren't there. Simple as that."

Zig shook his head again. "I get it, believe me, I do. But it's not me you have to convince. Have you listened to other bands, you know, to get some inspiration? Some old classics."

He leaned over the side of the sofa, where Kate noticed Ethan had about fifty LPs lined up against the wall and a pile of CDs beside them. He rifled through the LPs.

"You don't have much here," said Zig. "Looks like you left your good stuff behind in New York."

Ethan laughed. "You mean what you consider good stuff. I beg to disagree."

"You get my meaning. Most of this is Folk and Indie Rock with a bit of New World. That's not going to help you much, is it?"

"Since it's there to help me relax, I think it's just right." There was a bit of tension back in his voice.

It was only the sympathy she felt for Ethan that made her bring it up now, because she wasn't even certain it was something she wanted to share. Ever. The strong fear of where it might drag her hung heavy even now. "I don't know if this will help," said Kate, "but the other night, I was thinking about the 'House of Clouds' poem and its relationship to the artwork. And..." She paused, looked down at her beer. She took a deep breath. "I thought of a kind of song."

"About the 'House of Clouds'?" asked Ethan, brightening.

She nodded. "It's really only a rough sketch. Almost a fragment. But it was the 'moonlit cloud' that started me off."

A grin broke out on his face. "Really? Like what? What exactly? That is if you don't mind sharing it."

She shook her head. "No, it's fine." She recited a few phrases.

I will build a house of clouds,
For all the dreams I'm not allowed
With a canopy of trees
A tapestry of leaves
And deep inside would be a room
Where art and music bloom, for us.

"That's it," she said. "But the tune might go something like this." She hummed a bit, then began to put the first verse to the tune. "You know, a little like that." She shrugged.

Ethan started nodding. "I like it. It's good."

"It has me hooked," said Zig. "And I don't even know this poem."

Ethan and Kate looked at each other and laughed.

After a moment's consideration, Ethan stood and walked over to one of the guitar cases lined up against the wall. He opened the case and pulled out his guitar. It was his old Martin, the wood darkened and aged, the scuff marks almost integral to the wood pattern now. *A friendly guitar*, Kate thought. It had seemed that even when her brother had tried it out briefly. Now she found herself itching to try it too.

The thought must have communicated itself to Ethan, because a moment later she was startled to find Ethan handing it to her. "Here," he said. "Try it out."

Speechless, she took the guitar from him before she could even think to refuse and placed it in her lap, her hands automatically finding their place, the fingers homing into their positions. Ethan moved to another guitar case and withdrew an old Yamaha, heavy and dark, the shine dulled and completely worn through by the sound opening where his right hand would strum.

She stared at him as he resumed his place on the sofa. He nodded to the guitar he held. "My songwriting bash-around guitar. I've had it since I was a teen."

She smiled. "It's like an old, familiar teddy bear."

"Something like that," said Ethan.

He strummed the guitar and began fingerpicking. Kate found herself following him with the guitar she held, plucking the strings, finding the chords. She realized he was playing the melody she'd just given him, and she began to hum along with the two of them. Soon, he was humming too, eventually sliding into the lyrics she'd spoken earlier. His pitch was lower, but she matched in the upper octave, the two of them blending well, just as they'd done at O'Connor's, just as she'd always known they would from the first time she'd seen him singing "Suzanne."

She fell silent when they came to the end of the verse she'd created, but Ethan continued on, throwing out verses, adding "something, something" when a good phrase escaped him, a situation that occurred with increasing frequency, so that eventually she started to giggle, joining Zig's already loud sniggers.

Ethan, unable to help himself, began grinning, and that soon morphed into a laugh.

When his laughing made it impossible to sing, he halted his playing. "Okay, okay, you two. Enough of that."

"No, no," said Kate. "It was good, really. I mean aside from the 'somethings.'"

She laughed again, Zig joining her, while Ethan rolled his eyes.

Zig sobered. "No, really, man. It was cool. You added some good stuff there. It's different from your usual, but, yeah, it's good."

Ethan nodded his head slowly. "And therein lies the issue."

"What?" said Kate.

Ethan gave her a rueful look. "I think I've run out of songs that are suitable."

"Suitable for that band you write for?"

Zig snorted. "So make it like their style. You've done it before."

Ethan sighed. "Yeah, I suppose." He grimaced. "Anyway, it's not my song, it's yours, Kate. You should have it. It's about your artwork, anyway."

Kate shook her head. "No, it's yours. You were the one who saw 'The House of Clouds' in the view. If you hadn't called me and told me to come look at it, I never would have seen it, let alone made it into the artwork. You understood what that view could mean."

Ethan shrugged. "A collaboration, then."

She nodded. "A collaboration. But feel free to leave me out of the official credit if you do decide to use it."

"Why?" he asked curiously.

She gave a shudder. "I don't want any of that kind of attention. You say this band you write for is popular? Well, no thank you. I don't do well in the limelight now."

She'd tried to keep her tone lighthearted, joking, but it must have fallen short, because Ethan gave her a pained look and turned his head away. Zig eyed him, frowning.

"Sorry," said Ethan. "It wouldn't be a big thing, anyway. No one takes notice of the songwriters, anyway, trust me. Except maybe those who are really into knowing the full story, or collect LPs and actually read the liner notes."

Zig laughed and Ethan gave him a dark look. Zig shrugged. "Hey, I know all the songwriters on the albums I have."

Ethan pointed at him. "You're not normal."

"Neither are you," said Zig.

He indicated the collection on the other side of the sofa. Kate glanced at it, trying to see what albums and CDs Ethan had. She gave a soft smile, immediately recognizing a few of the spines of her father's band.

"I'm a songwriter," said Ethan. "Of course I look for other songwriters. Kate probably does too. That kind of thing always stays with you."

He looked at her expectantly and Zig fixed his gaze on her too, waiting for her denial. She grimaced. "Yes, I do. Can't help it, given my background."

Ethan just gave Zig a smug smile, his proof confirmed.

"But that just proves my point that a lot of people know who the songwriters are. Especially if it's their favorite band." He widened his eyes, trying to emphasize his words.

"It still doesn't make them famous," said Ethan, his voice firm.

Zig just shook his head. "You wish," he muttered.

THIRTY-ONE

The bar was quiet, except for Ethan's rich tones threading through the room. There was a large crowd there tonight, not even standing space available, let alone a vacant table. Word had obviously spread that this night at O'Connor's was the place to be to hear good music. Kate felt pride swell inside her at the thought and tamped it down as soon as it rose. But still, it was hard not to be at least pleased for him. He was so talented, and she could listen to him all day. She laughed inwardly at her fan girl thoughts. But then she'd been a fan girl all those years ago too.

She steered her thoughts away from that direction and caught Tom lifting his beer glass to his lips, his eyes narrowed thoughtfully as he stared ahead to the stage. It wasn't the first time she wondered what he was thinking. She wasn't certain, but she didn't think it had anything to do with Ethan's performance. In fact, she wondered if Tom had heard anything of Ethan's performance though the first set was winding down. She sighed. She'd been so wrapped up with Ethan's singing and playing, she'd really only registered his absentmindedness subconsciously. Something was wrong, and she had an inkling what it might be, beyond the obvious emotion they both shared. Grief. Her own came on her often enough, and not always at convenient or expected times.

A giggle and bout of whispering caught her attention. She glanced across the table where Zig and his new girlfriend, Tracy, sat. She was leaning against Zig, her phone out, taking a selfie. A minute later she turned it around and took a shot of Ethan up on stage, though Kate was certain there must be at least some part of Tom's head in it as well. Kate had to stop herself from frowning at Tracy. Tracy's youth was something Kate had noted when Zig had first introduced them tonight, just before the gig started. Ethan had already been onstage and hadn't been able to do anything more than wave over at Zig and Tracy. She could see what had attracted Zig, though. She was pretty enough in her jeans, Doc Martens, braided blonde hair, and long lashes that were visible from yards away. Tracy was also smart, and with her interest in gaming and music she was an irresistible package to Zig. Tracy had already taken several photographs of everyone and everything, posting them on Instagram and wherever else that was on trend. Zig had stopped her from taking videos, saying it wasn't cool. "Young" was the descriptor that threaded through Kate's mind and words like "sweet," "naive," also trailed behind.

She wondered briefly if Tracy was in a sorority, having no idea at this point what would be considered good sorority material now, especially since she'd never been in one. Tracy had the look, but she wasn't sporting a tale tell T-shirt or any other signifier.

Kate turned her attention back to Ethan in an almost deliberate move, hoping it might send a subtle message to Tracy. Zig didn't seem to be able to manage her or at least notice her lack of manners, his face showing an indulgent smile as he listened to her continue to whisper. This time Kate did roll her eyes. Tom leaned toward her and nudged her with his shoulder. A silent communication. She turned and grinned at him.

Fortunately, or not, Ethan took a break after that song, and Kate was saved from giving dagger eyes to either Tracy for her rudeness or Zig for bringing her. A moment later she was chastising herself. This was a bar and restaurant. They hadn't paid tickets. Not everyone felt the same about music and performers. And especially not this performer.

Ethan startled her out of her musings by leaning down and kissing her on the cheek, the fedora still perched on his head, glasses on, murmuring his thanks that she'd come. He did a quick clap on the back to Tom, uttered a brief thanks for coming, nodded quickly to Zig, but then turned his eyes back to Kate.

"I can't stay long. I have to talk to Pete about next week, but I wanted to ask...request...something of you first."

Kate gave a puzzled chuckle, conscious of Zig and Tracy behind her, staring. "Sure, what?"

He gave her a hopeful, tentative look. "Play a song with me in the next set?"

The surprise pulled a choked laugh from her. "What?" Then she was shaking her head, casually at first, but then with studied firmness. "No, Ethan."

"Why?" he asked her gently. "You're so good. We could just do one quick song. Your choice."

"No," her voice was loud, stern. She fought down the anger and the panic, forced it under control. "No," she repeated, her voice softer this time.

"You can do it, Kate," Tom said, his tone deliberately neutral. "It's nothing here. Just the usual crowd."

She looked over at him, her eyes hardening. "You don't even get it. I can't and won't. Simple as that."

Tom started nodding slowly. "Okay."

Ethan said nothing. He laid a hand on her shoulder and squeezed it gently. He looked over at Zig. "Hey, sorry I can't stop to talk, but I promise, after the gig, we'll have a chat and do proper introductions."

"Sure, man," said Zig. "Whatever."

Ethan left, and silence hung over the rest of the group. Kate picked up her beer, took a gulp, and then excused herself to go to the ladies' room.

The concert resumed shortly after her return. It took her a little while, but eventually, she was able to lose herself in the music and the tightness that had gripped her chest loosened.

The performance wound to a close, Ethan playing one encore and after, with the applause deafening around him. After the last encore, he gave a little wave and thanked the crowd. He tried to step down from the stage, but the growing number of people gathering there prevented him, all of them eager to speak with him and a few even brandishing pen and paper. At least no bared breasts and sharpie pens, Kate thought wryly. He was definitely getting a following, some of whom could even be labeled "groupies." But as he spoke to each person and signed offered pieces of paper, his eyes constantly looked up to find hers. They were rueful and apologetic, and she almost laughed.

A moment later she got up, and tugging Tom with her, made her way over to the stage. "We'll be roadies," she said.

Together she and Tom began to pack up the equipment and put away his guitar. Kate marveled at how compact Ethan had made everything, though even with this level of compactness it would have been impossible to manage it all on the back of the motorcycle.

Ethan came up to them, having finished with the gathered fans. "Thanks, you two. I appreciate it. For some reason in the last few weeks, I've had people wanting to talk to me."

Kate looked up and raised her brows, smiling. "You mean your groupies?"

He grimaced and shook his head. "Never groupies. Ugh. Just people who like the music." He pointed to the equipment. "Just leave it there. Pete will get someone to put it away. He stores it here for me. It's easier."

But of course he'd made an arrangement, thought Kate. He would ensure that he could make it all work.

"Great concert," Tom said. He gave Ethan a fist bump. "I think even Zig's girlfriend liked it in the end."

Ethan laughed. "Like that, is it?" He looked over at Zig and Tracy who were deep in conversation. "I suppose I should go and meet her." He glanced at Kate. "Come with me?" He gave a mock puppy dog face.

She laughed. "As if you need me there. I'm sure you'll have her eating out of your hand in no time."

He snorted and shook his head. "Not my intent. Not at all. It would just be nice to have you there. You've met her. You're a woman."

Kate laughed. "Yes. To both."

Ethan shrugged. "You know what I mean. It's Zig. He hasn't had a girlfriend in a while and, well, I want him to enjoy it."

There was so much unspoken there, so much that pulled at Kate.

"Of course," she said.

Tom grinned at Ethan. "I'll wait here and look after your guitar."

"You two want to come over to my place later?" asked Ethan. He looked at Kate. "I've been working on 'The House of

Clouds' and I'd like your input. If it's not too late. Or we could do it another time."

"Can't, man," said Tom. "Early start tomorrow. But you go ahead, Kate."

Ethan looked at her hopefully, and that hope filled her with a pleasure that momentarily unbalanced her. She shrugged, nonplussed. "Sure."

She followed him over to Zig and Tracy, who were still deep in conversation with each other at the table. When Zig caught sight of Ethan he smiled and stood, grabbing him in a half-hug. "Great set, tonight."

"Thanks," said Ethan. He gazed over at Tracy.

"Hi," said Tracy, sticking out her hand. "I'm Tracy. I loved your music."

Kate smiled inwardly, wondering how much Tracy believed it.

Ethan nodded. "Glad you both could make it." He looked over at Zig and grinned. "It was the only way I could get to see you, I decided."

Zig chuckled and shrugged. "Yeah, work's been crazy. And then well...we've been kind of busy." Kate felt Ethan's hand brush hers. Was he looking for reassurance?

"Sorry we didn't get to talk more," Kate said to Tracy, smiling. "Zig says you like music too. Do you go to many small gigs, or are you more of a concert-with-a-mosh-pit kind of girl?"

Tracy laughed, fiddling with one of the studs lining her ear. "Oh, I'm a mosh pit girl, no question about that. But this is good too. The small thing. I mean you can still really connect with the performers, but in a different way. It's like a different experience. But good."

Kate nodded reassuringly. Tracy was trying, there was no doubt, and Kate's annoyance over her earlier behavior began to slip away. Tracy continued to talk about different bands, Zig and Ethan chatting in the background, and Kate found her mind wandering. She could tell Tracy was interested and knowledgeable about bands, it just wasn't the kind of music Kate favored, or had even heard about. It reminded Kate once again how much she'd cut out that part of her life in the last several years. She was surprised how sad it made her feel.

Thirty-Two

The guitar felt good in Kate's hands, and she didn't know if that was more startling, or the fact that the music was flowing, and it felt so good playing with Ethan. They'd been at it an hour, or maybe more, she wasn't certain. They'd ridden back to the cabin on his motorcycle, Kate in back with his guitar strapped to her. That the whole experience had been completed without fuss and seemed so natural had thrown her off balance as she entered the cabin. But Ethan had just gone to the fridge, taken out two beers, and handed her one, not wasting a minute as he made his way over to the living room area. There, Ethan had given her the newer Martin, and he'd taken up the Yamaha with its warm, rich sound. There had been no questioning, no fanfare, he'd just taken them out of their cases and handed one over to her. He took a seat at the opposite end of the sofa to her, but she could feel the heat of his presence as she hunched over the guitar, tuning it and telling herself she was doing this to help with the song. It was nothing.

She'd felt subconscious and stiff at first, trying out a few chords while Ethan did the same, but then they just fell into playing together, blending, echoing, and inspiring each other, finding melodies, singing softly, if they knew the tune, or just following it. It had been so long since she'd done something like this. So long. And never, which startled and unnerved her, had it been like this. Effortless, flowing. Intuitive.

And then it was "House of Clouds." The song seemed to appear out of nowhere, working its way into their playing as Ethan led the way. She sang the first verse with him, a descant to his deep baritone voice. It gave her chills, the way it sounded, and as he moved on, singing a chorus, words he'd created since they'd talked, while she hummed and tried to follow his little modifications and flourishes. The words were moving, and she stopped playing after a while just to listen. He sang the chorus first.

> *Take me, take me, take me away,*
> *Take me away with you*
> *To the house in the clouds that we saw that day*
> *Where all our dreams come true.*

The song continued, verses spilling out, each one meaningful. When he'd finished, the room echoed with the guitar notes that resonated in the room and in her. He reached over the side of the sofa and retrieved some papers, holding them out to her.

"The lyrics," he said. "Sing with me. Like you did the first verse. And the chorus."

She took the sheets of paper from him, and after a glance through them, placed them on the coffee table in front of her. Ethan strummed the opening chord and launched into the song again. She was a little more self-conscious initially, worried about playing it correctly, as well as making out the correct words from his nearly indiscernible handwriting. Eventually, though, her nerves were lost in the absolute absorption of playing the guitar and singing with Ethan. It was a special connection, one that she was experienced enough to know was rare. And for a few moments, she allowed herself to sink into the feeling, to let her instincts, her emotions, run away with her. Only it felt like instead of going away, she was going toward. And it was that feeling that scared her the most.

She stopped almost immediately, her hands muffling the strings. There was no echo, only a dissonant sound of Ethan's surprise.

"Are you okay, Kate?" His tone was gentle, sympathetic.

She shook her head. "Sorry," she whispered. She swallowed down some of the tears that rose. Took a few deep breaths. "It's difficult for me." Her voice was still a whisper and she could hardly utter them.

Ethan put his guitar on the coffee table and took hers from her, setting it on the floor, to the side.

"Missy?" he said.

He took her hands, and she felt comforted, supported, but a moment later, she removed them and tucked them under her folded arms. Did she deserve comfort and support?

"What happened, Kate? Can you tell me that? I mean, I know she died. But how?"

Staring down at her feet, Kate took a few more breaths. "It was my fault," she said finally in a low voice.

"How?" His tone was gentle, probing.

She bit her lip. How could she explain to him? Slowly, she searched for the words. "We were best friends. Since kindergarten, really. We somehow just knew that we were so much alike." She looked up and gave him a weak smile. "You know?"

Ethan nodded. "You're lucky to have had that."

She gave a tight shrug. "We did everything together. We both discovered we liked music. The old hairbrush act. We were nine-year-old stars at that." She gave a soft laugh. "My mom used to egg us on. She thought we were hilarious. And Missy, she loved coming to my house because, she told me, it was music all the time there." She glanced up at Ethan again. "Her family wasn't into music like that. Didn't really understand why she was so caught up in it all. And then, after my mom died, Missy suggested we form a band, be a kind of power sisters band like my mom wanted. And so we did. We did well, too. Didn't really care about anything else in high school." Kate snorted. "Well, not much. I mean Missy had Mark, and was into him, but the music, our band, that's what came first."

Kate looked down again. It was the next part that drew her to her beer, lifted it to her mouth, and made her down the remaining half of it in one large gulp. She waited a moment for the alcohol to flood her body, but maybe it was her nerves, her adrenaline already using up so much of it, that she felt nothing. No easing. She pushed on, desperate to finish the story.

"Then, I went to college. I mean I was still living at home, but it was different. I had classes. And Missy, well she had the music and a job for a while. But we weren't with each other all the time. And I guess, without realizing it, we changed. And she started to resent the time I spent at college. Said I wasn't dedicated to the band enough. That I didn't want music. Why was I an English major, she'd ask me." Kate took another breath, sucked in her bottom lip, sneaking a glance at Ethan. "And I'd made the mistake of telling her about you."

Ethan raised his brows in surprise. "About me?"

Kate nodded. "I'd seen you play that first week. The showcase."

"'Suzanne.'"

She gave a small smile. "Yes, 'Suzanne.' As you know, that's a special song in my family. Well, for my parents. Anyway, I told her about you. How talented you were. And she just shrugged it off. Then I went to your gigs a few times." The modified truth made her redden. She'd been to every gig of his she could manage. But that was part of the point. She sighed. "Lots of gigs, to be honest. She began to see you as a threat. Started accusing me of wanting to pair up with you, to break up our band." Kate shuffled a bit. Made herself look up at him. "And the fact is that it wasn't far off the truth. I loved your music. Your playing." She didn't have to explain that it was more than his musical abilities that caught her attention, or the other ways she imagined they might be together. And for that part, she was glad.

Ethan's eyes were intense, so focused on Kate they nearly hypnotized her. "You wanted to play with me?" he said softly.

She looked away and nodded. "She could sense it. My denials were useless. We just knew each other really well. And nothing I said, or Mark would say, convinced her otherwise. She began to go a little crazy, I think. Looking back on it all. She started hanging around with other people. Drug users. Maybe it gave her what she needed, I don't know. But it got to a point where she started missing gigs, bailing out on any kind of meetings, or even going out with Mark. And if she did come, she'd be abusive. Sarcastic or just plain mean. Totally unlikeable. I started avoiding her and eventually, so did Mark."

There was only the end to explain, and then she would be finished. Her hands were clammy, and her heart quickened its pace. "One night, Missy was out with her new friends." She gave *friends* a sarcastic tone. "I'm not sure what they were on. Acid? I don't know. I never bothered to find out. But they went up to that rock over the lake. The one Tom took you to the other day. And she jumped off and drowned.

"Now, you could say it was an accident. And that's what everyone said at the time. But they would be wrong. I know Missy. I knew Missy." Kate's voice broke. "She could swim really well. She took those drugs and jumped from the rock, because that was the way she could manage to end her life. Because without the music, everything was dead for her, so why not be dead herself?"

The tears were streaming down her face, and she brushed them away with the heels of her hand, but they continued to fall. She found herself in Ethan's arms, his hand rubbing her back while he uttered soothing sounds. The two of them stayed that way for a time, her head tucked into his chest, safe, secure. Kate found herself wishing it wouldn't end.

"Shit, Kate. That's terrible. And an awful burden for you to carry," Ethan said in a low voice. She could hear the deep tones vibrate in his chest. He started to stroke her hair. "Especially since it's not yours to carry."

She started to pull away, but he held her firmly in place. "It's impossible to know what goes through a person's mind, especially if they are confused and under stress, let alone taking drugs. You didn't put the drugs in her hand. You didn't lead her to the rock and push her off. Or hold her underwater. Kate, you were both entitled to grow and evolve as you got older. It would have probably happened one way or the other, anyway. Missy might have found something else that replaced the music. Or not. But in any case. It wasn't right for her to hold you to ransom over your growth and change."

The words ran through her mind, sinking in slowly, finding a few places to settle where she could turn them over and examine them later. For now, the idea of them and his comfort were what eased, just a little bit, the deeply rooted knot inside her.

She sat wrapped in his embrace, feeling his warmth, his touch, as he stroked her hair. Something shifted and the fingers in her hair became small, gentle kisses that moved to the side of her face, and then her mouth. The kiss deepened, and the feel of him, his mouth, his hands, the press of his body against hers, lit her up. Lifted her. She was floating under his touch, his beautiful graceful hands that moved across her body, stroking, brushing. He was there, entwined, entangled in her thoughts and then her body as she melted away, up into their house of clouds. This was a dream she could store there, she had no doubt about that.

———

Early morning light filled the room, casting a glow on Ethan's face as Kate slowly opened her eyes. His beautiful face, now in repose, was sculpted by the shadows and the bones that framed his face. His strong nose, the mouth, the forehead, his hair just long enough now that it fell across his brow. The urge to capture him, either on paper or in a photograph, was strong. But the lingering lethargy kept her in the bed facing him, transfixed.

He reached out for her, eyes still closed, drawing her closer and whispered low in her ear in a raspy voice. "What's got your attention so much?"

"You," Kate said softly.

He chuckled and began to nibble her ear. The nibbles turned into long, sensuous kisses that moved down her jaw and eventually trailed along the length of her, while his hands stroked her body. Soon they were moving as one, tangled and entwined like before. It was their own rhythm, a song, and it was a song that seemed so much a part of them and it was as if there was no other song but them.

And after, as Kate lay there in Ethan's arms, still transfixed by the echoes of that song, she allowed herself for a moment to play another song in her head. The song of "what ifs." Almost as soon as it appeared, she shut it down and shifted her weight off of Ethan, propping her head on her hand.

"You play more than instruments well," she said grinning. "And in just as experienced a manner."

Ethan frowned a moment, stroking her hair absentmindedly. "I'm not," he said. "Well, not that experienced."

She laughed. "Dude, you're in the music industry."

He arched an eyebrow. "Dude? Where, oh, where has the *bella Italiana* gone?"

She looked away, suddenly self-conscious. "Gone. If she ever was," she said in a low voice.

He continued to stroke her hair, studying her. "You don't think you'll go back?"

She shook her head, then did a one shoulder shrug. "Yes, no. Maybe." She glanced at him and forced a smile. "Not for a while, in any case. After this exhibition. I owe Giancarlo for all his help. So I should probably go back for a while. Maybe do one more exhibition for his gallery. Then, we'll see."

"But you and Giancarlo?" Ethan asked in a quiet voice.

She put her head in the pillow and groaned. A moment later she lifted her head. "I don't think so. Is that enough? I mean..." She gestured to the two of them. "Don't you think?"

He laughed and reached for her. "And that, my dear madam, deserves a major tickle for being a smart ass."

It took less than a minute for him to have her shrieking surrender, but in that time, she caught sight of a tattoo on the right side of his abdomen.

"Wait, wait," she said, catching her breath. She held up her hand and pointed, grinning. "You have a tattoo. You. Ethan Peterson. Have a tattoo."

He glanced down at it and shrugged, his eyes darkening. "Yes. You, Katherine Wilson, are very observant. I have a tattoo."

She leaned down to examine it, though it was easily visible, taking up at least a quarter of the right side of his abdomen. An eagle, wings spread, beak open, was splayed across his skin. The detail was exquisite and done by an obvious master ink artist.

"Wow, Ethan, that's amazing," Kate said, shaking her head. It was a tattoo to admire, but for some reason it seemed out of place on Ethan. Part of him, yet not part of him. Maybe because it wasn't the Ethan she pictured. She cocked a head at him, trying to understand. "An eagle, though."

He nodded slowly. "Yes, an eagle."

She studied it longer. There was something to it, she knew. And she could tell he wasn't going to enlighten her now, at least not yet. An eagle. On the right side of his abdomen. Something tugged at the back of her mind.

THIRTY-THREE

The snowflakes drifted around them, aimless and looking for adventure, Kate thought. The wind had a bite to it as she trudged through the hard packed earth, Tom leading the way, Max making his way carefully at her side, and Ethan following close behind her. The woods felt refreshing at first, but now, an hour later, she wondered if it had been a good idea to come here with a Thanksgiving picnic in order to do something different on this day that was meant for families. Kate had been surprised when Ethan had said he wasn't going anywhere. She'd decided not to probe, knowing enough that his relationship with his family was a painful topic. This picnic seemed at least an indication of their severity.

Given all those thoughts, she'd readily agreed to a picnic in the car after a loop walk in the woods. Now, as the snow began to fall, she wasn't so sure it was a good idea. But at least Tom seemed in good spirits. She'd noticed he'd been a bit morose lately. She'd made a point of calling him every day and even dropped by the store a few days ago. He'd been deep in discussion with Fred, but broke it off when he caught sight of Kate, even managing a grin. They'd gone to lunch, and he'd teased her a bit over Ethan. She'd brushed it off with her usual "haha, Tom," and told him there was nothing serious going on. Because that's how it should be. The only possible way it could be. In the week since they were together, she'd only seen him once, when he stopped by. She'd been working madly in the attic on her art, and she'd been distracted, but glad to see him. He hadn't stayed long, just enough time to share a mug of coffee and to kiss her quietly for a brief moment. It was only after he'd gone that she felt his absence and all her concentration and focus had vanished for the day.

On the walk now, he'd held her hand for the short while the trail had made it possible, Max dropping obligingly behind, but once it had narrowed, Ethan had moved behind her, and she could only fathom the thoughts going through his head as they walked. The trail they were taking wasn't the most conducive to conversation, something that left her uneasy and, along with the increasing chill, gave her more impetus to finish the walk quickly. She had too many thoughts crowding her mind and very few were welcome.

Maybe Ethan had sensed her growing unease, because a moment later she felt a hand rest on her shoulder, halting her a moment. He turned her to face him and lowered his mouth to hers, kissing her deeply. She let it happen, let herself fall into the moment, because she couldn't help herself, because it felt so intense and wonderful. And because it was their song, and she would do anything to hear it.

"There," he said when they broke apart, the faces flushed, her lips tingling. "I couldn't go any farther without stealing at least one kiss from you."

She shook her head slowly. "No theft involved. Not at all."

Max, now ahead, turned and gave a little bark at them, as if to tell them to hurry up. They laughed. Ethan leaned his forehead against hers. "God, I just wish we could go back to the cabin and slip under the covers."

She smiled. "Ah now, I'm not a foursome person. Especially not with my brother and my dog."

He chuckled. "Not at all. You and me. That's it. That's all it will ever be."

The words echoed inside her, both thrilling and scaring her. "Tomorrow is tomorrow," she said. "Now is where we are."

He whispered into her hair, and she strained to catch the words, but a moment later he kissed her forehead and let her go.

"Come on, we don't want Tom to think we couldn't do the Thanksgiving walking challenge."

He gave her a little push down the trail and she allowed her legs to move forward, puzzling his words. After a few moments, she gave up.

———

The meal was a combination of anything that their respective fridges could cough up and was mildly picnic-like. The three of them sat in the back of Tom's empty van, a plaid blanket on the metal floor, perched on cushions gathered hastily from the sofa and armchairs from home. Max had found his place near Kate. They kept their jackets on, and for a time Kate had tried to keep on her gloves, but gave it up as impossible a few moments later.

Arrayed in the center was cold ham, sliced provolone, a wedge of Brie, some loose cherry tomatoes, bagels and cream cheese, potato chips and Fritos with a tub of guacamole. Kate had even brought some leftover meatballs she'd had, thinking that they might be able to eat them with their fingers, but when Ethan tried to take one from his plastic plate to his mouth it shot out of Ethan's hold across the van, and they all dissolved into laughter.

"Yes, well," said Kate, when her laughter had subsided. "It seemed like a good idea at the time."

Tom pointed his finger at Kate, while he munched on a bagel filled with a pile of ham, cheese, and a squashed cherry tomato. "I've always said there is definitely nothing boring about your cooking, Kate."

"Sorry, Kate," said Ethan, wiping his hands with a paper napkin. "I really did want to eat that, honest."

"Oh, shut up, both of you," said Kate, grinning. She reached for her mug of coffee, newly poured from the large thermos they brought, and took a sip.

"Here," said Ethan, reaching into his backpack that had contained his share of the food. He withdrew a bottle of whiskey. "Try a bit of this in there to warm you up."

She laughed and then raised her brow as she saw the bottle. She didn't know that much about whiskey, but she recognized the top-shelf Glenfiddich label.

"I feel honored," she said, holding her cup out to him. "Such champagne taste you have."

Ethan laughed, a slight edge to it. "You can thank my dad for that one. His drink of choice."

"Pour some of that champagne in this direction," said Tom, holding out his own mug.

The words and the tone lingered in Kate's mind while she watched Ethan pour a shot into Tom's coffee. He rounded it off by doing the same for his own. They lifted their mugs to toast.

"To great taste," said Tom, clinking his cup against the other two.

"Great taste and great company," said Ethan, smiling at Kate.

"Hear, hear," said Kate. She took a sip, felt the bite of the whiskey and the peaty taste among the broader bitterness of the coffee. She looked over at Ethan. "Your father introduced you to whiskey?"

Ethan gave a harsh laugh. "No. He introduced my brother to it. My brother was the one who obliged me. He was fifteen, I was eleven. Corrupting his baby brother and all that."

"You have an older brother?" she asked. Had she known that? She didn't think so.

"Had."

The words took her by surprise, a surprise that was instantly replaced by a huge wave of compassion. "Oh, God, I'm sorry."

"That's shit, man," said Tom.

The words between them were few enough, but it conveyed everything they shared and understood, a threesome who had some ideas of the ins and outs of grief.

"Was it an illness?" asked Kate, her voice low.

Ethan studied his cup, his jaw tight. "No. A boating accident."

Kate felt the tightness in her chest. The vise-like grip that brought up all the emotion and pain of the last few weeks, stealing her breath, her voice. She reached out and gripped his hand. Tom had looked away, trying to get his own emotions under control, and for a moment all they could hear was Max's soft snoring as he lay sprawled out next to Kate.

"The irony of it was that Cam didn't even like whiskey. I was the one who liked it." He shook his head, the memory coloring his blue eyes a deeper shade.

"Cam?" asked Kate. "Was that his name?"

Ethan grimaced. "Cambridge Hollis Peterson III, for fuck's sake. That was his full name. But we called him Cam. Except Dad, of course. As if Cam could forget his lineage. Or that he was destined for great things."

"You were close?" asked Tom. He glanced at Kate, and she saw his face was flushed with barely controlled emotion. This was hard for him, she knew, but she could see he understood Ethan's need to say it.

Ethan leaned his head back against the side of the van. He sighed. "He was my older brother. My hero. I looked up to him."

Kate nudged him. "Instructing you in all things bad?"

He gave a choked laugh. "Yeah, something like that."

"Did he play an instrument?" asked Tom.

"Hell, no, he was tone deaf," said Ethan with a snort. "Teddi and I used to joke about it. She played flute."

"Teddi?" asked Tom.

"Dorothea. My sister. She's five years younger than me." He grimaced. "My parents wanted to spread us out. So that they had time for each of us." The last phrase, Ethan held his fingers in quote marks.

"Did she play classical music?" said Kate.

Ethan shrugged and then grinned. "A bit of everything. She was good. She liked to take some pieces and do her own take with a twist and in a completely different style. It was sort of an underhanded gibe to my father. He would ask her what composer that was and she would say something like, 'Oh, Daddy, that's one of the new ones. You wouldn't know him or like him.' My father thought he knew classical music just because he had a few LPs and had season tickets to the Boston Symphony, but he knew fuck all."

Tom looked at Kate and snorted. "We used to do that all the time, but in our house, we could never get away with it. My parents would either end up calling us out or joining in with their own twist."

Kate smiled, but it had a bittersweet quality to it because she realized that Tom had experienced a few more years than she had of that kind of closeness with her parents before her mother died. There were only a few faded memories in her possession of the scenes Tom had just described.

"Yeah," said Ethan. "But your parents were awesome."

Tom laughed and Kate found herself smiling. "Yes, they were."

The thought made her feel good, a sentiment that drove her to look across at Tom and communicate it to him. And when she did, she was filled with a quiet joy to see that he understood and shared it too. And as if sensing that it was a moment for her and her brother, but one that stretched out beyond them, to Ethan, she found his eyes and then his hand. A hand that a moment later, Max found and started licking.

Thirty-Four

Tom filled up the kitchen not only with the smell of eggs and bacon, but also with his presence. It was large and comforting, like the breakfast he cooked while she made toast and coffee and got plates ready. Kate wanted to hug him to her, a personal teddy bear and perfect on this late November morning. Black Friday. But for her, the blackness had receded a little, and it was a feeling she wanted to share with her brother.

He'd opted to spend the night after driving her home in his van following their ridiculous but surprisingly enjoyable walk and picnic in the van. She'd been glad for his presence then as she was now. The house had seemed especially silent and lonely, even with Max, the last few days. It was if the numbness of grief had receded enough to let these other emotions creep in. Except for the night she'd spent with Ethan, she'd found herself waking up at odd times of the night, unable to get back to sleep. Often, she'd find herself downstairs making herself a cup of chamomile tea, not so much because she believed it to be effective, but because it was soothing and gave her a focus. Max would take up his position next to her on the bed. He'd gravitated there from the floor by stealth, and she'd hadn't the heart to stop him, because it was so comforting. His soft breathing that descended into soft snores reassured her in the yawning darkness.

Now Max was out in the backyard having his morning "sniff and snuffle," as her dad used to call it. That and any other business that needed taking care of. That phrasing had also been her father's and had caused both her and Tom a good giggle when he'd said it.

She bumped Tom's side. "Hey, how's it going there, chef? You almost finished?"

Tom blinked and looked across at her. "Oh, right. Yes. Kind of."

Kate arched a brow. "Kind of?"

"No, no. I mean it's ready." He lifted the large frying pan off the burner and put it to the side. He glanced at her and frowned at her expression. "What?"

She shook her head. "Nothing."

She helped him plate up and tore a piece each of paper towel for napkins before they both took a seat at the kitchen table. A companionable silence fell over them as they ate.

"Yum, Tom," said Kate. "You've certainly improved your cooking skills."

He looked up and gave her a wry look. "Yeah, well, needs must and all that. Living on your own, with my kind of appetite and no real extra cash to eat every meal out gave me a certain encouragement to learn."

"No mooching off of Dad every time?"

Tom made a scoffing sound. "Dad? Please. You know the extent of his abilities."

She laughed. "Yes, I guess I do. On the rare occasion I didn't cook I soon wished I had."

"So, there you go. Quick lessons in things I liked to eat. A few cookbooks and a few carefully chosen girlfriends, and I was good to go." He grinned at her. "You'd be surprised how much playing the helpless guy really reels them in."

Kate shoved him. "You're terrible. And what's worse, I believe you."

He widens his eyes. "It was a fair trade. I wasn't the only one who benefited."

Kate gave a full belly laugh. "Oh my God. You really think you're God's gift to women?"

"Clearly. I'm not evolved. I don't know why you expected anything different."

There was something in the tone of his words that stirred something inside Kate. "Didn't Tamzin consider you evolved enough?"

Tom gave her a sharp look. "What makes you say that?"

She shrugged. "I don't know. She hasn't been around at all. You haven't even mentioned her. And, well, she had a certain style to her, a personality that seemed to..." She searched carefully for the right words. "She seemed to assume that everyone would want what she strived for."

"And what is that?" Tom's tone was studied, as he searched her face for something that Kate could only wonder at.

"Something large? Radical? Not mainstream? I don't know. It was just a feeling I had from her."

Tom nodded for a while and then started to chuckle. "You know Kate, for someone so screwed up, you do have some really deep insights."

She punched his arm, her old reactions to his sharp teasing coming to her naturally. "What? I'm not screwed up."

Tom stared at her. "Really?" His tone was sarcastic, with just the very hint of humor behind it.

"Stop it. Just stop. I'm being nice and all you do is try and yank my chain."

Tom grinned at her. "It's so good to hear you speak like Kate. The Kate I know."

She gave him a puzzled look. "What's that supposed to mean?"

He shrugged. "Nothing. Just, well, maybe I mean that we're finally used to each other again."

A slow smile broke out on her face. She nodded slowly. "Yeah. We are." She squeezed his arm. "And so, big brother, why isn't Tamzin buzzing around you anymore?"

Tom raised his brows. "Buzzing?" He shook his head and shrugged. "It came down to the fact that we wanted different things. She wanted me to be more edgy with my furniture pieces. Do unique art pieces that weren't straight commissions for boring things like 'living room furniture.' I asked her why it mattered to her. If I was happy with what I was doing, that should be enough."

"And it wasn't enough."

He pursed his mouth. "No. She and her friends had this idea of art and the life of an artist. I didn't fit in, as much as she tried to make me do just that. My vision is New England essence. Simple, gracious lines, but grounded in the landscape. Flowing like the waters, curving like the mountains, majestic like the trees."

Kate rubbed his arm. "That's an amazing vision. And it's you. I know that."

He gave her a full on smile. "Thanks. I'm pretty happy now with the way things are going. I've thought a lot about what Ethan suggested. About putting more emphasis on creating art pieces, commissions, and bespoke furniture. Expand it as maybe an online outlet for other artists. Possibly a cooperative. I've been doing a lot of research. Viability and all that. Putting together a rough business plan. I think it's doable, Kate. And I'd like to try. That is, if you don't mind. It would mean funneling some of the profits into it, rather than buying more stock and selling sure things, like we've been doing. And that means, well, there will be less coming in."

He stopped, waiting for her reaction, and Kate could only blink at him, her instinctive response only joy. She'd seen and heard the excitement in his voice. Understood the passion he was experiencing. She leaned forward and squeezed his hand, her eyes alight. "Oh, Tom, that's fantastic. Of course you should do that, if that's what you want. I have no problem with it."

Tom's face brightened further for a moment. He frowned. "But what will you do?"

Tom had implied this question just moments before, but now he'd put it baldly, and it floored her. It was a slightly different phrasing than the one she'd been asked earlier by Ethan. But however it was phrased, it was a question that had been humming underneath all her days, all her actions and even her sleep. What would she do?

She thought of how poetically, how musically Tom described his vision of his art. His music vibrated in him in so many different ways. And he let music and art bleed over into each other, blending, mixing and creating something wonderful at the end. He just couldn't help it. It was there. No barriers. No walls keeping it all separate.

Some of Ethan's words rose up to challenge her thoughts. Missy holding her to ransom against growth and change. Maybe it had been her own demons, though, that had held her to ransom all these years. Making her keep things separate. Separate countries, separate careers, separate lives. The old life discarded. A life she couldn't have. Wouldn't let herself have. But now, just as Tom's loves and passions all spilled into one another, her own were bleeding out of their so carefully contained areas and mixing in with others. Music, art, and literature. She hadn't been able to contain it. And now she wondered why, through all these years, she had tried to do just that.

———

Her hair was tucked up in a clip, with wild tendrils falling around her forehead and around her ears. It was halfhearted, Kate knew, but she'd been so distracted this morning with some ideas in her head for her artwork that she'd dressed hurriedly in some old yellow yoga pants she'd used years ago as sleepwear, and a heavy forest-green sweater with an old yellow mohair scarf of her mother's bundled around her neck. Topped off with her lime-green fuzzy slippers from high school, she could only laugh at herself when she climbed the stairs to the attic to start on her art projects.

But now that it was her usual brief break time, she knew she'd put off this phone call long enough. She sat back in her chair up in the attic studio, cradling her cup of coffee made from the little coffee maker she'd brought up here. The laptop sat in front of her, waiting. Giancarlo would be just locking up the gallery and about to head home. It was the best time to catch him, before the rounds of various social obligations took hold of him. She took out her phone, located his image and pressed the video icon. She would do this facing him. So he could see her. Understand.

The screen opened up and Giancarlo appeared. She could see he was in the gallery office still, dressed in a charcoal gray suit, deep purple tie and pale violet shirt that contrasted well with his olive skin. His dark hair was tousled a little, as if he'd just run his hand through it.

"Katerina," he said, his eyes alight, a smile on his face. "I'm so glad to hear from you."

She felt a stab of guilt. She'd only texted him a few times since he left. Basic sentences that conveyed basic information stating that she was doing well enough, progressing with the exhibition pieces and hoped to complete the allotted amount. Information that she'd shared from a sense of obligation. A sense of obligation sharpened by guilt. Giancarlo was so good and kind to her. He'd done so much for her, encouraging her in her pursuit, and even though she knew it had been more his vision in the end, rather than her own, it didn't negate how much he cared for her.

"Your clothes, your hair, Katerina," Giancarlo said, his eyebrows raised, a worried look on his face. "Are you well? Would you like me to come? I can arrange for a short stay, if it would help."

She gave him a wan smile. "No, no, really, Giancarlo. I'm fine." She gestured to herself. "Just working. I don't really think about what I'm wearing, or how I look when I work. You know that."

Giancarlo gave her a pained look. "*Tesoro*, look, can we talk? I am feeling awful about how we left things between us."

Kate felt the tears threaten. She took a deep breath. "I'm sorry. I hate to cause you pain. But it wouldn't have been right for me to make decisions when I was unable to even understand what I wanted in the next breath, let alone for the rest of my life."

Giancarlo looked away a moment, biting his lip. When he focused on her again, his eyes were alight with hope, fear, anger and several other emotions that flickered briefly, before he extinguished them all and nothing was left but a neutral blankness.

"And now?" he asked in a careful tone.

Kate forced the words out. "And now, it seems my life is here. In America. I think. At least that's what I can see for my immediate future. My art, I feel that here. And I may move to

New York eventually, but I'm not sure." She stared at Giancarlo, could see the puzzlement in his expression, but she willed him to understand. "I'm so sorry, Giancarlo. I owe you so much. I love you for all that you've done, all that you made happen. But now, I can't see my way to marrying you."

The pain was back, she could see his chest rise and fall as he fought to get his emotions under control once again.

"Katerina," he said, his voice a raspy whisper. "Please. You don't have to make this final. Take the time you need. Take all the time. Just do not say it's over. We've built so much. We have so much. My love, it's there, real. For you. But you've had such a difficult time, my darling, so, so much to take in, to understand and decide. I understand. There was pain in your past, and now that pain is strong inside you. You think I don't notice the dark circles under your eyes? Do you think I don't know that you don't get the sleep you need? Please, don't make decisions now. Just work on your art pieces."

Kate began to shake her head. "Giancarlo, no. It's not only that. It's so much more. It's my life. Yes, the old is coming back. The music, all of it. It's becoming part of me again, I think. I don't know. But other parts are coming with it..." She wasn't certain how she could phrase it without hurting him. Had she moved on? It seemed so with Ethan the other night. She'd had no thought for Giancarlo. And it wasn't fair to him. She had to allow him to move on, regardless.

"Don't wait for me, Giancarlo. Don't. I have no idea what shape my life will take or who it will be with." There, she'd said it. "It's time to let us go."

His expression hardened. "Katerina, it is not just about what you want. You have obligations. I have obligations. There is a contract."

Her mind froze, her mouth dropping slightly as she struggled with the meaning of his words. "Contract?"

"Yes, you remember? You signed a contract when we first began this process. You are bound to me for your next two exhibitions. I invested a lot of money in you, Katerina. It is only fair. Your artwork is taking off, and I intend to become a part of it. After all, I discovered you." He paused a moment. "It is bad enough that I am only having a small percentage of the New York exhibition, so given Dante's *Inferno* as the subject matter for the third exhibition, it would be best if you created it here, in Italy."

His words did nothing to help her answer him. She remembered the contract, signed in a euphoria of joy that anyone would want her to have one exhibition, let alone three. And now that number three hung over her like an albatross. She could only stare at him for a few moments until she finally managed to end the call.

THIRTY-FIVE

Kate heard his footsteps on the stairs and the fugue that had seized her since Giancarlo's phone call was finally dispelled in the face of anxiety over whether she should mention this to Ethan. Was it really something she needed to share? She had no idea what their relationship was, not really.

The door opened with a slight squeak, and Max looked up from his spot on the old blanket she'd laid for him in the corner. The squeak was a recent development, one that might have been caused by the house contracting, tightening as the cold seeped farther and farther into the house. The little space heater hardly made a difference to the room anymore, and she knew she'd have to come up with some alternative arrangement soon. Really, the house needed more insulation in the space above. She'd have to talk to Tom about that.

These thoughts proved a welcome distraction from the huge issue that loomed in front of her, and so it was with surprise that she felt Ethan's hands rest on her shoulders and his kiss on her head. She jumped.

"Sorry, didn't mean to startle you," Ethan said, sliding his arms around her waist. "Still working, I see."

She could feel him studying the art piece on the table, and she realized at that moment that she welcomed it. His presence, his care of her work and passion for her art was meaningful and special, no matter that now it seemed to be tied up in Giancarlo-shaped knots. And with all that, too, in no way did she feel threatened, nervous, or the slightest bit undermined by the attention, or any of the comments that he'd made about it.

He kissed her neck, inhaling her scent. "You are such a talented woman. I am constantly amazed at what you see. How you see it."

She turned to look at him, her eyes filled with warmth and appreciation. "Really?"

He nodded. "Mmmhm. Definitely."

"Coming from someone who is doubly talented himself, I can't tell you how much that means to me."

He hugged her from behind, and she could feel his head shaking back and forth against her. "No, no. Not at all. Can't compare. You have a visual art that expands and blends in a manner I've never considered or thought about."

He pulled her up out of her chair. "But now, it's time to stop the tapping into the soul and feed the body. I brought us some take out. I thought we could share it together down in the kitchen."

She raised her brows. "Take out? What did you get?"

"Thai. Is that okay? I can order something else if you don't like it."

"No, no, it's fine. I love Thai."

He drew her closer, and she put her arms around his neck, making an effort to feel natural. To dispel the ghost of Giancarlo that hovered over her yet again. She kept her tone light. "I might have to find a way to thank you for your thoughtfulness. Any ideas?"

He leaned down and kissed her, deepening it for just a short while, brushing his tongue lightly along her lips. She could taste him, his essence, and she wanted to know it, to have it become so familiar that she could summon it at will.

He drew back and swept a tendril of hair away from her face.

"I do have a suggestion," she said. "I might have to remove all the other ones from the box, to ensure it wins."

He smiled at her. "No arguments here." His eyes roamed her face, his fingers still resting against her cheek. She savored his touch, his gaze, feeling the glow it gave her and the heat that was beginning to spread inside her, the thought of Giancarlo fading away for now. His touch, his kiss, that was all it had been, the Thai food and her empty stomach seemed unimportant now.

He smoothed her hair, which had become even more wild, almost half of it now escaped from the clip she'd put in this morning. She could almost laugh when she thought about what he must be seeing. But she didn't care. Not at this moment.

"You look so beautiful," he said, startling her.

She laughed. "Hardly."

He shook his head. "Definitely. You look natural, so much a reflection of your art, your"—he gestured around them—"surroundings. This image, for example. It's like you're a part of it. And it's a part of you."

She looked down at the mass of trees with their splashes of fall color. The reds, the golds, the amber browns, the green of the pine. Noticed again the gold of her yoga pants and the forest green of her sweater, which she had donned again today. She had to admit they were colors she loved, and the fall in the woods was something she'd missed sorely in Italy.

He leaned and kissed her briefly again. "You're a Rossetti girl," he said. "My very own Rossetti girl."

She laughed and shook her head. "I think there was only

one."

He smiled at her. "And now there's another one."

———

Kate fed the dog and put him outside. The two of them would walk him later. Though lately it was more an amble than anything else, but she didn't mind that, especially if Ethan was with her. Ethan had unloaded the cartons from the bag and had pulled out utensils from the drawer. She'd told him she would rather not struggle with chopsticks tonight, she was too hungry, and he had only laughed and said she'd be fine, until she poked his ribs with the chopsticks and promptly broke them in half with her hands.

A moment later, she pulled out the plates before he could protest. She knew when he was on his own he just ate out of pots, or the take out containers. He didn't even have to tell her; she had noticed his sink and things he had and hadn't said. She could only imagine what his life was like in New York. At least when he was with her, she would insist that he sit down and breathe. It was the ordinariness of the moment, and though it might have seemed mundane, Kate found that she could treasure it. She could set everything aside. A quiet moment, spent with someone she cared about. No frills, no fuss. No expensive dress to be anxious over, no cuisine to worry about eating properly or understanding its importance. She loved that Ethan had on an old, washed-out sweatshirt that said Somerton Lake College and old jeans and black boots, and that his hair hung unevenly into his forehead. And she also loved that they were sharing a dinner that had come out of boxes and cost a fraction of what a meal at any of Giancarlo's restaurants in Rome would have cost.

"Do you go out in New York much?" she asked. "To clubs

and things?"

Ethan looked up from his meal, considered a moment. "No, not really. I try and avoid that kind of thing if I can."

"Do the band members ever take you with them?"

He looked away from her, frowned. "They try. Sometimes."

His obvious discomfort puzzled her. Was it his family's disapproval that caused him to avoid any publicity? "Do you see anyone of your family anymore?"

He looked back at her, allowing her briefly to see the pain in his face, before he looked down. "Only Teddi. But that's rare. She's caught up in her life up in Boston."

"What does she do?"

"She's just finishing up law school," he said, a wry smile on his face. "My father, I'm sure, has her earmarked for his company, but she has her own ideas."

Kate smiled at that. "Does he know yet?"

He shrugged. "She says she's saving it up for a big reveal when she has it all lined up."

"Do you know what that is?"

"I have my suspicions. And I also suspect he won't be that enamored of her chosen area."

"Which is?"

"Immigration law." He shook his head, his smile growing rueful. "She's been doing a bit of advocacy for asylum seekers at a volunteer center. I wish her luck with it."

"Wow," said Kate. "That's quite a direction to take."

"Well, she has another few months to work it all out."

The question that had been lurking in the back of her mind ever since Thanksgiving last week surfaced. "Will you see her at Christmas?"

He jabbed his fork around his plate. A large sigh escaped. "No. She'll go home to my parents. I might see her New Year's Eve, though. She's thinking of coming to New York for that."

"Oh, that would be good," Kate said, mulling over the implication of his words. "Will you be in New York for Christmas?"

He looked over at her a moment, studying her face. "What are your plans for Christmas?"

"Mine?" she asked. All and any ideas she might have had fled her mind as she stared into his deep blue eyes, now filled with curiosity, concern, and something else that she might speculate would be hope. "Ah, I'm not sure. I haven't talked with Tom. I mean, with Tamzin out of the picture, I assume we would be spending it here."

She thought how it might feel. Being there, for Christmas. A Christmas without her dad. It would be her first Christmas in Somerton Lake in a while. She'd made it home one Christmas three years ago but had left after a few days. A rushed, hurried affair that she'd been too jet lagged to remember, really. But that had seemed best at the time. Now, though, it seemed stupid and selfish, and it was time she would never get back. She pushed the thought away. She could start making up for that stupidity with Tom, at least. She glanced over at Ethan. And maybe including one more would help toward making it a new kind of memory.

"Would you consider coming here for Christmas?" she asked.

Suddenly, it seemed important that he accept. An acceptance meant he wanted to be with her. That spending time with her, at Christmas, and especially this Christmas, would be something he would want to do.

A slow smile spread on his face. "I will if you promise I don't have to cook anything."

She laughed. "I would never do that. But I will make you assist."

"Hmm. I think I might be able to handle that."

Thirty-Six

Fine curls of sawdust clung to Tom's quilted down vest and dark beanie like snowflakes as he leaned over the clamped section of wood and honed it carefully with the planer, his breath misting the cold air. So focused was he on his work that he hadn't heard Kate come into the workshop, though the metal door had clanged lightly against the door frame that separated the workshop from the storeroom of the furniture shop. She watched him for a while, his strong fingers gripping the tool, his bent profile catching the backwash of the light from the angled window. She had an itch to photograph him like this. Her brother, artist and craftsman at work.

She'd come here at his request to take photographs of some of his pieces to use for the website, but she realized that she needed pictures of him at work. To show rather than tell that here was a man who took time and care over his creations. She removed her camera bag from her shoulder and set it on the counter. Her pea coat, she decided, would remain firmly buttoned. Whether she still wasn't used to the cold, or it was the way the workshop trapped the cold in its own special way, penetrating her to the core, she was glad she had on thick socks and her mother's Fry boots as well as the beanie she'd stuffed on her head, her hair spilling out from under it.

"Kate," said Tom, looking up. "I didn't hear you come in."

He began to set down his tools, but Kate held up a hand. "Wait, don't stop. I want to get a shot of you at work."

He grimaced but did as he was told. Over the course of the next half-hour she put him through his paces, until he grew fed up and brought a halt to it.

"You don't need any more of me, surely," he said. "That's enough."

"Oh, you'd be surprised how appealing pictures of you at work can be," she said, grinning. "To the potential buyers."

He gave her a suspicious look.

"Really, Tom. With your tight buns on display, you'll have all the women in the state, young and old, asking you to make things for them."

"I don't what I like less, you saying the word 'buns' in reference to my rear, or women looking at them online."

She laughed. "Oh, I'm sure you'll get used to it. Especially when the orders come flooding in."

He snorted. "I don't know about that. But if it's enough to get by, that will satisfy me."

She squeezed his arm. "That won't be a problem, I'm sure."

"What won't be a problem?"

The metal door opened and Ethan entered, followed by Zig and Tracy. Ethan made his way over to Kate, his leather jacket unzipped and showing a thick royal blue wool sweater underneath that only seemed to emphasize his broad frame. A beanie was pulled down low on his head, and though he was wearing his glasses, it didn't hide the fact that his eyes matched his sweater. He slid an arm along her waist and leaned down to kiss her briefly on the lips. Pleasure washed over her at his touch and attention.

"Pictures of Tom's buns on his website," Kate said, mischief in her eyes.

"What?" said Ethan, assuming a mock-scandalized tone.

"Don't listen to her," said Tom. "She's just trying to cause trouble. She's here to take pictures of a few commissions I finished recently." He pointed to the far corner where a beautifully crafted maple coffee table with a curving top and strips of walnut inlay stood alongside a burled walnut armoire.

"Wow," said Tracy walking toward them, her heeled boots clicking across the workshop floor. She wore tights and a short corduroy skirt topped by a fitted parka with a fur hood. Her blonde hair was tipped with blue now, a new style that worked well for her. "You made these? These are seriously cool."

Zig followed close behind, his tall, wiry frame looking taller in his skinny jeans and sneakers. "They are really impressive. I mean it." He ran his hand along the coffee table.

"Thanks," said Tom.

"Ethan, man," said Zig. "You should get him to make you some stuff. It would look great in your New York apartment."

Ethan nodded. "I'm ahead of you there. I've actually been thinking about it already."

"Really?" said Kate looking up at him, her eyes shining. She was so pleased for Tom.

"I'm not cheap," said Tom, deadpan. "I don't know if you can afford me."

Ethan laughed. "I'll send in a negotiator."

"Give him the family discount, Tom," said Kate.

"Can I be part of that family?" asked Zig. "I wouldn't mind having a special cabinet for all my LPs."

"Zig, you'd have to take out a mortgage for all the cabinets you'd need to house your LPs decently."

"You should see how many crates he has stacked up his place, Tom," said Tracy, moving toward him. "All filled with LPs."

Tom looked at her and then at Zig. "Yeah? Maybe I can do a special deal for you. You give me half of your LPs of my choosing, and I'll give you a great price for the cabinets. That way you'll need fewer of them, and it will cost you less. Win-win."

"Win nothing," said Zig, laughing. "Nice try, though. But you're welcome to come and look at them anytime. Emphasis on look. And maybe play. If I okay it. But they don't leave the apartment."

Tracy smiled at Tom, her eyes wide, assessing. "It is a good collection. I promise. You should come over and see it. I should know. I do some deejaying on weekends."

Zig came up behind her and put a hand on Tracy's shoulder. "She's good too. You should hear her play sometime." He looked over at Ethan and Kate. "All of you. Maybe we could make an evening of it."

Ethan squeezed Kate's waist, as if sensing the dread that rose up in her. "Sure. Maybe sometime. Christmas is coming, though, not sure if I can manage before then."

"I know I can't," said Tom, crossing his arms, his hands tucked under. "I have too much to do here with the holiday orders. Especially now that I'm changing directions with the store."

"You're going for it?" asked Ethan. At Tom's nod, Ethan grinned and leaned over to punch his arm. "That's awesome. I'm happy for you."

Tom responded to his enthusiasm with his own grin, his eyes lighting up. Kate was so glad to see Tom feel this moment of joy.

"It'll be great, Tom," said Kate. "This time next year, you'll have orders coming at you from everywhere."

"Here, here," said Zig.

"I have no doubts," said Ethan.

"I hope you're right," said Tom. "But in the meantime, I have to put in the work. Not long now until Christmas."

"You staying here for Christmas, Ethan?" asked Zig. "You know you can always come to me for Hanukkah."

Ethan arched a brow. "Hanukkah? Really? You mean you actually celebrate it?"

Zig shrugged. "Minor detail. I think there's a menorah somewhere."

Ethan laughed. "Well, thanks, anyway, but I'm going to spend it here. Kate's invited me."

"She has?" asked Tom. "Good. Because I was going to if she didn't. Wait. Where are we having it?"

Ethan and Kate exchanged looks and shrugged.

"You could all come and have the Hanukkah experience at my apartment."

"Dude you'd have to google Hanukkah to know what to do. You're the most un-Jewish Jew I've ever met."

"Just come over, Zig," said Kate. "Wherever we end up having it." She turned to Tracy, who'd been studying Ethan. "You're welcome to come too."

Tracy looked at her, surprised. "Oh. Thanks, but I'll be going home to my parents' house in New Jersey."

"Oh," said Kate. "Of course."

"Why don't all of you come over next week to the cabin?" said Ethan. "I'll get a tree, and we can decorate it or something." His eyes danced with amusement. "Decorate it creatively."

He looked down at Kate, his arm still encircling her waist. She'd been glad of its presence the whole time. Not just for the warmth, but the comfort, the solidness of it. And the sense that it felt right. It was a thought that shifted something in her that finally settled into place. A hand, a presence, a sense of him. The word echoed in her mind. Home. The unease that had taken hold since her video call with Giancarlo, incessant like a low background buzz, faded a little.

THIRTY-SEVEN

The tree was enormous. Kate had to laugh when she saw it first, the scent of pine overwhelming her as she walked in the door, Tom following her close behind, as it stretched up in all its vast glory in the living area by the window that faced the lake. They'd both been loaded down with odd-sized boxes, the booty of scouring the basement, the attic, and the closets for all the Christmas decorations from every Wilson family celebration through the years. It had been Tom's idea. With this approach, it would only be the decorations themselves that held the memories, without all the extra weight of the surroundings. And maybe having them erected and hung somewhere else, somewhere different, would take out some of that sting too.

She put the boxes down on the floor just inside the door, glad the weight was gone. Tom deposited his box beside hers, stretching back up and grinning over at the tree. "You tied it to the curtain pole?" he said.

Ethan, who had been struggling under the tree, trying to position the trunk in the stand he'd somehow managed to obtain, climbed up from under it and frowned. "You have a better idea?"

Tom laughed and shook his head. "You disappoint me. I would have thought you were an expert."

Ethan gave him a surprised look. "Why would you think that? I'm not the one proficient in all things wood."

"Oh, let him fix it," Kate said to Ethan. "I know he's dying to do it. He was the self-appointed Christmas tree erector at our house from the moment he could hold it by himself."

"Have at it, lumberjack," said Ethan, stepping back.

He came over and kissed her, lingering at her ear. "You smell heavenly. What scent is that?"

She pulled back and smiled at him. "Vanilla cookies."

"Really? They make a perfume of that?"

She shook her head, laughing. "No. I made some just before we came over. They're in the truck, along with some other things we brought. I'll just go get them while Tom plays tree engineer."

"I'll come and help," said Ethan.

He followed her out to the truck, and just as she was about to open the door, he pulled her into his arms and kissed her, parting her lips, brushing his tongue along her mouth, tasting her fully. She sighed with the pleasure of it, forgetting for a moment her surroundings, thinking only of the feel of him against her, his own scent, strong and masculine, speaking to her in ways she couldn't even name.

In the last week they'd spent most every night together, mostly at the cabin because she couldn't bring herself to use her father's old bed, for too many reasons she wasn't about to artic-ulate to herself, let alone Ethan. He'd never said a word, just crawled into her old bed and tucked her in beside him, while Max curled up on the floor beside them. Though it might have been awkward for him, she felt so safe, securely wrapped up in his body, his soft breath steady against her neck. It had been a good week, and she found that her spirit was lightening slowly, all thoughts of her contract and its implications tucked tidily away. There was plenty of time for that after Christmas. She would have this now.

He broke away finally. "I've been wanting to do that for so long."

She smiled at him. "I've only just arrived."

"I always want you, Kate. You don't have to be here for me to want you."

She felt herself soften further under his words. She pressed her head against his chest. "I can't seem to stop wanting you, either, Ethan. It hardly seems real."

He brushed her cheek with his hand. "It is real," he said in a low voice.

A car pulled up with a crunch of gravel, and Kate looked up to see Zig behind the wheel, Tracy beside him in the passenger seat. The two of them got out of the car, Zig reaching in and pulling out a bag from the back.

"You two enjoying some outdoor recreation?" Zig asked.

Tracy came up beside him and gave him a little shove. "So funny."

He put his arm around her, pulling her into him. She looked around her, taking in the cold fog drifting off the lake. It would freeze soon. The dock looked stark against it. She took out her phone, and pulling in Zig, took a selfie of the two of them, with the lake and dock as background. His extra height meant that Zig had to lean down at an awkward angle, his blond hair falling into his face, brushing his wire-rimmed glasses that reinforced the Lennon look he unconsciously mimicked. Tracy was wearing her parka again, the blue tips of her blonde hair resting against the fake-fur-trimmed hood. They made a quirky pair, but she seemed good for Zig.

Kate watched Tracy, her focus so intent on getting the right shot, Kate found it amusing. Her own approach was so much different, as was the content, but she guessed the intensity was the same. Zig seemed to indulge the whole experience like a besotted puppy and that, too, amused her.

"I feel like a parent watching his child fondly, realizing he's growing up," said Ethan, in a low voice.

"You mean it's as though we're sending them off to the prom?"

Ethan gave a low chuckle and kissed her ear. He released her and opened the truck door. "Go on in, when you're ready," he told Zig. "Tom's already in there sorting out the tree."

"Ooh," said Tracy, her voice filled with excitement. "There's a tree?"

"Of course," said Ethan. He bent down in the truck and pulled out a storage container. "Is this the right one?"

Kate laughed. "They're all the right one. Just hand me that one and pick up the other two that should be there."

"Aye, aye, captain," said Ethan. A few moments later they were entering the cabin and saw that Zig and Tracy had taken off their coats, and Zig's bag was resting on the kitchen counter. Zig unpacked it, and Kate saw that it was various wines and a bottle of whiskey.

Zig held up a small foil package to Kate. "I brought this stuff for you to make mulled wine."

Kate lifted her brows. "For me to make?"

Zig shrugged and grinned. "I don't have a clue. And well, you know your way around this kitchen pretty well by now, I assume."

She opened her mouth to utter an outrage and closed it a moment later, settling for a shake of the head. Better to let that pass. And besides, she found she actually liked the idea that she and Ethan shared a space.

"Don't worry," Ethan said, coming up behind Kate, the storage containers safely deposited on the kitchen table. "I won't hold you to that." He picked up the package and skimmed the directions printed on it. "I'll do it if you like."

She laughed and took the packet from him. "I'm not complaining."

Tom called from the living area. "Okay, folks. Tree is officially in place."

Tracy, clapped and lifted her phone, taking a picture while Kate gave her a bemused look. "Are you an avid Instagrammer?"

Tracy laughed. "Um, actually I do a TikTok collage reel several times a week. I just love putting it together. My week, and all that. I also do one for gamers. Talk about levels, characters, that kind of thing. But I sometimes still post on Instagram."

Kate looked at her in disbelief. All of that seemed so foreign to her. A website, that was where she'd left her skills last. Maybe she should do some Instagram for Tom? She couldn't imagine doing it for her own work, but she should probably consider it.

She moved over to Ethan, who was opening one of the storage containers. "Do you do any of that stuff?" she asked in a low voice.

He looked up. "What? Instagram and TikTok?" He gave a shudder. "God no. I don't do social media."

"Do you have a website, though? For your music and song-writing."

He gave her a guarded look. "No. No, I haven't found it necessary. At least not yet."

"But you're writing your novel. Don't you need a platform for that?"

"Come on guys," said Tom. "Enough canoodling in the corner, let's get started."

"First things, first," said Zig. He moved over to the cabinets and pulled down several drink glasses from the top cabinet over the refrigerator. "We need to fortify ourselves before we do anything else."

THIRTY-EIGHT

Kate looked up at the tree from the living area floor. The tree was half-decorated, but already its festive air lifted the room from temporary housing to a home. Garlands, lights, and ornaments all fought for attention, and though she knew it looked overdone, she didn't care. Tom, red-faced from his exertion hanging lights around the edge of the window frame, seemed to be enjoying himself, a fact helped by the few glasses of wine and a tumbler of whiskey he'd drunk after Zig had offered to drop him off at his place.

The mulled wine Kate had made had disappeared, the food had been consumed, and somehow decorations had been unpacked and hung with a lighthearted manner. Now, Ethan reached in and pulled out a painted blue clay blob sprinkled with glitter with a deep depression in the center. He set it on the coffee table and started to laugh. Tom jumped down from the chair, his last string of lights in place, looked at the clay object, and joined Ethan.

"What in the name of Christmas and the elves is that?" Ethan asked.

Tom only laughed harder. Zig looked up from the snow

globe he was playing with and joined the other two. Tracy, tucked in the corner near the sofa, had started looking through the pile of Ethan's albums shoved aside earlier, looked up, and scrunched up her face.

"Wow," she said. "That is seriously ugly."

Kate swept up the clay object into her arms. "Stop. You're mocking true art."

"Did you make that?" asked Zig, when his laugh had subsided.

"I did. And I'll have you know it's a candle holder."

"A candle holder?" asked Zig. "You definitely were following your own drum there, Picasso."

"I was a child genius. I made this for Christmas when I was five."

"I can see why your parents kept it," said Ethan, grinning.

"They knew a great doorstop when they saw it," said Tom.

Kate lifted her chin, striking a haughty pose. "It needs a candle to have the full effect."

"It's beautiful, Kate," said Ethan. "In a very arty way, of course, it makes its own statement."

Kate made a face as the laughter continued, and her spirits lifted. The holder was obviously a piece only a parent would have praised. And it had come out for most Christmases, a candle in place, along with other equally amazing childhood projects. It felt good to see it in Ethan's hands, giving her a private look as he studied it. She felt only warmth that he could share that small bit of her childhood and understand. She could feel that understanding, and she acknowledged it with a smile.

"Wow," said Tracy, picking up one of the albums. "You have some early Prometheus Bound albums. That is so cool. I love that band. They are the best. And so mysterious."

Kate glanced at Ethan and saw he'd paled.

"Oh my God, here's the first one in LP. I only have it on my

Spotify playlist. It's tough to get hold of." She held it up to the rest of the group, her eyes shining. "It's the only album that has an image of the band in it. And even in this album all you can see of Elijah Harmon is his torso. The others at least you can see their faces. When they perform, he wears a sweatshirt with the hood up so you can't see his face."

"Who's Elijah?" asked Kate.

"He's the lead singer," said Tracy. She beamed at Kate. "This is such a good album. You should have a listen." said Tracy. She looked over at Zig. "You have some of their albums, don't you? Do you have the first one?"

Zig nodded, his eyes carrying a trace of amusement. "I do. Somewhere."

"What are they like?" asked Tom. "I've heard of them, and think I might have listened to one or two of theirs along the way."

Kate looked over at Ethan again, wondering if he would mention that he wrote songs for the band, but he only stared down at one of the ornaments he'd picked up from an open box.

"Ethan writes some of the songs for them," said Zig. "Or with them."

Ethan looked over at Zig and narrowed his eyes.

"No way," said Tracy, swiveling her head around to face Ethan. "You have got to be kidding me. That is seriously unbelievable."

"Oh, that's right," said Tom smiling at Ethan. "I think Dad mentioned something about that. Good one."

Kate watched the exchange silently, trying to understand Ethan's emotions. Was a distraction needed?

"Hey, why don't you play one for us?" asked Tom. "Give us an idea what they're like. Or give me an idea, in any case." He looked over at Kate. "Do you know Prometheus Bound?"

Kate shook her head. "No. But then I'm not a current music expert. I'm afraid my recent forays have all been in opera."

"Opera?" asked Tom. He laughed. "Opera? Really?" He shook his head. "Can't imagine it, sorry."

She stuck her tongue at him. "I like my art to be informed by a broad experience."

He leaned over and picked up the clay candle holder. "I can see that your pieces are informed by something."

"Ethan," said Zig, "why not play 'Navigation'? Give them an idea of what your song was like before it became a Prometheus Bound song."

Ethan and Zig shared a silent exchange that Kate tried to decipher. She knew of his feeling for the band, but was it something more?

Ethan sighed and rose, and retrieved his 1920s Martin parlor guitar. A sweet, clear sound emitted from it as he struck up the notes, his fingers skimming over the strings and framing the chords. Soon his own warm, rich baritone filled the room.

Navigation, navigation, steer me home to you.

The boat's too small, the waves too tall
And the water is all around me.
The hunger gnaws and the seagulls call
And I can't see what they see.

And now it's night, the stars are bright
And I don't know where they point me
They fade from sight, it's nearly light
And their meaning is still a mystery
Navigation, navigation, steer me home to you.

It's your sweet touch I miss so much
And the feeling you always gave me
These thoughts I clutch, they are my crutch
And the dream of all that we might be

A storm comes past, it breaks the mast
I hear you say you believe in me
The boat won't last, it's fading fast
And then you say, soon, you'll be free.
Navigation, Navigation, steer me home to you
Navigation, Navigation, steer me home to you.

Kate was stunned as the last notes rang out into the silence of the room. The music had been in a minor key, a Johnny Cash feel blended with Leonard Cohen and so many other influences that Kate subconsciously knew. The words, well, she could listen to them over and over, she knew, and still feel the gut-wrenching pull of them. She barely heard Tracy's words, she was too caught up in her own reverie as the song echoed in her head.

"That is sooo different," said Tracy. "I mean, I can't believe it's the same song at all."

Ethan snorted. "Yeah, well. Things happen. Producers have a vision and all that."

"That's a boss song, Ethan," said Tom. "I wouldn't have changed a thing. What's the band's production sound like?"

Ethan shook his head. "You don't want to hear it."

"Oh, no. You should definitely play it!" said Tracy, rising. She pulled out the LP. "Where's your turntable?"

Ethan frowned at her.

"Come on, man," said Zig. "Play it. It won't hurt anything. It's completely different."

Reluctantly, Ethan rose and carefully replaced his guitar in its case. He took the LP from Tracy and headed to the bedroom.

Kate looked at the album cover, still in Tracy's hands. "Can I have a look?"

Tracy handed it over to her. "The design is amazing. There's so much symbolism and all that. It relates to the songs."

Kate nodded absentmindedly, her curiosity overwhelming, and trying to imagine what kind of band would take over that song and change it so much Ethan was reluctant to play it. It made her question how he felt about the other songs he'd written for them. No wonder he suffered from writer's block.

She looked on the back of the album and took a brief look at the list of songs. The last one was "Navigation." Beside it, where the songwriter was credited, was the name Elijah Harmon.

The album was folded out, and when she opened it the image of the band greeted her. It was a black-and-white photograph that emphasized the contrasting shadows that fell in almost deliberate angles across the band members' bodies and faces, carving and chiseling them in their bare-chested poses, each facing slightly different directions. Greek Gods, or a study in Greek sculptures. The concept was clever, tying into the band's name. At its center was the lead, a torso, neck, and hint of a chin and the edge of his low-hanging jeans, barely visible. His arms were splayed out, palms up, as if he had stigmata. Chains were fastened at both wrists, pulled taut to the sides to eventually vanish at the sides of the image. It was stark and stunning, the lighting playing off the muscles of his chest and abdomen. And in the center of the stark, sculpted torso was a tattoo. An eagle, its beak open, placed on the right side of the abdomen, just where the liver would be.

Kate stared at the image, the beat of her heart suddenly loud in her ears. The torso, bound by chains remained unmoving, the eagle still posed to peck as the sounds of Prometheus Bound's version of "Navigation" wafted out of the bedroom. Ethan had been right to dislike it, because the overproduced, loud, rock song with its flangers, bass guitar riffs, keyboard, and drums obscured the simple beauty of the song. But even the overproduction couldn't disguise the voice. The familiar deep, rich baritone, only barely changed by a rougher-edged quality and a lower key that no doubt reflected the producers' approach and vision. The song finished and Kate heard Ethan remove it from the turntable and close down the stereo system.

A moment later, Ethan walked back into the room. Kate looked up at him, her eyes wide, her mind frozen.

"God that's awful, if you ask me," said Tom. "What were they thinking?"

Kate leaned over and handed the album back to Tracy, muttering her thanks. Tracy stood and took the LP back from Ethan, studying him carefully, her eyes narrowed.

"Am I crazy or what?" she asked. She turned to Zig. "It's him, isn't it?"

Zig gave Ethan a panicked look and shook his head. "No, what? No."

She swung back around and grinned at Ethan. "I am right. Can't miss that voice. I've heard it often enough. When you were playing the guitar just now, I thought it was possible, and listening to the record only confirmed it."

"I think they just used a voice similar to his," said Kate, interrupting.

Her mind was whirling, trying to make sense of what she knew to be the truth. A truth that even Tracy had picked up. And the voice inside her. A voice that kept repeating "Why didn't he tell me?" over and over, the sense of betrayal so strong it nearly stopped her breath.

"Oh, that's definitely the case here," said Tom. "If you knew what record producers can do, you'd be amazed. In fact, you are amazed because that's definitely what happened here. But if you listen to the flanger action and the woof and reverb you can tell there's been some distortion there."

Kate heard Tom's garbled and jargon-filled explanation with a detachment that was born of her own numbness, conscious, all the while, of Ethan's eyes on her. She was afraid to meet his gaze, see whatever message they contained, because she just didn't know. Didn't know what she was feeling except betrayal. It was just too much.

"It's what Tom said," Zig told Tracy. "I mean, I don't know all the ins and outs, but Tom does. He's an expert on it. His father was in the music business for years."

Tracy gave him a doubtful look before turning to study Ethan one last time, a look that Kate saw for just a moment before she turned her gaze away. The neutral expression on his face, the forced shrug, tugging at her in ways she just couldn't make sense of. Ethan the reluctant rock star. She forced down the sudden wave of hysteria that rose inside her.

Zig popped up and lunged for an ornament inside one of the boxes. "We have a job to finish here. Ethan, man, you're falling down on the job. Our glasses are empty."

The glasses were refilled, the remaining ornaments unpacked and hung on the tree. Kate helped, though she was desperate to leave. Her actions were automatic, just going through the motions. After about a half-hour Zig made his excuses, corralling Tracy into her coat. Tom prepared to leave, and Kate found herself following suit, asking Zig if he could drop her off as well. Zig had tried to hide his surprise with a loud assurance, so Kate had collected her empty containers and her bag, conscious of Ethan's unspoken plea and brief hand on her arm as she left the cabin.

THIRTY-NINE

Sitting at the kitchen table, Kate stared at her phone, hardly able to believe the images, let alone the number of likes, shares, and screaming comments on the screen. Tom had called her to tell her to warn her about Tracy's Instagram posts that were nearly vibrating with all the action they were getting and how high they were trending. Kate didn't dare check TikTok for those statistics. And a Google of the band's name had left her panicked and wondering about the impact. She could only be grateful that, despite all Tracy's Instagram activity, her photography skills were woefully inadequate, and the one photo of Ethan, the one at O'Connor's, was mostly obscured by the back of Tom's head. And the part that showed Ethan had only half of his bowed head and his guitar. The post of Tracy and Zig at the lake were largely filled with her face and little of any significant points of the lake and dock. Though, as much as this might reassure her, the location was named. And that was the problem.

Tracy had definitely not believed any of the hastily created misdirection about Ethan. It had been laughable really, though Kate had never found any humor in it. Tracy had taken matters into her own control and decided sharing the scoop of the music world was worth the sacrifice for whatever fallout would happen to her and anyone else. Kate had no idea where Zig was in all this, but couldn't imagine he would have betrayed Ethan in this manner.

Kate could only be grateful that Tracy didn't know her last name, though she knew it would be only a matter of time before others figured it out. Or neighbors posted it, and her own location was exposed to everyone. She had no idea how Ethan was feeling, or what it meant for him. She'd refused to answer his phone calls or texts, too confused and filled with emotion to talk. The shock that he'd kept it from her, the knowledge that she hadn't known who he was really since she'd returned, left her shaken and filled with uncertainty. It was like she'd lost someone close to her, someone she loved. Even Tom's words of reason, spoken only this morning on the phone, had done nothing to help her out of the fog that seemed to surround her.

The back door opened and a helmeted figure wearing a leather jacket, jeans and heavy boots entered. She didn't need Ethan to remove the helmet to know it was him. She hadn't heard his motorcycle draw up, but given her distraction, it wasn't surprising.

He removed the helmet, shaking out his hair. He'd omitted the glasses today, his eyes, haunted and dark rimmed, were clearly visible. Dark stubble covered his chin.

"Kate," he said, his voice raspy. "Sorry for coming in like this. I had to talk to you and...it was the best way to ensure a bit of privacy."

She looked at him, the pain so evident in his face. "I'm sorry, too, Ethan. About Tracy's actions. You certainly didn't deserve that."

"Do you mind if I sit?" he asked, studying her carefully.

She shook her head, sighing inwardly. She'd needed to talk with him, and it looked as if now was the time. "No, go ahead. There's coffee there if you want."

He laid his helmet on the table and fixed himself a cup of coffee silently. Kate sat in her seat staring at her mug, her fingers gripping the side.

When he'd taken his seat, his mug before him, he reached out and gripped her hand. "I am truly sorry. I didn't want you to find out like this."

She looked up and gave him a weak smile. "Or do you mean you didn't want me to find out?"

He shook his head. "No, no. I was going to tell you. Soon. I-I just was trying to find a way to do it." He ran a hand through his hair. "I mean. God, I don't know. I felt like such a bastard, not telling you before."

"And why didn't you? It's not exactly a minor detail about your life. Or were you afraid that I might post something on Instagram?" She flushed, ashamed that she'd spoken those words. They'd just poured out of her mouth, even though she knew he wouldn't have thought that.

Ethan was shaking his head vigorously. "No, no, Kate. I know you and Tom both would never—"

Kate cut him off. "I know. I'm sorry I said that. I didn't mean it."

"You have every right to be angry." He scrubbed at his face. "Your father knew. He understood why I never told anyone. I mean, he understood that I hated the whole notion of being a rock star. It isn't me. And, maybe, after a while, that's why I didn't say anything. Because it isn't me. It's a different life. One that is so foreign to who I am and my music. My real music. I just didn't want it entering this part of my life."

"But it is part of you, Ethan. And part of your life. You can't get away from that."

He shook his head, staring down at his hands, now fisted. "No. I didn't want it. It was thrust on me."

She saw the struggle he experienced in his taught body, the tight jaw, and the anger in his eyes. "Prometheus Bound," she said. "That was you, wasn't it?"

He made a derisive sound. "My own little private joke. The producers, the record company, they loved it, though. Said it gave the band an edgy image. I was just showing the horror I had of it."

She shook her head. "I'm sorry it's been such an awful experience for you."

He sighed. "I know I should be grateful. I know every other musician would kill for the opportunities I've had."

"Exactly," she said. The fog was starting to dispel, leaving only the sharp stab of loss. Another loss and one she wasn't certain she could move on from. "You need to try and change your outlook. Surely you can use this to build a different music career."

He gave a scornful laugh. "You'd think. But they don't want any of the kind of music I'd like to be involved in. No, I decided, after this album, the contract is done, fulfilled. I'm out. That's why I've been writing the novel. To give me a different direction. One that can be for me, and one that I like."

"And let Elijah Harmon die."

He looked pained at her comment. "Yes. Elijah is dead anyway. It was my brother's middle name."

"Oh, God, I'm sorry. I didn't realize. But why choose that?"

He sighed. "It was a stupid jab at my father, but it still protected my family from the embarrassment of having a rock star in the family. Harmon was my mother's maiden name. My grandmother." He grimaced. "It all seems childish now, though."

"But why not just turn it all down? Why go through with being part of a band, a sound that you don't want or like?"

A myriad of emotions filled Ethan's expression. "I don't know. I think at the time I was hoping that I could prove to my father I could make my music pay. Only it ended up not being the music I wanted or felt was my music. It would have been better if I'd taken the classical music road from the start." The last words were spoken in a tone both bitter and forlorn.

Kate felt a sharp pain of empathy hearing his explanation and the obvious pain he felt. "Well, I hope your novel works out. You deserve that. And it's definitely a talent you have."

"Thanks," he said. He took her hand again. "I'm sorry, Kate. Really I am. You have to believe that I truly intended to tell you."

She nodded, fighting back tears. "I believe you. But I wish you had told me earlier. It would have made things easier for all of us."

He gave her a puzzled look. "What do you mean?"

Instinct drove her thoughts and she uttered them before she could think on it further. "It would have saved us both from becoming too...involved. Stayed just friends."

He frowned. "No, what? This doesn't change anything, Kate. My feelings haven't changed. And I can't believe yours have changed. Kate, I love you."

Kate gripped the mug tightly again. She had to get the words out, fight the tightness in her throat. "No, Ethan. It can't work. It probably wouldn't have worked, anyway. It was a mistake to think it had any possibility of becoming anything more than a brief relationship. I mean, I've only recently broken off an engagement. My father has just died. How can I be certain of anything? I hardly know myself and what I want, let alone coping with all that being with you might entail."

The thought of paparazzi, the press hounding her, taking

photographs of her all the time. It would be so much worse than when she was with Giancarlo. Tears filled her eyes. "I can't do it. I just can't."

"Please, Kate," said Ethan, his voice cracking with emotion. "Don't decide anything yet. Please. Let's just wait for this thing to die down. It will, I promise."

She studied her hands and the phone beside them, a reminder of all the comments, likes, shares, and follows of the Instagram posts. It had to be right, this decision. She could do it. This loss, this pain she felt now. It would go. "You don't know that, Ethan. You and your band are huge. And the mystery behind Elijah Harmon is too big to go away. They'll find you. If they haven't already. And when they do, your name will be out there."

"No," he whispered. "No. I won't let it. I'll protect you from all that, Kate."

She finally looked up and tried to smile, but the tears were welling hard, slipping down her face silently. "I know you want to believe that, Ethan, but you and I both know that you won't be able to."

Forty

Christmas music filtered into the office where Kate had her laptop, checking one last reference for the exhibition catalog. Out in the gallery, Cassidy was helping to unpack the crates that had been delivered only a half-hour before. Except for the music, it was hard to believe Christmas was the day after tomorrow, and even now Kate couldn't understand why Cassidy would choose to play such insipid music in her gallery, especially with the gallery closing until after New Year, and the need to please potential buyers all but ended.

The gallery was in transition. All the walls were bare of anything but the new paint recently applied, covering any marks and remains of holes and mounts from the previous show. If only Kate could cover over the holes and remains of what had been her life up until this point. What had seemed like a purposeful transition before was now becoming more aimless, especially since she'd finished her pieces for the show. All but one, in any case. Something about House of Clouds wasn't coming together. It didn't seem finished. All the others she'd worked on almost without stop in the last few weeks, rushing them off one by one to the framers. Now they were all here, waiting for Cassidy's final approval. Except for that one piece. And any joy she might have felt at this accomplishment was only a pale, faded imitation of any initial excitement about this exhibition. Right now, it was difficult to muster any interest. Giancarlo's interests hung over her still, but the greater pain of the loss of Ethan's presence in her life was more intense, despite any efforts to rationalize it or push it aside.

Cassidy leaned into the office, her lean figure beautifully dressed in a dark rust-colored jumpsuit, her hair a crown of wound cornrows. "You have to come out here and see them lined up against the wall, Kate. They're absolutely stunning."

Kate forced a smile at her enthusiasm, knowing she should be relieved to hear Cassidy's praise. She had doubted herself at the last minute, her relentless work and absorption in the project she'd thought had colored her abilities to dispassionately assess the pieces. Doubts that had seemed to increase in the light of Giancarlo's silence and Ethan's. But as she made her way to the gallery, a brief email sent that morning from Giancarlo stating curtly he hoped all was in order for her exhibition, she'd found any nerves had disappeared in a fog of disinterest. Was it the looming trip to Italy to begin the next exhibition? Or the fact that she dreaded his appearance at the opening of this exhibition?

She made her way out to the gallery where Cassidy and her assistant Trey had each of the framed pieces set up in a line along the walls. They would be spread out once they were hung, spilling over into the midsection that divided the front section from the back section of the gallery space. Kate surveyed the result and found herself tearing up, unable to explain to herself why. The framing was perfect. They were ivory-white with palest of pale green, taupe, blue and amber mats, depending on the image and the poem. Cassidy had helped, giving the benefit of her experience and knowledge of her own gallery space. A joint effort. An effort that had its origins in Giancarlo, something she'd rather forget.

She'd been tempted to call Ethan in the last few weeks' time and time again as the yawning absence made her days so much less than they'd been. An absence that had taken up space in her heart and permeated all the emotions she'd managed to muffle. As much as she tried to tell herself it was better for her to find her own way through these next months, her heart remained unconvinced. It remembered his scent, the touch of his fingers across her lips, along her hip.It didn't hear the rationale that it was best not to be drawn into promises and possibilities until she knew what she wanted for herself. A mature notion, a good decision. And, she told herself, she knew what she didn't want, at least. Besides, Ethan had left Somerton Lake the same day they'd spoken, his fear of the press driving him back to New York. At least that's what Tom had said. It had been a wise choice, Kate knew. And she'd taken refuge in the attic, working away at all hours, Max her only company, while people knocked and knocked on the door, occasionally calling up to the windows. Tom had secluded himself in the store workshop, while Fred fended off any unwanted attention. It had lasted a week. Surely that was enough to convince Kate she'd been right in what she'd said to Ethan. She reminded herself of that countless times.

"What do you think?" asked Cassidy. "It's going to be fab. The best show this winter. I just know it. I feel it in my bones."

"Oh, honey, it's going to be the talk of the town," said Trey.

Trey's large, round, dark-rimmed glasses winked in the overhead light, his closely cropped hair accentuating their size. He crossed his arms, staring at the array of artwork, his tightly fitted fuchsia-colored T-shirt hugging his muscled arms. He'd slung his forest green jacket on the only chair in the room, and Kate could see from the lines it was expensive. She hadn't met Trey before, but Cassidy had assured her that he had an unerring eye when it came to hanging works in her gallery. When they'd met he'd appraised her just as he was appraising her artwork now, and it drew a smile from her, deciding she liked him.

The three of them stood discussing the art, Trey moving forward to shift and position pieces in groups, getting a feel for their arrangement in a tactile approach that Kate found reassuring. It was absorbing to see her vision blend with first Cassidy's and then Trey's.

Trey picked up the "Two Trees" piece. The trees were maples, half-cast in silhouette, leaning into each other, with the phrases "gyring, spyring" repeated in drifting letters around the half bare trees. "This is a feature piece, I think," he said, walking over to the short center wall. "One that we want people to see when they first walk in."

"I still have one more," Kate said. "It's bit bigger than that one. You might want it to be in that place instead."

The gallery bell rang, once, twice, three times in succession before a pause, and then it rang again.

Cassidy sighed. "I'd better get that. It's probably some customer desperate to buy a last-minute Christmas present." She grinned. "They can be the best, though. Money's no object and all that."

"Oh, darling, reel them in," said Trey.

Kate gave a small laugh. Trey held up the piece against the wall. "I don't know, I still think this one has 'feature' written all over it."

"How about we keep it as a possible, or see if we can fit both?"

Trey shook his head. "The theme, the message of both, has to work. No, just get that piece here pronto, missy."

Kate nodded, resolving to finish it as soon as she returned to Somerton Lake, the day after Christmas. Tom and she had both decided that since she was going up to New York City so close to Christmas Day, they would spend it in New York City. Tom would join her tomorrow, Simon looking after Max for them, once the store was shut. It seemed best. There was plenty to do in New York City. Plenty to take their minds off of things.

"Kate, there's someone here who says he has to talk to you."

Kate turned around, her mind frozen at the thought it might be Ethan, but the figure who entered the gallery was Zig.

"Kate," said Zig. "Do you mind if we go somewhere and talk?"

She found herself momentarily at a loss for words, but finally managed a nod.

"You can use the office," said Cassidy. "We'll just go out for a quick coffee."

"I'm sorry. Do you mind?" Kate asked Cassidy. She wanted to get this over with, and this arrangement seemed the best way.

"No, no, not at all," said Cassidy. "Go right ahead. We'll be off after we get our coats."

It only took a few minutes before Zig and Kate were alone in the office, Zig looking drawn and exhausted. He'd unzipped his gray puffer coat, and she could see underneath it, he was wearing sweatpants and an old sweatshirt.

He dragged his hand through his hair. "Sorry, Kate. I don't mean to bother you here, but it was the only way I could think of to see you."

She gave him a puzzled look. "How did you know I was here?"

"Tom. He told me when I went to ask him where you were at the workshop. I tried the house, but there was no answer."

Of course. It would have been Tom. "Why are you here, Zig?"

"I had to come, first of all, to apologize for everything." He gave a ragged sigh. "For Tracy. Her behavior. The way—" He broke off, a gesture filling in the remaining words.

"It wasn't your fault, Zig. You didn't know she'd do all that."

"No, no. I should have. I mean I knew she was really into Prometheus Bound. I just didn't think anything of it. I mean, I never thought she would put together that Ethan…" He let the sentence drift off. "Well, that he was who he was. And I never imagined that she would connect the two voices." His face contorted with emotion.

She put her hand on his arm. "Zig. It was her doing. Not yours. You didn't post the pictures. Or tell everyone on social media. She did. She's the one who was responsible."

Zig shook his head. "It's nice of you to say that, but I played a part, I know. And now I'm just gutted that Ethan and you had to suffer like this."

"No, no. My decision about Ethan isn't your fault at all. And Tracy, well she just made it happen quicker."

Zig shook his head. "Don't say that. He's a wreck over what happened. You and Ethan, well, you're meant to be together. When he told me you were back in Somerton in October, I thought, finally it can happen."

She gave him a puzzled look. "I don't understand."

He gave her a surprised look. "It's always been you for Ethan. Since college. Sharing classes, all of it. From the first moment he saw you at the showcase, it's been all about you. I mean 'Navigation' was written for you. Really, they all were."

"What?" Kate looked at him, speechless for a moment, a roaring sound filling her ears. "No."

"Yes. And then he heard your music. It just blew him away."

"That can't be right." She fought the roaring, the sudden pain that rose up, unwanted. "I mean, he never said anything."

Zig snorted. "You were with someone else. From here. Some guy name Mark?"

"Mark? No." She fought to make sense of his words. "He was Missy's boyfriend."

Zig looked stunned. "But your bandmate told Ethan that Mark was your boyfriend."

"When was this?"

Zig shrugged. "At one of your concerts. Ethan used to go to them. Slip in the back. And one time your bandmate came up to him on a break and told him to back off. That you had a boyfriend, and he wouldn't appreciate Ethan sniffing around."

Kate shook her head, disbelief, anger and pain mixing into a one great wave of emotion that threatened to overwhelm her. She fought to shove it away. "No," she said in a whisper. "She couldn't have."

Zig nodded. "She did. Knocked Ethan a bit, because you'd never indicated you'd had a boyfriend in college. But then you weren't on campus often. He did mention he saw you a few times at soccer games and practice, but after a while he didn't make anything of it."

Kate gave a small shake of her head. "Of course not." She put her head in her hands. "Oh, Zig, this is all too much, really." She blinked, trying to breathe. Seconds passed, she took a deep inhale, and forced out the words she knew she had to say. "Zig, when it all comes down to it, I'm not sure it changes anything."

Zig looked stricken. "Don't say that. Just hold tight, give yourself time to absorb it all. Let this commotion die down. Because it will. Ethan's already had the media handlers issue a statement denying everything."

She gave him a surprised look. "But there's no guarantee that will do anything but fuel interest."

"Maybe," said Zig. "But that interest will move on.

Christmas and New Year's Eve. They'll all be concerned with their own personal lives."

Kate gave a bitter laugh. "Oh, Zig, I can tell you that's not how it works."

Zig took her hand and squeezed it. "Please, Kate. Just let it be for now. Don't make any final decisions."

She grimaced, wondering how to fend him off. "All I can promise is that I won't be going anywhere until this exhibition is out of the way."

Zig nodded, and Kate noted the hopeful expression, the slight lift of his shoulders, and realized he had more confidence about her future with Ethan than she did. But then she knew what her future looked like, at least in the immediate sense, and she knew there was no room for Ethan in it. Only Giancarlo and her commitment to him.

FORTY-ONE

The menu Kate held had Chinese characters beside the English words, which made her smile to think that she was here ordering Dim Sum on Christmas day instead of turkey with stuffing. It certainly was a different experience and in no way reminded her of Christmases past. The music that filtered into the dining area had little Christmas flavor to it either, rather it supported the Asian ambiance of the dragon murals and carved teak tables and chairs. Kate wasn't certain how she and Tom had ended up there for dinner, but she knew, given the overbooked restaurants that had surrounded the midtown hotel they were staying in, she should be grateful they'd found anywhere. She hadn't imagined how many people preferred to eat out at Christmas, or enjoy a New York City Christmas break. Still, Tom didn't seem to mind the choice of food, either.

The waiter took their order, and Kate found herself sipping an Asian beer that she'd never tried, relishing the cold bite to it. Tom had joined her, though the pursed lips and half-frown let her know they didn't share opinions on its flavor.

She held her glass up to him. "To a Christmas with a difference."

He laughed. "Definitely different." He clinked his glass with hers.

"How's the ankle?" she asked him. They'd spent the afternoon trying to ice skate at Rockefeller Plaza in a burst of spontaneity that had ended up being both fun and distracting.

"Are you insinuating that my ice hockey days are done?"

"Since you never had any ice hockey days, how can I be insinuating that?"

He shook his head. "I did play a bit."

"When you were ten, and I think it lasted only a month."

He put a hand to his chest. "You wound me. It was a whole season."

She laughed. "On the bench. At least that's what Dad told me."

"I was very good on that bench."

She shook her head. "I can't believe I can't perform a spin anymore."

Tom shrugged. "I turned my ankle. What can I say? Years pass, and we get older."

The words seemed to take on a meaning in that moment that brought all the carefully tucked-away emotions to the forefront again. She looked away. "Yes," she said in a small voice.

Tom reached out and touched her hand. "Hey, hey. I didn't mean it like that."

She nodded and put her fingers to the edges of her eyes, as if to push back the tears that could well at any second.

She took a deep breath. "Sorry, I don't know what's gotten into me."

Tom squeezed her hand. "Understandable. You've had a lot going on."

She looked at him. "So have you."

He shrugged. "Maybe, but you had a lot more baggage there in the first place."

She frowned. "What do you mean?"

Tom gave her a direct look. "I think you know what I mean."

She shook her head. "No, I don't."

He sighed. "Oh, Kate. Are you sure you want to go into this now?"

"What do you mean 'go into this'? What exactly needs 'going into'?"

Tom studied her a minute. "Missy," he said softly. "Giancarlo, Ethan."

"What about Missy?"

Kate could feel the beat of her heart as the silence stretched between them. "What are you thinking?"

Tom spoke slowly. "I'm thinking that you blame yourself for something that had nothing to do with you. Not really. I'm thinking that Missy was a troubled, anger-driven person because of the inadequacies of her parents after they split. I'm thinking that Missy, afraid of losing anyone else in her life, sought to control the people she held dear. And maybe she didn't mean to do it, but it led her to manipulate and lie. She controlled you, Kate. By the way she acted. By the way she made any action you took to be your own person into a personal betrayal of her. She did the same with Mark."

Kate was too stunned to speak for a moment. "No," she said finally, her voice weak. "You're wrong."

Tom shook his head. "Kate, it was so evident. Even Dad remarked on it. He said he tried to speak to you about it, but you got angry and said he'd never liked Missy in the first place, so he let it go."

She blinked at him, trying to make sense of his words. How could it be? She vaguely remembered her father talking to her about Missy, but she really had thought it was plain dislike of how close she and Missy were. Then she thought about the number of times Missy had criticized or ridiculed any boy that Kate had taken an interest in, or who might show some interest in her. Especially Simon. She'd made it impossible for Kate to be around Simon without flushing seriously at Missy's condemning words like "prig," "stuck up," or "boring." But Missy had Mark as a boyfriend. They'd been together since eighth grade. Neither of them had really had any other relationships before that. Had Missy really tried to keep Mark by her side, regardless? No, she thought. He'd adored her. Zig's words about Missy warning Ethan that Mark was Kate's boyfriend echoed through her mind.

She looked up at Tom. "Do you really think so?" Her voice broke mid-sentence, and she felt his hand squeeze hers again. Reassuring, comforting. She took a deep breath. "God, I don't know."

"Well, I've said it now. It's what I think. You're not to blame for any of Missy's decisions or actions. You have to stop punishing yourself. Starting with your music. You used to thrive up there on stage. Music is in your blood. You can't get away from it."

He sat back. "When you first went off to Paris, Dad was gutted. He let you go, figuring you needed time away to find your way back to yourself again. He knew that Missy's death cut deep. Me, I thought you were running away, afraid to face the fact that Missy wanted to punish you in the worst way possible.

"Then, after you settled in Italy, I thought maybe you found a different part of yourself, and through that, happiness. The fact that you could hardly stand to be a minute longer than necessary at home in Somerton Lake, I put down to the reminders it held. Though again, it broke Dad's heart."

Kate felt a deep pain hearing the impact her decisions had on both Tom and her father. Deep down, she'd know she'd been hurting them, but she'd refused to acknowledge it at the time.

Tom leaned forward again, his expression earnest. "And though you never said much about Giancarlo, I hoped, we hoped, that he was the person who would get you back to yourself. Help you create a good life. But when you came home for Dad's birthday, well, it wasn't the Kate I knew. Not at first. Dad said to me, jokingly, 'Where's my little fiery girl gone?' But we both knew it wasn't a joke. Then, when I met Giancarlo, well, I mean he's okay, but then when you two were together, I thought this isn't who she's meant to be with. The real Kate isn't there, not with him."

She opened her mouth to protest, but shut it. She took a deep breath. "I owe him a lot," she said, finally, not able to bring herself to tell Tom of Giancarlo's latest actions. "He helped me so much after art school. Getting me started, assisting me in finding a focus for my art, encouraging me when I did." The words were what she'd always told herself. Now, she wondered if it was more directing, leading, than encouraging.

"I know, and it was really good of him to do that," said Tom. "Your art is important. I can see that. And it's amazing that he helped you uncover that part of you. But it was as though it had to unfold in his way. That you had to pursue it under his guidance." Tom grimaced. "I'm sorry, but in some ways he's like Missy."

She pulled back, away from his gaze. "No, you're wrong."

"Am I?" Tom held her eyes.

She looked away, confused at all he'd relayed. "I can't believe that. Giancarlo loved me." But what kind of love had it been?

"I don't doubt it," said Tom. "And how do you feel? A few

weeks ago I would have said that you were heading in a direction that was where you should have been a long time ago."

She turned sharply to look at Tom. "What?"

"With Ethan. You two are like two halves of a whole. Inevitable as one. What you share is special. Don't throw it away. Believe me, I know what I'm talking about."

Kate started shaking her head slowly, denial her automatic response to the sudden pain that took hold of her. She made herself breathe. "No, Tom. That's where I know you're wrong. Ethan and I aren't inevitable. You think I have things to work out. Well, he has just as many, if not more. And the spotlight is no place to work them out. I can attest to that. I'm no celebrity. You may think I thrived on stage, but it was among friends. I was playing because I wanted to share my music with people who loved it, enjoyed it. There were no celebrity extras attached to it. Simple." Simple. But she knew it wasn't. The emptiness she'd feel at times only to be replaced by the ache, the crippling sadness, if she didn't lock it up tight.

"Ethan's no different from you, Kate. He wants a simple life. And he'll get there. I know him."

"You know him?" Her tone was mocking.

"I do." He reached for her hand. "But whatever happens, whatever you decide, I want you to know that I will be there for you. You can count on me."

The tears welled now, and she tried to brush them away as they spilled over. "Thanks," she said after a moment. "I have no idea what I'm going to do."

Tom gave her a reassuring smile. "You'll figure it out. I can tell that now."

Kate forced a smile in return, hoping that his words were true. At this point it didn't seem that way.

Forty-Two

Kate stirred her espresso, feeling the tension grow, despite her jet lag. Outside the café, in the Piazza Navona, the streets were wet and slick, and umbrellas jostled for space as they swept by. A dreary January morning, and few were eager to linger at the stalls or shop windows like most days, when the weather was dry and clear. It was the damp chill that would prevent those from lingering now, as much as the rain. Kate was thankful for the winter coat as well as the umbrella she'd had the foresight to pack. Her hair was another story, and even now tendrils were finding their way onto her face as the café door opened and with it, a gust of wind.

She looked up and saw Giancarlo. He was immaculate as always, and the trench coat he wore was expensive, but all the clothes and attention to detail didn't hide the drawn and cautious look on his face. Kate felt her anxiety grow. He caught sight of her then, and his face gave away little more. She nodded, and he made his way over to the small table she'd chosen, dropping a kiss on each cheek.

"Katerina, how good it is to see you," he said, his tone neutral. "Would you like another espresso?"

"No, I'm fine," she said. "You go ahead."

He nodded and went to the counter to place his order. A few minutes later, he returned with his espresso and took the seat opposite her.

"You are well?" he said after taking a sip. His eyes searched her face. "You look tired. Have you been sleeping and eating enough?"

She gave him a tight smile and gripped her cup. "I'm fine, really. It's just a bit of jet lag. I only got in yesterday, remember."

"Yes, yes. I know," he said. He reached out and covered her hand. "Why did you not tell me you were coming? You had no need to book a hotel. You could have stayed with me."

She looked away. "No, Giancarlo, that wouldn't have worked." She took a deep breath and made herself face him again. "I'm here for a visit, and that's all. And to collect my things."

His eyes narrowed. "You know that's not necessary. Not at all. You may leave your things here as long as you wish. They will be waiting for you. When you return to create your next exhibition."

Kate gave her head a firm shake. "But that's just it, Giancarlo. I am not returning. At least not to create the exhibition. I reviewed the contract, and it doesn't state anywhere that I have to create the exhibition in Italy. Nor does it state what type of art the exhibition should contain. Only that it should be in keeping in with the established brand of the creator. Which it will be." She gave him another tight smile. "So I think it's best for my creativity if I work in America." She released her breath. She'd rehearsed those words since she'd made the decision to come, in the days following her talk with Tom on Christmas day.

Giancarlo raised his brows. "I see. You have obviously studied the wording carefully, but that doesn't lay aside the obligation you should feel, or my reach, should I decide not to promote the exhibition." His tone was clipped, but Kate could hear the trace of hurt there.

She looked away, biting her lip. "Giancarlo," she said, her voice strained. "I am not doing this to humiliate or hurt you, no matter what you might think."

She could feel him tense, anger suddenly palpable. "I assure you, this is business. And I know the art world very much more than you do, Katerina." He enunciated her name sharply.

She looked at him, suddenly tired. "Yes, you do. I know that. And if you feel that you can't promote the artwork I create, or turn them down, that's up to you, but I will have fulfilled my obligation."

His eyes shuttered and he gave a short nod. She knew she'd won this point, but it felt like a hollow victory.

"Your exhibition in New York next month. I will attend it. It will be expected."

Kate pursed her mouth and forced a nod. She could concede this small win to him, even though she couldn't predict how he would use this opportunity. Would he try to win her back, or find some way to derail any potential success? Or was it really just a business decision for him? She realized now how little she knew this man sitting in front of her.

"I am not Katerina, Giancarlo. I am Kate. Kate Wilson, an artist with her own vision."

Giancarlo's face darkened. He shook his head. "In the art world and here in Italy, you will always be Katerina."

FORTY-THREE

Kate took a sip from her champagne glass, trying to appear calm. The room was crowded with critics, art collectors, other art aficionados, minor celebrities and those who were connections of Cassidy's. Kate knew very few of them, though Cassidy had made a point of introducing her to as many as possible. And even though Kate had repeated their names, smiled, shook their hands, and made small talk, she couldn't remember any of them. Except for the influencer Komiko, with her bold Asian-styled kimono, huge obi sash, and high platform boots. It might have been the outfit, or the surprising words of praise, but Komiko had registered in her mind.

There were many other outfits that were bold and made statements. Her own seemed very bland in comparison. She'd chosen to wear her hair up, with an amber-colored ribbon worked through the small braids she had twisted around and across into a bun, with loose curls spilling out on either side of her face. The dry February weather had given her hair more curl than frizz, and for that she was grateful. Her mother's dark green crushed velvet dress paired with a gold-and-rust silk scarf draped and tied around her neck, amber tights, and black velvet shoes that topped off the look. It suggested Pre-Raphaelite with a little bit of a twist, and she hoped it complemented her exhibition theme.

Tom approached her, dressed in a suit she remembered from the funeral. She gave him a grateful smile as he leaned forward to kiss her cheek. "Sorry I'm late. Simon had a tie emergency."

She looked behind him and saw Simon dressed in a dark suit, pale blue shirt, and no tie. She grinned. "An emergency?"

Simon gave her a wry look. "The emergency was that I thought I had a tie with me, but I didn't. I left it back at the office."

"I told him he looked more bohemian without the tie. Perfect for a gallery opening."

Kate laughed, taking in his precise haircut, shirt and suit. "Oh, Simon, you definitely look bohemian."

"Thank you," he said dryly. He leaned over and kissed her cheek. "Congratulations, by the way. Your show is stunning."

She flushed with pleasure. "Thank you."

"It is perfect," said Giancarlo, coming up behind Kate and slipping his arm around her waist and squeezing it. She stiffened and withdrew from his grasp. "She will be the talk this season. Cassidy was just telling me. You've created quite a buzz."

"No surprise there," said Tom. He glanced at her champagne glass and then her, reading her body language. "Do you need a refill?"

She stared blindly down at it. She hadn't realized it was empty. "Thanks."

"I'll get it, Tom," said Simon. "You stay and talk."

Simon slipped away before any protests were made, and Kate followed his retreat, her mind scrambling to try and appear as though she was enjoying the occasion. Had it been a success?

She'd been so intent on trying to engage with the people who came up to her or Cassidy had introduced and forcing away her anxiety at Giancarlo's looming presence, which had translated into directing and overriding most of her comments during any interactions, she hadn't had time to notice anything else. And any discussion about the show had been vague statements she'd made about the works and their themes. She hadn't really heard any of the responses, she'd been so aware of Giancarlo's constant attempts to claim her in a physical manner, either with an arm around her waist, a kiss on her cheek, a hand on her shoulder, she couldn't concentrate.

In the weeks leading up to the exhibition, she'd fought the worry over varying actions Giancarlo might take at the exhibition. And now that it was here, she'd tried to reassure herself that this was something relatively benign and easily handled. It would be over soon.

Her gaze suddenly caught a figure at the entrance wearing a fedora hat pulled low and a dark suit jacket with a cream sweater underneath. He turned her way for just a moment, and she saw the flash of dark-rimmed glasses catching one of the spotlights. She didn't need to see his face, or the brief moment his eyes lit on her to know who it was. She felt fixed to the spot, unable to move, Giancarlo's arm once again around her waist. She knew the moment he saw her and then Giancarlo beside her. He turned away and disappeared into the crowd.

Kate stared at the place where he'd been, a place swallowed up a moment later by two other people, talking animatedly to each other. The pain she'd worked so hard to lock away unleashed itself with full force. She started to move toward them, her hand resting on her heart, instinct pulling her forward. Simon moved in front of her, a filled glass in his hand.

"There," he said. "That didn't take long."

She looked around the room again, hoping she might see

him, even though in her heart, she knew he'd gone. She felt bereft, a wave of sorrow washing over her so powerful she felt the need to sit down. He'd come to her exhibition. Had he intended to see her, greet her at least? Maybe talk with her? She realized she wished for it. That deep inside, she'd hoped he might be here and that maybe they could talk. Now it was probably too late. He'd left assuming things that weren't true. A future for her that she had rejected.

———

Sitting in her makeshift studio in the attic, Kate flicked through the images on her computer aimlessly. Her next project evaded her. She couldn't settle on any of the ideas and wonderful possibilities that she'd had last autumn. They didn't seem the right choice, or even worth exploring. Perhaps the overwhelming success of her exhibition had subconsciously daunted her. Not even the knowledge that it would release her from Giancarlo once and for all inspired her. At least she'd made that clear after the exhibition. He'd taken his profit and with it, any desire to see their relationship continue, except on a limited professional basis.

Now, she felt numb rather than thrilled. Her only emotion had been sadness that "House of Clouds" had sold, even at the exorbitant price she'd set in the hopes it wouldn't find a buyer. Whatever the reason for her current state, she felt directionless, uninclined toward any idea.

She continued to skim through the photographs, hardly taking them in. Eventually she found some amount of comfort, a quietness settling within her. Without realizing, she stopped on an image. It was the picture she'd taken of Ethan by the dock all those months ago. She studied it carefully, her artist's eye appraising it, but something else, something far too emotional, prompting her to search it for a clue, a method to find her way. A few minutes later, she found herself applying filters, trying out different approaches, as an idea formed, and almost unconsciously she pressed forward with it.

When she was satisfied, she arranged the paper in her oversized printer and waited to see the results. It was just a test run in order to see the color resolution. The image began to appear, revealing itself slowly, like an emanation. When it was complete, she took it from the computer and moved to her table, where she assembled her pens and bottles of ink carefully, refusing to dwell on what she was doing or even why. She considered the ink choice, knowing it would have to be perfect for the words and the image. For now, she would experiment with the sepia and maybe the navy.

Even as she dipped the ink, she knew it would be sepia. She began to form the letters, the words coming easily. There was no need to look them up or write them out as a prompt. They'd been in her for so long, they'd become a part of her. "Suzanne." She knew the rules for copyright, but this piece would be just for her.

So deep was she immersed in the calligraphy that it took a few minutes for the sound of a loud knocking to penetrate her mind and to recognize its meaning. Slowly, reluctantly, she put the pen in the empty weighted inkwell and made her way down from the attic to the front door. A tiny flicker of hope, of possibilities, formed inside her. She opened the door and the hope changed to surprise.

"Mark," she said, staring at him.

He shifted uncomfortably in his fitted down jacket, knitted hat, and heavy walking boots. He rubbed a hand over his wind-burned face.

"Hi, Kate. Sorry if this is a bad time."

She backed away from the door. "No, no, come in."

"There's no need, really. I'm just off to the lake, to the rock." He paused a moment. "It's the anniversary of Missy's death." He cleared his throat. "It's something I do, well, have done for the past few years. Go there." He looked away, down the street. "I, uh, just wondered if you wanted to come this year. I mean, don't worry if you'd rather not. I just thought I would ask."

She looked at him, too stunned by his words, by his presence, even to form a thought in her head, let alone answer his question.

He looked over at her, the silence lengthening. "No, no. Never mind. I can tell this was a bad idea." He turned. "I'll see you, Kate."

She watched him make his way across the wooden porch. "No, wait," she said, the words tumbling out of her. "Sorry. It took me by surprise, that's all. I'll come. Just let me get ready a moment." She opened the door wide again and gestured for him to come in.

———

Their breath made large plumes as they made their way up the incline toward the rock. It was a bitterly cold day, the wind coming off the lake, and even the exercise couldn't dispel the penetrating chill that seeped under Kate's jacket and through her hat. Her feet were feeling a little numb, but she was still nimble enough to negotiate the last scramble to the rock. Even Max seemed to find the cold too much, his breath coming in frosty pants as he lumbered behind her. Mark turned and, holding out a hand, pulled her up the last few steps to the flat surface on top. She found herself beside him, looking out over the lake. Max came up beside them, refusing to sit on the cold rock.

Looking out, Kate could see that it had been cold for long enough that a thin film of ice covered the lake, winter birds landing on its surface. A flock of Canadian geese flew overhead, the distant honking providing the only sound in the stillness of the winter day.

Beside her, Mark fixed his gaze on the lake. "It was milder that year. No ice on the lake."

Kate nodded. "I remember."

He looked over at Kate and gave her a sad smile. "I know you do."

She touched his arm and then, on impulse, gave him a hug. His arms slid around her, and he returned the hug tightly. When they released a few moments later, Mark put his hand in his right pocket and withdrew a flask. He removed the cap, took a swig, and offered it to her.

"A toast, of sorts," he said, wryly.

She took a large mouthful. The bite made her choke a little at first, and she coughed to clear it. The fiery liquid of the whiskey felt good as it burned its way down.

"Oh, come on now, you can't choke on whiskey. Missy would never have approved."

Kate laughed at his statement, not only because the sudden hit of alcohol made her giddy, but because it was true.

"She would have somehow made it into an idea for a song," said Kate.

Mark snorted, taking back the flask and having another little sip. "You're right about that. You'd have been the one to come up with lyrics, though. You wrote killer lyrics."

"Oh, but she could put some mean twists on the tunes."

"Tunes you wrote," said Mark.

Kate shrugged. "We were a team. She had a great voice."

"She did. Even when she was yelling, there was something melodic about it."

The truth of the statement struck Kate as funny. She laughed.

"She was melodic a lot," said Mark. "When you think about it."

"Some would say she was passionate."

"Hmm. Yes, I can testify to that."

Kate snickered, and Mark shoved her, his face a study of seriousness, but the glint in his eyes betrayed him. "I meant she cared deeply about things."

Kate grinned. "You mean she felt things deeply."

Mark laughed, shaking his head. "Yeah, well."

"You two. Making out up here. I remember that."

Mark raised his brows. "What? When?"

"You thought I'd left. It was senior year. Summertime. Just before graduation. We came to have a swim. The moon was out, it was great. After we came up here, I decided I was tired and started back to my car, but I dropped my keys somewhere along the way. I retraced my steps back here to ask you both to help me look, but..." She grinned widely. "You two were playing a game of find-the-wiener. I seem to remember that I hadn't expected two moons out that night."

Mark gave her a look of horror, and Kate burst out laughing. "Don't worry, I didn't see much. Just enough to know that I didn't need your help that badly."

Mark joined her laughter after the moment. "We were such kids."

"And you were smitten. No other word for it. She had you wrapped around her finger."

Mark nodded. "Until she didn't."

"Until she didn't." Kate paused. "So much melodic voicing," she added.

"Some of that constant melodic voicing was misplaced."

Kate considered his words. Had Missy provoked the anger

and tension with Bunny? She tried to recall exactly what had begun the animosity between the two. Zig's words about Missy stating that Mark was Kate's boyfriend threaded through her mind.

"She feared being alone," said Kate. "The way her parents ignored her. She did everything she could to ensure we wouldn't leave."

"True. And in the end all she did was drive us away."

Kate shook her head and Mark leaned into her, draping his arm around her shoulders. He lifted the flask in the direction of the lake. "To Missy. A talent lost. We miss you." He took a small sip and handed it to her. She put it to her mouth and took a small swallow.

"To Missy," she said, softly. "We miss you."

Mark squeezed her shoulder. His warmth spread to her and took the edge off the chill, easing the tension in her shoulders and around her heart. She lay her head on his shoulder and stared out at the lake, sharing the moment with him.

Forty-Four

The guitar nested in Kate's lap, her fingers idly picking a tune as she hummed along. She hadn't thought too much when she grabbed her guitar case, unzipped it, and withdrew the guitar. It had just happened. The tune had tickled her mind this morning when she woke up, and once she'd donned an old pair of yoga pants and her brother's old battered Henley shirt and a sweatshirt, she'd taken the guitar and sat on the bed, just idly strumming and plucking. Anything to get the music earworm well and truly excised and out into the air. Now, an hour later, the tune was taking a real shape, and she realized she was hungry and in desperate need of coffee.

She made her way to the kitchen, humming the tune. It felt right, and the words that were starting to emerge in her head slipped easily into place, as did its title, "Conch Shell." A winding path full of whispers and ocean sounds. As she sat down at the kitchen table with a few slices of toast and mug of coffee, the song filled her and gave her such a burst of joy, she suddenly felt a need to share it with Ethan. A moment later, the pain of the thought hit her. She stared at her phone, debating, the coffee mug in midair. She put the mug down, scrolled through the contacts, and hit Ethan's. Almost immediately the phone went to a message stating the number was disconnected. Kate listened to the message to its completion, stunned. She put the phone down, the pain that rose whenever she thought of Ethan now sharpened, razor like. Tears welled in her eyes and she brushed them away, forcing herself to take a deep breath. And another. She looked at her half-eaten toast and pushed it away, unable to face it any more. She rose and stared through the window at Max ambling around the backyard.

With sudden purpose, she grabbed his leash by the door and called for him. A walk. That would help. Though the ground was wet with melting snow, Max wouldn't care. Max ambled over and up the porch steps into the back door. Nothing hurried about him. The whitened muzzle told her constantly what his gait only reinforced, but now she noticed, too, that there was a listlessness about him lately. Was he still grieving her father? She reached down and began to pet him, stroking along his ears and under his chin like he loved. He nuzzled her in return, and the exchange of affection helped her spirit improve. She could only hope that it did the same for Max. She couldn't bear to lose him as well. And she realized she couldn't even consider moving to New York City because that would mean Max wouldn't be able to come with her. And even though she knew Tom would take him in a heartbeat, that was unthinkable too.

She rose, thinking to get her coat, but her phone began to ring, interrupting her. She picked it up from the kitchen table and saw that it was Tom.

"Hey," she said. "What's up?"

"Hi, I didn't wake you, did I?" She could hear the humor in his voice.

"Oh, ha very ha."

"Are you in the middle of something?"

"Not really, no. I was just about to take Max for a walk. Why?"

"Can you walk him to the workshop, then?"

"Of course. Any reason you want me there?"

"Nothing in particular. Just something I want to show you."

She brightened. "Another piece? Did you want me to bring my camera?"

He laughed. "No, you're fine. No cameras needed yet."

"Okay. We'll see you soon."

Kate tucked the phone in her pocket and moved to the closet for a coat. She took her father's old puffer coat. It was ridiculous looking, but it was warm. She looked down at her sneakers and decided to exchange them for her scuffed old Doc Martens in the back of the closet. After shoving a knitted hat on her head, her hair mostly tucked inside, she attached the leash to Max's collar and left the house. The cold hit her face immediately and burned her lungs. She fumbled on her mittens, trying to keep the leash firm in her hand, though she knew there was little risk that Max would break loose.

The walk to the store and Tom's workshop was more lumbering than brisk with Max along, and by the time they were nearly there, Kate's nose was frozen, and her feet were starting to feel a bit numb, the damp pavement and cold of the slowly melting snowbanks penetrating through her layers.

Once she reached the store and made her way around the back, where Tom's workshop was located, she was ready to be inside and have a hot drink. She hoped that Tom had put in the new coffee maker she'd given him for his workshop for Christmas. The last time she'd been here, he said it was still back at his apartment.

She opened the door into the small hall that led to his workshop and office at the side. She could hear voices coming from the workshop. "Tom?" she called. "Is it safe to bring Max into the workshop or should I put him in the office?"

"You can bring him in," Tom said.

She made her way to the workshop entrance. Tom was leaning against one of the work tables, his arms crossed. She looked at the figure seated on a chair across from him, stunned, her breath gone, her eyes feasting hungrily. Ethan sat there, a guitar resting in his lap. His hair was longer now, but less ragged. Even more surprising was the neatly trimmed beard he wore. It made him look different in a way she couldn't quite pinpoint. Not older so much, but perhaps worldly? His eyes were tired, but there was a distinct light in them that she hadn't seen in a long time.

"Ethan," she heard herself say. She gripped Max's leash tightly.

He set his guitar on the floor, rose, and approached her hesitantly. "Kate. How are you?"

The words seemed at once ridiculous and natural, and Kate found herself nodding. "Okay, I guess."

He reached her and leaned down, kissing her cheek briefly, before squatting down to greet Max with a vigorous rub on the head and under his chin. Max replied with sloppy nuzzling and tongue gratitude.

"Congratulations on the success of your show," Ethan said, looking up at her.

"Thanks," she said, her voice feeble, breathless.

Her emotions were awash with happiness, confusion, anxiety. Part of her wanted to leave, remove herself from this possibility that was opening up, a possibility that could present so many things she wanted and so many that she feared. The other part of her kept her rigid, fixed to this spot in the workshop, her eyes wide and apprehensive.

Ethan rose, looked at her, uncertainty coloring his expression. "I, uh, came by because I wanted to run a song by you and Tom."

"A song?" she asked. She glanced at Tom. He raised his brows innocently.

"Yes. I value opinions from both of you." He looked over at Tom. "I've played it for Tom already, and he's told me what he thought."

"You played it for Tom?" Her mind was having trouble catching up with the conversation, the dynamics and everything else swirling around inside her, clouding her mind.

"Yep, he did," said Tom. He stood and began to head toward the office at the back. "Since I've heard it and given my opinion, I'll leave you to hear it and voice yours."

She opened her mouth to protest, to ask questions, but nothing seemed to come out. The office door shut behind Tom with a soft snick. Max leaned against her leg, his weight providing a reassurance she realized was comforting.

She looked at Ethan. He was studying her carefully, mapping her. "You're going to play the song for me?" she asked, trying to think of what to say, to fight the surge of hope that was taking hold. And the certainty that she wanted that hope, the possibility of Ethan. "What's the title of the song?"

"It's called 'Prometheus Unbound.'"

She blinked at him, a burst of energy shooting through her. She cleared her throat. "Are you into Shelly now?" she asked softly. "Or is it just this particular play?"

Ethan narrowed his eyes, considering. "Definitely just this particular play. Or maybe even just the title of it."

She nodded slowly. "And it has significant meaning for you?"

"It does," he said, drawing closer to her.

She looked up into his eyes. Saw the hope there clearly. "You've left the band?"

He nodded, bit his lip. "I'm cut loose, on my own. It cost me, but not enough for it to matter. Not nearly enough. I just hope I haven't lost other, more important things along the way."

"Things?"

"People. Or rather person. One in particular. One I hope feels for me what I feel for her. What I felt long ago and still do."

The rush of emotions nearly overwhelmed her, but first and foremost was the burst of a mixture of love and relief that told her what she'd known all along, but had been too afraid to admit. That it was Ethan and always had been Ethan.

A slow, joy-filled smile formed on her face. "Can I hear the song first?"

He laughed and took her into his arms. "You are the song," he said before he leaned down and kissed her slowly, deeply, and with all the emotion of the best love song there is.

Forty-Five

Six Months Later

Kate fiddled with the pickup connection on the end of her guitar. Her nerves were really starting to act up a bit, even though she'd assured Ethan a few moments before she was fine. They'd rehearsed the whole set until it was better than perfect, and there was no reason for anything to go wrong. But since it was the first time they would be playing together in public, she couldn't help herself. Even now she second-guessed herself, wondering why she'd finally agreed to Ethan's suggestion they try out playing a gig. See if it was something they might explore together. The two of them as a duo, singing in local venues around the region. Singing their kind of music, their songs, both old and new. No pressure, because she had her budding art career to give her direction, with Ethan her biggest fan. He'd bought the "House of Clouds" painting to prove what he'd said. As for Ethan's own direction, he had his literary aspirations along with a healthy bank account. So maybe music would work.

She searched O'Connor's and saw that Tom was now seated

in the front, his new girlfriend, Holly, there beside him. Old girlfriend, actually. Someone Kate vaguely remembered from high school who'd dated Tom briefly in their senior year, but she'd broken it off after a month because she'd told him it wasn't going to go anywhere. Now, after over a decade spent on the West Coast, she was back, working as a vet in the next town. Kate gave Holly a nod and grinned at her brother, raising her brows up and down in an exaggerated manner. He frowned back, mouthing at her to behave.

Beside them was Ethan's sister, Teddi, here for the weekend. In the last few months since Ethan had left the band, and at Kate's encouragement, he'd met up with his sister several times and through her had made tentative connections with his parents. It was all very fragile, but Kate had hope for it.

Ethan came up behind her, rested a hand on her back and kissed her behind the ear. She suppressed the shiver that came over her at his touch. After all these months, she still found it difficult not to seize every opportunity to kiss him, to get as much of him as possible.

"You'll be so great," he said to her softly. "I can already tell we'll be on fire."

She turned to look at him, amused. "You can tell that already, can you?"

"I can. Because we can't fail to be anything else when we're together."

She laughed softly. "We'll see, Mr. Prophet."

He grinned at her. "I was thinking, instead of putting 'Navigation' in the middle, why don't we put it at the end?"

She gave him a puzzled look. "The end? Why?"

He nodded. "Because it is the end. I was steered home to you. You're my home. And here I am. With you."

She felt herself redden, a flush of deep pleasure suffusing her. "You're my home too." And hearing the words, she knew their truth, and even though she and Ethan were living in the house she grew up in, her home didn't have to be structured and linked or unlinked to any particular place. It was in herself and the person she'd become. And that person she'd become was inextricably at home with Ethan.

THE SONGS

HOUSE OF CLOUDS

> *I would build a House of Clouds*
> *For all my dreams I'm not allowed*
> *With a canopy of trees*
> *And a tapestry of leaves*
> *And deep inside would be a room*
> *Where art and music bloom, for us*

> Chorus
> *Take me, take me, take me away*
> *Take me away with you*
> *To the house in the clouds*
> *That we saw that day*
> *Where all my/our dreams come true*

> Chorus

> *And within these rooms of mine*
> *Are instruments of every kind*
> *With the beauty of birdsong*
> *Singing choruses at dawn*
> *When the evening comes in*
> *The stars will shine and never dim, for us*

> Chorus

> *And the paint that fills your brush*
> *Containing colors deep and lush*
> *For the magic you create*

Speaking truths that carry weight
And the deepest truth of all
Is the love within these walls for you.

NAVIGATION

Chorus
Navigation, navigation,
Steer me home to you

The boat's too small
The wave's too tall
And the water is all around me.
The hunger gnaws
The seagulls call
But I can't see all that they see.

And now it's night
The stars are bright
And I don't know where they point me
They fade from sight,
It's nearly light
And their message is still a mystery.

Chorus

It's your sweet touch
I miss so much
And the feeling you always gave me
These thoughts I clutch
They are my crutch
And the dream I have of all that we might be

A storm comes past
It breaks the mast
I hear you say you believe in me

The boat won't last
It's sinking fast
Then you say soon you'll be free.

Chorus

ROSSETTI GIRL

Out of nowhere she was there
With the fire in her hair
With her eyes of green and gold
Telling stories all untold
With her flowing graceful air
She gives a smile oh so rare

Chorus
My Rossetti Girl, my Rossetti Girl,
My Rossetti Girl.

Then she picks up her guitar
Plays it boldly, plays it hard
And the truth she sings out loud
She sings them slowly all uncowed
She wins me fast she wins me true
And I hope she feels it too

Chorus

By the time she ends the song
There's only one place I belong
She becomes my own north star
So I pick up my guitar
And with all my skills and art
Tell her all that's in my heart

Be my Rossetti Girl, my Rossetti Girl, Rossetti
Girl

When the song comes to the end

I hope her look's not as a friend
She lays her finger on my lips
With my heart now in her grip
She whispers sweetly in my ear
I will always be right here

As your Rossetti Girl, your Rossetti Girl,
Your Rossetti Girl.

MIDNIGHT

I don't know, I don't know,
Why you touched me so,
When I heard you sing that night.
Was it the song, was it your voice?
Or that you caught me in your sight?

It was only at midnight, only at midnight
I'd admit you were the one
Only at midnight, it was only at midnight
I'd hope that you would come.

ACKNOWLEDGMENTS

This is a different direction from my usual novels which either are historical or fantasy, but they always have a hefty dollop of romance. This story I have had in my head for a while and I tried mightily to subdue it, because it isn't in my usual wheelhouse, but it wouldn't let me alone. So I gave in and it somehow became filled with so much of what I love. Music, art, literature, poetry and for the first time a foray into song writing. I owe a great deal of debt musically to the encouragement of my talented niece, Miranda, and my exponentially talented nephew, Jesse. As usual, I also owe a great debt of thanks to my alpha team of readers, especially Jean, Claire and Babs, as well as Lizzie, who has blazed her own path in romance writing.

Also I want to thank my fantastic editor, Jessica Knauss who helped me realize how much I have become such a blend of terms, speech and cultures over the years. Also thanks as always to my amazing cover designer, Jane Dixon-Smith, whose creative genius has gone a long way to help make my books a success.

And most of all, I want to thank my brilliant readers, whose support down the years has helped to make my writing such a wonderful experience.

AUTHOR'S NOTE

Originally from Philadelphia, Kristin Gleeson lives in Ireland, in the West Cork Gaeltacht, where she works as a librarian. She holds a Masters in Library Science and a Ph.D. in history and for a time was an administrator of a large archives, library and museum in America. She also served as a public librarian in America and was a professional harper and storyteller for a time.

Writing as Kristin Gleeson, she has also published *The Celtic Knot Series* and *The Renaissance Sojourner Series*, an urban fantasy series, *Rise of the Celtic Gods*, as well as *In Praise of the Bees*, a novel of 6th century Ireland. A free novelette prequel, *A Trick of Fate* is available free on e-retailers. In addition to her novels, a biography on a First Nations Canadian woman, *Anahareo, A Wilderness Spirit*, is also available.

If you have enjoyed this book please post a review. It helps so much towards getting the book noticed.

If you go to the author website and join the mailing list to receive news of forthcoming releases, special offers and events, you'll receive *Along the Far Shores,* and *A Treasure Beyond Worth* a **FREE prequel e-novelette** and the ebook *Along the Far Shores.*

www.krisgleeson.com

Music is a big part of Kristin's life and many of the books have music connected to them. Listen to the music while you read- go to www.krisgleeson/music and download the files. Keep checking back as more pieces will be added to the library in the course of time.